the child
I never
had

BOOKS BY KATE HEWITT

the child I never had

KATE HEWITT

bookouture

Published by Bookouture in 2022

An imprint of Storyfire Ltd.
Carmelite House
50 Victoria Embankment
London EC4Y 0DZ

www.bookouture.com

ISBN: 978-1-80019-302-4
eBook ISBN: 978-1-80019-301-7

Dedicated to mothers everywhere, who are loving their children and doing the best they can and to Lynne, Happy Birthday! So glad you've joined us.

PROLOGUE

I can't believe I'm actually here. The air is warm, and more humid than in New York, with a stickiness that clings to my skin. I look around the busy airport—families laughing and walking together, a businessman rushing, a woman flicking her hair and talking on her phone—and with a lurch of panic I wonder what to do next. I realize I didn't actually think this far ahead, not really. Somehow I never imagined that I'd actually get here, that no one would stop me, tell me I couldn't go.

I guess I shouldn't be surprised that a seventeen-year-old can fly from New York to North Carolina, no questions asked. No one has even looked at me. No one cares what I'm doing here, where I'm going. No one cares at all.

I watch as a little girl swings hands with her mother, a father dragging suitcases behind. The mom bends down to listen to her, and then she tweaks the end of her pigtail as the girl grins. I swallow hard, force myself to focus.

I need to find a way to Mia's house—seemingly simple compared to getting on a plane, yet it feels like the hardest part of all, this final step.

What if she doesn't want to see me? I sent a text, but I didn't tell her I was actually coming. I'm not even sure I should have come, but it felt like I had to get out, go somewhere, away from it all. No one else would understand, and yet will she? I've convinced myself she will, that she'll understand what I've been through, that maybe she's even been through something like it herself, but right now I wonder if she'll even care.

My mother doesn't, I know that much. She pretends, with all her fake encouragement and listening, the way she purses her lips and nods her head, but it's all an act. I know I could never tell her about this.

As for her? The woman who gave birth to me?

The woman who has basically ignored you for most of your life?

I push that thought away as I hitch my backpack higher up on my shoulder, and scan the crowded baggage area again. An airport security guy catches my eye, frowns. I start walking toward the exit, as if I know where I'm going. Can you hail a cab in North Carolina the way you can in New York? I don't even know, and that makes me feel stupid. I'm seventeen, a street-smart New Yorker. I should know how to do this, and yet right now I just want someone to talk me through it, to hold my hand.

Outside, the air is even muggier, like walking into a solid wall of heat; it hits me hard in the face. I look around, taking a steadying breath of sultry air as I watch the buses and taxis stream by with grumbles of engines and heaves of exhaust, people streaming toward the parking garage, moving quickly, going somewhere.

Think, Daisy.

I know her address; I can hail a taxi; I can get there. What happens after that I am not ready to let myself think about. I tell myself that it's going to be okay, that it has to be. I couldn't stay in New York, not with the way everything happened.

I close my eyes, fight against the tears that crowd under my lids as I remember that night just two weeks ago—the memory is blurry, but all too real. His hand on my bare stomach. Their mocking laughter. The flash of a phone's camera. The scalding shame.

I take a deep breath and will the tears back. I don't want to cry, not here, in the middle of the sidewalk. Not when I've come this far.

And yet as I stare down at my phone with the message I sent this morning, seen but not replied to, my stomach cramps with fear. Maybe I shouldn't have come, or at least I should have told her I was coming, but I know I didn't for a reason. I didn't want to give her the chance to say no, the way she always does, putting off a visit because it's so much easier to send a card. But now that I'm here, minutes from her house, I have a terrible, leaden certainty that Mia, my birth mother, isn't going to be happy to see me at all.

1

SUZANNE

"I want to live with Mia."

As I hear Daisy say the words, I realize that, more or less, I've been expecting to hear them for the last seventeen years. They're a kick to the stomach, a knife to the heart, and yet strangely they also leave me feeling flat, or maybe just numb. The words *my real mother* hang in the air, unspoken yet audible, at least to me.

"All right," I say, trying not to show her how hurt I am by her announcement, delivered in such a hostile, challenging voice, although, in truth, I'm not even sure I know what I am feeling. Part of me wants to howl; another part to curl up on my bed and go to sleep. I smile encouragingly, determined to listen, to seem open and interested in this, as in everything else. Daisy may have decided she as good as hates me since Mark and I divorced, but I keep telling myself, with more and more dogged determination, that it's just the usual teenaged angst. The important thing is how I respond—with understanding and patience—and eventually we'll get through this. "So what has made you think you might like to live with Mia?" I ask in a tone that is meant to be interested and engaged, rather than revealing the dark creep of dread I feel inside whenever I think of Mia.

Daisy rolls her eyes, as if my question is absurd. Her eyes are brown—the same brown as Mia's—and her hair is bright pink—a little better than last month's midnight blue, although her hair now has the consistency of straw, thanks to how much she's dyed it over the last few years, sometimes a new color every few weeks. Stirling, her school, has a strict policy about hair color, but Daisy still manages to flaunt it—along with quite a few other rules, only toeing the line when she is forced to. She's wearing jeans that are more ripped than not, chunky black boots with steel toes, and a cropped top that shows the belly button piercing I forbade.

"Please tell me they at least sterilized the needle," I'd implored her, when she told me she'd had it done at some hole-in-the-wall down on St Mark's Place last year. Her only response was to roll her eyes, the same way she just did.

Daisy is my daughter. My adopted daughter, which feels like some sort of shameful caveat, and yet one I so often feel compelled to offer, often because she does first, and has since she was a little girl—from the proud "I have two mommies!" when she was a toddler to the later flatly stated "Yeah, I'm adopted"—to whichever passing acquaintance, as if it explains something. And maybe it does, because when I tell people, I see the flash of comprehension in their eyes, as if they are saying *oh, okay then.*

Apparently it changes something for Daisy, because now she wants to live with Mia. Her birth mother. And even though she hasn't had a real relationship with Mia in years, I am not entirely surprised. I've been waiting for this somehow, bracing myself for the moment when Daisy would turn away from me and choose Mia.

"I just do," she says, as if that is a reason.

"Yes, but what made you consider it now?" I cock my head, smile. "Tell me more about your thought process."

My determined "positive parent" speak, practiced so assiduously, makes my daughter groan as she slumps back in her chair. "Do you *have* to talk to me like you're my therapist?"

I take a deep breath as I wonder how I'm meant to talk to her. Does she want me to scream or cry or rail at her? I never do. I never let myself. I've read so many books on parenting and adoption that I am fluent in the language of "positive affirmation and promoting connectivity." I can recite all the well-meaning advice about understanding why they're lashing out and how adopted children might push you away because they're afraid you'll do it first. I know about "the primal wound" and how rejection is at the core of their being, even if you have the most open of adoptions, even if you were there to catch them as they emerged, red-faced and angry from the beginning, like I was—cradling Daisy close, amazed and humbled by the miracle of her being, the way her rage at being catapulted into this world turned to wonder. She stared up at me with her unblinking blue eyes and we formed a connection as sure and true as her first breath. I know we did.

In reality, though, it's hard to hold on to those truths in the hostility of the moment, when my measured, careful speech only infuriates my daughter and inwardly makes me cringe because it sounds both sappy and forced.

"It's just that I'm surprised," I remark finally. "You haven't seen Mia in over a year." Well over, and then not for nearly three years before that. The regular visits that once seemed engraved in stone, written in blood, have, in the last decade, became more and more sporadic.

Daisy's adoption was, in the current parlance, an open one. No secret birth certificates or uneasy questions for us; from the beginning, we were all on the same page, telling a story of more rather than less. Admittedly, when Mia suggested it the day after Daisy's birth, I didn't feel I had much choice, but I chose to believe that an open adoption could mean a child received more support, more resources, more love. At least that's how it was supposed to work. That's how it *did* work, at least for a little while, although sometimes I wonder if I'm putting a hazy rose-hued tint on the past, simply because the present feels so dispiriting.

But surely, back when Daisy was a baby, it was easier than this? I had only love, amazed and overflowing, for my daughter, and I felt nothing but gratitude for Mia, for giving her to me. I'm sure of it. I *wanted* it all to work. And yet now we are here—with Daisy as furious at me as she ever is, insisting she wants to live with Mia.

"I know I haven't seen her recently," Daisy tells me with a toss of her head, "but I follow her on Instagram."

So perhaps that's it. Mia's glossy picture-perfect life, viewed in pixels and artfully curated, is more appealing than my staid normality—even if Instagram, like every other form of social media, can often end up making you feel miserable, Mia Sullivan's Instagram more than most.

"Right." I nod. "So you've discussed this with her, then?"

"Not yet, but I'm going to." Daisy lifts her chin, truculent now, with that hint of vulnerability in her eyes that reminds me of when she was little, when I could sweep her up in my arms without her squirming away. When love felt simple and easy, as natural as breathing, as being. When did it change? When did Daisy become so prickly, so hostile, and is it my fault that she did? The question plagues and torments me, and I wonder if I'll ever find an answer.

"Okay," I say, because I can't think of another response. Despite my seeming acquiescence, I can't help but feel a sense of dread, of deep foreboding. Why Mia? Why now? "So... what are you thinking?" I ask. "A visit over the summer, to start?" I hear the damning note of hope in my voice. *Please, no more than that...*

"No, not just the summer." Daisy sounds defiant, but there is a tremble to her words that fills me with both fear and guilt. "I told you, I want to live with her. I thought I could do my senior year there. I want to get out of New York." Again with the lift of the chin, the flash of her eyes—and the tremble of her lips. I see it all, and it makes me sad and afraid and so terribly tired.

"Your whole senior year," I state, and now it's my lips that are trembling. So basically the rest of her childhood, her time at home, gone. She can't wait to leave. Leave me, and for *Mia,* with whom she hasn't spent more than a few hours at a time, and only one weekend for her sixteenth birthday nearly two years ago. I may not be surprised, but I am still devastated. "Daisy," I finally say faintly, "that's a long time."

"It's a *year*." This said with a lip curl.

I rise from the breakfast table where we've been sitting, basking in a pool of spring sunshine, the traffic on Madison Avenue gliding serenely along, five stories beneath us. I walk to the counter to pour myself a cup of coffee, stalling for time as I try to think of how to respond, how to feel.

Although I already know how I feel—horrified. Hurt. *Afraid.* Yet I don't want to show any of that to my daughter; I don't want to burden her with my emotions, make her feel guilty. As I stand with my back to her, I manage to compose my features into what I hope is an expression of friendly pragmatism.

"Why do you feel like you need to get out of New York?" I ask as I turn around.

Daisy shrugs, her gaze on her raggedy nails. "I just do."

"Did something happen?"

Her lip curls again. "No."

I'm not sure I believe her, but I am hesitant to press. The last week or so she's been even more withdrawn than usual, and frankly it had been something of a relief, not to have to deal with her snarls and sneers. Now I wonder if there was something darker behind it. "Are you sure?" I ask cautiously, and she looks up, her face suddenly twisting with anger.

"Yes, I'm *sure*, Mom."

I take a deep breath, let it out slowly. "What about Stirling?"

She shrugs, dismissive. "I've always hated Stirling."

At fifty thousand a year, with her having gone to the highly selective private school since kindergarten, and both Mark and I scrimping and saving to make it happen, she could have made her feelings known a bit earlier, but then I realize I never really thought she truly *loved* Stirling. She hasn't seemed to love anything for some time, but isn't that just the way teenagers are?

Or so I tell myself, because I don't want there to be another answer.

"So how were you thinking of approaching her?" I lean against the counter, my cup of coffee cradled in my hands, my eyebrows raised in inquiry. Inside I am shaking.

"*Approaching her?* You make it sound like she's a wild animal or something."

I take a careful breath, let it fill my lungs before I release it slowly, unobtrusively. *At least*, I tell myself, *she called me Mom.* I'm still that. "I just meant," I say, my tone as cautious as my breath, "that you haven't seen her in quite a while, and then only rather briefly. This... idea might come as a surprise to her." An unwelcome one, perhaps, but I don't want to say that.

"I saw her on my sixteenth birthday," Daisy counters, as if I don't remember when Mia sailed into town on a resolute wave of bonhomie; she picked up my daughter in a limousine, took her to a show on Broadway, mocktails in the foyer, shopping at Bergdorf's. It was so showily over-the-top it was practically obscene, but I did my best to act like it was such a wonderful surprise.

When she sailed out again on Sunday morning, Daisy went into a funk, as she always has after Mia's visits—locking herself in her room, refusing to eat, snarling whenever I dared to ask a question. That was around the time, I recall, when she got her belly button piercing.

"But have you talked to her at all since then?" I press, and Daisy's only answer is to hunch her shoulders. She looks so little all of a sudden, her chin tucked low, her pink hair sliding into her face, that I want to cross the kitchen and pull her into my arms. I won't, of course. I can't actually remember the last time I hugged my daughter. The last time I touched her, even.

"No, but I said I was going to," she mumbles, before looking up, defiant once again. "Do you think she won't want to see me or something?" She flings the words at me, and fatally, I hesitate. "You do, don't you?" Her voice hitches and I take a step toward her.

"Daisy..."

"Why can't you believe she might want to see me?" she demands, her voice rising to a tearful shriek. "That she might actually like spending time with me?"

"It's not that," I protest, although I'm not sure why Mia has dialed back her involvement in Daisy's life over the years. Whatever the reason, I already sense it's going to be my fault. "I'm just concerned, Daisy," I try, "because you haven't seen her in a while and she's been quite—" I stop as abruptly Daisy rises from the table, her chair clattering on the tiled floor as she gives me one last glare before stalking out of the kitchen. I hear the slam of her bedroom door and I close my eyes.

I think about going to apologize, but I'm not even sure what for, and Daisy wouldn't accept it anyway. It feels like no matter how hard I try, I end up in this place. Alone. As I walk to the window, I tell myself I don't need to feel this nameless dread that swells and recedes like a tide every time I think of Mia. Maybe Mia will welcome the visit—*the move*—and maybe

Daisy will benefit. If I feel like a failure because she chose to leave, then that's on me. I need to think about what's best for my daughter, but it hurts all the same. Unbearably.

And the truth is, I may not know what's best for my daughter, but I have serious doubts that it's Mia—Mia, who swans in when she feels like it, and out again in the same way. Mia, with her presents and cards and effusiveness, and not much more. Is that kind of careless fairy-godmother persona really what Daisy needs?

But there again, clearly she doesn't need—or want—*me*.

I turn to look out the window. It is a beautiful June day; the sky is a bright robin's egg blue, the sun streaming over Madison Avenue. If I crane my neck, I can see Central Park, its leafy trees nearly fluorescent in their fresh summery greenness. From Daisy's room, I hear the tinny, wailing sound of her angsty emo music. I lean my head against the glass and close my eyes. It's barely nine o'clock in the morning and I already feel defeated.

A few years ago—three, four?—Daisy and I would have planned this summer's day together. A trip to the library, a stop at our favorite coffee shop, browsing in a few boutiques on Madison Avenue, giggling at the outrageous prices. Or maybe we'd have taken the six train down to Union Square, and strolled through the farmer's market, stopping by the big Barnes and Noble to spend an hour leafing through books. I can picture Daisy sitting on the floor in front of the manga aisle, absorbed in the stories of the big-eyed cartoon heroes and heroines she adored.

When did those afternoons stop? Was it when Mark left, and she seemed to blame me for it, or was it before? Did it happen slowly, in such small increments that I could at least pretend I didn't notice?

I'm not sure, but I do know that I have loved Daisy with every breath in my being. That has never changed, and yet right now I wonder if it makes much difference. I tell myself to hold on, to see Daisy through this rough patch, because surely we'll get to the other side. Yet how can we, if she moves to Mia's?

Even though I know it will make me feel worse, I reach for my phone and swipe onto Instagram. I steel myself for the photos I know I'll see—yes, there is Mia, her dark hair pulled back in a high, glossy ponytail, her lithe body encased in Lycra. She's got her hands on her hips as she beams for the camera; written over the photo in a slanting Corsiva font are the words *You can do this, Ladies! Remember, if you believe your best days are ahead of you, THEY ARE!* No doubt it's about another one of her peppy challenges—intermittent fasting, or five a.m. workouts, or a complete reorganization of a closet.

Mia is a lifestyle coach, which, as far as I can tell, is a service aimed at middle-aged mothers to reboot their stalled lives through exercise and housecleaning. She is always starting some supposedly fun challenge that people can sign up for—for a price, of course. The courses seem popular; she always has dozens, or even hundreds, of comments on her posts.

My gaze moves from her most recent photo to the one she posted last night—Mia posts on Instagram every day, often more than once. Yesterday's photo is of her three little girls—Ella, Avery, and Sophie—all in matching polka-dot pajamas, curled up like puppies on the pristinely white duvet of a king-sized bed, presumably Mia and her husband Tom's. They are all blond and blue-eyed like Tom, their hair in damp after-bath ringlets, their faces rosily cherubic. Ella must be about nine now, Avery seven, Sophie just four.

I glance down past a couple dozen photos, back to Daisy's sixteenth birthday, to see if there is one of her, but there isn't, just as I'd suspected there wouldn't be. Mia had posted the photo of them toasting their mocktails on Broadway for Daisy's sixteenth birthday with the somewhat ambiguous caption "*A weekend with my best bud!*" but she must have deleted it since. Although she's occasionally posted photos of Daisy, she has never featured prominently in her profile. She's not quite a secret, but something pretty close to it.

I put down my phone and stare out at the bright blue sky. I've been worried about how Daisy might react if Mia doesn't want her to live with her, but now another, and just as frightening, question assails me. *What if she does?*

2

MIA

It's a single sentence, but it still causes my heart to lurch in my chest before beating out a staccato rhythm of panic. I am waiting in line at our local Starbucks for my coffee, having just dropped Sophie off at preschool. Outside, it's a beautiful Monday morning, hazy blue sky and plenty of sunshine, not too humid for a June day in North Carolina, and in twenty minutes I have an appointment with a forty-something mom who wants to get back into work after nearly fifteen years at home.

I don't have the emotional space to think about this now.

"Mia? Skinny soy latte?"

"Thanks," I say, managing a quick smile before swiping my coffee from the counter and heading outside to my car. The Instagram message is still on my screen; it was sent last night at eleven. I'd checked my Instagram first thing this morning, as I usually do, and spent ten minutes liking and replying to comments on my posts, but I hadn't bothered to look at any direct messages until now. Potential clients often contact me through social media, so I'd been expecting something work-related, not this. Not Daisy.

I click my key fob to unlock my car and slide into the

driver's seat. The air is hot and still, the smell of my coffee making my stomach churn. Or maybe it's the message. Why this? Why now?

I glance down at the screen, slowly scanning the words. *Hey Mia, Wondering if I cld come 2 visit U this summer?* Followed by a ream of emojis—fingers crossed, a heart, a rainbow, a face surrounded by hearts, and, inexplicably, a panda.

I put the phone down and lean my head back against my seat, closing my eyes as I fight the rush of guilt and love that floods me every time I think of Daisy, which is not often for exactly that reason. Visit this summer? What does she mean exactly? A weekend? A week? More? The most time I've spent with Daisy since she was four years old was a single afternoon. The weekend for her sixteenth birthday was a bit more, but it was a blur of busy, squealing entertainment; I made sure we wouldn't have a single moment to fill, a few seconds' space for the awkwardness to flood into—the uncertainty, the anxiety, the sorrow, the guilt. I made my choices a long time ago, and I'm doing my best to live with them, as hard as that can be.

Anyway, that birthday weekend was a year and nine months ago, which feels like a very long time. I think we've had maybe one or two texts since then, a single chat on FaceTime that only lasted a few minutes. Nothing more.

I take a sip of my coffee, and as I hold the cup, I realize my fingers are trembling. I force down a sour-tasting swallow before I put my cup down again. This has really taken me by surprise. Daisy and I don't have that kind of relationship—at least not since she was little more than a toddler. I take a deep breath and let it slowly flood my lungs, my whole being, doing my best to bring a sense of calm to the situation. It's what I'd advise my clients, but it's hard to practice myself, especially with regard to my daughter.

When I let myself think about her, the hot, tangled rush of guilt and love floods through me just like that breath, overwhelming me with its power. The rare sweep-ins for sudden visits, the generous Amazon gift cards and flowery Hallmark cards, the occasional two-word text or awkward fifteen-minute online chat—none of it makes up for the fact that I have deliberately chosen not to be a significant presence in Daisy's life. I know that, I accept it, I live with the guilt—because it felt like the better, wiser, kinder thing to do, hard as it was. I can't backtrack now, can I? *I don't want to.*

And yet Daisy wants to visit. She's never even met my daughters, save for Ella, once when she was little more than a baby. She's only met Tom twice. How can I have her come here and invade my life, threaten everything? It feels selfish and horrible to think that way, but I can't keep myself from it. The truth is, I'm scared—and yet refusing Daisy seems so unbearably cruel. I can't stand the thought of hurting her, and yet I know I already have. Many times.

I release a pent-up breath and start the car. I'm going to be late for my meeting, something I try never to be. I toss my phone onto the passenger seat, a problem for later in my busy day.

And for the rest of the day, I mostly manage not to think about it. About Daisy. I focus on my clients, which is easy because I love my job. I know there are plenty of people who pooh-pooh the whole idea of life coaching—who needs a coach to just *live,* right? When Suzanne asks me, oh so politely, about it, I hear her disdain behind her usual cool reserve. And yes, some of it might look shallow. Silly, even. Cleaning out your closets or running a 10K may not seem earth-shattering to most people, but it can actually be life-changing. I know, because I've seen it happen. I've experienced it myself.

Take my first client of the day—Lou Richards, forty-seven, hesitant, shy, a little overweight, a tiredness in her eyes that looks like defeat. I've seen women like her so many times. She had a good career in advertising before children, but fifteen years at home and a different perspective on life have made her wary of returning to that cutthroat, corporate environment. Plus, she tells me with a wryness that doesn't quite hide her shame, she doesn't fit into her old work suits, and they're out of date anyway.

She doesn't know where to begin with anything; she confides in me, over a pot of herbal tea before we begin, that she's thinking about taking a job as a lunch lady at her youngest son's school—it fits in with the school hours and holidays, and it wouldn't give her, or more importantly her husband Kevin, any stress or pressure. It's the easy way out, but it's obvious she doesn't really want to do it.

"It's the hairnets you have to wear," she tells me with a little, embarrassed laugh. "I hate them. They feel so... diminishing."

Of course it isn't really the hairnets. They're simply representative of the whole prospect for a woman with an MBA and a decade of high-flying corporate experience. She doesn't want to go back to that world, but she doesn't want this one, either. I understand completely.

"Tell me what you've been up to since you started staying at home," I suggest as I pour us both more tea. "Besides changing diapers and going to Mommy and Me sessions." I give her a conspiratorial smile; we've both been there. "What has kept you sane during these years?"

Lou looks like she doesn't know if anything kept her sane, or even if she *is* sane. We've both been there, too. But I wait, because I know it takes my clients a long time to reboot their brains, to think of themselves as something—anything—other than a mom. Other than a housekeeper, a cook, a secretary, a slave.

"Well," Lou says after a moment, her tone shy, "I've really enjoyed crafting." She almost looks scared, as if I'll scoff at this, but I never scoff at anything. And plenty of women have told me they like crafting.

"Tell me more," I say warmly, and so she does, haltingly,

and with my prompting, she gets out the photo collage books she's made through the years—of her children, of course. I murmur encouragement and praise as I leaf through the albums; they're all creatively done, with washes of watercolors and a sweet, whimsical flair. "You've got such a good eye for color and arrangement," I tell her as I close the last book. "Have you thought about harnessing those skills in your next career move?"

Lou looks startled, as I knew she would, by the way I'm talking. Words like *harnessing skills* and *career move* are foreign to her, maybe even dangerous.

She ducks her head and mutters something about how she's never thought like that.

"That's why I'm here," I tell her warmly. "To help you to start thinking like that."

By the time I go to pick Sophie up from preschool at one o'clock, I've managed to banish Daisy to the very back of my mind and I'm feeling that buzzy sense of excitement at helping Lou Richards start thinking proactively about her life. When I left, after two hours of talking, and more importantly, listening, she was looking into retraining in graphic design.

Of course, it might come to nothing; the first adrenalin-laden shot of possibility often morphs into hand-wringing uncertainty, but part of my job is to help women navigate past the self-doubt they so often feel. I know, because I've been there too, when taking those terrifying yet necessary steps is so very hard. I hope Lou has the strength of will to keep going. I know how much determination it can take.

As I wait with the other moms—and a token dad or two—by the preschool doors, I give everyone a friendly smile, but the chitchat is minimal. I haven't made many inroads with the various moms I've met through school drop-offs and pickups;

I've seen a few of them roll their eyes at each other when I come in my workout gear, or when I take a call from a client while I'm waiting. Let them scoff at my business, my lifestyle. I've made myself not care; I've worked hard to get to where I am, to be who I am, to feel confident and strong. I'm not going to let a few moms in sweatpants deter me.

Today there's the usual little knot of moms jangling car keys and balancing babies, travel mugs of coffee and phones as they chat away. I check my phone, doing my usual scroll of posts and liking comments that have come in during the day, while they talk about the upcoming summer holidays and whether their kids are going to do the day camp the county is offering at the local park.

Then the doors open, and Sophie rushes out, holding her latest creation—a finger painting that is still dripping wet.

"Whoa." I let out a little laugh as a blob of orange slops onto my wrist. I try to hold the dripping painting by my fingertips as I draw my daughter into a decidedly sticky hug. "What an incredible painting, sweetheart. You do love your finger paints."

"She certainly does." Mrs. Miller, one of the preschool teachers, gray-haired and cuddly when she chooses to be, gives me a slightly steely smile before telling me in a singsong voice, "Although, unfortunately, Sophie had trouble sharing again today, didn't you, honey?"

I stiffen, especially as I see—and feel—the curious and maybe even gloating stares of the circle of moms. Nothing like a little schadenfreude. "Oh?" I say neutrally, while Mrs. Miller pins me with her stern gaze.

"This is becoming something of a pattern," she tells me, and I keep my politely inquiring smile in place, my arm still around Sophie.

"Four-year-olds are still learning how to share, aren't they?" I remark. "It's part of why they go to preschool."

Mrs. Miller's gaze narrows. "At Little Hearts, Open Minds,

we take our responsibility of fostering a community of sharing and consideration very seriously."

"And I'm so glad you do, because that is how Sophie will learn," I tell her, keeping my tone just on the right side of saccharine. "Thank you, Mrs. Miller, for all your hard work nurturing our children." I widen my smile, laying my hand on her arm, and she jerks away from the dripping painting I'm still holding with something close to a glare.

Nothing like a little taste of her own medicine, I think with a savage sort of satisfaction as I shepherd Sophie to the car. *I can speak that lingo just as well as you can, sweetheart. It doesn't mean a thing.*

It's not until we're in the car, driving towards Target for a quick whip round the grocery aisles before Ella and Avery get home from school, that I ask Sophie what happened.

"So you had trouble sharing today, Soph?" I ask as mildly as I can. "Do you want to tell me what that was about?"

Sophie shrugs, scratching her nose as she looks determinedly out the window. My youngest daughter can be as stubborn as I am.

"Was there a toy you wanted to play with specifically?" I guess.

"I *was* playing with it," Sophie replies irritably. "And Amelia just *took* it."

"Which toy was it?"

"The princess crown."

Ah, yes. Although the preschool supposedly has a policy of only offering toys made from natural materials, a battery-operated, twinkling, plastic princess crown has somehow made it into their dressing-up box, and is the firm favorite of all the girls and some of the boys. This is not the first time there has been a tussle over it.

"So what happened?" I ask.

"I was wearing it and Amelia said it was her turn, but it

wasn't. She just *said.*" Sophie thrusts her lip out as she glares out the window, the injustice clearly rankling her. "I only had it on for a few seconds. Evie had it before me."

"Hmm. That sounds difficult."

"It was *unfair*," Sophie says with heartfelt emphasis. "But Mrs. Miller said I *had* to share." She speaks the last word with something like scorn, not exactly the sentiment I'm trying to foster in my preschooler, but, all the same, I sympathize.

"Sharing is important," I tell Sophie, "but so is fairness. Did you tell Mrs. Miller you'd only just put it on?"

"Yes, but she wouldn't listen." Sophie thrusts her lip out even further, her arms folded across her chubby little body. "And we're supposed to listen."

"Yes, you are." Inwardly, I sigh. The sharing maxim at school has become something of a Marxist diktat; as soon as one child declares they want a turn, the other has to cheerfully submit, no matter what. When I've done my mandatory three hours a month of volunteering, I've seen the gleam of triumph in a preschooler's eye when they've played the sharing trump card, knowing nothing can beat it. And sharing, I've discovered—making me think of Daisy even though I don't really want to—is hard.

I wonder how Suzanne feels about Daisy wanting to visit me. Does she even know? I picture her pursed lips, that prissy smile. I bet she's seriously annoyed by this latest development.

As we pull up to Target, I do my best to push Daisy firmly out of my mind. Going around a grocery store with a four-year-old is challenging at the best of times, never mind when said four-year-old is clearly in a mood and I'm all over the place, thinking about Daisy even when I try not to. By the time we emerge, sweaty and victorious with two bags of groceries, we're both irritable—and I'm running late to meet Ella and Avery's school bus, which puts me further on edge. I like being on time, in control, feeling both calm and purposeful as I meet each fresh challenge head-on. That's my MO, my brand, my anchor.

That message from Daisy, I realize, has really shaken me. It's stirred up emotions I've forced myself to bury, brought back memories I've done my best to suppress. I have struggled to get my equilibrium back all day, even when I was deliberately not thinking about her. Because that, of course, took effort; the very deliberateness of not thinking about her requires energy and emotion that I need for my work, my life.

I swear under my breath as I see the bus pulling away from the curb as I turn into our street, one of many identical ones in Carpenter Village that manages to be manufactured quaint without being too cringey.

"Mommy, that's a naughty word," Sophie informs me as I swing hard into our driveway. The bus is heading determinedly down the street, even though the driver had to have noticed me.

I jump out of the car as the bus continues down the street. "Wait... wait!" I'm running behind the bus like a madwoman, waving my arms, breathless, shouting. "*Wait!*"

Finally, thankfully, the bus slows to a stop and the driver, Anita, flicks her hazards on. I am panting hard as I jog up to the doors that open with a slow, accusatory exhale.

"You're late," Anita informs me flatly. "I waited for three minutes." Which is the school district's policy; if no one appears to collect their children off the bus, they're taken to some depot all the way on the other side of the county, and you're charged for every fifteen minutes they keep them there, until you show up, although that hasn't happened to me—yet.

"I'm... I'm sorry," I pant, my hands on my knees. "Thank you for stopping." I try to smile, but my lips tremble. This is one more hassle I can't handle today, and I can usually handle anything. I've made it my business—positive, focused, unflappable Mia Sullivan. She can solve all your problems. She can inspire you to live your best life now.

Which is a hard sell if my own life doesn't look pretty close to perfect—with the odd, vague, carefully phrased admission of how I'm not perfect at all to keep it real, of course. I became cynical a long time ago.

"*Thanks,* Mom," Ella huffs under her breath as she stomps off the bus, her little body stiff with affront. Nine years old and she is already acting like a teenager, never mind a tween. "That was *so* embarrassing."

"Sorry, sweetheart." I reach out to tousle Avery's blond curls. "You okay?"

"Yeah." She pushes up her glasses with her middle finger and then blinks at me owlishly for a second before trotting off after her older sister, who is already striding ahead. Meanwhile, Sophie has started bellowing from the back of the car.

"Mo—*mee!* You forgot about me!"

I offer Anita one more harried apology that she accepts with a terse nod, and then I hurry after my children.

The next couple of hours are taken up with a buzz of afterschool activity: unpacking groceries, backpacks, and lunchboxes; helping Ella with her fourth-grade homework, which is harder than I thought it would be; folding laundry; and finishing the chili for dinner, which fortunately I prepped in a crockpot this morning, so at least that requires minimal effort.

But I still feel uneasy and emotional as I grate cheese and boil rice for the chili, nagging Ella to set the table, which she does with a lot of theatrical groans and stomping around. By the time Tom comes home at nearly six o'clock, I still haven't managed to regain my equilibrium, although I do my best to act as if I have.

"Hey, what's up?" he asks as soon as he steps into the kitchen, blowing Ella a kiss and drawing Avery into a hug as

Sophie tackles his knees. We haven't even spoken yet, but he can clearly sense my anxiety already.

"It's just been one of those afternoons," I answer with what I hope is something close to a breezy smile. I haven't even managed to look at my work emails or Instagram feed all afternoon; today's happy family shot will have to wait till tomorrow.

"Oh? Why?" Tom pries Sophie from his knees to toss her high up in the air, while she chortles with glee. I watch from by the stove, feeling a tug of both affection and gratitude that he's so good with the girls, as well as a faint flicker of resentment that it's so easy for him, to waltz in at six o'clock and be the good guy. That's not fair, I know; Tom will give Sophie a bath, and check Ella's homework, and listen to Avery's piano practice. And yet, I can't help but reflect, I have the instinct, just as many of my clients do, that I should somehow be grateful he's giving his own children some attention.

"Just because. You know." I wave a hand to dismiss the whole afternoon and lift the pot on the rice. "Dinner's ready."

"Do I have time to change?"

Not really, I think, but I smile and wave him upstairs. Ella still hasn't finished setting the table. My phone buzzes, and with a needling of irritation, I see it's Suzanne, no doubt wanting to chat about Daisy's visit. I turn my phone off and help Ella set the table. By the time Tom comes down, dressed in a T-shirt and gym shorts, we're all seated, waiting for him to arrive. He gives me a grimace of apology and goes first to the fridge to get himself a beer before he joins us at the table and we all hold hands for grace.

Some of my equilibrium is restored as we start eating and Tom asks each of the girls about their day; Ella doesn't mention the bus debacle, and Sophie has thankfully forgotten the problem of the princess crown. I look at my happy family all around the table and feel a sense of rightness and safety, like we're cocooned in our togetherness, held together by our love.

My family. They mean everything to me.

Then I think of Daisy sitting there too, and it's like I've been given an electric shock. I jerk upright in my chair, and Tom gives me a fleeting, questioning look. I glance away, not wanting to reveal my thoughts.

Daisy here. Daisy in my life, getting to know my children and Tom, asking them questions, being part of my family. So much of me still longs for it even after all these years even as a small, insistent part of me backs away in utter dread, which makes me feel all the guiltier. I love Daisy, I do, but I can't risk letting the disparate parts of my life collide in such a way. It would be too complicated—for the girls, for Daisy, for me. And yet how can I refuse? I can't, and I don't even want to, not exactly, but... *Daisy.* Daisy here. It's impossible to imagine.

It isn't until we've finished the meal and the girls have slipped away to the playroom, that Tom glances at me from across the mess of dirty dishes, his eyebrows raised.

"So? What's been bothering you?"

"Just a bunch of minor hassles." I try to smile, but as I think again about Daisy visiting, I can't quite manage the simple curving of my lips. She wants to *visit.* She's never asked for something like this before; we've never had that kind of relationship.

Once you did, but you chose to let it go.

But I had to, for both our sakes. Didn't I?

"Mia?"

I snap my gaze back to Tom's concerned one. My eyes slide to the playroom; the girls are engrossed in a game that involves piling all the sofa cushions in the middle of the room and then flinging themselves on top, accompanied by squeals of either excitement or terror. They can't hear a thing. "Daisy sent me a message. She wants to visit," I say quietly.

Tom's eyebrows rise further and he sits back in his seat.

"Wow," he says after a moment, giving a couple of slow nods. "That's kind of unexpected, but okay, great."

Great? I swallow my skepticism, because really, I shouldn't be surprised. Tom arranged my visit to Daisy for her sixteenth birthday, a surprise for both of us. He's always been supportive, if happy to be at a distance. A weekend visit won't affect him too much. He sees it as an easy win, while I am trembling inside, trying not to reveal my fear, my longing, my confusion, my hope.

"What?" Tom asks, even though I haven't said anything. "What's the problem?"

"There's no *problem.* It's just she's never visited before."

"Yeah. So?"

"The girls don't even know about her." Something we agreed, early on, at my suggestion. *They're too young,* I told him staunchly. *There will be time later to explain, for them to understand. We'll tell them then.* And he agreed, as he agrees with most everything, happy to go affably along as I march ahead.

Now it looks like that time may have come. It's sooner than I expected—or wanted.

"Then this is a great opportunity for them to meet her," Tom says so very reasonably. "Get to know her." He pauses, while I start stacking plates on the table. "I always thought it was a little weird that they didn't, you know. I mean, considering it's been an open—"

"Yes, I know." I do my best not to sound defensive, but I must fail because Tom frowns.

"What's really the problem here?" he asks again, as if everything is so very simple when I know it's not.

"It's a lot to explain, you know? 'Oh, sorry, girls, you have a sister.'" My stomach cramps at the thought of such a conversation—Sophie's confusion, Ella's fury, even Avery's predictably placid acceptance. And what about Daisy? How will she feel about all of it? I can't bear to disappoint her, and yet I know I have already, again and again. None of this has been easy—for her or for me.

"Half-sister," Tom reminds me with a small smile.

I twitch irritably. "Do they even know the difference?"

He shrugs. "Enough kids in their classes have parents who are divorced, remarried. This isn't the 1950s or something, Mia. Blended families are practically the norm, even in North Carolina. It's completely acceptable—"

"We're not a blended family." I sound vehement, and Tom's frown deepens.

"I'm okay with Daisy being a part of our lives, you know."

Oh yes, I know. Tom has been so very laid-back about it from the beginning—except it's easy to be laid-back when you're more or less indifferent. I told him about Daisy on our third date—hopeful, hesitant, having no idea how he'd take it. I was only twenty-four, and I had a four-year-old daughter I'd given up for adoption but still saw fairly often. I knew it would be a big deal to a guy like him, working in tech, upwardly mobile, fancy-free.

Tom had been taken aback at first—I saw the flash of it in his eyes—and then he gave a little shrug, both accepting and a bit dismissive. "Cool," he said, as if I'd told him I was double-jointed, or could wiggle my ears. He made it sound like a quirk, when it was the essence of who I was. "How often do you see her?"

"Maybe once a month." Sometimes more than that, but I was reluctant to tell him so.

He nodded, shrugged, and then asked me if I wanted dessert. We didn't talk about Daisy again until almost six months later, when I hesitantly, so hesitantly, asked if he wanted to meet her, and he agreed, after an awful, endless pause. In the years since then, it's always been the same—he's happy for me to see Daisy once in a while, but he's never shown much interest in making the effort himself, and the truth is I've been fine with that. *Fine.*

Now he glances at me, eyebrows raised, the pause deliberate. "The question is," he asks, "are you okay with it?"

Am I okay with having Daisy as a part of our lives? As if that could ever be a simple yes or no. I rise from the table, taking the plates to the sink and depositing them there with a clatter. "No, I'm not," I say when the clink of dishes has subsided. I keep my back to him because I don't want to see the expression on his face. "Not really. Not anymore."

Tom rises too, following me into the kitchen. "Why is that, do you think?" he asks as we both stand by the sink, silent, staring at the mess of dinner. From the playroom, Sophie screeches in fury.

"It's not fair on either me or Daisy." I say the words woodenly. "Too much time has gone by, and we've drifted apart. It's too complicated, too confusing, to reintroduce things now." Even to my own ears, I sound like I am trying to convince myself.

Tom nods slowly. "Okay, yeah, maybe when she was younger. But now she's practically an adult—"

"You're not an expert on adoption," I say shortly, and he blinks. "Sorry." The word comes out in a sigh. "Sorry. It's just..." My lips tremble and I press them into line. "This took me by surprise. It brings up a lot of emotions. Memories."

"Oh, hon." Tom pulls me into his arms and I go reluctantly, because as nice as a hug can be, I'm feeling too prickly now, as if I'm covered in spikes, ready to draw blood. Tom doesn't mind, though; he just keeps his arms around me. "It'll be okay," he murmurs against my hair, and I have to press my lips even harder together not to let out a sound—a sob or a snort of disbelief or something in between. Tom has no idea. No idea at all.

Sophie screeches again and I pull away, knuckling my forehead. "She needs her bath."

"Okay." Equable as ever, Tom is willing to leave the discussion for now. But how long will Daisy be willing to wait for my answer, especially when she must know I saw her message this morning? I need to send a reply. I need to figure out how to handle this.

Even as these thoughts race through my mind, I find myself remembering a time when I didn't need to *handle* anything. When Daisy was little, when I swung her up into my arms or I waved from the street and she watched, her nose pressed to the window, a delighted smile stealing over her features when she caught sight of me. When my love for her felt like a pure, simple thing for both of us. I miss the woman I was then. I miss the little girl she was. But I also know we can never go back.

Wearily, I turn back to the dishwasher, only to be surprised by the ring of the doorbell.

Ella pokes her head out of the playroom, looking both interested and suspicious. "Who's at the door?"

"I have no idea," I tell her lightly. I wipe my hands on a dishcloth as I head to the front door. Through the frosted glass, I see the shape of a young woman, silhouetted by our porch light. Dark hair, a slight figure, a backpack slung over one shoulder. My step falters. I can feel Ella behind me, curious, craning her neck.

"Who is it, Mom?" she asks, but I can't speak. My heart is thudding, my palms turning damp. My fingers tremble as I undo the lock and slowly, with a terrible sense of dread and inevitability, open the door.

"Hey, Mia," Daisy says, as her uncertain smile slides off her face.

THEN

DAISY

There are balloons, and fizzing fake champagne, and a stretch limousine with a sunroof that she is standing through, her dark hair streaming in the chilly autumn air, as Daisy stands by the doorway of her apartment building, unable to keep from grinning. A techno version of "Happy Birthday" is blaring from the speakers of the limousine, filling the stately street with its bass beat, causing people to turn and stare. A few point. Daisy's smile widens, even though she doesn't mean for it to. She wants to play this cool, especially after the last visit, but she can't. Mia holds the bottle aloft, seemingly impervious to the bubbles streaming down her wrist.

"It's not every day a girl turns sixteen," she exclaims as the limo glides to a halt in front of the building. Her gaze skates to Suzanne, standing behind Daisy, and then back to the birthday girl. "I wanted this weekend to be special." She cocks her head, lips curving. "Is it too much?"

She doesn't wait for an answer as she laughs, shaking her hair back, while Daisy can barely speak; she is equal parts embarrassed and thrilled by the over-the-top gestures—the limo, the balloons, the music, the fizz, all of it—and she has no idea what to say. What to feel. Mia looks so glamorous in a slinky black cocktail dress, her hair blow-dried and fabulous, even after being ruffled in the breeze. Her makeup is perfect; gold bangles slide up and down her tanned arm.

With a grin, she ducks down from the sunroof and a few seconds later emerges from the limo onto the street. Her arms are stretched out, but Daisy doesn't know whether to hug her; they haven't hugged very often, if at all. She can't remember the last time they touched and she hasn't seen her since she was thirteen. This birthday visit, as over the top as it is, was announced breathlessly by Mia on a phone call just four days ago; the quiet celebratory dinner they'd planned for the three of them having to be rearranged.

"You've grown," Mia says, dropping her arms, and then she laughs, stopping abruptly, as if she realizes she should not have needed to make this observation.

Daisy still doesn't speak.

"Wow, Mia," Suzanne says, her tone just a little too dry, "you've really gone to town. Literally."

Another laugh, this one with an edge. "Well, like I said, I wanted it to be special."

Daisy senses the currents flowing between the women, electric with tension, worse than the last visit, although maybe that was her fault. She had asked too many questions. She made Mia angry with her, even though she tried not to show it—smiling in sympathy, touching her hand. Daisy can't help but wonder if her questions are why there hasn't been a visit in the two and a half years since. No one has said so, of course. No one has ever said anything.

She glances between Mia and Suzanne, but neither of them are looking at her.

"How have you been?" Mia asks, eyebrows raised. The question is aimed at Suzanne.

"Fine. Fine." Suzanne crosses her arms.

The September wind funnels down Ninety-First Street, turning sharp. Neither woman speaks for a moment, and neither does Daisy. It's her birthday, but right then she feels forgotten.

"I was very sorry to hear about your divorce," Mia says finally, her tone formal, and Suzanne jerks her head in a semblance of a nod.

"Thank you."

There is another silence, and Daisy wishes she could think of what to say. She wants to tell Mia how glad she is that she came, how grateful she is for all the effort she's gone to, but the words catch in her throat; she fears they will sound corny and fake. Besides, she isn't even sure she means them. Why hasn't Mia been in touch before now? It's been two and a half years, and the plans for this birthday extravaganza happened so suddenly, and so dramatically, that Daisy isn't sure whether to trust them. Trust Mia. Her birth mother isn't even looking at her.

And then she does—and the effect is startling, dazzling. Her large brown eyes fill with warmth as she gives Daisy her megawatt smile.

"Hey, birthday girl." Her hand flutters toward Daisy's shoulder and then drops, only her fingertips brushing her coat. "Are you ready to celebrate?"

"Yes," Daisy replies, and her voice comes out too loud, too strident. She almost sounds angry. She's conscious of how she must look to glamorous Mia in her baggy black dress, the fishnet tights and combat boots she thought were cool but now she fears make it look like she's trying too hard to seem rebellious, edgy. She dyed her hair platinum blonde a few weeks ago, but it's turned a blotchy, coppery orange. She has a pimple on her chin and she feels fat.

Mia's eyes widen, her dazzling smile dimming slightly as her liquid gaze sweeps Daisy from head to toe, and then she turns her smile back up again. "Great. Let's go." She glances back at Suzanne, who hasn't moved from the door, guarding the entrance to their building like a sentry, a gargoyle. She is flat-eyed and unsmiling. Daisy looks away from her. "We should be back by midnight."

From the corner of her eye, Daisy sees Suzanne nod, her arms folded, her expression closed. She doesn't want her to go, Daisy knows. She's never wanted her to do anything with Mia, although she's never said as much. Daisy can still tell. She'd think Suzanne was jealous, except it isn't as if she wants to do those things herself, is it? All she'd planned for her birthday was a stupid family dinner. She can't remember the last time things felt fun. Maybe when she was little, although she can't really remember. Before her dad left, anyway, although his absence has just made it all worse. Daisy didn't realize how much he smoothed over the silences, jollied them all along, until he'd gone. Their Wednesday pizza nights and weekend brunches are a poor replacement.

"Let's go," Daisy says, and clambers into the limo without looking back at Suzanne.

Mia gets in after her, and they sprawl in the leather seat while Mia reaches for some plastic flutes to pour the champagne.

"Non-alcoholic, I'm afraid," she says with a smiling sort of grimace. "Can't be *too* crazy."

"I don't mind." Daisy takes her flute and Mia clinks it with hers.

"To the birthday girl," she says, smiling, and they both drink.

But when Daisy lowers her glass, she sees that Mia is looking out the window, her high-heeled foot tapping a staccato beat on the floor. There is a tension to her body, a slight furtiveness to her manner. Then, with effort, she turns back to her, her smile wide but not quite reaching those dark, melting eyes.

"So, how have you been? How's school?"

They're the questions of an elderly neighbor, a distant relative.

Mia's gaze slides back to the window, Central Park blurring by, before Daisy even answers. The fake champagne tastes sour in her mouth as she swallows it.

"Fine," she says.

"Good. Good." Mia nods, her foot still tapping. "That's great." She turns back to Daisy again. "We're going to have so much fun."

"Yeah." Daisy knows what she's planned—a Broadway show, shopping tomorrow at Bergdorf's, dinner at Gramercy Tavern. It all sounds amazing, but right now it feels like so much her birth mom has to endure. She doesn't, Daisy realizes with a sick, plunging sensation, look like she wants to be here at all.

But then Mia tosses back the rest of her champagne and reaches for Daisy's hand. Her fingers are slender and cool as they tighten on hers.

"I'm sorry I haven't seen you lately," she says, and Daisy's heart leaps as her hand grows clammy in Mia's. It hasn't been "lately", it's been two and a half years, but in that moment she doesn't care. Mia's here now, and she's holding her hand.

"It's okay."

"How have things been with your mom?"

Daisy shrugs and Mia squeezes her hand again before releasing it.

"I remember you saying things were kind of tough before."

Yes, on an abbreviated Skype call a few months ago. Daisy had called her to tell her about her parents' divorce, her mother's tetchy silence, her father's determined visits, and Mia had listened with that particular, intense focus that made Daisy feel as if she really cared, as if she was seeing her in a way that no one else could.

Then, after about ten minutes, a child had whined for her in the background and, with a grimace of apology, Mia ended the call. They haven't spoken since, except to arrange this weekend.

"They're still tough," she says, the words squeezed through her throat. If anything, things have grown worse with her mother since her dad left. Suzanne is so silent, so remote all the time. Daisy feels she can't do anything right, and so she has stopped trying. But more than that, she's angry with Suzanne, and she's not even sure why, only that's it there all the time, as if she's swallowed a coal. It burns inside of her. She turns to look out the window. "She's really uptight."

Mia nods sympathetically. "That was my mom, too. I could never do anything right with her." For a second, her voice tightens and then she manages a laugh. "It's like they forget you're a teenager."

Daisy turns back to give a grimace of acknowledgment, even though she has no idea what Mia's mother was like, what Mia's *life* was like. Her birth mother has shared so little about herself. Daisy knows she has three little daughters, Mia has shown her photos, but she only met the oldest, Ella, once. She's met Mia's husband, Tom, twice, when she was little, but she doesn't remember much about him besides he was tall and blond and smiley.

There's a photo though, from their first meeting; Suzanne took it, and Daisy is standing between Mia and Tom, staring at the camera, bug-eyed, as if transfixed. Tom is smiling easily, while Mia's gaze is a little off to the side, as if something has just caught her attention.

Suzanne has made an album of everything—every visit of Mia's, every card she sent, even the gift tags from every present she gave, all kept in a beautiful book with a leather cover and thick, creamy vellum pages. Daisy can't help but think it's all a little weird, as if Suzanne is trying to prove something, although she's not even sure what it is. Still, she takes the album out sometimes, looks at it, reminds herself about when Mia was more part of her life—and she was more part of Mia's.

And every time Mia visits, she wonders—she hopes—if they might go back to those days, when she came around more, when she seemed so much more interested. Her therapist told her it was natural for the relationship to slip a little, as she got older; it didn't necessarily mean Mia was rejecting her. *Relationships ebb and flow,* the therapist said. *It's a perfectly natural process.*

But it didn't feel natural, not to Daisy. And as the limo glides toward Broadway, and Mia looks out the window again, she wonders. No matter what has been planned for this weekend, how much fun Mia wants them to have, Mia's distance *has* felt like rejection, at least a little, even though Daisy has tried not to let it. She's tried so hard.

But then Mia turns the music to a popular song on the radio and starts to dance, inviting Daisy to dance with her as she raises her lithe arms and tosses her head back, dark hair rippling. Self-conscious, Daisy sways a little in her seat and Mia claps her encouragement, making her smile. She tells herself they really are going to have so much fun this weekend.

She can almost believe it.

3

SUZANNE

On Monday morning, I leave Daisy still in bed as I go to work, trying not to fret as to how she'll spend this empty summer day. I encouraged her to get a summer job, so she could keep busy, but she never did, and I worry about her being too much on her own. She's such a solitary person as it is, slouching in and out of the apartment, spending hours lying on her bed, scrolling on her phone. I don't even know if she has any good friends; she never mentions them. She hardly ever goes out, and when she does, it's usually alone. At least I think it is, but I know so little.

When I've mentioned my concerns to Mark on various occasions, he always shakes his head, smiling in a way that feels condescending. "You've got to let Daisy be Daisy," he says, which just sounds like bad parenting to me. Aren't we meant to encourage our children to be their best selves, to learn and grow and develop? Yet more and more, I've realized how little control I have over anything. Over Daisy.

And I realize that all the more when I come home on Monday evening to an apartment that feels hot and airless, all the windows closed, and I find the note from Daisy on the kitchen table.

I've gone to Mia's.

It's not even signed. I stare at it, as if the scrawled words will rearrange themselves on the page, say something else. We'd left Saturday's difficult conversation to the side, hadn't talked about Mia or moving or any of it since then. Part of me had been hoping she might have even dropped the idea, realized it was never going to work.

Now I realize she was just biding her time, waiting for the right moment to run.

I go into her room, a sanctum I'm hardly ever allowed to enter, and it looks just the same—a rumpled duvet half-pulled over the bed, clothes kicked into corners, a tottering pile of dog-eared manga comics by her bedside table, a sweet, musty smell of body spray lingering in the air.

I run my hand over her duvet, my fingers tracing the dent in her pillow. Disbelieving tears prick my eyes and I blink them back. I know I need to call Mia, check that Daisy is safe, but I also know I need to get hold of myself first. This feels too much like grief.

Taking a deep breath, I sink onto her bed, my face falling into my hands. *She's gone.* She didn't even say goodbye, not so much as a text to let me know, never mind a hug. She knew I wouldn't find the note until she was already on her way to North Carolina, which is undoubtedly how she wanted it. How did we get to this grim place?

I allow myself another breath, more of a shudder this time, and then I rise from her bed. I go into my bedroom, kick off my high-heeled shoes, my toes aching along with everything else. Before Daisy, I was the senior cataloguer for nineteenth-century European art at Sotheby's. It was a job I loved—researching paintings, writing the briefs and biographies, creating a living history for each work of art. By the time a piece went to auction, I felt as if I'd owned the painting myself; they'd become a part of me, living and breathing and alive.

I was willing to give it all up to stay at home with my daughter. I didn't even hesitate; after trying so hard to have a family, I knew I didn't want to squander a second of motherhood. And, in retrospect, I have no regrets. Yes, Daisy can be challenging, and Mia hasn't made it any easier, but I love my daughter. I love her with a breathless intensity that feels like a fist squeezing my heart, or maybe plowing into my gut. Painful and real and consuming. I hold on to that truth like an anchor that can somehow keep us both afloat... even now.

I've gone to Mia's.

Is that really the best thing for Daisy now?

I remember how Mia seemed on her sixteenth birthday, how edgy and distracted, almost as if she didn't want to be there, even though it was her idea. I saw how uneasy she was about Daisy's appearance, despite all the fanfare. Daisy had just started on her rebellious Goth look then—peroxide blond hair, heavy black eyeliner, ripped fishnets, attitude. Stereotypical angsty teen, or so I tried to tell myself, but Mia, with her three little blond girls, looked a little bit shocked. This was not the daughter she was expecting.

And how will she feel when Daisy turns up at her door? Has Daisy warned her? Has Mia welcomed her? I have no idea. I don't know if Daisy got there safely; she might be seventeen, but she's never flown on her own before. I need to call Mia, make sure my daughter is okay.

I swipe for Mia's number on my phone as I walk into the kitchen and crack open a window to let some air in. The call goes to voicemail and I let out a sharp sound of frustration. I'm not surprised she isn't answering my call; she has always liked to deal with me—and Daisy—on her own terms.

"Hi, Mia, it's Suzanne," I begin, only realizing after I've started speaking that I should have thought through what I was going to say. "Daisy left a note here saying she was going to visit you, and I... I wanted to check she got there safely. Could you let me know? Thanks."

I cringe as I end the call. What kind of mother doesn't even know where her daughter is, or where she's going? I think of my own mother, briskly no-nonsense, of the generation that believe being a mother involves cooking dinners and folding laundry, not playing make-believe or pushing a swing. I doubt she has ever agonized the way I seem to.

I call Mark while I heat up some leftovers for dinner, even though my stomach is in knots, my appetite nil. I still feel the need to go through the motions.

"Suzanne?" He sounds wary before I've even spoken, as he always does, as if I'm going to snap at him, as if he needs to summon energy to deal with me. I don't understand how this dynamic has evolved, how somehow I've been cast as the difficult, demanding one, when I am careful—*so* careful—not to ask for anything, ever.

"Daisy's gone, Mark." My voice wavers and I do my best to steel it. "She went to Mia's."

"*Mia's?*" He sounds incredulous, which is somehow gratifying.

"Yes, Mia's. On Saturday she told me she... she wants to live with her."

"What?" Even more shock this time. "But why? I mean... she hasn't seen her in years."

"Since her sixteenth birthday."

"Yes, but... you know, even before then..." He trails off uncertainly. Mark hasn't actually seen Mia in about ten years. He has allowed himself to forget about her, I realize, in a way I have never been able to.

"I know they don't have much of a relationship," I tell him. "But Daisy doesn't seem to see it that way."

"Did she tell you why she wanted to go?" he asks, still sounding mystified.

I bite my lip, to stem both my annoyance and guilt. "You know she doesn't tell me anything."

Mark sighs. "She never mentioned this to me, and I saw her just yesterday." Mark has Daisy over every Wednesday evening for pizza and Sundays for brunch; his apartment isn't big enough to have her sleep over, but he does make an effort to show up, to be a part of her life.

"I called Mia, but she didn't answer. I don't even know if Daisy got there okay."

"Let me check her ATM card transactions." Even though we've been divorced for nearly two years, Mark still handles Daisy's finances, Stirling's tuition. We've never quite completely untangled our lives, although I suppose we have in his mind. "Four hundred and thirty bucks for a plane ticket to Durham." He sighs heavily. "And twenty for a taxi from Durham-Raleigh Airport. At least we can be pretty sure she got there."

A choking sound escapes me, and I press my knuckles to my lips.

Mark's voice gentles. "She'll be okay, Suzanne. And maybe... maybe this is for the best."

"How?" The word escapes me in something between a bark and a moan, and I force myself to claw back some of my control. I hate showing my vulnerability to Mark when he has so clearly demonstrated that he doesn't want it, or me. "It's just," I manage in a more even tone, "Mia hasn't been involved or interested in Daisy's life in a long time. I'm not sure she'll welcome her visit."

"But surely she agreed to Daisy coming?" Mark asks, his tone morphing from reasonable to taken aback as he realizes that she might not have. "Did she even know about it?"

"I don't know. Daisy hadn't asked her when she spoke to me on Saturday."

"I'm looking up the flight..."

I wait while he swipes and clicks.

"She got in around five-thirty. She might not even be there yet." We are both silent, considering what this means. "Have you tried Daisy?"

I am ashamed to admit I haven't, because she never takes my calls, answers my texts. "Maybe you should," I suggest, and I hear his sharp intake of breath, like he wants to berate me, but he doesn't.

"Fine," he says, his tone turning terse. "I'll call you back."

I wander around the apartment, feeling like I don't know what to do, as I wait for Mark's call. It's always this way between us now—I am the supplicant, trying not to be too demanding, while Mark acts as if everything is just a little too much.

When we were married, I believed we were equal partners. We both had good jobs, and we were both equally invested in Daisy's adoption. We'd looked into adoption after years of trying led to fertility tests which revealed Mark had a low sperm count. I took it with equanimity, but during our divorce, he accused me of blaming him, although I never did. I never even *thought* that way.

We met when we were both starting out in the city—me as an intern at Sotheby's, Mark in an entry-level job at Morgan Stanley. He'd gone to an auction with a bunch of bigwigs from work, some client thing, and he was barely twenty-two. He told me he was fascinated with me, with how coolly capable I seemed, so wonderfully different from his melodramatic mother, his alcoholic father. I was a calm, soothing presence, he said, and I liked how friendly and even eager he seemed, with his shaggy hair and crinkly eyes, the human version of a Labrador. He stuttered when he asked me out, and I played it cool, even though I was thrilled inside, amazed and wondering that I had actually caught his interest, that someone so friendly and full of zest for life wanted me.

A week later, we were officially dating, married two years after that, both of us just twenty-four. I was so *happy*, then, with a kind of quiet incredulity that it was possible to feel this way, to have this much. Even when we struggled with infertility, the ups and downs of pursuing adoption, I felt so very grateful.

And when Daisy came... I close my eyes as I remember the day we brought her home, just two days old. How we buckled her into her car seat, fumbling with the straps, laughing at ourselves, drunk on wonder. Usually I unconsciously edit Mia out of that memory, but now I recall she was standing in the room, ready to go home herself, slightly slumped, her expression closed, her stomach sagging emptily.

At that point, we'd only just agreed to the open adoption; I would have agreed to anything, knowing Mia still had six weeks to change her mind. And I convinced myself it could all work out, that I would make it so. Mark, Daisy and I were a family now. We had room for Mia... at least sometimes.

My phone buzzes, and I snatch it up. "Did you talk to her?"

"She texted me. Said she's okay."

I am not going to let it sting, that Daisy texted Mark and not me. I've known, deep down, that she's always had an easier relationship with him than with me, even if I don't really understand why.

"That's good. She's at Mia's?" I do my best to keep my voice neutral.

"No, in the taxi. Almost there."

"Does Mia know she's coming?"

"I didn't ask." He pauses, and I feel an instinctive need to brace myself. "She's seventeen, Suzanne," Mark says, and he makes seventeen sound like twenty-five, or thirty, sophisticated and worldly-wise. I want to remind him she's not an adult, she's a *child*, that even when she acts like she hates me, she still asks me to kill the spider she sees on the ceiling of her bedroom. I know how to make the peanut butter and banana sandwiches she loves; I've perfected the ratio of butter to banana. When her belly button piercing got infected, I swabbed it with disinfectant and managed to get the wretched thing out while she closed her eyes and tried not to cry. *She needs me.* Even if she doesn't think she does.

"I wonder, though," Mark continues slowly, "why she wants to visit Mia now. Did something happen?"

My ignorance both shames and convicts me. "I don't know."

"Even if she didn't tell you... did you notice anything?"

"She did seem more withdrawn this last week," I admit. *And it felt like a relief.* I close my eyes, force the words out. "Since last weekend, I think. She went to her friend Becca's for a sleepover..." And I'd been pleased, because she hardly ever went out with friends. I hadn't seen Becca since she and Daisy were in eighth grade. "Maybe something happened," I finish lamely. I am cursing myself for not thinking through his more, for not being aware and attentive and *on it.* The truth is, parenting mostly solo can feel like such a lonely slog sometimes, and I'd let myself go without realizing. I'd been grateful for the breather. "I should have realized," I tell Mark, framing it as an apology.

"It's hard," he replies, his tone thankfully without any recrimination. "I didn't realize anything, either."

We are both silent, absorbing this unwelcome development. Our daughter is gone. We might know where she is, she might, God willing, come back to us still, but she is gone. The emptiness reverberates through me.

"Okay, well," Mark finally says, a farewell. "Let me know how things go. When you talk to Mia..." Because, of course, I will be the one to talk to Mia. From the beginning, I have always been the contact point for her. That first visit, when she tiptoed into our house like she wasn't sure she should be there, Mark greeted her in a jolly voice and then beat a hasty retreat. It has, on some level, always been Mia and me.

Mia and me. It sounds like a children's story, one of those kiddie TV shows, with talking animals and lots of glitter, so very far from reality.

"I will," I tell him, and then we end the call.

I reach for my phone, check for texts, but there is nothing. I hesitate, and then I swipe to text Daisy. I glance at all the blue bubbles scrolling up the screen—unanswered reminders for dentist or hair appointments, telling her I'm going to be late and there's a casserole in the fridge, that the super needs to be let into our building to check the electrics. No replies to any of them.

I bite my lip as I think what to text. *I hope you're safe and that you have a good time with Mia. Love, Mom.* I send it, and watch the blue bubble appear, the message delivered. I wait a few minutes, staring at the screen, *hoping*, but as usual, no reply.

I put down my phone and gaze around the apartment, the empty space echoing with loneliness. Even though Daisy would usually be holed up in her room, I feel her absence, like a pulse. I wonder if she's arrived at Mia's, how it has gone. Will Mia return my call? How will she feel about Daisy in her life? And how will Daisy react, being so suddenly in Mia's?

In the last three months, Daisy has been suspended twice— once for skipping school, and another time for smoking in Stirling's courtyard. The private school she attends has a "three strikes and you're out" policy; if she's suspended again, she won't be asked back for her senior year. I wonder if that is behind her decision to visit, or even live, with Mia. Is she worried she'll get in trouble again? Does she want a new start? Or did something happen last weekend that I don't know about?

A sigh escapes me in something close to a shudder and I head to my bedroom, meaning to change out of my work clothes, but instead I find myself standing on my tiptoes to reach the cardboard box on the top shelf of my closet, behind a bunch of sweaters I never wear.

I ease it out slowly, carefully, and then perch on the edge of the bed as I slip the lid off and gaze down at the mementoes nestled within. Daisy's first pair of booties, knit by my mother, so impossibly tiny, made of soft white wool and trimmed with lace. A lock of her hair, dark brown and curling, kept in a small silver box, still soft. The first painting she brought home from preschool, a smeary watercolor of our family—three beloved, faceless stick figures. Tears catch at the back of my throat and I force them back.

Her preschool report card. *Daisy is a lovely, bright child, albeit sometimes quiet.* Then kindergarten: *Daisy is a shy child, but she can sometimes be disruptive.* That was right after Mia married Tom. First grade, when Mia had moved to North Carolina: *Daisy is a quiet child, who seems most happy in her own company. She tackles each activity with an impressive intensity. Sometimes it is hard to direct her to another task.*

Is it wrong of me to connect those dots? To blame Mia and her withdrawal from my daughter's life for the challenges she's faced? It feels too easy, but also too forced. Nothing is that simple; all children go through difficult stages. Their personality emerges, develops, changes. And it isn't as if Mia was around all the time, even back then. During the more open season of our open adoption, we saw her at most a few times a month.

But I still instinctively make those connections. I want to blame Mia for the way Daisy is, because if I don't, I might have to blame myself.

In any case, I wonder if any of it matters. It doesn't change where we are now, with Daisy in North Carolina, and me alone here, wondering why she has gone. Quietly, I replace the lid on the box and return it to the back of the closet.

4

MIA

I stare at Daisy on my doorstep, my mind spinning, my face slack. I am so shocked I can't even fake a smile, my bubbly persona gone completely flat. Daisy's uncertain expression hardens.

"Hey, Mia," she says, and there is a coolness to her tone that makes me ache, and thankfully kickstarts me back into effervescent action.

"Daisy!" My voice rings out, all false jollity, and yet part of me really is glad to see her. Part of me aches to hug her, draw her inside, and yet I stand here frozen, the smile on my face a rictus.

Daisy must know I'm faking it, but even so her wariness thaws, just a tiny bit, a fleeting look of hope lighting her eyes. Perhaps she is thinking that at least I care enough to pretend. It's a terrible thought, and it's not true. I care, I *do*, it's just that she has taken me completely by surprise. I'm not ready for this; I don't have a plan, and I don't know how to operate without one.

"My goodness, I didn't expect you so soon!" I laugh as I usher her in, my mind racing, racing.

Ella is peeking out from the playroom, her eyes wide. She doesn't even know who Daisy is. Upstairs, I can hear Sophie splashing in her bath, Tom's answering rumble. Panic ices inside me, freezes my brain. I have no idea how to handle this, no idea at all.

"I should have called," Daisy says, not looking at me, her head lowered, her hair sliding into her eyes. "But I really needed to—" her voice hitches "—to get out of New York."

I stare at her, my mind still spinning. *Get out of New York?* What on earth does that mean? "I'm..." I shake my head, trying to snatch at my scattered thoughts. "I'm so sorry." Daisy shrugs her reply. "I'm glad you're here," I tell her, and she gives me a look of such naked longing that it's hard not to cringe. I'm not entirely glad she's here, but I want to be. I will figure this out, I tell myself. Somehow. I will make this work.

"Mom," Ella calls from the doorway of the playroom, sounding strident. "Who's here?"

I take a quick breath, glancing between Daisy and Ella. "Ella, this is..." A terrible, telling pause. "Daisy. Daisy, Ella."

I don't miss the flash of bitter understanding in Daisy's eyes, that I didn't say she was my daughter, but how could I, when Ella doesn't even *know*? And right there, amidst my panic and fear and longing for Daisy, I feel a spike of anger. *She could have at least warned me.*

Ella takes a step towards Daisy, her gaze roving over her curiously, taking in Daisy's bright pink hair, the black eyeliner smeared underneath her eyes, the cropped top she's wearing that shows a belly button piercing, an old plaid shirt unbuttoned over it. Slouchy jeans and battered black combat boots complete her nineties grunge look. All of it unfamiliar and clearly fascinating to nine-year-old Ella, in her khaki shorts and pink sparkly top.

"Why don't you come into the kitchen," I tell Daisy. I am

scrambling, trying to think of a way ahead. What am I going to tell Tom? The girls? How long will Daisy be staying?

"Okay," she mumbles, and follows me back toward the kitchen.

I turn to Ella. "Why don't you go tell Dad Daisy's here," I tell her, and her eyes narrow. She knows when she's being fobbed off, but I have to give Tom some warning. Also, I realize, I don't want him bounding down the stairs in the next few minutes. "Tell him he can come say hello in a little bit."

Reluctantly, her gaze still fixed to Daisy's hunched form, she nods and turns toward the stairs.

As I walk into the kitchen, the counters freshly wiped, the dishwasher making its comforting, gurgling noise, I think of how just a few scant minutes ago I was wondering how I would handle Daisy. Now I realize with something edging toward hysteria, I will find out.

"Do you want something to drink?" I ask. "We have juice, water, tea...?"

"Um, water is fine." She is standing in the middle of the kitchen, looking lost, and I gesture towards the table by the French windows overlooking our backyard.

"Sit down," I say, and it comes out too much like a command.

She moves to the table, dropping her backpack onto the floor. She doesn't have a suitcase, I realize, and I feel a treacherous flicker of relief. She can't be staying that long, then, and yet... this is *Daisy*. Daisy, whom I birthed out of my body, whom I cuddled close, whom I swung hands with as we walked along Central Park. Daisy. My Daisy, I called her. My daughter.

But those days were a long time ago and I stopped thinking of her that way, for both of our sakes. It was too hard, too painful. Now, as I look at her hunched in one of our kitchen chairs, she is a stranger.

"Sorry I didn't call or something," Daisy says in a low voice as I put a glass of water in front of her. "I should have warned you I was coming."

Warn, I think, being exactly the right word, unfortunately.

I ease myself into a chair opposite her. "It's okay."

She glances up sharply. "Is it?"

The question hangs suspended between us for a few tense seconds and then she looks away.

"Yes," I say, my voice only a little stilted. "Of course it is." Daisy doesn't reply. "Does Suzanne know you're here?" I ask, as I think of her call earlier.

"I left a note."

A note? That's it? "Daisy, she'll be worried about you."

"I texted my dad in the taxi. They know I'm fine." She speaks so dismissively of both her parents, and I wonder how it all went so wrong. I chose Suzanne and Mark because they seemed so stable, so safe. Normal, friendly people. And also, I allow, because they lived in New York, and I was at NYU. I wanted Daisy close.

How things have changed.

I suppress a sigh as I rise from the table, too restless to sit. I start wiping the already clean counters. "So you said you needed to get out of New York? Why was that?"

She doesn't reply and I glance back, alarmed to see her lips tremble before she presses them together. Suddenly, despite the grungy clothes and the attitude, she looks very young, younger even than just seventeen.

"Daisy? Did something happen?"

"Yeah." Her eyes are glassy and my heart turns over, squeezes.

"Daisy…"

"I thought you might understand…" She trails off as Tom bounds into the room, just as I knew he would, all smiles and cheer. Could he not have given us a *few* more minutes? And yet did I really want to hear what Daisy was going to tell me?

"Daisy!" He says her name like he's reading out a contest winner. "It's so, so great to see you. It's been... what? Nine, ten years?"

She shakes her head, a shy smile curving her lips. "I don't actually remember."

"Neither do I." He laughs, and so does she, and I try to smile, join in the joke.

But I remember. The last time he saw her was the first Christmas after we moved to North Carolina. I was pregnant with Ella and asked Suzanne if I could see Daisy last minute, on Christmas Eve. I had told myself I wouldn't, that it wasn't fair to keep interrupting her life. But I did, and Tom decided to come with me, and it was as hard as all the other visits, when I had to hide how my heart was breaking, and I almost wished I hadn't gone.

Avery has come into the kitchen, peeking shyly from behind Tom. He glances at me, and I know what he's thinking. How do we explain this? I decide to take control of the situation.

"Avery, this is Daisy. Daisy, Avery."

Daisy smiles at her and Avery smiles back shyly. Ella has sidled in along the wall, and is watching us all, arms folded, eyes narrowed.

Then Sophie marches in, dressed in polka-dot pajamas, her hair in damp blond ringlets, clutching her favorite koala teddy bear. "Who are you?" she demands, and Daisy looks bemused.

"I'm Daisy."

"I'm Sophie."

We all laugh, uncertain huffs of sound, relieved to get this far.

"That's a nice koala," Daisy says, nodding towards Sophie's bear. "I have a panda at home."

She glances at me, and in a flash of poignant memory, I recall the teddy bear I gave her for her first birthday. She still has it? I think of the panda emoji she sent in her message. I feel a tumbling sensation inside, a mix of wonder and fear that I may still be that important to her.

Tom glances at me over the girls' heads. "Shall I make up Sophie's room?" he asks, slightly sotto voce, but obviously not enough, because Sophie's head whips round.

"My room?" She sounds as if she is caught between excitement and suspicion. "Why my room?"

"I thought Daisy could sleep there," Tom says easily. "And you can share with Avery."

Sophie purses her lips, thinking this through, and then she nods. "Let me show you my room," she tells Daisy, a gracious command, and Daisy looks at me, as if for permission. I nod, even as I desperately want to press pause on this whole situation. It feels too fraught, every moment a minefield. And yet it also feels inevitable, as Sophie lays claim to Daisy, taking her hand, marching her toward the hall, Avery following them. Tom has already gone upstairs to get clean sheets.

Ella gives me a narrowed, challenging look. "Who is she, Mom?" she asks as we trail after them.

"She's..." I take a deep breath. "I'll explain later, Ella, okay?"

Her eyes narrow even further, to suspicious slits. "Why do you have to *explain*?"

"Just..." I shake my head. "Please, just be patient."

As I come into the front hall, I see Daisy glance at the wooden sign in the hallway that states so proudly in its curlicue script "The Sullivans Live Here," along with the family portraits, one per year, above every step. Standard suburban decorating choices, yet now I cringe inwardly at the sight of our growing family—the first one of Tom and me when I'm pregnant with Ella, my hand resting on my bump with that proprietary satisfaction of the heavily pregnant woman, the last one of the five of us sprawled on verdant grass, all dressed in white T-shirts and denim. Daisy, of course, isn't in a single one of them.

"Nice pictures," she says, and her voice comes out just a little bit tight.

I briefly close my eyes as Sophie tugs on her hand and they head upstairs, with all of us following. "Thanks. I think Avery has her eyes closed in one of them, but what can you do?" I force out a laugh and then fall silent. Daisy doesn't reply.

"My room's here, at the end of the hall," Sophie says, leading Daisy toward the small, very pink bedroom, with its toddler-sized furniture. It's not the obvious choice as a guest room, but I know why Tom chose it. Sophie is the only one who would be excited to give up her room, who would feel special, proud rather than possessive.

Daisy steps into the room, tucking a strand of hair behind her ear, and I notice, for the first time, that she has a small, round birthmark right by her left ear, the same as I do. A shiver of recognition passes through me; I didn't think birthmarks were even genetic. Yet as Daisy steps closer, dropping her backpack onto the floor, I am struck afresh by the impossibly true realization: she is my daughter, no matter how I have tried to act or feel otherwise over the years. She's *mine*. I feel a surge of emotion, a thrill of terror.

I glance at my three little girls, standing together, watching Daisy and me, and I wonder with both trepidation and a new flicker of hope, what this visit, however long it is, will hold.

"Thanks for letting me stay," Daisy says as she scuffs her boot along the carpet. Her head is bent so she can't look at me.

"Of course, of course." I practically babble the words. "Girls, you need to get ready for bed. Ella, in the shower. Avery, PJs. Sophie, teeth." I give them my best I'm-your-mom-so-do-it look, and while I'm expecting the usual pushback, they all drift away to their various tasks without a murmur. I wonder if they sense the weirdness, the tension.

I glance at Daisy, having no idea what to say, what she needs to hear, and then Tom comes in with the sheets.

"Peppa Pig, the latest fashion," he jokes, and Daisy manages a smile.

"Are you hungry?" I ask, realizing she probably hasn't eaten. "We have some leftover chili."

"I'm vegetarian."

I probably should have known that. "No problem, I've got some veggie burgers in the freezer." I give her an encouraging smile, determined to seem upbeat, even though dread is lining my stomach like acid, and every muscle in my body is twanging with a terrible tension, so I feel both exhausted and wired. "I'll pop a couple in the oven," I tell her. "Go ahead and get settled in." Although since she only brought a backpack, I don't know how much that is going to entail. *How long is she going to stay?*

For a second, she looks at me with something like scorn, and I have the awful feeling that she sees right through me, that she has been able to read all my awful thoughts. "Thanks," she says, and there is a challenge to her tone. "I will."

Downstairs, I move on autopilot, digging through the freezer for the veggie burgers, slapping them on a baking tray. I am grateful at least that Ella is in the shower, unable to give me the inquisition she undoubtedly wants to, and Avery and Sophie are upstairs with Tom. I need a moment to myself, to recover, to regroup. As I search through the freezer for some buns, I realize I am actually shaking.

Daisy. Daisy here. Once I would have welcomed it, celebrated it even, thrilled to include her in my life, to show her everything. I would have taken her by her little hand, given her a full tour, pointed out pictures, told her stories. Of course, by the time we'd moved to North Carolina, I'd already decided to take a step back from Daisy's life, so that never would have happened in this house. It felt like a choice I had to make, for her sake as well as mine. Neither of us could straddle the divide, handle the strain, of being both everything and nothing to each other.

But, I recall, as I hunt for ketchup in the fridge, I once asked Suzanne if I could have Daisy stay with me, when she was about three. Just one overnight, a Saturday. My apartment was tiny, but it was in a good neighborhood, she would have been safe. Suzanne had said no. Regretfully, but firmly. Drawing a line. I understand why she did more now, but I still can't keep myself from resenting her anyway.

As I stand there, one hand on the fridge door, the memories rush at me in a way I try to never let them: holding Daisy as a newborn, kissing the top of her head. The moment I handed her to Suzanne, wrapped in a soft pink blanket Suzanne's mother had knitted. I'd wept while I'd put it around her and she'd blinked up at me with her big blue eyes. The moment she left my arms, I felt like crying out. Suzanne had tears in her eyes as she took hold of my daughter.

"Thank you," she said, as if I'd just given her a birthday present, and I wanted to slap her.

Later memories, too—the first time she'd toddled toward me. Suzanne had watched, smiling faintly. "She took ten steps yesterday," she said, while I caught Daisy in my arms.

It wasn't a competition, I knew that. I couldn't let it be, because I would always, always lose. I'd given Daisy up, no matter how often I saw her, and I knew she wasn't mine, not in that way. The leader of a support group I went to, back at the beginning, always said that "at the heart of adoption, there is loss." It was meant to be comforting, but it felt like failure. There's no way to come back from that. Ever. No matter how hard you try—try to let go, to hold on, to stand back, to step forward—it never feels like the right thing to do, every choice painful, like you're losing a part of yourself again and again, until there's nothing left but broken pieces.

But somehow, right now, I've got to scoop up those broken

pieces and turn them into some kind of whole, and I'm really not sure how. Me, Mia Sullivan, lifestyle coach extraordinaire, has no idea how to put her own broken life back together. In fact, I'm not even sure I should try.

"I've made her bed," Tom says quietly as he comes into the kitchen.

I close the fridge door, my breath coming out in a shuddering rush. "Is she still upstairs?"

"Yeah, Sophie's asked her to read her a story. The one about the whale and the snail."

"Oh." I feel a surge of emotion, a painful, poignant longing as I imagine Sophie on Daisy's lap, their heads bent together. It's the kind of image I've never let myself indulge in.

"It's sweet." Tom is silent for a moment. "Did she say why she came so suddenly?"

"No, but I think something happened. She said she needed to get out of New York."

"She did?" Tom's voice sharpens. "Is she okay? What do you think happened? Could it—"

"I don't know, Tom." I sound irritable, when what I feel is fear—and guilt. Always the guilt, along with the love, both twined together so tightly I can't tell them apart. *I gave her up. I let her go. And now I can't handle having her back.* "The girls don't even know who she is."

"We'll have to tell them now," he points out practically, and I let out a weary sigh.

"I know."

Tom steps toward me, his voice gentling. "You were going to have to tell them one day, you know."

"Yes, *one* day," I reply. "Ella is only nine." I wasn't ready for this all to be sprung on me so suddenly. I needed time.

"She's old enough to understand."

"On what level? We only told her about the birds and the bees a few months ago."

Tom cocks his head, his gaze sweeping over me. "Is that what this is about? You're afraid she'll think worse of you?"

I prickle, because it sounds like there is judgment beneath those words, and as we both know, Tom was a bit of a player back in his day—college jock and frat boy, cycling through girl-friends like a merry-go-round. "Did I say that?"

"You didn't have to." Tom's voice is gentle, and my irritation deflates; my eyes sting. I open the oven to check on the veggie burger, sizzling away. "Mia, it was a long time ago. And obviously we don't have to tell them the nitty-gritty."

Tom doesn't even know the so-called nitty-gritty. I told him I'd had a one-night stand when I was nineteen years old, with a man I never expected to see again. Plenty of women have done similar, of course, but it's not exactly something you want to confess to your nine-year-old daughter, and anyway it's not the truth. Not the total truth, which I haven't told anyone, ever, and certainly not Tom, although I've tried, so haltingly and painfully, more than once.

"I know that," I say, my back to him, my voice clogged.

I hear him walk toward me; he slips his arms around my waist and draws me against his chest. I close my eyes.

"I'm glad Daisy's here," he tells me. "I know it's unexpected, but we can help her, and maybe, who knows, she can help us. Get to know her half-sisters."

I want to believe in his rosy version of reality, but it's so *hard*. I can't even look at Daisy without feeling crushed by guilt. And what about my other daughters? Will they feel threatened, confused? Can this work, can it really be as simple as Tom seems to think it is? I wish it could, but it feels like nothing more than empty optimism, not reality. Not the reality I know.

"Okay," I manage as I step out of his arms. Upstairs, I hear the shower has turned off, and I know Ella will be down here soon, asking questions, demanding answers. "Hopefully you're right."

"And the girls?"

"I'll tell them tonight, before they go to bed." My stomach cramps at the thought—not just about what they think, but about what everyone else will. Daisy hasn't been a secret, but something close to it. My family knows about her, of course; my mother was the one who pushed me into giving her up for adoption, insisting it was for the best. *You have a wonderful future in front of you, Mia. Don't ruin it now, when you've come so far.* She never even realized how much I'd longed to hear that kind of affirmation from her—that she actually believed I could have a wonderful future, baby or not.

Since I gave Daisy up, however, my family has preferred to act as if she doesn't exist. My parents had not been supportive of the open adoption, suggested, in desperation, the day after Daisy's birth. *Why complicate things?* my father had said, his tone gentle but confused. My mother, naturally, had been more strident. *You'll just confuse the child, along with yourself. The pain won't be worth it.*

Sometimes I think she's been right about that, and yet even now I can't regret involving myself in Daisy's life over the years, although we've ended up here, as virtual strangers.

As for other people—friends, colleagues—I haven't told anyone. What I have—and don't have—with Daisy has felt private. Painful. But with her here now, and my girls knowing, it will all be brought into the open.

I have no idea how to handle her visit, what it might mean for her, for my children, for my marriage. Maybe I should have done things differently before; in fact, I *know* I should have, but in that split second when you can decide to say something or not and then you don't—how do you come back from that? Do you even try? I could second-guess myself forever, but I can't live that way. I made my choices. I will live with them. Or so I keep telling myself.

I take the burger out of the oven as Tom frowns at me.

"Don't you *want* to see Daisy?" he asks. "Spend time with her?"
There is a very slightly accusatory note in his voice that makes
me stiffen.

"It's not about what I want," I tell him as I get out a plate, a
knife. Upstairs, I hear the thumps and thuds of drawers being
pulled out too far as Ella gets ready for bed.

"What is it about, then?"

"What's best for the girls. Our daughters."

"Our daughters? And what about Daisy?"

"And Daisy, of course," I say, flushing, because he makes it
sound as if I don't care about her at all, and it is definitely not
like that. "Why do you care about her so much all of a sudden?"
I ask, because while Tom has been supportive, he has always
been happy for me to keep my visits with Daisy in the background; he certainly never pressed to come along, or for her to
visit here. What's changed?

"Because she's just a kid," he replies quietly, "and she may
be in trouble. You told me she was having problems with her
own parents, and they got divorced when she was only
fifteen..."

I hear the throb of emotion in Tom's voice and suddenly I
understand what this is about. Tom's parents got divorced when
he was twelve and it affected him deeply, going from what he
thought was a happy and stable family home to spending every
other week at his dad's bachelor pad, the other with his mom
and her new boyfriend whom he didn't like. Of course he feels
sympathy for Daisy suffering a similar fate, although when I last
saw her, for her sixteenth, she didn't mention anything about
the divorce, or her parents at all, really. In reality, we barely
talked; I made sure we catapulted from activity to activity, the
busyness covering the awkwardness, the strain that invariably
was there.

"I know," I tell him, "but by that point our visits had
already dropped off. I started to think it might be better for

Daisy if I started to withdraw from her life. Gradually, I mean."

Tom is silent for a moment and I force my gaze back to him. He looks troubled, rubbing his jaw, his forehead crinkled. "I know you haven't seen her in a while, but there have been video chats and stuff, haven't there?"

"A few." One or two.

"I didn't realize you'd made a decision to reduce contact." Again with that accusatory note. "You didn't run that plan by me."

"It wasn't a *plan*. It felt like it was just happening naturally, the visits becoming farther and farther apart. Open adoptions don't usually go on long term, you know? It starts out kind of intense in the beginning, and then there's usually a gradual parting of ways, which is healthier for everyone." At least that's what I read in the books on open adoption I forced myself to read. It helped me, to think what was happening might be inevitable, if also orchestrated.

"Okay." Tom is silent for a moment. "Now I know why you seemed less than thrilled when I surprised you with the New York trip."

"It was a lovely thought." I'm hardly going to admit the dread I felt when he'd shown me the tickets, told me about the hotel and limo he'd booked. I was forced to call Daisy just days before her birthday, act as if I was the one surprising her with this over-the-top weekend I hadn't even planned myself. Suzanne, I know, was less than thrilled by the whole thing, which I could sympathize with. It felt like too much even to me, but I know I can't even begin to make Tom understand.

"But it went well, didn't it?" he pressed. "You and Daisy in New York, painting the town?"

"Yes, it was... fine." What else can I say?

"You said you had fun," Tom insists.

I hear the girls come thudding down the stairs.

"We did. It's just... complicated. Like I said. Can't you understand that at least, Tom?"

His eyebrows draw together. "At *least*?"

"We can talk about this later." Already the girls are coming in, Daisy slouching in behind them, and I turn to them all with a wide smile. "Hey! Ready for your burger?" I sound so chirpy, I want to slap myself. Ella is still looking suspicious, Avery uncertain. Sophie, at least, only sees this as an adventure.

I put Daisy's plate on the table, and the girls gather round her as she sits to eat. Tom decides to make hot chocolate, even though it's almost bedtime, and suddenly it feels like a party, everyone excited, Daisy smiling shyly.

I watch them all, feeling strangely separated from the moment, the camaraderie. I'm so tired, and I'm also, I realize, unbearably sad. It's a sorrow I can't share with anyone; I know none of them would understand. I'm not even sure I understand it myself. Am I sad for what I never had with Daisy? Or what I had and lost? Or sad for what I am seeing here, the possibility of all four of my daughters together, enjoying each other's company, a possibility I never even let myself consider?

While Tom gets out a can of whipped cream from the fridge, I murmur something about checking on things upstairs and slip out of the kitchen. The tension knotting my shoulder blades eases a fraction as I head upstairs, busying myself hanging up damp towels and putting the girls' dirty clothes in the hamper. Tom has done a good job with Sophie's bed, the sheets pulled up tightly, the duvet turned back invitingly. Daisy's backpack is at its foot, untouched.

Downstairs, I hear Sophie squeal, and it takes me a second to ascertain that it's a joyful sound. Without even realizing why I'm doing it, I turn to my bedroom, walk toward my closet, where I keep a box of Daisy's baby things high on a shelf, out of sight, out of mind. I can't remember the last time I took it down, opened the lid, lifted out her first onesie, the plastic wristband from the hospital, a lock of her downy hair that I snipped when she was just one day old. Years ago, at the very least.

I take a step toward the closet, my arm outstretched, a longing running through me like a streak of lightning, and then I stiffen my shoulders, my resolve. I drop my arm and I turn around and walk out of the room.

THEN

SUZANNE

May 2018
3 years ago

They arrange to meet at Ladurée, a fussy, high-end tearoom on Madison Avenue, on the Memorial Day weekend, a belated celebration, Mia said, for Daisy's thirteenth birthday. It's twenty blocks from their apartment, too far to walk, so they take a taxi. Suzanne feels nervous, her stomach churning, her heart skipping every few beats. She does her best to hide it, making inane remarks about the weather, the park, as they travel down Fifth Avenue.

She can see that Daisy feels nervous too, and she isn't able to hide it as well. All morning it has come out in fits and starts, in anger and tearfulness, and now in a moody silence, as they exit the taxi and head into the restaurant, taking their places at a spindly table, and a waitress swoops down with fancy menus.

This visit was unexpected. Or really, not so much unexpected as a long time coming. It has been over three years since they've seen Mia, the longest they've ever gone without her visiting. The last time was a summer picnic in Central Park; Mia was pregnant with Avery, and Ella was a toddler, with blond curls like cotton candy, big blue angel eyes. Daisy was almost ten then, and young enough that she enjoyed playing with Ella, pushing her on the swing.

"Don't they get along," Suzanne had remarked, and Mia had smiled and nodded, her eyes narrowed as she watched her two daughters together. Suzanne had had the sense that Mia was already moving on, letting go. As she'd watched Daisy and Ella, she had rested one hand on the very slight swell of her bump, fingers stretched over it possessively. When she'd said goodbye, she'd walked away quickly, without looking back.

This visit already feels different. Mia called them a week ago, suggesting the tearoom—"Girls only, how fun." Her voice had been high and thin, bright and determined. Suzanne had felt suspicious; the last time they'd seen Mia, there had been a strange finality to it, almost as if she wasn't intending to visit again. Suzanne does not know what today will hold, or why, after so much time, it is happening at all. She tries to hide her worries from Daisy, but she fears her daughter feels them all the same.

Daisy is wearing a sundress that is too tight under her arms; she is at that stage of girlhood where she is not old enough for women's clothes but has grown out of the child sizes. Her body, with its new bumps and curves, the pimples that speckle her chin, embarrasses her unbearably, Suzanne knows, but she struggles to articulate her understanding without embarrassing Daisy all the more. The few conversations they've had about periods and boyfriends have been agonizing for both of them, and yet Suzanne persists, because that is what all the parenting books tell her do. *Be matter-of-fact*, they instruct. *Speak naturally about these subjects and they will become natural.* She is not finding that to be the case.

But perhaps, she reflects as she peruses the menu of delicate finger sandwiches and miniscule petits fours, she should not be surprised. As Daisy has got older, Suzanne has found parenting so much harder. Gone are the days when a bottle of warm milk and a lovely, long cuddle were what her daughter needed. Gone too are the days when Daisy would clamber into her lap, and Suzanne would wrap her arms around her chubby middle and hold her tight, reveling in the solid warmth of her.

Suzanne can't remember when Daisy started squirming away, when she didn't run to her with a scraped knee or a sloppy painting, needing her help or wanting her to share her joy. Perhaps it happened gradually, so gradually Suzanne could convince herself it wasn't happening at all.

Having Mia sweep in every so often, with her effusive hugs and her over-the-top presents, hasn't helped matters any, but Suzanne knows she can't blame Mia for the wary distance that has sprung up between her and Daisy now; they haven't seen Mia for three years, after all.

"When will Mia get here?" Daisy asks. Her finger strays to the pimple on her chin, which she begins to pick.

"Soon. She texted to say she's running a few minutes late." Suzanne has already told her as much five minutes ago, in the taxi. Gently, she takes Daisy's hand and draws it to her lap. Her daughter yanks her hand out of hers and gives her a glare. A droplet of blood appears on her chin like a bright pearl.

Suzanne looks toward the door, willing Mia to arrive. She realizes she wants to get the visit over with, so they can move on from it, begin the inevitably needed recovery. Mia's visits, even just her Skype calls, can feel like a thunderstorm blowing through their lives, stirring everything up, taking weeks, or even months, to settle again. The phone call to arrange is like the distant boom of thunder, Daisy's sudden outbursts of anxiety the streaks of lightning. Suzanne dreads it all, struggles not to show the frustration she feels at Mia's careless inconsistency, coming when she feels like it, making a fuss, and then dipping out again, to her real life. Her real family.

She's not sure when she started to feel this way about Mia's visits; did she dread them at the beginning, when Mia was so much more a part of their lives, or did it happen later, when the visits became more sporadic and surprising?

Of course, there haven't been that many visits since Mia moved to North Carolina. In fact, Suzanne can count them on one hand: the last one, that felt so final when Daisy was almost ten; when she was eight and they exchanged Christmas presents; when she was seven and Mia told them she was moving to North Carolina; when she was six, and she met Tom. Only four, but they have each made their indelible mark.

Daisy is picking at her chin again.

Suzanne lowers her menu. "It's okay to be nervous," she says, and her daughter doesn't look at her.

"I'm not nervous." There is a hint of impatience to her voice, of something close to scorn.

Suzanne doesn't reply; she doesn't want an argument. This has been happening more and more lately, every exchange difficult and jarring, so she feels as if she is constantly bumping into conversational corners, having to start again.

"Well, I'm a little nervous," she tries with a laugh, and Daisy shoots her a disbelieving look before her face lights up for no more than a second, a flash of excitement before she sits back in her seat and folds her arms, arranging her expression into something less revealing. When Suzanne turns to look at the door, she sees Mia coming in.

Every time Suzanne sees her, she is struck by how *glossy* Mia looks, as if she's stepped from the pages of a magazine, as if she's not quite real. How does she get her hair so sleek and shiny? How does her skin look airbrushed, her clothes creaseless? Suzanne considers herself no slouch when it comes to fashion—she tends to favor classic pieces, crisp white blouses, tailored black—but she knows she will never look as good as Mia.

"Daisy!" Mia's voice is effusive without gushing, and she leans forward to press her cheek against Daisy's before she drops a slouchy leather shoulder bag on the floor and shakes her long, dark hair—the same hair as Daisy's—over her shoulders. Her fingers flutter to her wrist, where she slides several delicate gold bangles up and down; the only sign, Suzanne thinks, that she is anything but entirely comfortable. "Sorry I'm late," she says as she sits down. "Have you ordered?" Her gaze moves to Suzanne without really looking at her. "How are you, Suzanne?"

"Fine, thanks." Suzanne does not know what else to say. It feels hard to believe that she once held a weeping Mia in her arms; that once Mia had offered her the same kind of comfort. That the last time they saw her, Suzanne half-wondered if they would ever see her again. "How are you?"

"I'm really well," Mia replies, and she gives a secretive little smile that makes Suzanne's heart lurch. It's the same smile she gave when she told her she was pregnant with Ella, and then with Avery. Is Mia having another baby? How will Daisy handle that? *Three* little girls to replace her. That is how Suzanne fears it will seem.

"You look well," she says, because there can be no denying it. Every time she sees her, Mia looks even more put together than before. Today she is wearing a pale pink maxi dress with little bows on the straps, its delicate hem sweeping the floor. She has open-toed sandals and her toenails are painted the same shade of pink as her dress; so are her fingernails.

Suzanne knows Mia has started her own lifestyle-coaching business; she has seen her posts on Instagram and been somewhat baffled that people can make a living from this. But perhaps that is something else that shouldn't surprise her. Everyone is so into wellness these days, being mindful and present and proactive. Raised by two no-nonsense and taciturn parents who could remember the war enough to mention it often, Suzanne feels at odds with this new brand of unabashed self-focus.

Mia, however, seems to thrive on it. She is brimming with confidence and energy, the subtle, expensive scent of her perfume wafting over them every time she moves.

Suzanne remembers her from fourteen years ago, twenty years

old and heavily pregnant, shy and stammering and so very unsure, her hair sliding in front of her face, her gaze always cast downward, filling Suzanne with sympathy. This Mia seems very different, and yet, Suzanne can't help but notice, she still can't quite look anyone in the eye. She has not yet spoken properly to Daisy.

Finally she does, after they've ordered—a full cream tea, complete with sandwiches, scones, cakes. "So," she says, plopping her elbows on the table in a way that manages to seem graceful. "I'm so glad to see you. I know it's been too long."

"You've been busy," Suzanne murmurs, but Mia ignores her.

"How is school, Daisy? Eighth grade, right?"

Daisy nods. There is an intensity to her gaze as she looks at Mia that unnerves Suzanne, and she thinks it unsettles Mia, as well. Perhaps it's because it's been so long since they've last seen her; a scattering of visits were postponed, only to then be canceled. First Mia was going to come for Christmas two years ago, then there was talk of them driving down to North Carolina for a weekend on the shore. Another time Mia floated the idea of spending the day after Thanksgiving with Daisy; she was going to her parents' in Maryland and it was only a couple of hours more to the city. None of it ever happened. There were always good reasons, heartfelt, even tearful, apologies, promises to reschedule. Everyone understood. Suzanne actually felt relieved, after she'd weathered Daisy's disappointment—stoic silence flaring into anger and resentment, a chronic condition, handled with care.

Now Daisy is looking at Mia with hungry desperation, almost as if she would eat her. Mia fiddles with her earring, laughs lightly every once in a while for no apparent reason, and somehow they stutter and stumble their way through all three courses of the tea. Mia draws Daisy out enough so she tells her about the eighth-grade art prize she won in school, and Mia effuses appropriately. When she turns her full attention on Daisy, it is like she is in a spot-light, bathed in a warm, approving glow. Suzanne watches Daisy unfurl like a flower beneath the sunlight of Mia's glance, knowing that as soon as Mia leaves and life returns to normal, her daughter will wilt.

"It's normal for there to be some ups and downs," Mark has said, when Suzanne has fretted about the emotional yo-yo she feels they are all dangling on. He has never been as fazed by Daisy's ups and downs, taking them in his stride. "I still think Mia's involvement is positive. Daisy loves the attention, and it's good for her to know her birth parents—or her birth mother, anyway."

As Suzanne is pouring out the last of their tea, grateful that they've managed to survive an only occasionally excruciating hour and a half, Daisy says to Mia in a voice that comes out in a low throb, "I want to know who my father is."

Suzanne's arm twitches in surprise and tea splashes on the table. A waitress glides forward to mop up the spill. Mia goes completely still, her face as blank and beautiful as a cameo.

"That's understandable," she says after a moment, tucking a gleaming tendril of hair behind her ear.

"Will you tell me who it is?" It sounds more like a challenge than a plea.

Suzanne puts the teapot down on the table. Her heart is thudding, her palms slick. This is a conversation they have never had before. All Suzanne knows about Daisy's biological father is that he has never been in the picture, not even at the beginning. Early on, Suzanne wondered if something painful had happened—had Mia been raped? Or was it an affair with a married man, a one-night stand, a relationship broken beyond repair? Something Mia never, ever wanted to talk about, and Suzanne has never felt she could ask.

Daisy has never asked Mia about him before, at least not that Suzanne knows about, but clearly it has been eating away at her, because as she looks at Mia, her eyes are blazing and her lips tremble.

"I can't do that," Mia says after a moment, her voice full of regret but also resolute. "I'm so sorry."

Daisy presses her lips together. "Why can't you?" she asks in a low voice that thrums with anger, and far worse, hurt. Suzanne realizes her daughter has been storing up this emotion, as if she were charging a battery. Her body is practically vibrating with pent-up feeling, and Suzanne had no idea it was there. She should have, she knows. Of course she should have.

Mia is silent for a moment, her face set like stone, and then suddenly, as with the twirl of a kaleidoscope, her expression changes, softening, her eyes melting like chocolate, and she leans forward to put her hand over Daisy's.

"Oh, Daisy, sweetheart," she says, "if I could, I would. You know that, don't you? But it wouldn't make any difference to you, okay? It wouldn't make any difference at all."

Of course it would, Suzanne thinks with a trace of scorn she's not used to feeling for Mia. It is so important for Daisy to know where she came from, who is in her history. At least that was the reason Mia gave her for having an open adoption in the first place. Suzanne remembers her insisting she didn't want to be some secret in Daisy's life, as she clutched her newborn baby to her, her face twisted in agony while Suzanne struggled to adjust to this new reality, not to feel like a thief.

"I still want to know," Daisy insists, her voice trembling along with her lips. Suzanne knows how much it is costing her to confront Mia—Mia, whom she has secretly, desperately idolized all along, even if she's never said as much. She's never had to.

Mia's face settles back into implacable lines. She shakes her head. "I'm sorry."

"Do you even know who he is?" Daisy demands. "Were you raped or something?"

Mia flinches, but when she speaks her voice is steady. "I can't talk about it with you, Daisy. I'm sorry."

Daisy lets out a shuddering breath and they all wait; Suzanne has the sense of a silent storm having ripped through the room, an invisible earthquake. There are new fault lines in these fragile relationships, riven even deeper, overturning all they thought they knew.

Daisy pulls her hand away from Mia's and then, in a movement sudden enough to make them both gasp, she pushes away from the table, knocking over her chair.

"Daisy—" Suzanne begins, as her daughter's face turns blotchy. Daisy just shakes her head and hurries to the bathroom. Suzanne glances at Mia; she looks troubled but also resolved.

"I'm sorry," she says again, and the words fall into the stillness.

5

SUZANNE

Daisy doesn't text me back, but Mia does. *Daisy's here, she's fine.* That's it. I veer between relief and rage. Was I not worthy of a phone call? I don't reply to her text.

It is strange, how utterly empty the apartment feels without Daisy. I'm certainly used to my own company, and yet her absence pulses through me, a throb of longing. I find myself dwelling on tiny, insignificant things that have suddenly become unbearably sweet: how she always leaves the knife in the peanut butter jar; the bass beat of her awful music vibrating through the apartment that I somehow miss; the childish panic in her voice when she's running late and she realizes she's lost her MetroCard and I can swoop in and hand her another one.

I tell myself not to be so melodramatic, that Daisy is visiting Mia, not *dead*, but I can't shake the feeling of grief that suffocates me like a shroud. Something has been lost, that much I know. Whether we can get it back again is uncertain.

The next afternoon, I leave work early to visit my mother at her nursing home in Montclair, where she's been for seven years. I try to visit her once a week, usually on Sundays, even though she doesn't always recognize me anymore. I used to take Daisy, but it became too upsetting for her, this old woman who sometimes knew her, often didn't.

I never know on any given day whether my mother will be either lucid or lost in memories of another time—when she was a little girl growing up in Delaware, or at college in New England, or married with a daughter. Me.

Today as I come into her room, she's a young girl again, giggling as she asks me where her sister is, because they're going to get an ice cream down at the corner drugstore. Her sister has been dead for thirty years. All the books on dementia I've read advise playing along with the person rather than forcing them to confront the truth, but I can't shake the feeling that it's cruel, to perpetuate a delusion like this. To lie.

"It's crueler to force them to continually remember painful episodes," one of the nurses told me, rather severely, when I mentioned it. I felt scolded, shamed; it seemed my daughter instincts were misplaced, along with my maternal ones.

At least today my mother is happy enough, excited for her ice cream, chocolate sprinkled with peanuts she tells me, her wrinkled face creased in a girlish smile. I murmur approving things, even as my heart aches with a feeling like homesickness. My mother is here, and yet she is not. I feel displaced, as if I am in an unfamiliar country, unable to find my way home.

I can't tell her about Daisy going to Mia's, the hurt I feel that she left so suddenly, my nebulous worries that it might all go terribly wrong. I can't explain that I am afraid Daisy will like it there, as much as I'm afraid that she won't. My mother won't understand and I'm not sure she has any idea who Mia is anymore. She only occasionally remembers Daisy. I yearn for her no-nonsense advice, even though once it might have chafed at me. *You can't coddle them forever,* she might have said, wagging a finger. Or *you need to tell Mia she's either in or out of*

Daisy's life. Actually, I realize with a weary wryness, I'm not really sure what my mother would say now. By the time Mia was starting to make herself more and more absent, my mother had Alzheimer's.

She was wary at the beginning, I recall, when I told her about our plans for an open adoption. "Do you really want to deal with that kind of complication?" she'd asked with a frown. "Someone who thinks they have rights to your child coming in and out of your life whenever they choose? I wouldn't stand for it, myself."

I'd explained, so positively and patiently, how Mia was an asset, a resource, to our family and our parenting. "We don't have to treat children like possessions," I told her, smiling and shaking my head. I was desperate to believe it; Daisy was just one day old, the news sprung on Mark and me so suddenly, while Mia had clutched her baby, our daughter. I convinced myself that it was a good idea, because I had to. "The more input and support we have," I told my mother, "the better."

My mother had pursed her lips and said nothing; she was of the "on your head so be it" school of thought, and I was grateful she didn't continue to lecture me. Now I think how she might have understood so much more about the complexities of the human heart than I did at the time.

"Where's my sister?" My mother's querulous voice rouses me out of those pointless memories. "What have you done with her?"

"I haven't done anything with her," I tell her as gently as I can. "She'll be here soon, Mom."

My mother's eyes narrow, her chest swelling with both indignation and suspicion. "Why is this woman calling me Mom?" she demands of the aide who has just come into her room with a wheelchair.

"There's music out on the patio, Elizabeth," the aide says in a voice that manages to sound both cheerful and calm. "Why don't you go out and have a listen? This nice young lady will come with you." She smiles at me, and I try to smile back, even though her words sting. I have to pretend not to be my mother's daughter. I've done it before, but it always hurts.

I realize it probably wasn't a good idea to visit my mother so soon after Daisy's disappearance; I had a faint hope of feeling connected, but instead I feel unmoored from both generations, lost in the middle and alone. I usually manage to steel myself for these visits, but I didn't have the strength today.

Eventually, with the help of the aide, I manage to cajole my mother out onto the patio, where a mariachi band, of all things, is playing a lively tune. My mother, who used to have a derision of any music that wasn't classical, hums along and claps her hands while I sit on a bench in the muggy heat and do my best not to wilt.

"She's been in good spirits this week," another of the aides, Tina, informs me with a smile for my mother, who is now singing along even though she doesn't know the words, and they are, of course, in Spanish. Neither fact deters her.

"I'm glad to hear that," I tell Tina. Even if she wasn't in good spirits with me.

"She keeps mentioning someone named Helen," Tina continues. "Helen this, Helen that. An old friend, I'm guessing, although from the way she talks, they had some beef!" She laughs while I shake my head, mystified but not really surprised. A few weeks ago, my mother went on about her boyfriend Myles Jepson, whom she had never mentioned to me in forty-three years of lucid motherhood. I don't know if she's made up these people, or shadowy ghosts from the distant past have suddenly taken on more resonance as the current day under-standably loses its appeal.

"I don't recall any Helen," I tell her with an apologetic shrug.

"A school friend, maybe," Tina suggests. "She talks like they had an argument, you know? 'Helen has a lot to answer for,' that kind of thing."

I shrug again, helpless, ignorant. I'm too weary and worn out to dredge up any curiosity for the mysterious Helen, whoever she was. "She must be from a long time ago," I say. No one important now.

Tina nods and gives me a smile full of sympathy, because we both know the more my mother sinks into the past with all of its shadowy ghosts, the more she forgets me.

As I head back into the city after sitting with her for a dinner of a medley of unappetizing purees, it's hard not to feel lonely, like an emptiness is whistling right through me. Daisy might be prickly and perverse, but I remember the rush of love I felt when I held her as a baby, when I breathed her sweet scent in, when I realized she really was mine.

Except, I can't help but think as I step into my empty apartment, maybe she never actually was.

I kick off my shoes as I go around opening windows, the sultry air and the sound of traffic below comforting and yet somehow making me feel lonelier, high up here all on my own.

I decide to call Mia, even though I'm somewhat dreading talking to her, because I really need to know what's going on. It's seven o'clock on a Tuesday evening, and her phone rings and rings, irritating me, before she finally answers it.

"Suzanne." Her voice comes out wary.

"Hello, Mia." I sound stiff even though I didn't mean to; I realize I haven't spoken to her in nearly two years. "How is Daisy?" I hate that I have to ask her for news of my daughter.

"She's..." Mia hesitates. "I think she's okay."

"You think?" My voice sharpens. "What do you mean?"

"I'm not sure what's happened." Mia lowers her voice; I can hear her moving through rooms, closing a door. "But something has."

My stomach lurches and I sit hard on a kitchen chair as I struggle with a sudden swoop of nausea. "How do you know?"

"I don't, she just said she needed to get out of New York." Mia's voice has sharpened. "You don't know what happened, I take it?" I don't miss the note of judgment in her tone.

"No, I'm afraid I don't." I will not explain my relationship with Daisy to Mia.

"Well, I'll try to get it out of her, I guess. I asked her last night if she was okay—physically, I mean."

"Physically..." Again I feel a lurch of nausea and I double over, one hand pressed to my stomach. "Do you think she was... assaulted?"

"I have no idea what happened, Suzanne, but Daisy assured me that she was all right... that way. She doesn't want to talk about it, and I'm reluctant to press at this point."

I am silent, absorbing all this news, struggling to push aside the hurt I feel that Daisy never confided in me, because of course she didn't. Our relationship hasn't been like that for a long time. And yet, I realize, I still thought, or at least hoped, that she'd come to me in a crisis. "All right," I finally say, and I still sound stiff. "Thank you."

Mia is silent, but I sense her struggling to say something. Finally she tells me, "I spoke to Daisy today and we agreed on her staying for a week."

There is something final and almost ominous about her words, and I realize Daisy must not have told her about her plan to live with her for the year. Did Mia give an ultimatum before Daisy could explain? My heart aches for my daughter, the disappointment and hurt she must have felt, and yet I am relieved. I am certainly not going to mention the plan to Mia.

"How did Daisy feel about that?"

"She agreed." I cannot tell anything from Mia's tone. Did Daisy go silent or surly, or did she sneer or rail? Or did she, as

I've seen her often enough before with Mia, simply nod and agree, doing her best to hide her hurt, her hope?

"Thank you," I say, "for having her."

"Of course." Mia sounds diffident. The conversation feels as if it has finished.

"Let me know if there's anything I can do," I say, uselessly, and after a murmur of farewells, Mia ends the call.

I call Mark to update him, my stomach still in knots from Mia's revelations. Why on earth did Daisy have to get out of New York? The phrasing feels melodramatic, almost farcical, like she's some gangster on the run. Part of me wonders if it's just an excuse Daisy gave to justify arriving on Mia's doorstep, but I feel in my gut, my heart, that it's more than that.

"Mia would tell us if something's really wrong, wouldn't she?" Mark asks when I've explained the situation to him.

"I... I think she would." I realize, despite eighteen years of relationship, of strained silences and difficult moments, of startling moments of both intimacy and animosity, I really don't know Mia at all.

"Maybe she can get to the bottom of this," he says heavily, "even if we can't. That was what we wanted, in the beginning, wasn't it? Another adult in Daisy's life to support her?"

I think of the optimism I made myself feel, back at the beginning. "I suppose it was." I hesitate, and then offer cautiously, "I just don't know if that adult should be Mia."

"Why not? She cares about Daisy, just as we do."

No, I think, *not* just *as we do*. Because Mia has flitted in and out of Daisy's life, and no one who really cares about someone does that. Do they? "She hasn't had much of a relationship with Daisy recently," I say as diplomatically as I can.

"Then maybe this will help."

I struggle with annoyance and, worse, the hurt I feel, that Mark is so optimistic about Daisy and Mia's relationship, but I tell myself that is petty, that of course we should both be hopeful that Daisy will gain something from this visit.

"Anyway," Mark says, his tone cautious but also with a hint of wryness. "You might like a bit of a break. Don't you think?"

I'm not sure how to answer, because while, yes, part of me would very much like a break from the sullen silences and endless hostility, the other part just wants Daisy back. Desperately. And anyway, it's not that simple. Even when she's not here, I'm still her mother. I still worry and long and hope. There's never a break from that.

"I guess," I say in a dubious tone, and Mark gives a little sigh.

"Let me know when she gets back," he says, a farewell, and I murmur my agreement before ending the call.

As I wander through the apartment feeling anchorless, I try to tell myself I am free. I could do my best to enjoy this liberty, unexpected as it is, as worried as I still feel. I could get a takeout, drink a bottle of wine, even go to a bar. I could do anything, anything at all, and yet I do nothing, drifting through empty rooms before, for want of anything better to do, I finally head to the kitchen and make myself a sensible salad.

If Daisy were here, she'd be in her room, listening to her music, door firmly closed. All I'd get out of her for the whole evening would be a grunt, maybe a few syllables. I'd likely feel lonelier, I realize, if she were here than if she wasn't, and yet I can't settle into being by myself.

I'm picking at my salad, sipping at my single glass of wine, when my friend Lynne calls, and I swipe to answer, grateful for the reprieve from my own company.

"I'm having a party tomorrow night," she states matter-of-factly, "just a few people, middle of the week, wine and cheese. You're invited."

"A party." I sound wondering, incredulous. *What is this strange thing of which you speak?* I can't remember the last time

I went to a party. Maybe when Mark and I were together, one of his work things. I've never been much of one for parties, something Lynne knows very well.

"I mean it, Suzanne," she says severely. "You need to get out more. You can be fun when you want to be."

"Fun," I repeat skeptically. It is not an adjective I'd ever apply to myself.

"All right, interesting. You are definitely interesting. Still waters run deep and all that. It's time you met someone who agrees with me."

"Met someone!" I give a hollow laugh. I cannot possibly imagine such a thing. I still miss Mark far too much.

"It's been two years—"

"I know."

"And Daisy will be at college in another year. You'll be an empty-nester at just fifty! You have your whole life ahead of you."

"Everyone has their whole life ahead of them." Or the rest of it, anyway. I take a sip of wine.

"Don't be pedantic," Lynne scolds. "Just come. Daisy can fend for herself for an evening."

"Daisy isn't here, actually." The words come out flat.

"Oh?" Suzanne clearly hasn't caught my tone. "Where is she?"

"She went to Mia's."

"Ah." Lynne, my oldest friend, knows all about Mia. She has heard my determined attempts to be generous about her, and my brief rages when Mia has announced one of her unexpected visits. "And how is that going? She's never visited her before, has she?"

"No, she hasn't." My throat is becoming tight and I don't have the emotional energy to explain to Lynne about how Daisy more or less ran away.

"All the more reason to come, then," Lynne declares. "You're footloose and fancy-free. I won't take no for an answer."

I am already shaking my head, even though Lynne can't see me. I can't go to a *party*. I'm far too tired and worried and sad. Besides, I'm terrible at small talk. And then I think, suddenly, rebelliously, *why not?*

"Suzanne?"

"I'll think about it," I hedge, still afraid to commit.

"*Come.* Seven o'clock. Bring a bottle of wine."

"Maybe."

She huffs a laugh before hanging up, and then everything is once more plunged into silence.

I eat my salad, methodically, like it's a chore. I wonder what Daisy is doing. Has she met Mia's daughters? She must have. We've only met Ella once, when she was a toddler. The other two are just photos on a Christmas card, in matching blond ringlets and red velvet dresses.

What will these three young girls think of Daisy? What will she think of them, this ready-made family for her to step into? The prospect brings a pang of jealousy, but worse is the stab of fear. What if they don't like her? She can be so difficult, distant and intense in turns, scowling when she means to smile, hiding her fear with anger. What if Mia is simply taking her on sufferance? *She agreed.* It sounded as if Mia had made the timeline, not Daisy.

I allow myself a second glass of wine, taking it to the window to watch as the sun sinks behind Central Park and the streetlights come on along Madison Avenue. If I narrow my eyes, the road becomes no more than a golden blur of headlights, the world retreating into a fuzzily soft focus, like one of those Instagram filters, turning reality both artful and vague. I check my phone, but there are no texts from Daisy, no quick "Got here okay. Love you!" that other mothers seem to receive in their stride, dismissive of the casual intimacy, taking it for granted as they slide their phones back into their bags.

I never would take it for granted. I know that, with every fiber of my being, I never, ever would.

As the lights far below blur into one, I take another sip of wine.

6

MIA

The night of Daisy's arrival, I tell the girls who she is. It's not an easy conversation, conducted in hushed whispers, because I don't want Daisy to hear anything that might be hurtful, and frankly probably all of it is, in one way or another.

"She's your *daughter?*" Ella's eyes round in disbelief, while Sophie slips her thumb into her mouth. Avery reaches for her book and sinks behind its pages. They are all huddled on our bed, the door closed, Tom perched on the edge next to me. Daisy is in her room, probably wondering where we've all disappeared to. "Were you, like, *married* before?"

"No. Not married." I try to keep my voice both light and matter-of-fact. "You don't need to be married to have a child, Ella." We did cover that when we told her about sex, but clearly it hadn't computed.

Her frown deepens as her gaze darts from me to Tom. "So where has she been all this time? Who has she been living with?"

"Mom gave Daisy up for adoption," Tom explains, making it sound as easy as filling out a form. "It was before we knew each other, and she was pretty young at the time. She thought it would be better for Daisy if someone else raised her. So someone else did." *Simple, right?* is what he seems to be saying, and I fight the urge to either scoff or scream, because it was not like that at all. It never has been.

"Suzanne," I fill in, my voice stilted. "She's Daisy's... her mother. And Mark, her father. You actually met them a long time ago."

"Did I meet her?" Sophie asks, taking her thumb out of her mouth, and I shake my head.

"No, just Ella, when she was little. They live in New York City. We haven't... we haven't been in touch much recently..." I trail off at a look from Tom that I can't interpret but which feels like disapproval.

"So why did she come here now?" Ella demands.

I try to smile. "She wanted to visit."

"You didn't know she was coming." Ella hurls this at me like an accusation.

"I didn't know *when* she was coming," I correct. "But I knew she was planning to."

"How long is she staying?" This from Avery.

"I'm not sure. A few days, maybe a week." I glance at Tom, who frowns. We haven't discussed the length of Daisy's stay, and I don't know what she expects, but that's the time frame I can just about handle. Maybe.

"And she'll stay in Sophie's room the whole time?" Ella asks, her tone turning shrewd, calculating. She's already counting up the beds in her head, wondering how her life will be inconvenienced by this development.

"What do you think, Sophie?" I turn to my youngest daughter.

"She can have my room."

I almost smile at her tone of benevolent generosity. "Great."

I rise from the bed, ready for this conversation to be over. I know they'll have more questions, especially Ella, but at least the truth is out now... or as much of it as I'm willing to tell them. There are some secrets I will always have to keep.

Later, after I've kissed Sophie goodnight, Avery and Ella sidle downstairs, looking around for Daisy, trying to figure out this new, if temporary, normal. While I am putting out lunchboxes and cereal bowls for the morning, Ella corners me in the kitchen.

"How old is Daisy?" she demands, her hands on her hips, as I place a banana and a box of raisins in each lunchbox.

"Seventeen." I am pretty sure I'd told her this upstairs.

"And when is her birthday?"

I turn to her, eyebrows raised, trying to keep it light. "September sixteenth. Why are you asking, Ella?"

She hunches her shoulders. "So you had her seven years before you had me?"

"About that, yes." Where is she going with this? I'm not sure I want to guess.

"And when did you and Daddy get married?"

I discard a slightly brown banana—Avery will refuse it—and replace it with a yellow one. "You remember we celebrated our eleventh anniversary last month?" I tell Ella. "Why are you asking all these questions, sweetie?"

She shrugs, her hair sliding in front of her face. "I'm just curious."

"Okay." It's natural for her to wonder, to ask questions. I know that, but it doesn't make it any easier to field them. "What do you think of Daisy?" I ask lightly.

"She's okay."

"I think she's hoping to get to know you."

Ella doesn't reply, and I keep moving around the kitchen, lining up cereal boxes on the counter for the morning. "Why is her hair pink?" she finally asks.

"Because she dyed it."

"And why does she have a tattoo on her arm?"

Ella must have been observing her very closely; I hadn't even realized Daisy had a tattoo. "Does she?" I ask, smiling. "I don't know. Maybe you could ask her about it."

"You said you didn't like tattoos."

I try not to sigh as I hold on to my smile. Children are human recording devices, designed to catch every offhand comment and preserve it for posterity, carve it in stone. "Did I? I don't remember."

"You did." She sounds accusing.

I turn to her, deciding it is time for some empathy, although she usually rebuffs my attempts to be understanding. "Ella, it's okay if you find it hard having Daisy here. I understand why you would."

Her frown deepens into a scowl. "Why do *you* think I would?" she throws back at me, and I hide a smile. Clever, irritating child.

"It's just a little strange, isn't it?" I continue. I am reluctant to introduce the idea of her feeling threatened, even if she is. "Because you didn't know about her before, I mean."

"Why didn't you tell me about her before?"

"I thought you might be too young to understand."

"Because I didn't know about sex," she surmises scornfully.

"That and other things," I answer, trying to smile. "Why don't you go see how Daisy is doing upstairs? Maybe she'd like to come down and be with us."

In answer, Ella merely huffs and flounces off to the playroom, where Tom and Avery are reading a book together. As I finish in the kitchen, I wonder if I should ask Daisy to join us. I'm not sure I have the energy for that, though, and in the end, Daisy stays in her room until Tom and I go to bed, and I tell myself that maybe it's better that way. We all need time to get used to being together, Daisy included.

"You know, this could actually be great," Tom tells me as we lie in bed, his arms around me. "It's summer, the girls finish school on Wednesday. I can take some time off work, we can have lots of fun. What if I book tickets for a Mudcats game?" He sounds endearingly eager, but I am too tired and anxious to be heartened by it. Everything, absolutely everything, feels difficult, including this.

"Yeah, maybe."

"And I could take the girls out so you and Daisy can have some alone time. Figure out what's going on with her, get to know her better. Bond."

A prospect that fills me with both dread and yearning. The push-pull of my emotions utterly drains me. "That sounds good," I say with an approximation of enthusiasm.

"Mia?" Tom's arms tighten around me. "I know this is hard, and I can't begin to know all you're feeling right now, but... I think it's good Daisy came to visit us."

A lump forms in my throat and I close my eyes. Tom has no idea how painful I find his words, the earnest sentiment in them. "I hope so," I manage. A few minutes later, I feel his body soften in sleep.

Lying there, sleep so far away, the dread and anxiety swirling in my stomach is replaced with a deep, pervading sadness for all I've given up, all I've lost. I feel the sudden urge to burst into tears, to weep and weep, and even in his sleep, Tom must sense it because his arms tighten around me once more, his chin resting on my head. I squeeze my eyes shut and push it all back—the tears, the memories—as I focus on simply finding a way through the next few days, whatever they hold.

The next morning, I wake up early. I don't have to, as there's no five a.m. circuit training or cardio routine this week. Last night, before I went to bed, I canceled all my meetings and classes, citing a family issue, and then I posted a photo of the sun setting over Topsail Beach and a message telling my followers I was taking a break from social media "to live each moment" for a while. I got the usual flurry of "stay well" and "enjoy your quiet" comments, and a few "I hope you're okay" with worried-face emojis. I replied to each one, as I always do, assuring everyone I'm fine but that I "just need to be." The vague and flowery language of Instagram, emoting so much while revealing nothing.

It was actually a relief to put my phone away, to unplug from the constant demand to document my life for my followers and clients, showing them that I'm both inspiring and relatable —and it also, I knew, meant I wouldn't have to post about Daisy. Not until I was ready, anyway.

Down in the kitchen, I watch the sun rise over the trees, the backyard suffused with pale, misty light. As I wait for the coffee to percolate, I wonder, with a tangle of trepidation and hope, what the day will hold. I need to talk to Daisy, and figure out what's going on with her. Why did she come here, really? What needs to be fixed in New York? Or, I muse, should I treat this as a visit, something planned? I could act as if I'd responded to her message, that she came here on my invitation, it was all arranged. But what would the point of that be—just to make it easier for me?

Daisy came here for a reason, I remind myself. Even if I don't know what happened, she needs help, and she looked to me—*me*—to offer it. That gratifies me as much as it scares me, and I try to take heart. Maybe all I need is a little more of Tom's optimism. Maybe Daisy coming here could be the best thing that has happened to any of us.

"Hey."

I turn at the soft sound, and as I take in the sight of Daisy standing uncertainly in the doorway of the kitchen, still dressed in her pajamas, her hair in a tangled cloud about her face, I feel an entirely unexpected jolt of recognition, as if I am looking at someone new, and yet at the same time someone entirely familiar.

I *know* her. I know that beaten-down yet determined look, the slump of her shoulders, the lift of her chin and the flash of hope in her eyes. I know it so well, because that was me, once upon a time. Standing here at dawn in an empty kitchen, I realize this is the first time I truly see myself in my daughter, and it reverberates right through me, like I've missed a step even though I'm standing still, frozen in place.

"Hey," I finally say, softly, and for a second her eyes widen and a smile flirts with her mouth and then slides right off as she rearranges her features into something I'm sure she hopes is cooler. *Oh, Daisy.*

"I couldn't sleep," she says by way of an explanation, moving past me without looking at me, defenses back in place. She sits down at the kitchen table, drawing her knees up to her chest. As she wraps her arms around her knees, I see the dark flash of her tattoo, but I can't tell what it is.

"Coffee?" I ask and she nods. I move to the coffeemaker, studying her covertly as I pour us both mugs. I can't help but think how vulnerable she looks, how guarded and cautious and *young.* So young. She is only two and a half years younger than I was when I had her. Something inside me clenches hard at the thought.

I bring the mugs over to the table, along with sugar and milk, bracing myself for whatever conversation lies ahead, yet part of me, strangely, welcoming it too. I want Daisy to open up to me, and yet I'm afraid of what she might tell me—and what I might feel. Just looking at her stirs all kinds of emotions and memories in me, ones I've suppressed because they're too painful to feel.

I think about when I held her, just six weeks old, the first time I saw her after I'd given her up, signed the papers. She smelled the same as the day she was born, underneath the fancy organic baby powder and shampoo Suzanne used. She'd smelled like my baby. Handing her back to Suzanne right then, knowing there was nothing else I could do, felt wrong on every level, and yet I did it. Even though I was howling inside, I did it. And I've kept doing it, ever since, even as part of me has been longing to snatch her up into my arms.

That desire has grown fainter with time, as it surely had to. Because you can't, I've come to realize, sustain that force of feeling when it's not being fed. When you know you're not the most important person in her life, you're not meant to be. How can she then be yours?

And so there was a gradual letting go, a deliberate easing away, my visits becoming more sporadic and yet no less intense, because I *missed* her. As Daisy grew older, the letting go began to feel more natural; this precocious six-year-old, this uncertain tween, this spotty teenager… they were all strangers to me, on some fundamental level, out of painful necessity, and even though it hurt, it was also a relief. I could let this girl go.

But now she's here and I can't, even though part of me still wants to, because it feels like it would be easier. Simpler, anyway. I won't do that this time, I tell myself as I join Daisy at the table. I won't let her down now.

We sit quietly in a pool of sunshine, sipping our coffee. I struggle to think of an innocuous opener, a way into deeper things. "Is it much hotter here than in New York?" is the best I can come up with, and inwardly I wince. Barely five minutes in and all I can talk about is the weather.

"Not too much." Daisy cradles her coffee cup, and again I see the tattoo. This time I can make out the image—a crescent moon, weeping what look like drops of blood. Is that just a teenaged Goth thing, or does it have some personal significance? It's grim, either way, and I feel an ache of sadness for this girl and whatever she's been through, the burdens she carries. How many of them are because of me?

A few more moments pass and I decide to address the hulking elephant in the room, crouching on the table right between us. "This is a little weird, isn't it?" I give what I hope is a commiserating smile.

Daisy looks up, her eyes narrowed. "Is it weird for you?"

"A bit." I'm not sure how far to go with this. "But it's also good. I'm glad you've met my... my other daughters." I stumble slightly over the word *other,* and I can tell she notices. Her expression hardens briefly and then she looks away, out the French windows, sunlight bathing the grass in gold, catching on every dewdrop as if they are diamonds.

"I met Ella before."

"Yes, but I mean, properly. So they remember."

Daisy is silent for a long moment, and I sense she is steeling herself to ask a question. I have to steel myself too, because I have no idea what might be coming next. "Why didn't you tell them about me?" she asks. She is still looking out the windows, her face averted. "I heard you in the bedroom last night, and anyway, it was obvious." Her breath hitches and she squares her shoulders. "Were you keeping me a secret or something?"

"Not a secret." I take a sip of my coffee, stalling for time. I want to be honest, but I don't want to hurt her, and I don't know if both those things are possible. "I just wanted to wait until they were older, and they could understand."

"Understand what?" She sounds aggressive, but I do my best to keep my even tone.

"Well, that... that you're my daughter, but, um, well, not Tom's." I wince; I can't help it. "You're related, but..." I trail off, because there is no good way to say this. "It just felt kind of complicated, I guess, but I've realized, now that you're here, I probably should have told them about you before. I don't know." I shake my head, trying for a wry expression even though every second of this conversation is agony. "It's hard to know if you're making the right decision in the moment. All you can do is try to figure out what's best for everybody and keep going. I'm sorry if I hurt you, though, by not telling them."

Daisy flicks her hair from her shoulders. "I don't care," she says, so indifferently I can see right through her. Of course she cares. And yet, I realize, part of me wondered if she still would, when I've been absent from her life for so long, and I am gratified—so gratified—that she does.

"Anyway," I say, "the important thing is that you're here. And I'm glad you are, Daisy."

Her lips twist as she glances back at me. "Are you?"

"I won't pretend this isn't... challenging," I answer carefully, "because it's new territory, for all of us. But I want to help you—"

"I don't need your help." The words come too fast, too hard.

"Then why did you come here, without even telling your mother?" I ask quietly.

She stares down at the table, digging at a little divot in the wood with a ragged fingernail. I wait, my heart beating fast, yet also with a strange sense of calm. I got this far, which is more than I thought I'd be able to manage.

"I just didn't want to be around my friends anymore," she says after a moment, without looking at me.

Surely that can't be it. "What happened to make you feel that way?"

She hunches one shoulder. "There was a party. I was stupid."

My breath catches. "Stupid? What do you mean?"

She shakes her head, the movement definitive. "It doesn't matter."

It does, I know it does. "Daisy, were you... assaulted?" I speak as gently as I can, even though inside I am shaking with panic. "Do we need to go to the police?"

Her eyes fill with tears as she bites her lip and shakes her head. "No. It... it wasn't like that."

But it was something. Something close to that, maybe? I can't bear to think of it. I gaze at her, my heart twisting with sympathy and concern, as well as guilt. Because somehow this is my fault, at least in part. If I'd been more present, or maybe more absent, *something*. If I hadn't given her up or if I'd never insisted on an open adoption, this—whatever this is—wouldn't have happened. I know I can't second-guess fate in such a way, but it's so hard not to. I've never stopped feeling guilty, for everything, and I can't stand the thought that I might have brought Daisy to this—whatever *this* is.

"I'm fine," Daisy insists, her voice hardening, and I decide that I've pushed enough for now, even though part of me wants to demand she tell me what happened.

"Okay," I say slowly. "I hope you feel you can talk to me about it, if you want." She nods, not looking at me, and I continue, "I'm glad you came here, that you wanted to come here, even if it... it surprised me at first. And I... I hope I can get to know you better, while you're here." The words sound stilted, but they are sincere. In that moment, I realize how much I mean them, even if it hurts.

And then, to my wonder and my hesitant joy, she looks up and smiles at me. "Thanks," she says quietly. "I... I want to get to know you better, too." Her face is full of uncertainty, and I feel a rush of emotion—of relief, of gratitude, of love.

"Good. That's good. I mean, it's great." I let out a slightly wobbly laugh. "Sorry. I feel like I'm second-guessing myself all the time, wondering what I say, how I sound."

She shakes her head slowly. "You always seem so confident."

"I've learned to pretend, I guess, for my job." I pause. "When I was younger—in school, college... I was pretty insecure." Incredibly insecure, actually. Trying my best to be invisible, because that felt so much easier.

Her eyes widen and she leans forward a little, clearly wanting to learn more. "You were?"

"Yeah, pretty much. I'm dyslexic—I'm not sure you ever knew that?"

She shakes her head. I'm not surprised, since I don't really tell anyone, but Suzanne knew, and I wouldn't have put it past her to score a petty point. *Thank goodness Daisy's not dyslexic like you are, Mia.* But no, that's not fair, that's not Suzanne's way. It's actually what my mother said, when Daisy was about six, one of the few times she mentioned her at all.

"Well, I know it's not such a big deal anymore, lots of people get help and it's fine, but..." I blow out a breath. "When I was growing up, it was a little different. And my parents..." I stop, because I don't want to badmouth my parents to Daisy. She's never met them, but maybe she will one day, although, I acknowledge, she probably won't.

"What about them?" she prompts.

"They were always disappointed that I didn't do better in school, that I wasn't a superstar like my younger sister, Kerry. She was an amazing student, athlete, everything. Straight As her whole life, president of her high school, delegate for the model UN." I can't quite keep a note of bitterness from my voice. *You can never be like Kerry* was the unspoken refrain of my childhood. Admitting to them I was pregnant at nineteen just confirmed all their low expectations, solidified their disappointment.

Daisy makes a face like she knows exactly what I'm talking about.

"Anyway, I wasn't," I tell her. "I found reading and writing really hard—still do." I smile self-consciously. "I actually dictate all my texts and posts. Siri is a lifesaver." Daisy nods, and I continue, "My parents used my dyslexia as the reason I wasn't like Kerry—which it was, I guess, but they kept trotting it out all the time, like it was the reason behind *everything*." I shake my head as memories I've kept back float to the surface, make me both cringe and burn. "We'd be at a Christmas party or something, totally unrelated, and they'd introduce me, 'This is our older daughter, Mia. She's dyslexic.' Like it explained something about me, about why I seemed stupid or quiet or shy, whatever. I hated it, how they pigeonholed me. Everyone would look at me in pity, like I was—I don't know, substandard." I hear the throb of emotion in my voice and I let out a little, self-conscious laugh. I wasn't expecting to reveal that much.

Daisy's face, however, lights up with understanding as she nods vehemently. "That's how I feel about my mom. She's always telling people I'm adopted, I mean, like, *everyone*. And I just want to be introduced as me, you know? Without this... this addendum. As if it explains why I am the way I am."

"Yes, I know." I try to ignore the ache I feel deep inside, that being adopted is Daisy's cross to bear, the burden she carries. *And that's my fault.*

I push the thought away as I smile at her in sympathy, and she smiles back, and for a few seconds both of us are united in this shared experience.

"No one wants to be labelled, right?" I say, and again she nods, as if I've said something profound. Maybe I have.

I imagine Suzanne informing everyone that Mia is adopted; I can hear her saying it, in that prim little voice, and I feel a sudden flash of fury. If she wanted Daisy so much, why does she keep her at arm's-length? Talking about her adopted daughter like she's not the real thing.

Whereas you didn't talk about her at all... and there was a reason for that.

It is another thought to push away as Sophie comes into the kitchen, her thumb in her mouth, her koala bear trailing the ground. "Daisy!" she exclaims, and her face lights up. The ache in my heart eases as Sophie scrambles into Daisy's lap, and Daisy puts her arms around her, anchoring her there, with a sweetly self-conscious smile. I feel as if I could cry with both joy and sorrow. I never expected moments like these, but how many more have I missed? Or were they never really possible at all?

Briefly I let myself imagine an alternate reality where I stayed involved in Daisy's life all along. Maybe Ella would have looked up to her. Built-in babysitter, Tom might have joked. We could have done a yearly vacation, weekly Skype calls... who knows how it might all have turned out, happy families times two?

Of course, I tell myself, it would never have been that easy. I doubt Suzanne would have agreed to that level of involvement, and would Daisy really have been content with being some sort of honorary but-not-quite member of this family? But for a few seconds, as I watch Sophie snuggle on Daisy's lap, I can almost imagine it, an alternative reality suffused with a happy, rosy glow.

Except, of course, I know it would never have actually been like that.

"How long are you staying, Daisy?" Sophie asks, tilting up her face to look at her.

Daisy tenses, and then glances uncertainly at me.

"Um, I'm not sure," she says, as I race to think of how to handle the question. "A little while, I guess."

"Maybe a week?" I meant it as more than her 'little while', but from the way her expression freezes, I know she's not thinking about it like that.

"Yeah, sure," she says, and I wonder what she had in mind. Two weeks? The summer? I realize I should call Suzanne and let her know what's going on.

"Yay, a whole week," Sophie says, and Daisy smiles.

"Yes, a whole week," I agree. "We'll have so much fun. Tom wants to take us all to a Mudcats game, and I thought maybe you and I could have a spa day." I hadn't thought of that until this moment, but I mean it. I meet Daisy's gaze, and her smile widens, just a little, but it's enough. As I get up from the table, I find I am smiling. "Pancakes for breakfast?" I suggest, and Sophie squeals in delight. Daisy puts her arms around her and gives her a little squeeze. This is my reality, I tell myself, and I am going to make the best of it.

THEN

MIA

June 2014
7 years ago

It's a beautiful June day, the kind that belongs on postcards. The Central Park reservoir is a sparkling blue oval, shimmering under a brilliant summer sun, and the trees are exploding with cherry blossoms and bright green leaves. Skyscrapers glint in the distance, like flashes of light on a mirror. Everything feels vibrant and alive, bursting with life and possibility.

On a grassy knoll by the Ancient Playground, Mia waits, holding Ella's hand, scanning the crowd for Daisy and Suzanne. It has been eighteen months since their last visit, the Christmas after she'd moved to North Carolina, when Daisy was eight.

Mia had come up to visit on Christmas Eve, irritating her parents by missing their annual cocktail party, an event she can barely endure, with all the silent, sneering comparisons to her sister. Tom had insisted on coming along, and she'd told herself it could all be okay, that it could work, the three of them. That she could see Daisy without it tearing her apart.

And it did work, sort of. At least it hadn't been awful. Daisy had been quiet; Mark in the background, as he often was, Suzanne looking so stiff and prim. Mia had been pregnant with Ella, holding hands with Tom, longing to include Daisy in their little family, even though she knew she couldn't. Daisy had been thrilled with her present, at least, an American Girl doll, the latest kiddie craze, costing over a hundred dollars. Still, Mia didn't like to think she'd had to buy her daughter's affection. In the car on the way back to her parents' house in Baltimore, she had wept, tears dripping silently down her cheeks, her face turned to the window so Tom wouldn't see.

Back then, she had been heavily pregnant, having just moved to North Carolina, her whole life changing. She'd known it, and yet she hadn't wanted Daisy to know it. She'd thought, for a little while, that she could somehow keep it all balanced, these two parts of her life strong yet separate, like parallel tracks, running in symmetry. She should have known it didn't work that way, that she'd have to give something up. And, in reality, she *had* known all along that it would be Daisy. It would have to be.

"Mia!" Suzanne lifts one hand in greeting as she calls her name. She is strolling down the cobbled sidewalk alongside Fifth Avenue with Daisy by her side—she's grown so big, Mia thinks with a lurch of emotion, a sudden stinging behind her eyes. She will be ten in September, and she already reaches past Suzanne's shoulder.

"Hey there." Mia swings Ella up onto her hip and it isn't until after she's done it that she realizes how it might look, a defensive, proprietary gesture, as if Ella is a human shield, when that's not how she feels.

Daisy blinks slowly and says nothing. She was so quiet the last time she saw her, Mia remembers. It was only when she'd opened the American Girl doll, complete with a change of outfits and her own bed, that she'd smiled. She'd hugged her then, Mia remembers, her cheek pressed against her shoulder. Mia had clasped her in her arms and seen Suzanne's stony gaze over the top of Daisy's head.

She pushes those memories aside as she focuses solely on Daisy now—nine years old, her dark hair in two neat French braids, her brown eyes unblinking, her body caught on the threshold of change—legs lanky, cheeks dimpled and soft. She's wearing a pair of denim shorts and a pink top with a scattering of sparkles across the front. "This is Ella, Daisy. Say hi, Ella?" She takes Ella's chubby hand in hers and waves it while Ella squirms; it's a silly thing to do, she knows. Ella is fifteen months old. She is not going to say hi. She doesn't even want to wave.

"Shall we go into the playground?" Suzanne asks, in her level way. Mia has never known how to read Suzanne. She has always been so calm and unflappable, which was reassuring at the start, when Mia craved a mother figure, someone to shepherd her through the frightening and surreal experience of having a baby but not her own child. Suzanne had been so kindly understanding when Mia had blurted she wanted an open adoption, the day after Daisy was born. There had been a quiet confidence to her that had comforted and heartened Mia, back in the beginning, a certainty that it could all work out.

But over time Mia has started to wonder if there is actually anything much underneath Suzanne's calm exterior, if she actually *feels* things. She has to remind herself how Suzanne held her on the day she gave Daisy up, and how—just once—she herself was able to offer the same kind of comfort to Suzanne. Two women bound by loss, brief moments of intimacy in a relationship that has otherwise felt as if it's on sufferance, and entirely transactional, with a woman who barely bats an eyelid at anything.

Mia glances at Daisy, who is not looking at her. Her arm twitches at her side with a need to touch her, to gently tug on her braid or press that soft, childish cheek. Instead, she holds onto Ella more tightly, and the toddler squirms, letting out a screech of resistance.

"Sure, let's go to the playground," she says as Ella tries to lurch out of her arms. "Ella loves the swing."

She sets her daughter on the ground and watches, smiling faintly, as she toddles towards the baby swings on delectably chubby legs. She is relieved at how uncomplicated her love for Ella is, how sweetly simple. It feels both easy and pure, while her love for Daisy is difficult, shot through with darkness, with guilt and pain, and has been, right from the beginning, too hard for her to bear, no matter how much she wants to.

"Would you like to push Ella on the swing, Daisy?" Suzanne suggests, and Mia catches her breath as she watches Daisy follow Ella, and then, clumsily, lift her and fit her into the baby swing. Her little legs are so chubby, they barely fit in the slots, and her dimpled fists clutch the chains with an endearing authority. Ella has been obsessed with swings since she was about four months old. Was Daisy similar? Mia remembers pushing Daisy on the swing, but she can't recall if she loved it the way Ella does. She never had Ella's exuberance, Mia knows, her self-belief as she storms through life, only a year old yet ready to conquer, while Daisy has always been quieter, more cautious.

"Look how alike they are," Suzanne says, and Mia gets the sense that it costs her something, to say this.

Mia doesn't think they look anything alike—Ella pink-skinned and blue-eyed, her hair an angelic halo of blond curls, Daisy dark-haired and sallow, the same as her.

Suzanne nods towards them, Daisy pushing Ella with careful diligence, while Ella bellows, wanting to go higher, faster. "They both have that same focus and intensity," she explains, and Mia realizes it is true. They are both completely absorbed in the swing, Daisy in pushing, Ella in soaring ever higher. The knowledge is unsettling, the separate spheres of her life colliding in a way she can't be entirely comfortable with, even as part of her craves the completeness of the whole. "So how have you been?" Suzanne asks, and gives her a direct, unflinching look. "Life seems busy. Daisy said you were training to be a… a lifestyle coach?"

Mia doesn't think she's imagining the delicate dubiousness as Suzanne poses the question. "Yes, that's right," she says. She rests one hand on her middle. "I'm also expecting again." The words sound so old-fashioned, her voice ringing with self-conscious pride. "I'm seventeen weeks along. Due in November. Another girl." She can't keep herself from smiling. "We just found out."

"Oh, my goodness." Suzanne looks taken aback, before she quickly masks it. "Congratulations." She glances at Mia's middle, which is only slightly rounded, the small bump hidden by her loose, embroidered top. "Were you planning to tell Daisy today?"

Mia hesitates. Was there an edge to Suzanne's voice? "I was thinking about it," she says, and hates how uncertain she sounds, how unsure she feels. Suzanne has always possessed that ability, to make her doubt herself, without even trying. "Do you think I shouldn't?"

Suzanne glances back at the two girls, Daisy diligently pushing, Ella screeching to go higher. "I think it might be wise to save that news for another day. Maybe let's focus on just Daisy and Ella getting to know one another." She turns back to Mia with a smile that doesn't seem like anything more than an upturn of her lips. "Don't they get along."

Then what's the problem? Mia thinks as she watches the girls. Her daughters—except she knows she can't think like that. She will not allow herself to, not anymore. "Do you think it would upset Daisy?" she asks. "If she knew I was having another baby?" She doesn't want to upset Daisy, and yet part of her, she realizes shamefully, is almost pleased that Daisy might be upset. That she might care that much.

No, she thinks quickly, not pleased, not that. But gratified, perhaps. She wants to be important to Daisy, even as she recognizes that she can't be—or at least not as important as she wants. She's known that for a long time.

Suzanne purses her lips, the expert offering her considered view. "It might. Daisy doesn't always articulate her emotions, but she does feel things very deeply."

"Was she upset to learn about Ella?" Mia thinks of the last visit, when she invited Daisy to put her hand on her bump, when she was trying so hard to make everything seem like it was working, when she'd known all along, with a leaden certainty, that it wasn't. That it couldn't. That there could be no such thing as an open adoption when secrets were being kept.

"There were some behavior issues," Suzanne says after a pause, and it irritates Mia how she talks about Daisy in the same way someone might talk about training a puppy, resents how unemotional she sounds.

But what can she do about it? She has no real say in Daisy's life anymore. Even these visits are possible only on Suzanne's sufferance, because Mia knows, just as Suzanne does, that open adoption agreements are not legally binding, but merely a matter of good will. She chafes against it all, even as she recognizes she was the one who moved away, who made the choice to step back. It doesn't mean she has to like it, and she never has.

The push and pull of her own heart is exhausting, and she knows it must seem confusing to Daisy. The visits she canceled, because she was afraid to come, to care. The sudden, expansive notes, scrawled in glittery cards, a few twenties stuck in for good measure, after weeks or months of silence. What, Mia wonders, does Suzanne think about it all? She does not approve, of that she is sure. She cannot really blame her.

"Did you bring a picnic?" Suzanne asks, which is what they'd arranged, and Mia lifts the pretty straw basket she brought, a checked cloth covering the top.

"Yes, I have enough for everyone." She'd made sandwiches that morning at her parents' house, her mother standing over her like she couldn't be trusted with a sharp knife. But then her mother has always been that way—disapproval masked as concern, exasperated with her seeming faults, determined to direct her life. To her, Mia knows, Daisy is nothing more than the detritus of a long-ago mistake that is better forgotten. That's what she called her, she remembers, when she came to the hospital, determined to make sure Mia saw the adoption through.

"This is a mistake, Mia, that you can fix. That's how you have to look at it, for the sake of your future."

"Daisy is not a mistake," Mia had replied, her voice throbbing with emotion. She'd been clutching her daughter, only two days old, her body still battered from a long, difficult birth. "And I won't have her be a secret."

Famous last words, Mia thinks now, because that is exactly what Daisy has become.

"That's so kind of you," Suzanne says, without much enthusiasm. "Shall we find a place to eat?"

They head back to the grassy knoll by the playground; Mia spreads a blanket, while Suzanne inspects the grass for broken glass or dog dirt.

"You can never be too sure," she tells Mia, which she imagines to be her life motto.

Daisy chases after Ella, who is chortling with delight.

When they are all seated, Mia hands out the peanut butter and jelly sandwiches, brandishing a plain jam one for Daisy triumphantly. "I know she doesn't like peanut butter," she says to Suzanne, and then realizes she should have said it to Daisy.

"Daisy likes peanut butter now, actually," Suzanne replies with a small, conciliatory smile that makes Mia grit her teeth. "Don't you, Daisy?"

"It's okay," Daisy says, and takes the jam sandwich. She is caught in the middle, even in this.

"I thought toddlers shouldn't have peanut butter, in case of allergies," Suzanne continues as Ella takes apart her sandwich and begins smearing it all over her face.

"Ella didn't have peanut butter until she was over a year." Mia hates that she is defending her parenting choices, hates that Suzanne is making her, and over *peanut butter*.

They eat in silence, Daisy's head bent over her sandwich, and a sudden sorrow, something akin to grief, sweeps over Mia; she feels the heaviness of it, like a cloak she cannot shake off.

Why am I here? She thinks, and for the first time since Daisy was born, since she held her in her arms and kissed her soft, damp head, she feels it would be better if she wasn't.

The picnic lurches onward, in awkward fits and starts. Ella gets peanut butter in her hair, and Daisy nibbles at her jam sandwich. When Mia offers to take Daisy to the slide, wanting to spend a few moments with her away from Suzanne's watchful gaze, Ella bursts into tears and won't be left with Suzanne. Mia balances her on her hip as she watches Daisy dutifully climb the ladder and then slide down, the whole affair seeming depressingly joyless.

"Do you like the slide?" she asks Daisy, and her daughter—yes, her *daughter*—just shrugs. Ella grabs Mia's hair with a hand that is sticky with peanut butter.

Mia feels as if she is watching everything from a distance, almost as if she isn't here at all, and she realizes she has been waiting for this moment, knowing it would come.

It would be better for Daisy if I didn't see her anymore.

The words hammer through her as she follows Daisy around the playground, clutching Ella. Of course this day was coming. Meeting and marrying Tom, moving to North Carolina... she has been taking deliberate steps away from Daisy for years now. And yet it isn't until now that she realizes how far she has traveled.

Suzanne approaches them, her arms folded. "It's getting late," she says, with an unnecessary glance at her watch. "Mia, would you like to come back to the apartment with us?"

The invitation, Mia knows, is perfunctory. She glances at Daisy, who is looking down at her feet. A few years ago, she would have jumped up and down, tugged at her sleeve. *Yes, Mia, yes! Come back!*

But she can't come back. Mia's throat thickens and she holds Ella closer to her. "I'm sorry, but I can't. It's a long drive back to Baltimore."

"Of course." Suzanne nods, and Mia crouches down to Daisy.

"Bye bye, Daisy," she whispers, and her voice chokes. "I had such a fun time with you today."

Daisy looks up at her, her dark brown eyes solemn and unblinking. She doesn't reply. Once Mia would have clasped her to her, kissed her cheek, ruffled her hair. Now she can't bear to do any of it, because she knows this is a goodbye different from all the others. Will she see Daisy again? She can't stand the thought of walking away forever, and yet she knows it will never be the same. Something has changed—inside Daisy, inside her. It had been changing all along, but now she understands how different they both are.

She touches her cheek once, lightly, and then she straightens and turns away without saying goodbye to Suzanne, afraid she will break down. As she hurries from the park, clutching Ella, she tells herself this is for the best, even if it feels, utterly, that it isn't.

7

SUZANNE

My friend Lynne lives in a high-rise in the mid-sixties, a modern one-bedroom apartment that she bought after her divorce a year ago. Her husband Bill was a notorious philanderer—traveled for work, had a woman at every Marriott hotel from here to San Francisco. He finally left Lynne when a woman in Chicago told him she was pregnant. Now he's acting out domestic bliss there with her and their nine-month-old baby. Lynne is always at pains to tell me how much happier she is on her own.

As I head up in the elevator, clutching my bottle of wine, I check my reflection in the gilt mirror, worried I look like a crow in my tailored black trousers and matching turtleneck. I'm not very good at parties. My chitchat always comes out sounding stilted, or worse, censorious, and I feel more on edge than usual, considering the yawning silence from my daughter.

Daisy still hasn't texted or called me. I've been telling myself it's no big deal, but if I'm trying to convince myself that I'm not worried by the lack of communication, it's not working. The truth is, I feel desperately hurt that Daisy hasn't sent me so much as a single word to tell me she's okay, she's sorry, *something*. I'm also—irrationally and unfairly, I know—angry at Mia, simply because she is there, taking care of Daisy, learning her secrets, instead of me.

The doors open and as I step out into the hallway, I see a man standing in front of Lynne's door, fixing the cuffs of his button-down shirt. He gives me a self-deprecating smile, blue eyes crinkling, as he reaches down to pick up the bottle of wine he'd placed between his feet.

"Caught in the act." His smile is easy, relaxed. He looks to be about my age, maybe a little older. "You're here for Lynne's party?"

"Yes." I manage a smile even though I feel too fragile for a party, small talk, all of it.

He holds out one hand to shake. "I'm Peter."

"Suzanne." I take his hand; it is warm and dry, and he gives a firm handshake, without squeezing too much.

"Shall we?" he asks, and then he presses the doorbell.

I can hear music and chatter from inside the apartment, with the occasional raucous, staccato burst of laughter; clearly the party is already in full swing, even though it's only seven forty-five.

Peter slides me a sideways glance and, after a few more seconds, presses the doorbell again. We both let out a little huff of laughter, to dispel the awkwardness of the moment. I fold my arms, a bottle of wine still clutched in one hand.

Then I hear the clack of heels and in the next moment Lynne throws open the door. She is wearing a slinky black cocktail dress that makes me feel as if I dressed for work. "You're here, you're here," she exclaims, waving her wine glass about as she presses her cheek to mine, and then to Peter's. "You've already met? How *perfect*." That single word, laden with satisfied innuendo, makes me suspect she was thinking of Peter specifically when she said I should meet someone.

I glance at him, but he is smiling at her, unperturbed.

"Rioja! You know what I like," she says as she takes the wine he proffers before shepherding us both in.

I dump my bottle on the makeshift bar in the corner of the living room; it's a long, narrow room that is crammed with people I don't know, with a balcony overlooking Central Park, a perfect green rectangle from fourteen stories up.

Lynne has disappeared into the kitchen, taking Peter with her, and so I fetch myself a glass of red and edge to a corner of the living room, trying to cultivate a look of alert interest on my face, as if I don't mind standing off by myself, which I actually don't, although I feel as if I should.

I've never been particularly social. My parents didn't really socialize much, and I've always preferred to lose myself in a book or a painting than stumble through getting to know someone—a fact that has felt shameful, like something I have to hide. Everyone's meant to be so extroverted now, documenting their lives for social media, freeze-framing every moment for public consumption, the way Mia does. If she were here, she'd probably be holding court in the middle of the room, throwing her head back and laughing... but why am I thinking of Mia? Why am I comparing myself to her, especially when it has nothing to do with Daisy? As usual, all my thoughts lead back to my daughter. I wish I knew how she was doing.

"You look as if you're inwardly writhing in agony." I turn to see Peter strolling up to me, holding a beer and smiling. "Either that or you're constipated," he continues, cocking his head as his gaze sweeps over me in kindly assessment.

I flush, because even though I know he's just joking, I did not grow up in a house where bodily functions were ever talked about.

"Just trying to work up the energy to talk to someone," I tell him with a small smile, and take a sip of my wine. "I'm not really one for parties."

"I'm not either, actually," he replies. I find that hard to

believe, because he looks very relaxed, one hand in the pocket of his khakis, the other loosely holding his beer, his expression open and friendly. It feels like something people say but don't really mean, the same way Lynne rolls her eyes when she says "teenagers," safe in the knowledge that her son just made Phi Beta Kappa at Cornell.

"How do you know Lynne?" I ask.

"She was friends with my ex-wife, actually," he replies with a slight, rueful grimace. "When we divorced, she got the pets and I got the friends. Pretty good trade, I'd say."

I'm not sure how to respond and he winces.

"Sorry, that sounded glib." He looks genuinely apologetic, and I find myself softening.

"How many pets were there?" I ask, smiling, and it makes him laugh.

"Two cats. And I'm allergic, so…"

"And the friends?"

"Actually, mostly just Lynne. We're both lawyers, so it seemed natural to keep in touch, especially after Melinda moved out to California. Sorry, I'm rambling. The last thing you want to hear about is my ex-wife." He shakes his head wryly.

"At least you got all that information out of the way," I tell him, and again he laughs, which heartens me, because it feels like a long time since I've made someone laugh, or even smile. I realize I am enjoying myself, surprisingly. At least a little bit.

"You?" he asks, and I'm not sure if he's asking if I'm married, or he already knows I'm divorced and wants the details. Has Lynne briefed him?

"No pets, and the ex stayed in the city. We didn't have a lot of mutual friends, so we didn't have to negotiate on that point, fortunately." My few friends were mostly from the art world, Peter's from his college days, a couple of work colleagues.

Peter nods, smiling. "Any children?"

"One, a daughter. Daisy." Just saying her name feels like a

splinter lodging inside my heart. *Daisy, who is gone.* I hesitate and then add, "She's adopted."

"Is she? An international adoption?" He speaks like it is a foregone conclusion, and I am startled.

"No, no, domestic. We adopted her as a newborn."

"Oh, I just thought it must be international, since you mentioned she was adopted. As if it would be obvious." He shrugs apologetically, and I take a sip of wine to get my bearings.

Why *did* I mention she was adopted? There was no need, absolutely none. Daisy wasn't here to offer the information herself, and yet I did it anyway, as if it explained something.

"I guess I'm thinking about it a bit more at the moment," I tell Peter. "She's visiting her birth mother right now."

"Oh?" He raises his eyebrows, looking bemused. "Is that a good thing?"

"Umm..." I let out a shaky laugh, and Peter gives me a sympathetic smile. Suddenly I feel as if I could burst into tears, and I glug my wine to cover my distress. I cannot cry in front of this stranger at a party full of people I don't know.

"It must be tough," he says quietly, and I know he must see how close I am to losing it. "Did she look her up when she turned eighteen or something?"

I let out a choked laugh. *If only.* "No, actually, it's been an open adoption from the beginning. Her birth mother has been involved all along."

"Oh. Right. I didn't realize that was a thing."

Neither had I, until Mia suggested it. "Yes, it's become much more common. Hardly any adoptions are closed anymore." Something the case worker pointed out to us when we discussed Mia's request for ongoing contact. I take a steadying breath, grateful that reciting these facts has put me on surer ground. I am not going to cry. "Anyway, what about you? Do you have children?"

"Two boys. And if we're going to go in for confessionals, one is a drug addict and the other isn't talking to me." His commiserating smile is brittle, his eyes briefly clouding with pain as he takes a slug of beer.

I have no idea what to say. This isn't the usual humblebrag of Manhattan parents—"Everett got a baseball scholarship, he was really lucky" or "Annabel is staying in the city for college —yes, Columbia." In fact, it feels like the opposite, the airing of our secrets, our weaknesses. So much so that I find myself saying, "Well, my daughter doesn't speak to me, either. In fact, most of the time, she acts as if she hates me, and has for a while now, although it's grown even worse since my husband and I got divorced. And before you say 'that's teenagers for you' or something similar, please don't. I hear that all the time." I smile, meaning to lighten the mood, but the words came out like bullets and my smile feels tight, stretching my skin.

Peter nods slowly. "Okay, then. I won't say it. I promise."

I nod back, and silence descends. It has to be one of the oddest conversations I've ever had. I feel as if we know each other after just a few minutes, and yet we're complete strangers. As the silence spins on, I feel the prickly embarrassment of having said too much, even though he did, too, and yet I'm glad I said it.

"So an open adoption," he remarks after a few moments when we've been sipping our drinks. "How does that work?"

"I'm not sure it does." The words pop out before I can think them through. I can't believe how honest I'm being. It feels reckless, heady, like jumping off a bridge—a burst of adrenalin, a sudden weightlessness as the words leave me. And I don't think I can even blame the wine; I've only had a couple of sips.

"I can imagine," Peter replies soberly, "that there's a lot to navigate."

"You could say that." I realize I sound bitter, and as much as

I feel a compulsion to unburden myself, I bite any further words back. "Anyway. You said you were in law?"

He chuckles softly. "Nice segue."

"Thanks." I laugh too, a dry, raspy chuckle.

"Yes, I'm in law. Corporate, very boring. I doubt you want to hear about it."

"Oh, I do," I assure him, and he laughs softly, recognizing my desire to deflect.

"Right. Well, as much as I could bore you to death with stories about litigation and loopholes, I won't." He smiles, his eyes crinkling in a friendly way. "Shall we go outside?" He nods to the balcony, which, thanks to a light drizzle, is empty.

I nod and follow him out, squeezing through the crowd until we are standing on the rectangle of concrete, protected from the rain by the balcony above. I breathe in the misty air, grateful for the opportunity to clear my head. Swallow the last of my tears.

"So how long is your daughter visiting for?"

"A week, I think."

"You think?"

I know he's just making chitchat, or maybe just trying to be nice, but every question feels like a wound, and yet ones that need to be lanced. "She left without telling me," I explain. "And Mia, her birth mother, hasn't actually seen her in almost two years, and not for nearly three years before that. She's been drawing away gradually, whether it was deliberate or not, I don't know. And I have no idea if she even wants Daisy there or not." My throat aches and I sip my wine. I tell myself, again, that I am not going to cry.

"I'm sorry," Peter says after a pause.

"Sorry, that was a lot to take in." I try for a laugh and don't quite manage it. "Maybe we should talk about the weather."

"That's about as boring as corporate law, and anyway, it's

raining." He glances at me, looking sympathetic, sincere. *Kind.* "Why do you think she went to Mia?"

I gaze out at the dark rectangle of park, surrounded by the blur of city lights. "I don't really know. Maybe because Mia's glamorous and young, at least compared to me. And Daisy's always had this... fascination... with her. She breezes in and out of our lives and I think Daisy feels like she never gets enough of her. She's always wanting more." More of Mia and less of me. It's not a competition, I *know* that, but it's so hard not to feel inferior. Lacking.

"I'm sorry," Peter says again. "You must be worried."

"Yes." The word comes out in a suffocated squeeze of my throat. Yes, I am so very worried. I'm worried that the visit won't go well, and Daisy will come back hating me more than ever, and I'm worried it *will* go well, and she'll go live with Mia, and I'll lose her forever. I swallow hard. I can't say any of that to this man, kindly as he is. I can't tell him about the constant dread I feel, and how I'm not even sure why or what for, yet in some ways, I realize, I've been feeling that way all my life, waiting for the worst to happen. Is this it? Has it finally come to pass? No, I think. Of course not. There is always worse.

"I think," Peter says after a moment, as he stares out into the night, "one of the hardest things about parenting is standing by and watching your children make mistakes. Pretty disastrous ones, sometimes." He sounds as if he is speaking from experience.

"Yes," I agree quietly. "Although sometimes I wonder if I'm the one who has made all the mistakes."

He gives me a sudden, charming grin. "Of course you have," he says, and I let out a huff of startled laughter. "We all have. So what? That's life. I make a dozen mistakes before breakfast. The important thing is how you handle them—saying sorry, moving on."

"I suppose," I reply, because, of course, he's right, but it never feels that easy.

"Look, I hope this isn't too sudden or weird..." He pauses, and I glance at him, apprehensive, yet also a little bit hopeful. "But would you like to go out to dinner sometime? Or to a museum? You're an art historian, right?"

I narrow my eyes deliberately. "Lynne told you about me?"

He laughs, abashed. "Busted. I think she's hoping to set us up, and to be honest, I don't mind." He gives me a frank look that has me blushing. When was the last time someone looked at me in genuine admiration? It is, I know, a balm for my battered soul. "Well?" he asks, smiling. "How about it?"

I gaze out at the city, shrouded in darkness, sparkling with lights. Daisy is five hundred miles away, and I'm all alone. I can't remember the last time I've gone out, enjoyed myself, done something different. There is nothing keeping me back, I realize, but my own anxiety. And, I acknowledge, maybe I need a distraction from my ever-present, nameless fears.

I turn to Peter. His hair is gray and curly, his eyes very blue and his smile relaxed. I take a deep breath and smile. "Okay," I tell him. "Why not?"

8

MIA

On Wednesday afternoon, Tom takes time off work so we can go to a Mudcats game. Daisy has been with us just under forty-eight hours, not that I'm counting. The hope I feel in her company, in her cautious smile, or the way she swings hands with Sophie, is tempered with an edgy fear that at any moment it could all go wrong. Yet as the hours pass, I start to relax, at least a little bit.

The days are drowsy and warm, and Daisy is happy to accompany us to the park, the pool. I suggest a shopping trip, since she's only got her backpack of clothes, and she agrees shyly. I look forward to buying her things, to be able to give her something.

I keep an eye on Ella and Avery, trying to assess how they are adjusting to Daisy's presence. Avery is quiet, as she often is, and I catch Ella looking at Daisy with a shrewd, calculating look that I try not to worry about. That's Ella's way, we've always joked she's a little lawyer. She needs to figure out how Daisy fits into her life. We all do.

As we head into the baseball game, I take the opportunity to fall in step with Avery, my middle child, so often lost in the shuffle.

"How are you doing, sweetie?" I ask. "Do you like having Daisy here?"

Avery gives me a wary look. "Yeah, I guess."

"Maybe we can play a board game later," I suggest, because Avery loves games, is always asking for a family night. "One more person for Candyland."

She looks away. "Ella says Candyland is babyish."

"Oh, does she?" Nine years old and growing up way too soon. "Okay, how about Twister?" Again, Avery gives me that cautious, uncertain look, like she wants to ask me a question but she's afraid to. "Avery?" I press. "Won't that be fun?"

"Maybe," she replies, but she sounds dubious. She slips her hand into mine and squeezes tightly. I squeeze back, the only reassurance I know how to give in this moment.

The baseball game is exactly what I wanted it to be—noise and activity, popcorn and peanuts and cotton candy, a cheerful excitement humming through the crowd. I watch out of the corner of my eye as Tom leans over to chat to Daisy, explaining the game. On the way here, we discovered she'd never been to a baseball game, doesn't really know the sport. I felt dismayed, wondering if this was a mistake; Tom took it as an opportunity to widen her interests.

That, I think, is the difference between us distilled into a moment; Tom is relaxed, assuming everything's going to be okay, always looking on the bright side. It's a choice he made deliberately, after spending several months in rural Thailand and surviving an earthquake while he was there, less than a year before the big tsunami. He'd gone there after graduating early to teach English, and apparently the experience gave him some sort of enlightenment, or at least the perspective to live each moment to its fullest—something he's done ever since, both admirably and a tiny bit irritatingly, because he's so very deliberate about it.

It's a great story, but not everyone has an earthquake to shake up their lives. Or at least, not a literal one. And as much as I want to relax and *be in the moment* like I said so sanctimoniously on Instagram, it still takes a lot of effort.

I am heartened when Avery says something to Daisy, shyly, and Daisy laughs in return. Tom can't resist giving me a "see?" look, and I manage a smile. Maybe I have been overreacting. Maybe it is all going to be okay, like I want it to be.

As we are leaving the game, I make everyone pose for a selfie, beckoning to Daisy to come stand by me. "Let's mark this for posterity," I say, and her shy smile both encourages me and breaks my heart. I put my arm around her as we press our faces together, Ella on my other side, Avery by Daisy, Tom holding Sophie. I'll post this on Instagram, I think, never mind my so-called break. I want everyone to see Daisy and me together, even if I'm not quite ready to explain who she is.

"Cheese!" I call out gaily, only to hear a woman say in the tone of doing a double take, "*Mia?*"

I lower my phone to see Trina, one of the preschool moms, out with her family. She has a toddler on her hip, and her daughter by the hand. Amelia, I remember. The one who took the princess crown. Trina's eyes widen as she catches sight of all of us.

"Mia! How nice to see you. I don't think I've met your older girls." Her curious gaze roves over Ella and Avery, whom she undoubtedly knows about, thanks to the mural of family trees on the preschool wall, painstakingly filled in at home and proudly brought back. Daisy isn't on ours, of course. "And who is this?" she asks as she glances at Daisy. I can see her narrowed gaze taking in Daisy's pink hair, belly button ring, and tattoo, and storing it up all for later gossip. I remember that she was the one who rolled her eyes when I took a call as we waited for preschool to let out. "Your niece?" she fills in. It almost sounds as if she knows the truth, and is daring me to say it. "She looks just like you!"

I open my mouth, but I find, to my shame and horror, that I can't speak. I can't say who Daisy is, not to this woman.

Trina waits, eyebrows raised, a smile like a smirk on her face. Or am I imagining that? I still haven't spoken, and from the corner of my eye, I see Tom give me something close to a glare, and Daisy's face hardens.

"Yeah, I'm her niece," she says, and then she strides ahead, leaving us all behind.

"What's going on, Mia?"

Tom's voice is quiet, gentle, and yet I still cringe as he closes our bedroom door behind him with a definitive click. Downstairs, the girls are absorbed in the latest offering on Disney; Daisy is with them, silently scrolling on her phone. We've just gotten back from the baseball game, and my awful silence when stupid Trina asked me if Daisy was my niece reverberated through us all for the entire journey. No one spoke, except Sophie once, to ask in a sweetly piping voice, "Why did you say you were Mommy's niece, Daisy?"

Daisy didn't even reply.

"I don't know," I tell Tom now, trying to keep my voice low, for Daisy's sake. She'd heard us in our bedroom once before, after all. "I guess I froze. I didn't mean to." It's not as if Tom is the one who should be hurt, and yet that's how he looks, all crumpled and sad, and it both annoys and alarms me. Why is he so invested in this? Just because Daisy's parents are divorced?

He drives his hands through his hair before dropping them slowly to his sides. "I just don't get it. You're going to tell everyone about her, right? I mean, you'll have to?"

"Yes, of course I am. It's not as if I've kept her secret." Much. I have posted photos on Instagram, my family knows about her, but, no, I don't go shouting it from the rooftops. "It's just *personal*," I tell Tom. "And Trina, the mom who asked, is... not my best friend. Okay?"

Tom walks over to the bed, sinking onto its edge while I watch, torn between frustration and fear. "Why do you sound so angry?"

I try not to roll my eyes. "Tom, please don't act like my therapist right now. I'm not angry. I'm just..." I blow out a breath. "Defensive. I know I messed up, and I will apologize and explain to Daisy. But I don't need a lecture from you about it."

He looks hurt, his face crumpling a little more before his eyes flash. "I'm not lecturing."

"Whatever." I move to the window, my back to him, because I don't trust the expression on my face. Everything was going so well, and yet it only took a second's hesitation to blow it all apart. I *knew* it would be like this. It's felt like this from the start, in one way or another. All it would ever take was a moment.

"All those times you went to visit her," he says slowly. "I never went. Why was that?"

I stiffen in disbelief. "Are you saying that's my fault? You never offered, you know. Not *once*."

"It felt like you didn't want me to." Which was true, at least after a while, but I struggle not to feel angry.

"It felt like *you* didn't want to," I tell him. "Please don't rewrite history, Tom. When I first told you about Daisy, you didn't ask about her again for six months." I turn around, my chest heaving as I remember how much that had hurt. "And whenever I said I was visiting her, back when we were dating, you were happy to let me go. Alone."

Tom's mouth drops open. "Mia, I was twenty-six years old—"

"When I was *twenty* years old, I had a child, one I painfully gave up for adoption. Don't tell me you were too young or some crap like that."

He slumps on the bed, his elbows braced on his knees. "Why haven't you said any of this before?"

"Because *you've* never said any of this before. What's changed for you, Tom?"

He is silent for a long moment. "I guess my feelings have changed since Mark and Suzanne's divorce," he says slowly. "I feel protective of Daisy in a way I didn't before. I want to help her."

"And do your feelings trump mine?" I ask, knowing that isn't a fair question. Knowing it all too well.

"Of course not—"

"Then let me go about this my way," I cut him off. "I care about Daisy, but it's more complicated than you clearly think it is."

"Stop telling me it's complicated like that's the end of it," Tom replies, and now he sounds as irritated as I am, which is alarming. We don't fight, not usually, but then we also rarely plumb these kinds of emotional depths. "Do you want Daisy in your life or don't you?"

And isn't that the million-dollar question.

I don't answer, and Tom rises from the bed. I hear the squeak of springs, and then him walking toward me, my back still to him.

"Mia?"

"It's not as simple as that."

He starts to speak, but I raise my hand as I speak over him.

"There are other people in Daisy's life. She has parents, you know—"

"Parents who are divorced—"

"But they're not *dead*. They're still taking care of her. I've always been at the periphery, even from the beginning, and that *hurt*. I'm not sure it can ever be another way." Early on, I read a memoir about open adoption, written by both the birth and adoptive mother—or first and forever moms as they liked to call themselves. It was a beautiful story, completely inspiring how they worked together and got along, both providing support and love for their precious son, who grew up incredibly well-adjusted and overflowing with love and appreciation for both his mothers. By the end of the book, I wanted to throw it against a wall.

Real people don't work that way. They aren't that well-adjusted, that self-aware, that forgiving and understanding and open. Or maybe I'm just a wreck. Either way, even though Suzanne and I were both trying to be positive and proactive at the beginning, it's never been easy—at least not for me. And as time went on, it only got harder. Those two perfect moms wrote that book when their son was only nine. Who knows what he went through later? What they did?

"You still haven't answered my question." Tom comes to stand right behind me, his hands heavy on my shoulders. I have an urge to shrug them off, but I don't. I stare out the window at the hazy summer day as my vision blurs and my breath hitches. "*Mia.*" He squeezes my shoulders gently. "I'm trying to support you—"

"It doesn't feel like it." Now I do shrug him off, and wipe my eyes before he can see. "It feels like you're disappointed in me, because I can never be good enough for you—*or* Daisy."

His mouth drops open. "What—"

All right, this might be not so much about Tom, but about my mother. My family. Me. How inside I've felt like a failure, trying to measure up, knowing I never will. "Tom, I'm trying, okay? And this morning I had a good conversation with Daisy. So can you just let us find our way naturally, together? There are bound to be some bumps along the way, but it actually was going okay, you know? I feel we made some progress."

He looks like he wants to say something, but then he presses his lips together and nods slowly. "Okay. Good."

I straighten my shoulders and head toward the door. "I'm going to see what they're up to," I tell him, meaningfully, although really I just want to end this conversation. There was too much truth in what Tom was saying. There are too many secrets I have to keep, and while part of me longs to just let it all out, I know I can't. I made my choice a long time ago, and it's too late for that. Far, far too late.

THEN

SUZANNE

December 2012
9 years ago

The apartment smells of cinnamon and evergreen. Suzanne insisted on a real Christmas tree this year, eight feet tall, big and bushy. Before Daisy, they had a tabletop tree, tastefully artificial and out of the way. It seemed silly to celebrate Christmas without a child.

"You know this thing cost eighty bucks?" Mark demanded good-naturedly as he dragged the tree into the apartment, shedding needles. "And I don't even know how we'll get rid of it. Jason in 2B told me we need a bulk pick-up appointment, and they're all already booked through January."

"We'll find a way," Suzanne said, smiling. "And having a real tree will be so nice for Daisy."

Daisy has been, Suzanne is gratified to see, entranced by Christmas and all it entails this year. She is eight years old, the perfect age to enjoy the festivities. Suzanne has made her mother's seven-layer bars and gingerbread men, which Daisy decorated with icing and sprinkles. They played Frank Sinatra's Christmas album and Mark laid a fire; they decorated the tree as dusk fell outside, the ornaments glinting in the firelight. It even snowed, just a little, but still. It's all so perfect, it almost feels painful; she's afraid to enjoy it too much.

And yet *this* is what she dreamed of, all those years ago, when they were waiting for an adoption to come through. This was the moment she'd held in her mind like a promise, a gift. The three of them around the tree, making a memory. The lighting soft, the music playing, Daisy's hesitant smile as she reaches for a candy cane to put on the tree. It really is perfect.

They haven't had a Christmas like this since Daisy was born. The first two years she was too little, and when she was three, they went to Suzanne's mother's. The following year it was Mark's mother's turn, and all the drama that entailed, and the year after that, his father's, which was dinner in a Chinese restaurant in San Francisco while he got steadily drunker, hardly a festive occasion. The next year was back to her mother's, and then when Daisy was six, Mark surprised them with a Christmas Caribbean cruise—he'd had a stressful few months at work—and when she was seven, they all came down with a terrible stomach bug and spent the whole holiday racing to the bathroom or groaning in bed.

Now Daisy is eight, and they are finally—*finally*—having the Christmas Suzanne has always wanted. It's going to be perfect. It already is. It's the twenty-third of December, and Suzanne is eager for Christmas Day, even as she is anxious not to squander a single moment. Tomorrow they'll go to the candlelit Christmas Eve service at the Brick Church, just two blocks away, and where Daisy attended preschool. They'll have a quiet dinner of shepherd's pie and they'll hang their stockings by firelight. She can't wait for Daisy to see the presents she's bought her. She hasn't gone overboard, or at least not too much, but every other year has been such a washout, and Daisy is finally of an age where she *gets* Christmas, where she can look forward to it and understand and celebrate.

Suzanne has bought her an American Girl doll—ridiculously priced, over one hundred dollars, and that's not including all the outfits and accessories. She chose the Molly McIntire doll, because with her dark hair she looks a little bit like Daisy, and whenever they've passed the American Girl Doll store on Fifth Avenue—three stories dedicated to nothing but these dolls—Daisy has liked to look at Molly best. She can't wait to give it to her. She's sure Daisy will be thrilled; she'll throw her arms around her, she'll kiss her cheek, just the way she used to.

Except, Suzanne knows, Daisy is not very physically affectionate with her anymore. The spontaneous hugs, the sleepy morning cuddles, have trailed off in the last few years. She knows it's part of growing up, but it feels far too soon. She has stopped asking for hugs or kisses, not wanting to pressure her daughter. Not wanting to be refused. Still, she hopes.

She has just tucked Daisy into bed and is humming under her breath as she cleans the kitchen when the phone rings. The landline hardly ever rings, and she feels a clutch of anxiety. Is it her mother? She'd had to go into assisted living six months ago, and Suzanne still feels guilty about it.

But it's not her mother; it's Mia.

"Hi, I hope it's not too late?" Mia sounds breathless.

Suzanne glances at the clock above the stove; it's a little past eight. "No, no, it's not too late. Is everything all right?"

"Yes." Mia sounds slightly annoyed that Suzanne has asked, but why is she calling on the twenty-third of December, sounding so rushed? "I'm in Maryland actually, visiting my parents. And I thought I could come up to New York tomorrow, to see Daisy. I have a Christmas present for her." A silence follows this, while Suzanne struggles with how to respond. "Suzanne?" There is an edge to Mia's voice. "Is that all right?"

"Yes, of course," Suzanne replies after another tortured pause. She doesn't want Mia to come, but what else can she say? It would be cruel to refuse, and it would make things awkward between her and Mia. More awkward, because she cannot pretend it has always been easy so far, and yet she *wants* it to be easy. She continues to believe that an open adoption can work, that it is only their insecurities and anxieties that keeps them from having the kind of relationship she was determined to envision at the beginning—connected, supportive, real.

"I thought I'd come around noon," Mia says. "And stay till dinner, if that's okay? Then I won't infringe on your evening."

Yet she'll still be here for most of the day. "Yes," Suzanne says, a bit woodenly. "Fine. Great."

"That's not a problem, is it?" There is a sharpness to Mia's voice that Suzanne registers. She has heard it before, whenever she pauses or prevaricates. If her response isn't instant enthusiasm, Mia, although she never says so, is annoyed. "I haven't seen her in over a year."

"Yes, I know, Daisy has missed you." Mia has been diligent about sending a birthday card, a Thanksgiving card, an Easter card, even a Valentine's Day card, generous gift cards or cash included with each one, so Mia is never out of mind. Suzanne had thought it might be easier with Mia in North Carolina, but in some ways it is harder.

"And I've missed her. Is she there? Can I talk to her, tell her about tomorrow?" There is a stridency to Mia's voice, along with a desperate eagerness. Suzanne knows she does not like having to ask.

"I'm sorry, she's in bed. Asleep," she adds, even though she's not sure Daisy is, yet. "But she'll be thrilled to see you, I know."

Mia lets out a huff of disappointment. "I've really missed her," she says again, her voice going soft.

"I know you have." Suzanne tries to gentle her tone. "I know moving so far away has to have been hard on you."

Mia doesn't reply, and Suzanne wonders if she has somehow said the wrong thing. She often feels she does, with Mia. Things she meant as merely a remark are taken as a criticism or slight; she can see it in Mia's face, and she's not even sure Mia is wrong, because she does resent her. She tries not to—oh, how she tries—but it's there, a kernel nestled in the very center of her soul.

"All right," Mia finally says, sounding resigned. "Tomorrow, then."

When the call ends, Suzanne finds Mark in the living room. He is flicking through channels on their TV, the volume low for Daisy's sake. A small classic six, it is not that big an apartment.

"That was Mia. She's coming tomorrow, to visit."

Mark sits up straight. "She is? Why didn't she tell us before?"

Suzanne cannot tell if he is annoyed or not. They have both been as accepting as they know how to be, of Mia's involvement. It has always felt like a sacred trust, to keep her in Daisy's life, to honor the promise they made.

"I suppose she just decided." Suzanne keeps her voice even. She has never confessed to Mark how helpless and raw Mia's visits can make her feel. She keeps up the pretense that they have an open and healthy relationship, because she hopes that if she acts like they do, then one day it really will be. And, she tells herself, it's not so bad. A couple of hours. Daisy will be thrilled, although afterwards she'll likely be sullen, mute. That is the part Mia never sees.

"It would have been nice if it was just us, this time," Mark says after a moment. It is the first time he has ever said such a thing.

"Well, Daisy will be glad to see her," Suzanne replies robustly. She feels the need to be cheerful, to convince them both this is actually a great idea. "And we have the rest of the vacation by ourselves, after all."

Mark doesn't reply and she bustles around the room, tweaking a few ornaments, straightening a few books.

"Besides," she adds, to herself as much as Mark, "Mia has never come for Christmas before."

"This is our first Christmas, just the three of us at home," Mark points out. "Without being sick, anyway."

"We'll still have Christmas Day."

Mark doesn't reply, just aims the remote at the TV and flicks to another channel. They have never talked honestly about Mia, and Suzanne suspects it is because they don't want to admit how they really feel. It seems so petty, to resent your child's birth mother's presence, paltry as it is, in their lives. Or *first mother*, as some in her support group like to call the birth mother. Suzanne prefers birth.

It will be fine, she tells herself as she goes back to the kitchen to finish emptying the dishwasher. Daisy will have a lovely time with Mia, and Suzanne will make sure she has an early night, to recover from the excitement—or perhaps the stress—of seeing Mia. Suzanne can never tell which it is. They might have to skip the candlelit service, but that's okay. Daisy would have been bored, anyway. And they'll still have Christmas Day.

She keeps telling herself that when she announces to Daisy that Mia is coming, and Daisy spends the rest of the morning in a state of strained excitement, pressing her nose to the window, knocking things over, suddenly bursting into tears.

She tells herself that when Mia sweeps in, heavily pregnant and bearing gifts, accompanied by Tom, who apparently decided to come at the last minute. He is joking, jovial; Daisy doesn't look at him.

And Mia looks beautiful, radiant, Suzanne thinks. She looks like Venus on the half-shell—blooming, brimming with life, in a flowing dress of crimson velvet. Daisy stares at her bump, while Mia hands her the present, wrapped in shiny red paper, tied with a satin bow. Suzanne registers the shape of her box and her heart sinks. She struggles to keep the expression on her face friendly, interested, as Daisy unwraps an American Girl doll, Molly McIntire no less, with even more outfits and accessories than she'd bought, and then hugs the doll joyfully to her.

"Thank you, Mia," she says as she cradles the doll. "This is just what I wanted. This exact one."

Mia watches her with a yearning sort of look while Daisy gives her a quick hug before scrambling off the sofa to play with her doll. Tom squeezes her hand and Suzanne rises from the sofa, knowing there is a rigid look on her face.

Mark shoots her an uncertain glance; Suzanne doubts he fully understands the significance of the doll. Suzanne bought all the Christmas presents herself. He won't realize what it means, how tomorrow she won't have a big present to give Daisy.

"More coffee?" she asks, and nobody answers.

9

SUZANNE

In the end, Peter and I don't go to dinner, or at least not just to dinner. He calls me on Thursday, the day before our date—if I can even use that word—and says, "Dinner is boring and predictable, why don't we meet in the afternoon?"—I've already told him I get off at three—"We could go to the MoMA instead, and have drinks afterwards on their outdoor terrace? We can eat after that, if we're so inclined. You can teach me all about the art," he finishes, and I laugh lightly.

"I specialize in nineteenth-century European art," I remind him. So many people think if you're an art historian you know everything about every painting, ever.

"Then we can just look at the pretty pictures," he replies, unfazed. I like how uncomplicated he makes everything seem.

By Friday, the day of our date, and halfway through Daisy's week with Mia, I have reached a fragile equilibrium. Daisy still hasn't texted me, and I managed to refrain from texting Mia, checking her Instagram instead. Last night, she posted a selfie of her next to Daisy, her family around her; it looked like they were at a sports stadium, maybe for a baseball game. Mia and Daisy's faces were pressed cheek to cheek, and Mia had captioned it simply: *Living my best life NOW.* I scrolled through the comments, my stomach churning as I scanned them: *Twinning & winning... You guys look so beautiful... Wow, Mia, is that your daughter?!* She hadn't replied to any of the comments, but the evidence was clear. She and Daisy were having a fabulous time. The photo felt as if she were staking her claim.

I dropped my phone onto the table, feeling a weird mixture of both painful envy and deep relief. They were okay. Daisy was okay. She wasn't silently suffering; Mia wasn't simply enduring the week. That was really good news, and so much better than what I'd been fearing.

And yet... *Daisy was having a good time.* A great time, without me. And while I would never begrudge my daughter her happiness, I couldn't keep from feeling not just jealous, but hurt. How, after a little more than forty-eight hours, could Mia and Daisy be cheek to cheek? I'd struggled and suffered with Daisy for years. I couldn't remember the last time she'd touched me, never mind a cheek press or an actual hug.

Tears smarted and I pressed the heels of my hands to my eyes. I was not going to cry because Daisy was having fun. I would not be that petty a person.

And so, by Friday, when I am hurrying off the Fifth Avenue bus toward the MoMA, I have made peace with the whole idea. Mostly. I have told myself I have, anyway. And at least Mia hasn't posted any more aren't-we-having-fun selfies. She hasn't answered any of those comments, either. I've checked.

Peter is waiting outside, hands in the pockets of his chinos, his pale green button-down shirt open at the throat. I can't help but give him a slightly skeptical look; I've come from work and am wearing a pair of tailored gray trousers and a pale pink blouse with pearls. I fear I look remote rather than casual.

"You don't look like a lawyer," I say as I stop a few feet in front of him so we don't have to do an awkward kiss on the cheek. I'm not ready for this to actually be a date.

"I take Thursdays off," he replies. "Perks of having made partner."

"It must be nice," I tease, smiling to take any sting from the words, and he cocks his head to the door.

"Shall we?"

For the next hour, we occupy ourselves with the art, which lessens the potential intensity of having another conversation like the one at the party. No confessionals now, just a few pithy comments about the relevant works, and I dredge up all the trivia I know about modern art, which Peter takes with more enthusiasm and interest than perhaps is warranted.

Then, on the fifth floor, we come to the painting *Christina's World*, by Andrew Wyeth. I stand in front of it first, surveying the stark landscape of brown grass, a girl sitting in a field, legs sprawled out behind her, a wide, bleak sky above and a farmhouse of dusty gray clapboard in the distance. After a few minutes, Peter joins me.

"I recognize this one."

"Yes, it's pretty well known. One of my favorites, actually, although I'd kind of forgotten about it." I give a small laugh as Peter raises his eyebrows in inquiry. "I first saw this when I was pretty young—maybe eleven or twelve? It was on loan to the Brandywine Museum of Art, in Chadds Ford, outside Philadelphia. They don't actually loan it out anymore, it's become too iconic."

"And?" Peter asks. "Why did you like it so much as a kid?"

"I don't really know," I admit. "Art is like music or poetry, isn't it—you can have a visceral reaction to it, a feeling of intense longing or sadness or joy, and you can't even articulate why."

Peter nods in understanding. "And which was it for you?"

"All of them, really, or maybe something in between." I feel self-conscious admitting so much, and yet I keep going. "I saw so much possibility in it—a young girl, the wide field, the open sky. It was all hers for the taking." I shake my head slowly, fighting a sense of embarrassment now, and worse, of nameless loss. "Later, when I started studying art history, I discovered the story behind the painting—Christina, the girl there"—I nod to the canvas on the wall in front of us—"she actually had a degenerative disease that meant she couldn't walk. They used to think it was polio, but it might have been something else. Anyway, she refused to use a wheelchair, and crawled everywhere instead. When I looked at it again, when I was older, I saw how that was true—she was sprawled there, almost like she'd fallen. And the landscape is so forbidding and bleak—typical Wyeth, all gray and brown." I shake my head again. "Something that I remembered as being so inspirational was actually tragic."

I glance at him, wondering if he's bored by my musings, but he looks alert, interested.

"Anyway, I felt a bit—silly, I suppose. To have gotten it wrong."

"But did you get it wrong?" Peter returns with a smile. "After all, beauty is in the eye of the beholder, right? Although, I have to admit, it's all a little too brown for me." He laughs and I smile.

"Yes, you're right, art is open to interpretation, but in this case, there was a real story behind it." I give a little laugh as I shake my head. "I think I definitely got it wrong."

"Look." Peter steps closer to the painting, pointing to the curator's notes on a plaque next to it. "There's a quote about it by Wyeth himself. 'The challenge to me was to do justice to her extraordinary conquest of a life which most people would consider hopeless.'" He glances at me, his eyes and smile both warm. "Sounds like you might have got it right, after all."

"I've never heard that quote before," I admit. I feel emotional in a way that is unsettling; we're just talking about a painting, but it feels like more.

"Expert that you are," Peter teases.

"Nineteenth-century European art, remember." I give him a small smile back, and it almost feels like we're flirting, except I'm not sure I really know how to flirt.

I step closer to read the plaque myself. *The title,* Christina's World, *indicates that the painting is more of a psychological landscape than a portrait, a portrayal of a state of mind rather than a place.* I glance at it again, the tension in Christina's body, as if she's poised to launch herself forward, the bleak grays and browns, the wide-open world. Maybe it really could be seen both ways. Maybe anything could.

"I still like it," I tell Peter, "whatever it means. Brown as it is."

He laughs and we move on to the next painting, Edward Hopper's *Gas.*

By five, we are heading to the terrace café, and Peter orders us glasses of wine, even though it feels a little early. It's not often I go on a date, I tell myself, even as I try to act like this isn't one.

"So," Peter says when we're both sitting at a table, midtown Manhattan laid out before us in a grid of glass and steel, "How long have you been divorced?"

I nearly choke on my first sip of cool, crisp Chardonnay, surprised by such a direct question. "Almost two years."

He nods slowly. "Still pretty new then."

Yes, and still raw. I nod. "What about you?"

"Seven years." He pauses to take a sip of wine. "She fell in love with someone else. Admittedly, I was working all the time —distracted, tired, irritable. I was trying to make partner and while I billed all the hours, she fell in love with our son's English teacher. They're still together."

"I'm sorry."

He shrugs, accepting. "What about you?"

"What about me?"

"Why did it end?"

Is that what people do, I wonder, in this new world of divorced dating? Share their war stories, show their battle scars?

I realize I don't actually have much to say. "To be honest? I don't really know."

"You don't?" This surprises him. "You must have an inkling."

"A bit, I guess. There wasn't anyone else." I'm quite sure about that; Mark insisted. I run my finger down the stem of the wine glass, to catch a bead of moisture. "Mark, my... my ex, simply sat me down one evening and said this wasn't working, and he wanted a divorce."

"And you didn't discuss it, or at least ask why?" Now Peter sounds incredulous.

I pause as I recall that painful conversation. I remember how resolute Mark looked, how stunned I felt—and yet, at the same time, completely unsurprised. The same way I felt when Daisy said she wanted to live with Mia. Instinctively, I turn to glance at my phone, checking for a text, but it's in my bag and I won't bring it out now.

"I must have," I tell Peter.

Surely I didn't just meekly nod and agree when my husband said he wanted to leave me. It's just the conversation is a blur, something I've chosen not to remember. And yet I can remember exactly how I felt sitting there, my hands tucked between my knees like a child, everything in me cringing and whimpering even as I stayed silent, motionless.

"He told me he couldn't live with someone who didn't love him," I say after a moment. That is the one torturous verdict I remember Mark delivering so flatly; it hurts to say it now.

"*Did* you love him?" Peter asks, which I suppose is a fair question.

"Yes, very much so." I shrug and put my glass down. I feel restless now, like I need to move. "I really didn't know what he meant, by saying that. But you can't argue someone into believing you love them. Either they do or they don't, and anyway, it was probably an excuse." Yet for what? Did Mark get tired of me, bored of marriage? He'd never seemed so, but it was what I had feared. That I simply wasn't enough.

"Sorry, I didn't mean to kill the mood with the questions," Peter remarks wryly, perhaps sensing my disquiet. "You get to my age and you just want to cut through all the crap, you know? Figure out what's really going on."

"Yes, I can understand that." I've recovered my equilibrium, thankfully, and my voice is level, even rueful. "I don't talk about it very much, so I might have been a bit... raw."

"Two years isn't that long."

"Maybe not."

Fortunately, we ease off the heavy conversation then, and Peter is skilled at making friendly chitchat, so I feel more myself by the time we leave the MoMA, enough that when he suggests dinner at a little French restaurant he knows around the corner, I agree.

It's a cute little place, with leather booths and wooden chairs, lots of little tables crowded in a long, narrow room. The menu is standard but delicious—steak frites, escargot, French onion soup. We eat and chat about work, about art, about living in the city—both of us have been in Manhattan for over twenty-five years—and I remember how good it feels to go out, to have friends. Between my work, my divorce, and Daisy's hostility, my personal life has disintegrated into nothing. It feels good to get a remnant back.

It's after eight by the time we wander uptown to get a cab at Columbus Circle. Since Peter lives in the east seventies, it makes sense to share, and he insists the driver drop me off first.

"I had a good time tonight," he tells me as we speed up Columbus Avenue to cut through the park. "I hope you did, despite my prying about your divorce."

"I did have a good time," I admit. "I'm not used to anyone asking me about that stuff, that's all."

Peter is silent for a moment, the light from the passing traffic flashing across his face, washing it in white. "It can be so lonely," he finally says, quietly. "Can't it?"

It's as if his words have opened up an ache inside me, allowed all the emotions I've held back to rush through. "Yes," I reply, just as quietly. "It can."

I'm grateful that Peter doesn't make a big to-do of escorting me to the door; he simply squeezes my hand and says he'll call soon, as I slip out of the cab. Although I'm a little bit relieved to end the extended tension of a first date, I feel that loneliness he'd just talked about sweep through me as I unlock the front door to my building. I had a good time. I am hoping, I realize, somewhat to my surprise, that Peter asks me out again. And yet, I am alone, now more than ever.

My footsteps echo through the foyer as I head to my mailbox and unlock it, withdrawing the usual flyers and junk mail—and a long, white envelope with Stirling's embossed crest on the back.

My heart stutters for a second—Daisy has already received her report card, and the bill for next year doesn't come until August. It's addressed to both Mark and me; I've continued to receive all the school's correspondence and pass on whatever information he needs.

I wait till I get back in my apartment before opening it, all the while telling myself that it's probably just a fundraising letter, or the headmistress's newsy update about all the successes Stirling girls have had in the last year. Except it doesn't feel like that sort of letter. There is something official about it, something forbidding, although perhaps that is just my usual nameless fears rising to the surface yet again. *You always think something is going to go wrong,* Mark has told me—in the past it was with wry affection, later it was more accusingly.

I close and bolt the front door and kick off my shoes. In the kitchen, I stand by the sink and pour myself a glass of water, and all the while the letter waits.

Finally I open it, and for once my nameless dread has a reason, a source. The letter is brief and brusquely to the point. *It is with regret I must inform you that after a particular incident has been drawn to our attention. I will not be asking Daisy back to Stirling for her final academic year.*

I stare at the page, its typewritten words looking so indifferent, uncaring. Daisy has been expelled? And it didn't even merit a phone call? And what *incident*? This, I realize, must have something to do with what happened, why she left.

A shudder rips through me as I let the letter fall onto the countertop. Again I feel that mingling of both shock and despairing inevitability. I am not surprised, and yet I am reeling. This has to be why Daisy went to Mia. What, I wonder, do I not know about?

10

MIA

I don't find an opportunity to talk to Daisy until later that evening, when Tom is upstairs giving Sophie a bath and Avery and Ella are in the playroom, having yet more screen time. Some days are just like that, I tell myself as I go upstairs to find Daisy; no one is an entirely engaged, interesting mother all the time. I certainly am not, no matter what my Instagram profile indicates.

Daisy is lying on Sophie's toddler bed, which is about a foot shorter than a normal bed. Guiltily I wonder if I should have given Daisy a bigger bed, a better room, but there was no time and so I push the thoughts aside to gaze at her directly.

"Hey." I stand in the doorway, unable to gauge Daisy's mood, with her head bent over her phone. "I'm sorry about earlier, after the game. When that lady asked me about you, I... I froze for a minute. She's not someone I'm close to, and I didn't want to tell her about you like that, but I'm sorry if it made you..." I search for a word that won't make things worse. "Uncomfortable."

Daisy doesn't even look up from her phone. "I get it," she

says in a flat voice, and I feel crushed, because I think she *does* get it, and I hate that she does.

I inch into the room, perch on the edge of the bed. "I really am sorry, Daisy."

She flicks her hand at me before returning to her resolute scrolling, liking posts as if she's being paid by the click. "Whatever."

Such a dismissive word, three syllables that convey some-one's utter disdain, their complete indifference, and yet she's not indifferent. I know she's not. I stare at her—her bent head, her deliberately lowered gaze. Her knees are drawn up to her chest, and my hand is resting by her ankle. I long to touch her, but I feel like I don't have the right. My heart aches with both love and regret.

"I've made a lot of mistakes," I tell her quietly. "I know that. And I'm not just talking about today."

She looks up at me quickly, one blazing glance. Then she looks down at her phone again, without saying anything.

I think of all the cancelations over the years, the abbreviated calls, the gushing cards because I couldn't come but neither could I stay away. When I held her when she was born, when I pushed her out of my body, I never thought it would be this hard to both hold on and to let go. This painful tug of both possessive love and complete denial. How is that supposed to work? The answer, so obvious, comes instantly: *it isn't.*

Yet here is Daisy in my house, with my family, needing something from me that I don't know if I can give, and yet I want to give it. I want to try.

"I thought we could go to a spa on Friday," I venture hesitantly. "There's a place in Raleigh that's really lush. Manicures, massages... there's a sauna and a hot tub, too." I sound like I am pleading. "Tom will have the girls... it would just be the two of us."

She doesn't look up as she gives one terse, indifferent nod. "Okay, fine," she says, as if she doesn't care either way.

I murmur my thanks like a supplicant and creep away.

By the time we set off for the spa on Friday morning, I am feeling both determined and fragile. Yesterday we went to the park, Sophie commandeering Daisy for the swings, the slide, making me remember those afternoons I took her to the playground—from when she was tiny, bundled up in a bucket swing, to later, when I felt so at a loss, at the very periphery of her life.

All through the day—park, pool, dinner, bedtime—Daisy occupied herself with the girls or her phone, and we didn't get a chance to talk, not that I went searching for one very hard. It was enough, I told myself, to just be, and yet today I am hoping to get to the bottom of whatever sent Daisy hightailing it out of New York, to me.

She is quiet as we drive to the hotel in Raleigh, and I try to keep the chat going, telling her about the treatments, the amazing facials and the wonderful massages, what I usually have done.

She puts one hand to her hair, looking both self-conscious and hesitant. "Do you think I could get something done to my hair? I know it looks pretty ratty."

"It doesn't look ratty," I protest, even though it does. "Maybe a bit dry from the dye." I pause, feeling my way through. "Do you dye it often?"

"Every couple of months or so." Daisy shrugs as she looks out the window.

"Your school is okay with that?" I am thinking of the tattoo and piercings as well, because I know she goes to some hoity-toity private school, probably the kind with a lot of rules.

Daisy gives another shrug. "Not really. But I don't care."

It seems like the perfect opening, one I can't refuse. "So, about the other weekend," I say. "That party."

I wait, but she doesn't say anything.

"What happened, Daisy? Why did you say you'd been stupid?" I keep my voice gentle.

She doesn't speak for a long moment, and I turn into the driveway of the hotel, driving slowly through the parking lot to give her time to speak.

"There was this guy," she begins, her voice sounding tight. "I thought... I thought he..." She breaks off and shakes her head. "It doesn't matter."

My heart feels as if it is twisting inside my chest. I can only imagine what she might tell me, and I ache for her, for me, because I *know* this story, and it hurts so much. "It does matter," I tell her, but she just shakes her head again.

I decide to leave it for now, since we're at the spa and we want to have a fun time together. There will be time later for a heart-to-heart, I hope.

The next few hours or so is taken up with spa stuff—we pick our treatments from a menu and Daisy decides to have a facial and manicure, while I speak to one of the beauticians to ask if she can have her hair done, too. It will take longer, but I don't mind.

There's no real opportunity to talk during the treatments, and while I'm having a massage—badly needed—Daisy is led away for her hair. When we meet up for lunch a couple hours later, both of us swathed in white terrycloth robes, she looks fresh-faced and young, her hair a shiny, sleek waterfall of chestnut that swings as she moves.

"Do you like it?" she asks shyly, putting one hand to her hair as she joins me at our table in the atrium restaurant, sunlight pouring through a domed skylight. She is glowing.

"It's amazing." I mean it sincerely. She looks younger,

happier, even. *She looks like me.* Without thinking, I reach over to tuck a strand behind her ear, and she jerks back a little, before giving me an apologetic half-smile. "You look beautiful," I say quietly, and her eyes fill with tears.

"At that party," she blurts. "There was a guy, and I... I thought he liked me."

I still, my hand near her cheek. "Did he hurt you, Daisy?" I ask quietly. "Did he... did he do something you didn't want him to?" Out of the corner of my eye, I see the waitress coming toward us with menus, and I wave her away as discreetly as I can, keeping my gaze on Daisy.

"No, not exactly." Her voice wobbles and my heart aches and aches. *Oh, Daisy, what happened to you?* "I mean, no. Not like that. Not really." Is there ever a "not really" in this kind of situation? I remain silent, waiting for her to say more and she sighs, a shuddery sound. "I'm kind of a loner at school," she states, and then looks down at her placemat, as if she's embarrassed by the admission.

"That's okay," I tell her, "I was too."

She looks up, her expression almost comically disbelieving, and I give a small smile. "You were?"

"Yes, I was. I told you I was insecure, right? Well, I was really shy, too. I hated speaking in class, or being called on, or anything like that."

"Because of your parents? The dyslexia?"

"Yes, at least in part. My mother in particular is a very... forceful person." I think of her standing above me, hands on her hips, when I told her I was pregnant, my voice shaking with fear, knowing I was disappointing her more than ever before. *You have to give it up for adoption.* It was the first thing she'd said. No "I'm glad you told me" or "I'm so sorry you've been going through this alone." Just that diktat, given as if there was absolutely no other option—and she convinced me there wasn't.

"I just wanted to sink into the background," I tell my daughter. "Be completely invisible."

"You've changed," Daisy says frankly, and I incline my head in rueful acknowledgment.

"I did, but it took time and effort. It was hard, to put myself out there, but I really wanted to be different. I wanted to feel... in control of my life." Even if it was just a new hairstyle, better clothes. It gave me a swing in my step, it helped me stand taller, and it enabled me to move on. *Sort of.* It's that kind of confidence that I try to give to other women now.

"What made you do it?"

I swallow as I realize I should have seen where this conversation was headed. How can I talk about anything with Daisy without it leading here? She stares at me intently, waiting for my answer. "Losing you," I tell her quietly, and she flinches, as if she might cry, before her expression irons out.

"Why did you give me up?" she asks, an edge to her voice that is both wobbly and hard. "I mean, did you really have to?" She swallows and looks down and I hesitate, torn between telling her as much of the truth as I can, and a deep, desperate desire to prevaricate yet again. Do I really want to do this now? Weren't we talking about this party, that guy? But maybe we need to have this conversation first, or as much of it as we can.

"I was in college," I tell her carefully. "Only a sophomore. And it... it was a one-night stand. The... the guy involved, he wasn't someone I really knew. In fact, I never expected to see him again. He was older than me, he was leaving the college..." I trail away because Daisy is giving me a hard, questioning sort of look.

"So you were this shy, insecure girl, and you had a one-night stand with some older guy?" She sounds skeptical, and rightly so. He never would have looked at me normally.

"We were study partners. Remember I'm dyslexic? I was failing my economics class, and the professor asked him to help me. One of his roommates brought some beers over... I didn't actually drink much, because I'd never drunk much of anything before, but he did." I speak slowly, as if in a foreign language, picking through the details that feel safe to tell her, although, the truth is, nothing about this conversation feels safe. My heart is racing even as I try to keep my voice even. "He got drunk. I'd always had something of a crush on him. A big crush, actually, even though I knew he barely knew my name. Before I even really knew what was happening, we were..." I trail off as Daisy watches me, eyes narrowed, lips slightly parted, everything in her still and tense, as if she is holding her breath. "It was my first time," I tell her quietly, which is the truth.

I look down at my placemat, and the waitress takes that moment to come forward with the menus. We take them with murmured thanks, and I stare blindly at the usual offerings of a place like this—smashed avocado on toast, Cobb salad—wondering what Daisy thinks of me. What she is going to ask next.

"Did you want to keep me?" Daisy asks, her voice sounding small.

"I... I was conflicted," I admit painfully. It's so hard to think about those days, when I felt as if I was sleepwalking through life, trying to pretend I wasn't pregnant. "I didn't know how I could keep you, with being in college and... and the dad not around." I swallow and force myself to go on. "But I was thinking about it. But then, when I finally worked up the nerve to tell my parents, my mom made it clear she thought I should give you up for adoption. And it made sense—I had no money and two more years of college. A couple could give you so much more than I ever could. But it was hard—really hard—to make that choice." Harder than perhaps she'll ever be able to understand.

Daisy is silent for a long moment, her gaze on the menu,

before she looks up. "Why didn't you tell me any of this before?" she finally asks quietly.

I force myself to hold her forlorn gaze. "When you were thirteen? That seemed so young. It didn't feel appropriate to me."

"You said you *couldn't* tell me," Daisy says. "You made it sound like some big secret. I... I thought you might have been raped." There is the lilt of a question to her voice, despite what I've already told her.

"No." I swallow. "Nothing like that. But what about you, Daisy? And this guy? You haven't told me—"

"Did you try to find him?" she cuts me off, her voice rising, turning plaintive, a tiny bit aggressive. "To tell him about me? So he could know he was a father?"

I fight the urge to close my eyes. I can't have this conversation, I can't, and yet I am. We are. And Daisy deserves the truth —or as much of it as I can give her.

"I couldn't. This was 2004, remember. There were no smartphones, no WhatsApp or Facebook or Instagram. He'd left the college. I didn't know him well enough to have his phone number or email or anything. The truth is, I barely knew him at all."

"But since then," Daisy presses, and I see that unsettling, intense gleam in her eyes that fills me with dread. How on earth did I think it might be possible to talk about this, to any degree? "You must have looked him up on Facebook or something since then." She leans forward, her whole face ablaze with curiosity, with need. "You must know where he is now."

"I..." I stare at her helplessly, having no idea how to answer that. I can't tell her the truth. I *can't*.

"May I take your order?" The waitress saves me, even if I know it is only a brief reprieve. We stumble through our orders, and then she is gone, and Daisy is still staring at me, unwilling to let me off the hook.

"You know where he is, don't you?"

"Yes," I admit, only because I know I can't pull off a lie.

A look of triumph blazes in her eyes, and then she deflates. "And you still won't tell me?"

"Daisy..." I take a deep breath, my mind scrambling to find an answer that will satisfy her. "*He* doesn't know. I've never told him. He doesn't even remember me. He didn't remember that we'd—the next morning, I mean." I am blushing with humiliation and shame. "How can I tell someone who doesn't even remember who I am, or that he slept with me, that he has a daughter?"

"I'm sure plenty of women do it all the time," Daisy replies evenly. "Since men are such schmucks."

"They're not all schmucks," I say automatically, although I recognize I'm not exactly selling her own father to her. I close my eyes briefly, needing that second's respite. "The thing is, I need to tell him first. I can't tell you before I tell him, can I?" I try to smile, but my lips tremble.

"*Will* you tell him?" Daisy asks, her voice a throb of raw feeling. "Contact him on Facebook or whatever? So I can meet him?"

"You want to meet him that much?"

She looks thrown by the question, as if she never expected me to ask it, to consider her request seriously. And, in truth, I don't know if I can. "I... I don't know," she admits reluctantly, looking down again, one ragged fingernail picking at the edge of her placemat. "I guess... I guess it would depend."

"Maybe we both need to think about it, then," I say, and my breath comes out in a long, low sigh as relief courses through me. Disaster averted, for now, but I still don't know what happened to her at that wretched party.

THEN

DAISY

September 2011
10 years ago

Mia is coming to say goodbye. Daisy knows this, although at seven years old she doesn't really understand. Why does Mia have to go? Why is she moving so far away? Her mother told her it was far, and even showed her on a map, but the colors of the different states blurred in front of her. She's never even heard of North Carolina before. She asked Suzanne if it was near Grandma, who had just moved to New Jersey, and for some reason Suzanne's eyes filled with tears. It made Daisy feel as if everything she said was wrong.

Now she is standing by the window, waiting for Mia to come. She always stands by the window when Mia visits; when Mia turns the corner, she looks up from the street, grinning and waving wildly at her. Daisy always waves back.

Today, though, she doesn't think she'll wave. She feels angry, but she isn't sure why. When Suzanne was helping her pick out her clothes this morning, she threw her favorite sparkly top on the floor.

She screamed that she hated it, even though she didn't. Her mother didn't say anything, just stooped to pick it up, her expression so very placid, and somehow that made Daisy feel even angrier. She wants this day to be over, and yet she doesn't want it to begin. She presses her forehead against the glass, hard enough to hurt.

"Daisy." Her name sounds like a rebuke as her mother puts her hand on her shoulder, drawing her back. "You'll hurt yourself."

But she *wants* to hurt. She can't explain that either, and so she twitches away from her mother, turning from the window, and she misses the moment when Mia comes around the corner, looking up as she always does—and sees an empty space.

A few seconds later, the doorbell rings. Daisy whirls back to the window, but it is too late. Mia is gone.

But then, of course, she is there—Suzanne is at the door, and Mia is coming through with a waft of familiar, flowery perfume. Daisy stands in the doorway of the hall, hanging back, suddenly shy and unsure. Once, she might have run to Mia, before things got strange. *Before Tom.* She's only met him once but she feels he's changed everything, and now Mia is going away. She remembers, from visits before, how Mia would swing her up, high, high, and then settle her on her hip, so Daisy could put her arms her around neck. Now Daisy hesitates, and Mia's lips tremble as she speaks.

"Hello there, darling Daisy."

She always calls Daisy that. Daisy used to like it, but now she's not so sure. Maybe it's babyish. Maybe Mia doesn't mean it.

"Daisy," Suzanne reproves gently, "say hello."

That makes Mia frown, or maybe it's Daisy who is making her frown. Maybe she should have run up to her as always. And then she does, hurtling herself forward into Mia's arms, which come around her tightly, too tightly. Before Mia can swing her up, Daisy squirms away.

"I'm sorry, it's been difficult," Suzanne murmurs, and Mia does not reply. Daisy runs into the living room.

After a few seconds, Mia follows her, standing in the doorway while Daisy kicks at the sofa and then throws herself onto it. She doesn't know what to do, how to be. When Mia normally visits, she is full of chatter and activity, telling her this or that, tickling her, making her laugh. Daisy shows her her books, her toys; once they played Candyland. It all felt so much easier than this.

Now Mia perches on the edge of the sofa, her hands clasped in her lap. She looks so beautiful, as she always does—her dark hair is in gleaming waves around her face, and she's wearing a pretty flowery skirt that looks silky, and a white flowy top. She also looks very serious. Daisy doesn't like it.

"How have you been, Daisy?" Mia asks. "Your mom says you're liking school?"

Daisy shrugs. She's just started first grade; she likes the paints they can use and the tubs of crayons, the waxy feel of them between her fingers. She also likes getting a gold star when she practices "good listening" like her teacher, Mrs. Francis, says. And she likes her best friend Annabel, who picks her as partner for gym and holds her hand when they go into lunch. She doesn't feel like telling any of that to Mia right now, though.

"You know I'm not going to see you for a while," Mia says, and, looking down at the floor, Daisy nods. "I'm really going to miss you. A whole lot."

Daisy's throat grows tight but she says nothing, just stares at the floor.

"I'll make sure to write lots, though, you know? I might type them, because I'm not always so great at handwriting."

"I'm good at writing," Daisy says abruptly, looking up to see Mia smile as she brushes at her eyes.

"I bet you are. Do you think you could write me letters? Maybe your mom could help you."

Daisy looks for her mother, but Suzanne is in the kitchen. "I guess," she says uncertainly. She's not sure if she's ever written anyone a letter before.

"And I will visit—just not as often. But I'm thinking I might come during the summer… we could go to the park, maybe. Or even the circus! Would you like the circus?"

Daisy stares at her blankly. She is not sure about the circus, and the summer feels like a lifetime away.

"It won't be that long," Mia says, and she does not reply. It feels as if Mia is going away forever.

Suzanne comes into the living room, that look on her face that Daisy recognizes. She is trying to be cheerful, but it's as if she's wearing a mask. "Perhaps you could take Daisy to the park now," she suggests. "It's such a lovely day out."

Mia flinches, looking guilty. Daisy knows that look, too. It's the look Mia always has on her face when she says she wants to do something but can't. She's been seeing that look more and more recently, although she doesn't know why. Mia used to come around so much more than she does now, and she hasn't even moved yet.

Suzanne must know that look, too, because for a brief moment her face turns hard.

"Even if only for a few minutes," she says.

"Yes, of course." Mia's voice is bright, too bright. "Would you like that, Daisy?"

Usually Daisy loves going to the park with Mia, but today feels different and she isn't sure. She senses her mother's brittleness, Mia's silent misery, and, wanting to escape both, she nods.

A few minutes later, in a flurry of coats and shoes, they are downstairs and then out on the sidewalk, in a buttery spill of sunshine. It is too warm for a coat and Daisy squirms out of hers, leaving Mia to carry it as she skips ahead. She doesn't know why, but she doesn't want to hold her hand the way she usually does.

"Careful, Daisy," Mia calls, sounding panicked, as they head down the wide, cobbled sidewalk that runs alongside the park. Daisy shoots her a scornful look and keeps skipping. She knows how to get to the playground by herself. She doesn't need Mia. But then her shoe hooks on the edge of a cobble and, with a startled gasp, she goes flying.

She hits the cobbles hard, scraping her hands, her feet, her chin. For a second she is too shocked to cry or even make a sound; she is breathless, the wind knocked right out of her, the world reeling.

"*Daisy!*" Mia flies to her, kneeling on the ground, taking her into her arms. And then Daisy begins to cry as she curls into her, noisy sobs that shudder through her, more than the scrapes warranted, but it feels good to cry. It feels right. "Oh Daisy," Mia croons, rocking her right there on the sidewalk. "My Daisy." Her arms tighten around her as Daisy clings. "You're mine," she says into her hair. Daisy can feel the dampness of Mia's tears on her face. "You're mine." Daisy clings harder.

After a few seconds, though, people have to step around them, and other people are watching, whispering.

Mia eases back, blinks back more tears as she tries to smile. "You're not actually bleeding," she says. "Just a little scraped."

Daisy scrambles off her lap, wiping her face, feeling embarrassed, almost as if she did something wrong. Mia stretches out her hand, and after a few seconds Daisy takes it. They walk in silence, holding hands, all the rest of the way to the park.

11

SUZANNE

I barely sleep the night after my date with Peter, thinking about the letter from Stirling, what it means for Daisy. My mind is spinning with questions, with fears, with endless, anxious uncertainty. *What incident?* Why did the school not inform us earlier? And why didn't Daisy tell me what happened? The answer to the last is, unfortunately, obvious. She no longer tells me anything, but I am sure this is why she fled to Mia.

The next morning, I call Mark at seven-thirty, while I am gritty-eyed, making coffee.

"Suzanne?" he asks, his voice full of alarm. "Why—"

"It's Daisy."

He draws his breath in sharply. "What—"

"I got a letter from Stirling. She's not being asked back."

His breath comes out in a rush. "I thought she'd been in an accident or something—"

"Mark, she's been *expelled.* This has to be why she went to Mia's—"

"Does it?" He sounds skeptical, but I am sure. "Why do you say that?"

"Because we know something happened. And now this

letter… she must have known it was coming." I can't believe he can't connect the dots. "What is she going to do for her senior year?" The answer comes quickly, even though I want to reject it: *Live with Mia.*

"Suzanne," Mark says quietly, "are you more concerned about Daisy not being asked back, or why she wasn't?"

At first I don't know what he's asking; I can't separate the two. "Both, Mark," I reply sharply. "Because they both matter. But if something has happened that… that we need to deal with…" I trail off as anxiety makes my stomach clench. What on earth could it be? Mia told me it wasn't—*that.* But can I even believe her? Or whatever Daisy told her? *My little girl…*

"Okay." Mark is silent for a long moment, while I clutch the phone, needing him to say something, to help me. Help Daisy. "Reasons aside," he tells me slowly, "This… this isn't the end of the world, is it?"

For a second I can't speak. No, it isn't the end of the *world,* of course it isn't. But this is our *daughter,* and she's been expelled. "Don't you want to know why?" I ask. My voice sounds despairing, and yet holds an edge.

"Yes, if it is something serious." He pauses. "But you know what Stirling is like, how strict they are. She's already been suspended twice, she flouts their uniform policy almost every single day, and her grades have definitely been slipping. Surely this can't come as too much of a surprise?"

He's right, in a way, and yet it still does, to me. It's a blinding, breathless shock, a suffocating feeling of failure and fear. "And all those things should be our concern," I insist. "If she's failing school—"

"She's not *failing,*" Mark interrupts me. "And anyway, at Stirling, they think failing is a B."

There is some truth to that, unfortunately, but I persist. "Still, it all reveals a concerning pattern—"

"Of typical teenaged behavior."

Again with that old chestnut.

I decide to try a different tack. "Well, the reason they gave for the expulsion—"

"She hasn't actually been expelled, right?" he cuts across me. "Just not asked back, you said. There is a difference."

Technically he's right. Stirling has a policy of having to ask every single student back, every year, like a party they have to keep getting invitations to, admission never a guarantee. Daisy won't be the first girl who wasn't asked back, but for her senior year? It's a blow, there can be no denying that. Plenty of girls have limped through their last year, I know, simply because it would be too difficult to switch.

"The reason," I continue, raising my voice a little, "is because of a specific incident."

He draws his breath in sharply, and I am gratified that I am finally getting a reaction. "What incident?"

"I don't know, but it must be why Daisy went to Mia's. They just wrote that an *incident* has come to light—"

"An excuse, maybe?" he asks hopefully, and I wish it was.

"No, an excuse would be 'Daisy no longer exemplifies the admirable traits of a Stirling girl' or something like that. Something *happened*, Mark. Mia said the same thing." My voice practically vibrates with anxiety, and my stomach hollows out. *What is my daughter hiding?*

"All right," Mark says calmly. "Then we need to call Stirling, and ask what this incident is. Make an appointment with Mrs—?"

"Hull." I am relieved that he sees the need for such measures, even if he can't remember the name of the headmistress. "I think we should both go in to meet her."

"I agree. Text me when you've made the appointment?"

Because, of course, I will do it, not him.

After I end the call, I pace the kitchen, struggling with the need to do something productive, something that will *help*. I consider calling Daisy, but I already know that conversation won't go well. And yet I ache to call her. To reach her. Instead, I am going to find out what happened from a stern, censorious woman whom I can't help but think doesn't even like her.

I consider calling Mia, but I can't bear the thought of asking her yet again about my daughter, begging for her help, needing her wisdom.

As I stare out at the muggy June day, the bright blue breaking through the gray humid haze of high summer, I wonder what Daisy is doing, thinking, feeling. She's probably asleep, and I picture her curled up in bed, her pink hair spread across the pillow, her face softened and turned childish in sleep. I miss her. As prickly and difficult as she can be, I miss her so much.

I call the school and am able to make an appointment with Mrs. Hull for this afternoon. She's only been at the school for three years, and I have actually only met her a handful of times, at a few school events, and then only to say a restrained hello. Mark and I have never been able to attend the school's yearly charity gala, a silent auction with tickets costing five thousand dollars apiece, plus the bidding, of course, which often runs into the six figures for a single item, with almost every guest duty-bound to buy something.

It's that kind of thing that has made us question, over the years, why we chose to send Daisy to Stirling, but the fact remains that it has the best student to teacher ratio in the city; it has an award-winning extracurricular program and a nurturing preparatory division; and, not to be underestimated, it has the highest percentage of Ivy League admissions of any school in New York. Not that Daisy had to go to an Ivy League college, nor was I even sure I wanted her to. But the kind but firm approach the school excels in was, I'd always thought, good for her.

Now I wonder. Now I find myself questioning everything,

and it is a terrible, terrible feeling. What if all the decisions I've made have been wrong?

Mark and I meet outside Stirling on Ninety-Fourth Street, both of us having left work early. Mark, as usual, looks hassled, his hair ruffled, his jacket creased. I used to love his adorably rumpled look, thought it made him more approachable, perhaps because it was so different from my own upbringing, where my mother had an almost religious devotion to ironing. Now, however, I am annoyed by how unkempt he looks. Couldn't he have made more of an effort for this meeting?

We are ushered in almost immediately to Mrs. Hull's inner sanctum, a wood-paneled room with framed certificates and tasteful displays of students' artwork, some of which is better than stuff I saw at the MoMA yesterday. *Just yesterday.* Already my date with Peter feels like a lifetime ago, a moment in time, brief and uncomplicated compared to this.

"Mr. Thompson, Mrs. Thompson." She nods graciously at us both but doesn't rise from behind her desk, which doesn't bode well. We take two leather club chairs, which put us several inches below her—a cheap trick, I think, as I sit up as straight as I can. "Thank you for coming."

"Of course." I clear my throat, determined not to let my voice wobble. "I must say, Mrs. Hull, we were quite shocked by the letter we received." I give her a direct look, but her cool expression gives nothing away. "And neither of us were aware of any *incident.*" If admitting my ignorance weakens my position, so be it. I need to know what has been going on with my daughter. Daisy's well-being is paramount right now.

"The incident I referred to in my letter concerns Stirling Academy's social media policy," Mrs. Hull replies, unruffled as always. "As I am sure you are aware, we have strict rules about what Stirling students are permitted to post on any social media platform. Every Stirling student signs our social media contract at the beginning of every academic year."

"Yes, I know." I speak tightly; I can't help it. What on earth did Daisy post on social media? I have no access to her accounts; I held out longer than most, not permitting her to have any social media until she was sixteen, when most of her peers were posing for selfies at ten or eleven years old. I thought at sixteen she was mature enough to handle it. Was I wrong?

"It recently came to my attention that images of Daisy have been posted online which compromise Stirling's reputation."

I feel a cold flush sweep through my body, like I've swallowed a bucket of ice. "What *images*?" I can't bear to think about what they may be. Why isn't Mark saying anything?

"They have since been deleted, but they were provocative, to say the least."

"Did you see these images yourself?" Finally Mark speaks up.

Mrs. Hull's lips tighten. Clearly she finds the whole discussion distasteful. Well, so do I, and worse, I find it frightening. "I saw screenshots," she replies.

"Will you please show them to us?" Mark asks evenly, meeting her gaze, and I am glad for his sangfroid. I feel as if I could shatter.

After a second's pause, the headmistress reaches for her laptop, flips it open. A couple of clicks and then she angles the screen toward us.

At first I can't figure out what I'm seeing; it's all a blur, a blur, I realize, of naked limbs, hair spread out on a sofa. It's Daisy, half-dressed and heavy-lidded, her shirt unbuttoned to reveal a black lacy bra. There is a male hand on her bare stomach, fingers spread, like he's branding her. My own stomach clenches, nausea swooping through me. *Daisy. Oh, Daisy. My poor girl.* Mark makes a small sound of distress.

Mrs. Hull turns the laptop back toward her and closes the

screen with a definitive click. She doesn't speak, as if that screenshot has said it all.

"Daisy obviously didn't take that photo," I say when I trust my voice to sound level, even though inside I am reeling, weeping. I know teenagers get up to all sorts; last year I forced myself to have an incredibly awkward conversation with Daisy about birth control, all the while advising her to wait. And yet... that photo seems so *grim*. So soulless, so sordid, and what if she didn't want it to be taken? "And she didn't post it, either," I add, sounding defiant. At least I'm assuming she didn't.

"Our social media contract covers indecent images of our students, whoever has posted them," Mrs. Hull returns smoothly. "I'm afraid she has violated the contract regardless."

"But she surely didn't *choose* to post it," I protest, incredulous. "Someone must have taken advantage of her. She might have been assaulted." My voice breaks and Mark, to my gratification, reaches for my hand. "This is not her fault," I whisper. "You should be supporting her, not... not blaming her."

A flicker of sympathy passes across the headmistress's face and then disappears. "I appreciate this is distressing for you," she says, "but I'm afraid I must abide by the school's policies. All Stirling students are responsible for their behavior, Mrs. Thompson."

As if Daisy is the first Stirling girl to get drunk at a party or be in some salacious photo. When did she even *go* to a party? She's been on the fringe of her class for years, hanging out with a few rebellious loners like her. She didn't go to any *parties*—except, of course, she must have, most likely when she told me she was having that sleepover. And I was so pleased at the possibility of a blossoming friendship, but now I realize it had to have been a ruse. A lie.

"Who posted the image?" Mark asks. "Because they've violated the contract, as well." Gently, he squeezes my hand and I struggle not to cling to him.

Mrs. Hull's lips thin. "It was not a Stirling student."

A boy, then, I think. Some callow, callous jerk who thought it was funny, no doubt, to take advantage of a girl and then brag about the evidence.

I am incandescent with rage, devastated with heartbreak, but I know there is no point in showing it to this uncaring woman. She has clearly already made her decision, and she won't be moved from it. I glance at Mark, and he gives me a short nod, as if he understands what I'm thinking and he agrees.

"Thank you," I tell her shortly, and Mark and I both rise from our seats.

I don't miss the look of relief that passes across Mrs. Hull's long, stern face. She was worried we'd make a fuss—and we *could* make a fuss, I know, because this cannot be right. No matter what their stupid social media contract is, plenty of Stirling girls have cavorted all over the likes of Instagram, I'm sure of it. She's picking on Daisy because she can; because Daisy isn't an exemplary Stirling student, and because we aren't rich enough to donate a hundred thousand dollars for the new library, or whatever it is the average parent coughs up to keep in the school's good graces. Daisy isn't the one to blame here; the anonymous boy who's going to get away with it is.

We all say stiff goodbyes, and then we are outside, stunned and silent, both reeling and fuming.

"Do you think Daisy is okay?" Mark asks after a few seconds as we stand there in the oppressive heat. "Should we... should we go down there? To North Carolina? Talk to her?"

"She's coming back on Monday." I arranged Daisy's flight back to New York by text, never actually speaking to either my daughter or Mia, and now I wonder if it will even make a difference, to have her back here. She still won't talk to me, will she? She chose to go to Mia rather than tell me about this. Why would she choose me now?

"We could sit down with her together..."

"She'd hate that."

Mark nods his dismal agreement. "Yeah, maybe. But we should still do something."

"But what?" The realization swoops through me, how powerless I am, and yet I still have to try. "I can try to talk to her," I offer dispiritedly. I feel so downcast, burdened by it all.

Mark sighs and we start walking down the street, although I'm not even sure where we're going. Back to the apartment we once both called home? Or will Mark head to the subway, to return to work?

"I never liked Stirling anyway," he says after a moment, and I let out a tired huff of a laugh. "I mean it. It was so snooty, so up itself. Look at Mrs. Hull. She was so prissily sanctimonious about it all, when you know Daisy's not the first girl who's had her photo posted online. She was *blaming* her." His mouth tightens as he thinks of that photo, and I almost reach for his hand, as he took mine, but then I don't.

"It's a good school," I say wearily, because that much is true —and I don't want to think about that photo.

"But maybe not the right one for Daisy," he states heavily.

"No, maybe not." It hurts to admit that, that maybe I was wrong all these years. I wanted to give Daisy the best—the best education, the best environment. But maybe she would have thrived in a place that was—what? Less academic? Had fewer rules? The truth is, I don't even know what would have been best for Daisy. My daughter is an enigma to me, and I'm so tired of not understanding her, yet I still want to try.

"So you think you should talk to Daisy about this photo?" Mark asks. "You don't want me there?"

"Let me try on my own first." When Mark and I have sat down with Daisy together, we've fallen into a good cop/bad cop routine that doesn't work for any of us. Maybe I should talk to Mia first, find out what she knows. Would she even tell me?

"Well, whether we do or not, we need to think about what

school she's going to next year," Mark says. "Because if we want to try for private, we'll need to hustle."

"It's too late for private." Nobody enrolls their child in a private school in Manhattan in *June*. High school places hardly ever come up, and if they do, there's a mile-long wait list of eager applicants, checkbooks at the ready.

"Okay, well there are some good public schools..."

I shake my head. The good public schools are heavily oversubscribed, and places were allocated months ago. New York City doesn't operate like most of the United States, where a student just trots along to their local high school and registers. They have to apply, and any school that's rated highly will have a waitlist even longer than the private schools'.

I sigh wearily, scrubbing my forehead with my knuckles. A headache has started to throb at my temples, but worse is the weary despair I can already feel flooding through me, so putting one foot in front of the other feels like too much effort. What's the point, when it comes to this? "Daisy," I tell Mark, "told me she wanted to live with Mia for her senior year."

"The whole year?" He sounds taken aback. "What does Mia think about that?"

"I don't know. I don't think Daisy has told her yet." I'm pretty sure Mia must have suggested a week's visit without realizing what Daisy had been hoping for.

"Well," he says after a pause, "it would solve the school problem, I suppose."

"*Mark—*"

He holds up one hand placatingly. "I know, I know. It's not that simple. At this point, I'd be surprised if Mia agreed. But, Suzanne..." He hesitates and I brace myself for whatever is coming. "Maybe Daisy would be better off with Mia right now?" he says gently. "I know you don't like to think that, but Mia loves Daisy. I think we both can agree on that."

"Can we?" I try not to sound bitter.

"I know she must have struggled with how to be involved. It has to be hard, knowing when to come close, when to back away."

"She hasn't seemed to care much how it all affected Daisy."

"We don't know that."

I hate how fair he's being. I hate realizing he might be right. Can I blame Mia for having trouble finding the balance? It was Mia Daisy went to when she was in trouble, not me. I think of the selfie I saw, Daisy and Mia pressed up close together, so they looked practically conjoined. Maybe Mia will agree to it. Maybe she'll be thrilled. And for the first time, even though I am still deeply reluctant, I do not feel a shot of panicky dread at the thought. For the first time, I actually think that maybe, just maybe, it could be a good thing. For Daisy... and for me.

"Think about it," Mark says, and I nod.

"I will."

After Mark leaves to head back to the office, I realize I can't face going back to work, and so I take the train to Montclair to visit my mother. I'm not sure I'm in the right frame of mind, or if she is, but I need to be with someone who knows me, or at least did, once.

Fortunately, today is one of the days my mother remembers who I am. She perks up a little as I come in the room.

"Oh, Suzanne! What a nice surprise!" She smiles at me from her armchair by the window, and I place my purse on the table as I take the other seat in the room.

"Hi, Mom." It's so good to see her, to know that she knows me, that I feel as if I could weep.

"You're looking rather gray, aren't you?" my mother comments, frowning at my hair, and I let out a watery laugh. I haven't kept up with my salon appointments. "You really shouldn't let yourself go," she adds severely, and I nod, because this is classic Mom: love given out in stern, medicinal doses. I'm still grateful that she cares enough to say.

"How have you been?" I ask her, and she shrugs, twitching a crocheted blanket she made years ago over her knees, even though the room is sleepily warm.

"Oh, all right. Although I do find it irritating how one of the aides treats me like a child. 'Now, now Elizabeth,'" she mimics, pursing her lips. "I may be losing some of my marbles, but I haven't lost all of them. Not yet, anyway."

"No, you certainly haven't." I'm so thankful she's lucid today that I find myself blurting, "Daisy has been expelled from school, Mom. And she's visiting Mia—you remember Mia?"

"Mia." She frowns, nodding. "Yes."

This is enough to have me continue desperately, "She wants to live with Mia for the year. Her last year of high school, which means she's basically left home already." I swallow hard while my mother listens, a slight frown on her stern, wrinkled face. "And something happened at a party—I know it's probably just the usual thing kids get up to these days, but it makes me feel sick inside, and I know Daisy won't let me talk to her about it. I can't talk to her about anything anymore, and sometimes I wonder if I ever could. I feel as if I'm second-guessing everything, my whole history, my whole self... and I don't know what to do. I don't know what the right thing to do is, or if there is one, or if... if Daisy and I were doomed from the beginning."

Tears have slipped from my eyes without my realizing and I wipe my cheeks, trying to draw in a steadying breath, but it's too late. I have to say more.

"I do wonder," I confess wretchedly. "If it's because she's adopted. If it's because of... of Mia. I know I can't blame Mia for everything, I don't even want to, but... it's like I've been parenting with one arm tied behind my back. I'm so tired of it all, and then I feel guilty for being tired, guilty for thinking that maybe it's better for Daisy to live with Mia. Part of me..." My voice drops to a whisper. "Part of me just wants to be shot of it all. Shot of her." A sob escapes me and I press my fist to my mouth. I can't believe I just said that. That I thought it, even for a few seconds.

My mother stirs restlessly in her chair. I don't think I've ever talked to her so honestly or rawly before in my life. We've never had that kind of relationship; it's all been brisk how-do-you-dos and not that much more. I'm not expecting sympathy; if anything, she'll say something like "Well, you knew what you were getting into when you agreed to that open adoption" or similar, as she has done in the past.

I look up, my face still wet with tears, steeling myself for her usual acerbic advice, but when I blink her into focus, she is frowning in confusion.

"Daisy?" she asks. "Who's Daisy?"

I lean back in my chair and close my eyes. I feel utterly spent, hopeless.

"No one, Mom," I say after a moment. "Never mind."

"No need to get so upset, then," she says, sounding sniffily affronted, and I open my eyes and rise from my chair.

"Shall we go into the dayroom?" I suggest. "I think they might be playing bridge."

My mother brightens at this, even though she's long ago forgotten the rules of the game she once played with razor-sharp acuity. As I help her into her wheelchair and push her out of the room, I think of all the things she's forgotten—not just the skills, but the memories. Most likely she won't ever again tell me the story of how, when I was four years old, I once stuffed boiled cabbage down my shorts instead of eating it, and she only found it, all wilted and revolting, when I was getting ready for bed. Or how I used to hide under my bed during thunderstorms, and she'd have to pull me out by the ankles. She'll never reminisce with me about the scholarship I won to Vassar, or the first time I took Mark to meet her—my dad had died the year before—and she'd said in a stage whisper, "He's quite... *messy, isn't he?*"

My heart aches with all the things she'll never do, the memories I have as good as lost because I no longer have anyone to share them with. And now if Daisy stays with Mia... I'll have lost my daughter as well as my mother. I feel more adrift than ever before, as if the last fragile threads that have anchored me have finally snapped. I am now unmoored from the relationships that once defined me, perhaps both of them too far gone to ever get them back.

12

MIA

Daisy's visit is going pretty well. In fact, I could cautiously use the word great, although perhaps that's pushing it, considering how tentative and new everything still seems. Nothing *bad* happens, at least, and good things happen, too. After our lunch, Daisy didn't press for any more answers, and I was grateful for the reprieve. I didn't ask more about the party, the guy, feeling I should wait until she was ready to tell me.

I was grateful that we seemed to reach a rhythm, when our conversations weren't laden with issues of import. With secrets. When we could just be, enjoying each other's company, learning this new way of relating.

We played an epic game of Monopoly, with Sophie insisting she was on Daisy's team, and even Ella thawing, because she loves Monopoly, along with Avery. Tom met my gaze over the game board as we squabbled over whether Boardwalk was worth New York *and* Tennessee. I smiled back, grateful that we were back on our footing, the tension about Daisy having eased a little.

That night, as we went to bed, he took me in his arms, nestled me against him, and just like always, I fit, hooking my head underneath his chin, my arms around his waist, our legs tangled. "I'm sorry," he whispered against my hair. "I'm sorry I wasn't more understanding."

I nestled closer. "I'm sorry, too."

"This is hard, for both of us," he admitted. "I should have realized that. It's not... it's not easy, but I think it's going well."

"Yes, I think so, too." And for the first time I actually believed it.

On Saturday, while Tom took the girls to tennis, I took Daisy shopping, and was quietly pleased when she bought something other than the oversized T-shirts and ripped jeans that have comprised her current wardrobe. Seeing her come out of the changing room in a cute denim skirt and pink polo shirt was weirdly jolting, because with her newly dark hair and that shy, hesitant smile, I could have been looking at a younger version of myself.

"Do I look too weird in this?" she asked anxiously. "I feel so preppy, but it's what everyone wears here, right? I feel like such a try-hard in my other clothes." She gave a little, uncertain laugh, and I dared to put my arm around her.

"You look great," I told her, and she leaned into my hug as my heart swelled with love and gratitude. We were *doing* this. We were doing normal things like any mother and daughter, admittedly with some stumbling steps, but it was happening. When the sales lady mistook us for sisters, I didn't mind, and I even dared to tell her, laughingly, that Daisy was actually my daughter. Daisy beamed, and I felt like I'd given her a gift.

I posted another selfie on Instagram, with us in matching polos and denim skirts, our hair blending into one: *My best bud!* I captioned it, a little guiltily, because while I could admit to the sales lady that Daisy was my daughter, I wasn't quite ready to admit it to the whole world, and face the fallout.

The time would come for the lengthy Instagram post explaining exactly who Daisy was—because I know I'd been somewhat ambiguous about that, over the years—but I needed the mental space to think about exactly what I wanted to say, how I wanted to say it. For the first time, though, I was almost looking forward to writing that post, to coming clean... mostly.

After our shopping trip, we went to the Lake Johnson Park pool, lying out on deckchairs while the girls swam and Sophie splashed in the baby pool, before Daisy joined them all, giving Sophie piggyback rides in the water, racing Ella, doing handstands with Avery. It gave me an almost painful sense of joy to watch them all together, hear their laughter rising above the sound of their splashes. *What have I missed out on?* was the question that kept hammering through my brain, my heart. *What have they?*

I could have tormented myself endlessly by envisioning an entire, alternate glittering reality where everything was perfect and happy all the time, but I knew life wasn't like that. Ever. Even if I'd been honest from the start, if I'd done my best to include Daisy more in our family lives... there were no guarantees, and Suzanne might not have allowed it anyway. She'd been pretty grudging about my infrequent visits, after all.

Better not to second-guess, but to simply enjoy the moment, savor the week and all of its pleasures, for besides the daily outings, there were all the wonderful little moments, too: noisy dinners around the table, a movie night piled in the playroom, a twilit walk with the girls on their bikes and scooters around the neighborhood, as the crickets chirped their incessant, happy chorus.

On Sunday, we went to the beach, bodysurfing the waves, all of us getting sticky with sand and pinkly sunburned, and then suddenly it is Sunday, the day before Daisy leaves, and somehow it feels as if it has all gone by so very fast. We eat dinner out, a boisterous table for six at the Cheesecake Factory, and then it is eight o'clock, the girls are in bed, and I am wiping down the kitchen counters, Tom doing some work in his home office in the basement, when Daisy comes to find me.

"I can't believe I'm going tomorrow," she says shyly, and I stop with my wiping to place my palms on the counter and give her a commiserating smile.

"I know, I can't either. This week has gone by so quickly." I pause, wanting her to know how sincere I am. "I've really enjoyed it."

"So have I." She takes a step into the kitchen. "Actually, I was wondering if I could ask you something?"

"Of course." I do my best to suppress the surge of unease I feel at her question. We've had a wonderful time this week, far better than I could have ever expected, but what we *haven't* had is any more serious discussions. It's been such a relief, to get to know Daisy without front-loading every conversation with questions about the past. I'm not sure I'm ready for any now, but I am also conscious I haven't pursued what happened to her at that party. She hasn't seemed to want to, and I haven't wanted to push.

Daisy takes another uncertain step into the room, and I gesture to the table by the French windows, freshly wiped down. "Why don't we sit?"

"Okay."

We sit opposite each other in the quiet of the kitchen, and I fold my hands on the table as I wait for what she has to say, trying not to feel apprehensive.

"You remember I told you about that party... that guy?" she asks, her dark hair falling in front of her face to hide her expression.

"Yes, I do." I am glad she feels she can come to me about that, even as I dread to hear what she might say. "Do you want to tell me about it now?"

She hunches one shoulder, her head still bent. "Maybe it wasn't that big a deal, I guess. I went to a party... I got a little drunk... there was this guy I liked. Not that he even knew I existed before that night."

My heart aches. *I know this story.* "And what happened?" I ask gently when it seems as if she's not going to say anything more.

"We started fooling around." Her head is bent as she picks at her raggedy nails. "I was pretty drunk. I didn't even know what was happening, at first." She bites her lip, and I reach for her hand, overcome with empathy. *My poor girl.*

"Did he assault you, Daisy?" I ask gently.

"No," she says quickly, too quickly, pulling her hand away. "I mean, I *liked* him."

"That may be, but it doesn't change the facts. If he... if he touched you when you didn't want him to—"

"I don't know." A tear slips down her cheek and she dashes it away. "I was surprised, but I was... I mean, I was *flattered.* I don't know."

Another tear trickles down her cheek, and I reach for her hand again. I understand her confusion. I remember that incredulous feeling of wonder, even as the doubt starts to seep in. You push it away. You tell yourself just to enjoy the moment, the way he makes you feel, because he *does* make you feel so special, so wanted. *Alive...*

Daisy wipes her cheeks, takes a breath as she gathers her composure. "Look, it's not about that. Not completely, anyway. It wasn't what we did, it was afterwards. I realized he didn't feel the same way I did. At all. He took a photo of me looking pretty out of it, you know, when we were... well, fooling around." Her shoulders twitch. "He put it on the Board."

I stare at her blankly. "The Board?"

"It's this website for private-school kids in the city. It's, like, secret. No teachers or parents or anything know about it. They can't find it, either. It has a password and stuff. Some techie guy at Browning started it, I think, like, ten years ago."

"What is it?" I ask as dread swirls in my stomach. It sounds hideous.

"It's this site where guys post photos of girls they've hooked up with—like revenge porn, I guess, but not that bad. You know, not too... explicit." She shrugs. "It started out as this big burn on girls, but then it became, like, a status symbol, if a guy put you on it." She makes a face. "Stupid, I know."

"Right." I swallow. I am imagining Ella navigating this sort of dark, sordid world in just a handful of years and I can't stand the thought. "So that's why you wanted to get away from school? Because you were on this... this board?"

"No, not exactly. I mean, I knew he was putting me on the Board as a joke, you know? It wasn't ever going to be a status symbol for me, because I'm not... I'm not one of *those* girls." I don't need to ask who those girls are, because I already know. The swishy-ponytailed, sleek-limbed popular girls that every single high school has, the kind of girls who strut down the halls and who can make your life a misery, so you just hope you stay invisible. "But it hurt, that it was all just a big joke to him, that he was laughing about me with his friends, because I actually cared." Her voice throbs with emotion and my eyes sting. This is, in its own strange way, so close to my own story. I understand her hurt, as well as her anger—I see both flashing in her eyes, hear them vibrating in her voice. "Anyway, I got back at him," she tells me, and for a second she looks both guileless and defiant. "I sent a photo of us together to his girlfriend, and she broke up with him."

"He took a photo of the two of you?" I say in surprise. "For this board?"

"No." There is a hint of scorn in her voice. "I Photoshopped him into it. I'm pretty good with that kind of stuff. He was so pissed off. And then..." Her voice wavers, her defiance disappearing in an instant. "All his friends started messaging me, saying all this awful stuff about how I was a skank and I should die and they were going to tell everyone and..." She chokes back a gulping sob. "It was so awful, having everyone hating me like that. All the girls in school knew, they were laughing at me in the hallways for the whole last week of school. I was like you, I've been practically invisible, and when everyone started with the messages and the whispers... I realized I wanted to be. Invisible, I mean. And even though school ended pretty soon after, I knew it wouldn't stop. I had to get away."

"Oh, Daisy." I am near tears myself, imagining what she has gone through, what she has endured alone. I should have pressed harder earlier, I think, but then I wonder if she would have been ready to tell me. I'm glad she's told me now.

She dashes at her eyes again, with the heel of her hand. "And the guy—he messaged me to say he was going to send the original photo of me to my school. And I'm pretty sure he did."

"Why would he do that?" I consider myself social media savvy, but I can't keep up with the awful, online labyrinth that Daisy has to deal with.

"Because the school has this social media policy where you can't have any *questionable* photos online. Everybody does, they're all hypocrites, but I'm pretty sure I'm going to be expelled for the one he sent." Her breath comes out in a defeated shudder.

I blink, a bit startled. Just how bad was that photo? As if she can read my thoughts, Daisy says quickly, "It was just me lying on a sofa with my shirt unbuttoned. It wasn't, like, you know, *really* bad."

I nod slowly. I can hardly be the one to make judgments about something like this. "I'm so sorry this happened to you," I say, because that much is certainly true. My heart aches for her, for all girls who've found themselves in a similar situation. And, in a slightly different way, for me. For the girl I was, so long ago.

"I thought you might understand," she says quietly.

"Because of... of what happened with my... you know, my birth father. He took advantage of you, didn't he?"

I hesitate, not wanting to draw so clear a comparison. "I understand how you're feeling," I say carefully, "but your birth father didn't take advantage of me, Daisy. It was completely consensual. I don't want you to think—"

"But you were surprised, like I was, weren't you?" she insists. "You weren't sure—"

"No, I was sure." I speak quickly, firmly, although inside I am trembling, appalled at the conclusions she has leaped to. I think of years ago, when she asked me if I'd been raped. Perhaps I should have answered her more clearly then, but I couldn't bear to talk about it. To tell my secret. I still can't, but neither can I let her believe our situations are that much the same. "I was naïve," I tell her, "but he... he was kind. It wasn't... it wasn't like that."

Her lip curls. "He didn't even remember you."

"That wasn't his fault. Please." My voice sounds panicky. "Don't think badly of him."

She glances at me in dawning suspicion, no doubt wondering why I am suddenly defending this mystery man so much.

"So what are you going to do?" I ask, desperate to change the subject. "If you are expelled?"

She hesitates, and then says shyly, "I... I was hoping I could come here." I blink, and she continues uncertainly, "For my senior year."

I can only stare, scrambling to think of something to say, because while Daisy was explaining everything, I was not imagining that *this* was the question she wanted to ask me.

"Okay," I say blankly, and then as her face lights up, I hasten to add, "I mean, I can see why that could seem like a solution." I cringe at how uncertain I sound, and her excitement dims as she gives me that disconcertingly intent stare, the one I haven't seen since our lunch at the spa.

"So are you saying I can?"

"Well... it's not that simple, Daisy." I try to smile as my thoughts race. "I mean, what about your mom?"

"My mom?" This said with more than a touch of scorn, which only saddens me. "She won't care."

"I think she will." Daisy doesn't reply, and I find myself compelled to say, "You know she loves you very much?"

Daisy moves restlessly in her chair. "I think she *believes* she loves me," she corrects.

"What do you mean by that?"

She shrugs. "She's always doing the right thing. She reads, like, a million parenting books. And whenever she talks to me, she sounds, like, I don't know, a robot. Or a therapist. Or maybe a robot therapist. But she doesn't sound like a *mom*." She glances up at me, her gaze defiant. "It's like she's not a real person."

I'm not sure how to take that, because of course Suzanne is *real,* and yet I know what Daisy means, sort of. There is a polished purpose to her that I mistook for friendly confidence when I first met her.

"I know she can sometimes seem a bit... distant," I say carefully, "but I'm pretty sure she loves you. A lot." I think of Suzanne cradling Daisy, after I first gave her to her. I was biting my lips, trying not to sob, while she looked down at this scrap of humanity in joyful wonder.

"You sound like my dad." She lowers her voice to a gruff bark. "'Your mother might not be very adept at showing her emotions, Daisy, but I have never doubted her love for you.'" She rolls her eyes. "Whatever, okay? She'll agree to me living here, I know it."

But the question is, will I? A *year.* A whole year. I can't even imagine it. We'll have to move the girls' bedrooms around.

Sophie's bed is really too small for Daisy; Avery and Ella would have to share. Can I really have an eighteen-year-old girl in my house? Do I even know how to parent a teenager properly? I feel a lurch of panic, like I'm jumping out of my skin even as I sit across from Daisy, so very still. *I'll have to tell Tom...*

"Don't you want me to come?" Daisy asks plaintively, and I can't tell if she's being manipulative or she's genuinely afraid that I don't. Does it even matter which?

Because I *can't* say no. Can I?

I think of Ella, Avery, Sophie. What effect will this have on them, to have an older sister foisted on them without any discussion or choice? Ella might have thawed a little over the course of the week, but she still seems a little wary of Daisy. And Avery has been so quiet, I still don't really know what she thinks about it all. Sophie will take it in her stride, but what about when Daisy is tired of being her plaything? What responsibility do I have to my daughters, my younger ones? What responsibility do I have to Daisy?

"It's not a question of whether I want you to or not, Daisy," I tell her as carefully as I can. "We need to consider all the implications, the repercussions..." I trail off helplessly as anger flashes again in her eyes.

"What implications?" she demands, her voice rising. "That people will finally know I'm your daughter?"

"I meant for your parents, for your life in New York," I reply steadily. "And for my family, too. You might not have noticed, but Ella's been having a bit of a hard time. I'm not saying it's right or wrong, just that it's strange for her. There's a lot to consider."

Daisy doesn't reply, just presses her lips together and folds her arms. She looks angry, but she also looks so *young*. And I know she's lashing out because she's afraid I'm going to reject her. *Like I have before.* And, in truth, I can almost hear myself saying the words: *Daisy, honey, that's such a good idea, but running away from your life in New York isn't the answer, really, is it? You need to face your problems. I can help you...*

Talk about hypocritical. How can I say something like that to her, when I've been running away, more or less, for thirteen years? Part of me wonders if maybe I should just let it happen. I'll tell Tom, I'll tell Daisy. It would be such *a relief...* but it might cost me my marriage. My family. Daisy, too. Is it worth the risk? Do I have a choice?

I don't think I do. Not anymore.

I need to let Daisy live with us, and I need to tell Tom the truth I've been keeping from him for all these years. The truth that has been eating at me from the inside out, that has made me run from Daisy even as I long to be with her, because I'm so scared of what could happen, what I could lose if anyone finds out. The truth, unshakeable and seemingly impossible, that it is actually Tom who is her father.

THEN

SUZANNE

October 2009
12 years ago

Suzanne flies around the apartment, straightening a coaster here, twitching a throw pillow there. Every time Mia comes to visit, she goes into full spring clean mode, making sure the apartment looks like a movie set, immaculate yet cozy. Today she feels the need even more, because for the first time Mia is bringing someone with her. Tom. Tom Sullivan.

The name rolls around like a marble in her head. She has heard it before, a few times. A little over a year ago, Mia told her about him, trying his name out as if she wasn't quite sure of it, looking to Suzanne almost as if for approval.

"I'm seeing someone," she'd offered shyly. "A guy I met at one of NYU's alumnae events, actually, although we didn't really know each other in college. Tom. He's really nice."

"That sounds lovely," Suzanne had said, and meant it, because surely Mia deserved some happiness, some stability, after that other guy—whoever he was—had left her high and dry, pregnant and alone? Suzanne has never learned the details of Daisy's conception; Mia hasn't offered and she hasn't felt she could ask, had presumed it wasn't a secure relationship, maybe not even a relationship at all.

"It is," Mia had said, with a funny, incredulous little laugh. "It is." This time she almost sounded as if she were trying to convince herself.

Suzanne hadn't heard anything more, and a few months later she'd dared to ask if things were going well with Tom—saying his name with peculiar, self-conscious emphasis—and again Mia had given that funny little laugh and said that yes, they were.

That had been the sum total of their conversations about him, until a phone call three days ago. Mia and Tom were engaged, and she wanted him to meet Daisy.

"Mia is getting married," Suzanne had told Mark that evening, when Daisy was asleep. "To Tom."

"Oh?" He'd looked guarded, as he often did when it came to Mia, although he had always acted as if he'd approved all along of the open adoption that had been foisted upon them right after Daisy had been born. Suzanne was the one who had scrambled to do the research, who had read the books, who had made herself believe it could work. Now she realizes she feels a tremulous flicker of relief, that Mia is getting married. That she will have a life of her own that does not revolve around her visits with Daisy. Maybe she will even have other children, when the time comes, her own family and not just Suzanne's.

"She wants us to meet him," she continued. "Daisy to meet him, I mean. She's coming on Saturday."

And now it is Saturday, and as has become the habit with Mia's visits, Suzanne feels a knot of anxiety in her stomach, a sense of needing to steel herself for what is ahead. Last night she'd told Daisy about Mia's visit, and that she was bringing a friend. She'd left it as long as she could, because she has learned once she tells Daisy Mia is visiting, her daughter, at only five years old, has no understanding that she is not coming right that second and so every minute of waiting is endless, excruciating.

Already Daisy is exhausted; she woke up at five that morning, has been standing by the window with her nose pressed to the glass for the last hour. Suzanne tries not to let it sting, that her daughter looks forward to Mia's visits as if she is Santa Claus, or a fairy godmother. Of course she does, she tells herself, because that is how Mia acts— bestowing presents, giving Daisy the kind of undivided attention and undisguised flattery that an everyday mother cannot. *It's good for Daisy*, she tells herself, even as her daughter descends into sullenness or tantrums after almost every one of these visits.

Was it always this way? Suzanne wonders. No, she thinks, it was not. At the beginning, when Daisy was a baby, Mia was another welcome pair of arms. Suzanne appreciated the help, the break, although something pierced her deeply inside when she caught Mia crooning to Daisy, drawing her so close.

Then, when Daisy was around a year, she grew clingy. For a short time, she wouldn't let Mia hold her, and as much as Suzanne guiltily enjoyed scooping up her daughter with a grimace of apology for Mia, that stage was difficult, as well. Mia upped her visits, coming almost every week, in an attempt to break Daisy's clinginess. It worked, and by the time she was eighteen months old, Daisy was toddling very happy into Mia's arms, and has been ever since.

And while Suzanne knows she has struggled with Mia's involvement, with her insistence on coming for birthdays, last-minute requests to spend an entire Saturday with Daisy, unannounced arrivals *because she was in the neighborhood*, she realizes now that Daisy's tantrums really only ramped up a year or so ago... around the time Mia started to see Tom.

And, Suzanne thinks, counting on her fingers, there haven't been nearly as many visits since then. Yes, there has been the occasional Saturday, a trip to a tearoom for Valentine's Day that Daisy was really too young for, but there has not been the regular onslaught that there was in the past, and while it has been a relief, not to have Mia coming over so often, it has still been hard, because Daisy has reacted badly after each visit, like coming down from a high, the inevitable crash after a sugar rush.

Is she wrong to make the connection, though? Suzanne wonders. Is Daisy *missing* Mia? The possibility makes Suzanne feel sad—both for her daughter and for herself.

The doorbell rings, and Daisy whirls from the window. "They didn't come around the corner!" she cries, already distressed.

"They must have come the other way," Suzanne soothes. She is, unreasonably, perhaps, she acknowledges, annoyed that Mia skipped this ritual. Doesn't she know how important it is for Daisy? Or is she only thinking about Tom now?

To be fair, Suzanne tells herself, it must be nerve-wracking for Mia, to introduce your fiancé to the child you had with another man, even if that child is adopted and not entirely a part of your life. She takes a deep breath and heads to the door.

"Mia!" As always, she sounds far more pleased to see Mia than she really is. "And you must be Tom." She smiles at the affable, fresh-faced-looking young man, in his late twenties perhaps, with ruffled blond hair, a round face, and crinkly blue eyes. He looks, Suzanne thinks, like a little boy in a grown man's body; his good humor is infectious. "I'm so pleased to meet you."

Tom shakes her hand, and then Mark's, and then they come into the hallway, crowded in the narrow space, while Mia hovers, nervously tucking her hair behind her ears, reminding Suzanne of a butterfly.

"Daisy is in the living room," she says, and Mia glances at Tom, her face full of undisguised apprehension, making Suzanne wonder if there is more to this story. Has Tom been reluctant to meet Daisy? Does he not want the complication of a child, even one they will only see occasionally? The thought fills her with a tangled mix of relief, foreboding, and anger on Daisy's behalf. She does not want her to get hurt, but she fears she already has.

Mia heads to the living room, Tom strolling behind. Suzanne has the sense she is walking on her tiptoes, even though she isn't. As they all come through, they see that Daisy is standing with her back to the window, one hand pressed against the glass, as if she has been cornered, so different from previous visits, when she flew to Mia in a tangle of limbs.

"My darling Daisy," Mia says, and her voice trembles. She glances at Tom, an almost panicked look in her eyes, and after a second's hesitation, he steps forward.

"You must be Daisy," he says in that too-jolly voice adults use with children who make them uncomfortable. "I'm Tom."

Mia, Suzanne sees, isn't even looking at Daisy; she's gazing at Tom with an intentness that borders on desperation. Loyalties have shifted, imperceptibly perhaps, but the tectonic plates of their relationship have moved, and even at just turned five, Daisy can sense it.

"Can I get you some drinks?" Mark asks, and Mia shakes her head.

"No thank you, we thought we'd take Daisy out." She glances at Suzanne, not quite seeking permission, but something close to it, because this was not discussed during their phone call. And while Mia has taken Daisy out by herself before, Suzanne is hesitant. As kindly as Tom looks, he is still a stranger, and he seems uncomfortable with children, although Suzanne acknowledges that lots of twenty-something guys probably are.

But Daisy is Suzanne's child in the eyes of law; it is her legal responsibility to care for her, not Mia's. Sometimes, in these moments, she almost forgets that. She has to remind herself, anchor herself in that truth, that she gets to say what happens to her daughter.

"Where were you thinking of going?" Suzanne asks, and she sees a flash of ire in Mia's eyes.

"Just to the park."

Suzanne glances at Mark, and he gives a little shrug, granting permission or absolving himself of responsibility, she isn't sure which, but it irritates her. She turns to Daisy, who has not moved from the window. "Would you like to go to the park, Daisy?" she asks. "To the Ancient Playground? You like that one, don't you? With the pyramids."

Daisy gives her a darkly suspicious look, and Suzanne's heart aches. She wants to sweep her daughter up into a tight hug, although Daisy has started squirming away from her hugs. She wants to protect her, but right now she's not even sure what from.

"Daisy?" she prompts, as Daisy remains silent, looking from Mia to Tom and then back again.

"Do you like the swing, Daisy?" Tom asks, his tone still too jolly, and she nods, then shakes her head. She does like the swing, Suzanne knows, although she is hesitant to go too high. She imagines Tom pushing her high, to give her that thrill, and her heart lurches with fear.

"We'll have so much fun, my darling Daisy," Mia says, and once again her voice trembles. She looks almost as if she might cry, and with a pang of guilt, Suzanne relents.

"Of course you will, Daisy! You love the playground, and I'm sure Mia and Tom will get you an ice cream afterwards." A little bribery never hurts, and Mia almost always gets Daisy an ice cream afterward, even if it's just before dinner. "Shall I get your coat?"

Daisy glances at Suzanne, and her eyes look so huge, so dark. Wordlessly, she nods and walks up to Suzanne, slipping her hand into hers. Suzanne leads her into the hall, helps her put her little arms into her coat. A shudder goes through Daisy, or maybe Suzanne, she's not sure.

Instinctively, Suzanne drops to her knees and wraps her arms around Daisy. To her surprise and gratification, Daisy wraps her arms around her, burrowing her head against her shoulder. They don't hug very often; Daisy has never been one for physical affection, and Suzanne never wants to push. Yet now they wordlessly wrap their arms around each other, clinging together for a few second before, reluctantly, Suzanne eases away, grateful for the moment of affection, of solidarity.

"You're going to have such a good time, Daisy," she promises, as Mia and Tom come into the hall.

Suzanne stands up, taking a few steps back as Mia comes forward and takes Daisy's hand. She glances again at Tom, that apprehensive look that Suzanne doesn't understand, but one also filled with a desperate sort of hope.

"How about a photo?" Mark suggests, brandishing his camera, and dutifully the three of them pose, Mia and Tom on either side of Daisy, holding her hands, like a family.

For a second, Suzanne considers the awful, awful possibility that Mia might be imagining she can somehow get custody of Daisy, that she can make her own little family, the three of them.

But, no... that's impossible, surely? She's being paranoid, even to think of it, to wonder or worry for a second. Daisy is *hers*. Hers and Mark's. They signed the adoption papers five years ago, there is no turning back.

Yet as she carefully closes the door behind the three of them, watching as they walk to the elevator, Mia holding hands with both Daisy and Tom, she cannot keep from feeling a swirling dread in her stomach, a sense of new dangers lurking, that she never let herself think about before.

13

SUZANNE

As Daisy comes out of the baggage claim, I almost don't recognize her. It's been years since her hair has been anything close to her normal color, although she did dye it an unrelenting midnight black for a while, rather than bright pink or blue. But it's not just her hair, it's everything. Her clothes, her makeup, her *manner*. I am so startled that I simply stand there as she comes toward me, pulling a suitcase I don't recognize, wearing a sundress covered in daisies that reminds me so much of Mia.

Her hair ripples in glinting waves around her shoulders, and instead of her usual dark eyeliner, she's wearing some sort of bronzer or blush that gives her a natural, sun-kissed glow, helped, I suppose, by a week in the southern sun. She looks so different, but she also looks better, healthier and happier, and I don't want to examine too closely how that makes me feel.

"Daisy." I take a step toward her, my arms fluttering at my sides. I want to hug her, but there's one thing about her that hasn't changed, and that's the scowl she gives me as she hitches her backpack higher on her shoulder and brushes past me.

"Hey."

I swallow any hurt as I hurry to fall in step. "Good trip?"

"Yeah."

"I saw some photos on Mia's Instagram." I do my best to speak lightly. "It looked like you were having an amazing time."

"Good *grief*, Mom." Daisy slides me a disbelieving look from under her lashes. "You are such a stalker."

"Well, I just wanted to see how you were doing." I keep the tone light, but it takes effort.

Daisy walks faster, almost as if she wants to lose me in the crowds surging out of Newark Airport.

"Are you hungry?" I ask as we emerge outside into the muggy heat. "I called an Uber, but we could stop somewhere. Pirandelli's?" I name our favorite pizza place, over on York Avenue, although I don't think we've actually been there in years.

If I'm imagining a friendly catchup over slices of veggie pizza, it's not to be. "No." Daisy hunches her shoulders. "I just want to get back to the apartment."

I don't miss the way she says *the apartment* rather than *home*, and my heart lurches in my chest. I'm not going to talk about Stirling, or her being expelled, or what on earth she's going to do for the next year, not yet. I wanted to have some normal chitchat first, a chance to reconnect, but unsurprisingly it seems that's not going to happen.

We wait in silence for the Uber to come, and then neither of us speaks all the way home, my few, hesitant attempts at conversation completely rebuffed. Back in the apartment, Daisy disappears into her bedroom. I text Mark that she's arrived back home safely, and then I sit in the kitchen and stare out the window, wondering what to do.

I need to talk to Daisy about her plans, whether she has talked to Mia about living with her, but also about what happened with that party, that photo. I dread both conversations, and I know having them will be like slogging through a swamp, soul-sucking and dispiriting and difficult, no matter how much I want to help her. For want of anything else to do, I start making dinner, taking comfort in the familiar, mind-numbing motions of peeling and chopping. I am just putting some onions and garlic on to fry when my phone rings—it's Peter.

I haven't spared a single thought for Peter since our date, and I'm not sure I can get my head around thinking about him now. Still, after a second's pause, I take the call.

"How are you?" he asks immediately, his voice warm. "Daisy got back today, yes?"

It's unsettling somehow that he remembers, but also a tiny bit gratifying. "Yes, just now. I'm making dinner." I sound inane, but I feel lost.

"I was wondering if we could see each other again. Maybe Friday? Shakespeare in the Park has their first week of the season—they're doing an updated version of *King Lear*, set in some urban dystopia, the stage is all graffiti and steel. I don't know if that's your thing...?"

I can't remember the last time I went to one of those summer plays—a picnic in the park before we watched the stage light up as dusk settled softly around, Belvedere Castle looming behind the stage like its own ready-made set. Maybe when Mark and I were dating. Certainly before Daisy.

"That would be fun..."

"But...?" Peter prompts, a wry note in his voice, because I know I sounded dubious.

"Things are a bit complicated right now, with Daisy—"

"Things are always complicated with children, aren't they?" He speaks gently. "I'll get the tickets anyway, since they're free. You can let me know if you're up for it. I was thinking Friday night. The weather looks good—this humidity is finally going to break."

I can't decide if he's being pushy or just kind. "Okay," I say. "Thank you. I'll let you know." I can't imagine going to the park on a date with everything the way it is, but I appreciate his effort.

I've just put a veggie lasagna in the oven when Daisy finally emerges from her room. Again her appearance gives me a jolt—she looks so like Mia, back in the beginning, when she was a shy college student. I remember how I sometimes felt as maternal to her as I did towards the child she'd given me. She'd come to the apartment, watch me cradle Daisy in one arm, fitting her bottle into her mouth with the other as she sucked happily, kicking her chubby legs in satisfied joy.

"You're so good at that," she said wistfully.

"Only from practice, trust me," I told her with a laugh. "I was all thumbs the first few times. Here—why don't you try?" I'd gestured to Daisy, three months old, and she'd taken her clumsily, giving me a shy smile, her heart in her eyes.

I'd been so magnanimous then. We'd signed the adoption papers just six weeks earlier. Already I thought I was an expert —calm, competent, in control of the physical necessities of managing a baby who so clearly needed me; it was all the emotional chaos later that threw me. I was confident enough to encourage Mia, to let her love my child. I stood back while Mia fed Daisy, fumbling to hold her, milk dribbling down Daisy's chin. Mia looked as if she could cry.

"It's all right," I said, wiping the dribble with a muslin cloth. "It takes a bit of getting used to, that's all."

That wasn't the first time Mia had visited, as I recall. Maybe the second or third, but she hadn't fed Daisy yet, she'd barely held her. She'd seemed so adrift then, having given birth, gone back to college, caught between two worlds and so clearly grieving. Of course I felt magnanimous. I felt sorry for her; she seemed little more than a child, and I knew she needed help and care. It had seemed simple, then, easy. I can't remember when it started becoming complicated, when Mia's visits began to make me grit my teeth, brace myself. And now we're here.

"So." I turn to Daisy. "Tell me about your trip."

She lifts one shoulder in an indifferent shrug as she slouches into a seat at our little kitchen table. I move to the window, haul it open with a screeching protest because the kitchen is warm from the oven.

"I saw you went to a baseball game," I prompt helpfully.

"Yeah, it was fine. Good." As I turn around, one shoulder propped against the window, she glances at me from under her lashes. "I talked to Mia about living there for my senior year."

I keep my expression of friendly alertness, cocking my head as I give a small, encouraging smile even as my heart sinks. "Oh? Yes?"

"Yeah, she said I could. She's looking into whether I can go to the local high school and stuff, but she said she'd get back to me this week." Daisy glances down at her nails; they're not quite as raggedy as they used to be. "School starts early there, like in the middle of August, so I'd need to leave pretty soon." She glances up, guileless, seemingly uncaring what effect her words might have on me.

"Wow, that's a lot to take in," I manage as I move to the stove, open the oven door to needlessly check on the lasagna. It's barely turned warm.

"I told you about it before."

"Yes, I know. I just... You haven't seen much of Mia in a long time. Only a couple of visits since you were..." I blow out a breath. "Seven or so? When she moved to North Carolina."

Daisy shrugs. "She's always been in touch, though."

Scrawled notes, a couple of giftcards, but I'm not going to belabor the point. "Yes, she's very good that way."

"So...?" There is a note of impatience in her voice that tears at me. Am I just a hurdle for her to jump over, so she can get to the good stuff in life?

I turn back to my daughter. "Are you asking my permission?"

For a second, uncertainty flashes in her eyes. She lifts both shoulders in an "I don't know" motion.

I take a deep breath. "First, I think we should talk about Stirling."

Her expression turns guarded. "What about it?"

"A letter came while you were away, from the head-mistress." I pause, waiting for her to offer some acknowledg-ment, but she just stares at me, her wary look turning hostile. "Maybe you'd been expecting this, but you haven't been asked back for your senior year."

She does not look at all surprised. "Guess it's a good idea to go to North Carolina, then," she drawls.

"Maybe, but, I have to ask, Daisy... what happened at that party?" She goes still, and I continue steadily, "We went to speak with Mrs. Hull. She showed us a screenshot she'd been sent, of you at a party. She said the reason you haven't been asked back is because you violated the school's social media policy."

Daisy rolls her eyes. "As if I'm the only one."

"I know, I'm sure there are other Stirling students who have had similar photos taken of themselves." I speak evenly, trying not to betray my distress, my sadness, that this is the world we live in. That this is the world my daughter inhabits, the one she doesn't want to talk to me about. "Daisy, it... it doesn't matter, how you got to that party or why I never heard about it." I am trying to reassure her that I'm not angry that she lied to me about it all, but if I'm expecting anything resembling gratitude or affection, I am disappointed. Her lip curls and she looks away. "I just need to know... for your sake... that nothing happened that you weren't comfortable with. That you didn't want to happen." She turns back to give me a disbelieving look, and unsure if she understands what I'm saying, I state baldly, "Whatever happened at that party... was it consensual?"

To my shock, Daisy giggles, a nasty-edged sound. "Mom, you're *blushing.*"

It takes everything in me to hold her mocking gaze, to keep my voice steady. "I just need to make sure, for your sake."

"Yes, of course it was *consensual.*" She says the word like it's an absurd joke as she rolls her eyes, yet I think I see something fragile and hurting underneath her sneer, and it both heartens and saddens me. *Why, Daisy, why, are you pushing me away now?* "You sound like you're reading from a pamphlet," she mocks. "Did you look that up on YouTube or something?"

"And the photo?" I ask, forcing myself to focus on the matter at hand, and not let myself be hurt by her words. I am still holding her gaze, willing her to be honest with me. To be real.

"Whatever, okay? I don't care about the photo." She slides me a sideway glance. "Did Mrs. Hull mention anything else?"

"There obviously is something else, then." I hate the thought, and yet I knew there must be. A single photo, awful as it was, was never the whole, broken story.

She rises from the table. "No, there isn't. Nothing the school cares about, anyway." She starts walking out of the kitchen.

I care, I want to say, but I can't make the words come. She'd only mock them anyway. For a second, as I watch her walk away from me, I long to tell her how I really feel, the words bubbling on my lips, desperate to be poured out. *Daisy, I love you so much, it feels like I can't breathe and I'm so scared of losing you, except I wonder if I already have. I don't know how to reach you, I feel like I never have, and if you just gave me anything to work with, to hold onto, I'd take it and be so grateful. I love you. I love you.*

She's at the door and I swallow hard. We never said things like that in my family. I never questioned my mother's love for me, I saw and felt it in the way she ironed my clothes, and cooked my dinners, and came to every single spelling bee or sports day I ever had. But we never, ever spoke about it.

"Dinner is in fifteen minutes," I whisper.

Daisy doesn't look back as she answers. "I'm not hungry."

That same evening, I texted Peter and told him I'd go to the play. I felt reckless and desperate, like I needed to do something that wasn't simply sitting around and grieving the relationships I'd lost, feeling helpless, hopeless, alone. And not just about Daisy—when I left my mother's the other day, the aide, Tina, mentioned she'd been talking about Helen again.

"She kept saying Helen should have told her the truth," she said, looking concerned. "Whatever happened, it's bothering her. It might help if you talk to her about it, get it out in the open. Some of our residents need that kind of closure—old hurts and things come to the surface in their twilight and it can cause a lot of heartache."

I stared at her blankly, because I had no idea how I could help my mother with whatever problem she'd encountered with this Helen. I'd never even heard of the woman.

"Some people find it helpful to role-play," Tina suggested. "You could pretend to be Helen."

I opened my mouth, closed it. Pretend to be someone I'd never heard of? I was already having to pretend not to be her daughter sometimes. "I'll think about it," I told her and pushed it to the back of my mind.

As I get ready for my second date with Peter, however, it comes back to me; I'll be visiting my mother on Sunday and I really don't want to pretend to be anyone else. But then, I reflect, sometimes I feel like I'm always pretending to be someone else. A good mother. A loving wife. A capable art historian. Someone in control of their life, who doesn't feel deathly afraid inside, and the strange thing is, I'm not always sure what I'm afraid of.

I've given myself a good talking-to about Daisy's imminent departure; yesterday Mia phoned her to say she was able to enroll her at Cary High School, but she needed her birth certificate. Mia has yet to talk to me, but I understand that it is more between her and Daisy now; Daisy is almost eighteen, after all. At least, that's what I tell myself to keep from feeling angry about it, or worse, hurt.

"I suppose you can take it with you," I told Daisy, and she narrowed her eyes.

"Why doesn't Mia have my birth certificate, since she gave birth to me?" It felt a bit like a taunt, but I kept my reply matter-of-fact.

"I have copies of both your original birth certificate and the one that replaced it, when we adopted you. For all legal purposes, the second one is the one that counts. The one that lists your dad and me as your parents." Her eyes flashed and I continued in an isn't-this-interesting tone of voice, "In the old days, before adopted children really had a chance to know their birth parents, the original birth certificate would have been sent to the state registrar and kept as a sealed record. You never would have known it existed."

"Yeah, if you'd kept it a secret and basically lied to me my whole life," she retorted, and I managed a smile.

"I certainly didn't want to do that. Your dad and I always thought it would better for you to know your birth mother, to have more people who love you in your life." *And look how well that has turned out.*

"So can I have the certificate?" she asked, an edge of impatience to her voice.

"I'll put a folder together of all the documents you'll need," I promised her. There was so much more I wanted to ask—what subjects would she be taking at this new high school, how Mia's other children had taken the news of her living with them, whether she was going to apply to college and who would help her with the applications, not to mention whether I could visit, would she come back for Christmas—but I didn't. I doubted she would answer any of it, anyway, and there were only so many put-downs a person could take in one afternoon. I am trying to let my daughter go, but it's both hard and painful.

And so, on Friday night, I put on a spritz of perfume and my favorite pair of earrings to meet Peter in the park, and I tell myself I'm stepping into my new life—one I'm not sure I really wanted, single at almost fifty with my defiant daughter moving to another state—but it's the one I have, and I am determined to make the most of it.

The trouble is, I'm not sure if I can.

14

MIA

So it all basically happened the way I told Daisy, more or less. I managed to get accepted to NYU despite my parents' unflagging skepticism; I worked like a dog through high school, every assignment both painstaking and painful, and at NYU I majored in marketing, which thankfully didn't require an excessive amount of reading or writing. In my sophomore year, I took a required economics class, Predicting and Modeling Market Outcomes; Tom was a senior, a varsity baseball player and president of his not-too-wild fraternity, a smart guy but also a popular jock. The lecturer always picked him to answer his semi-rhetorical questions, scanning the lecture hall, eyebrows slightly raised, a faint smile on his face when he caught sight of Tom sprawled in one of the seats in the front, baseball cap crammed on his unruly hair, long legs stuck out in front.

"Tom?" he'd ask, and Tom would reel off the answer with an aw-shucks grin.

Of course I had a crush on him.

Of course I never expected him to notice me. At that point, I'd never even had a boyfriend, barely been kissed—my only experience being a quick fumble in the front seat of a rented limo with my prom date, a guy who'd asked me "as a friend." I was shy, awkward, often stammering or silent, sinking into the background as often as I could. Guys like Tom, who strutted around the campus, who took everything as their due, so much so that somehow he didn't even seem arrogant about it, just accepting, didn't even *see* girls like me.

And then the kindly professor called me into his office, because I was failing his class. I stammered out about my dyslexia; he looked at me with sympathy and suggested I have a tutor. The next thing I knew, he'd paired me with Tom, and somehow, right before our final exam in December, Tom was asking me over to his apartment for a study session.

In retrospect, I think the professor had probably asked him to meet with me weekly, but that hadn't happened and so Tom was doing his best to make up for it, and keep in the old guy's good graces. I was both thrilled and petrified, changing my outfit three times, putting on lipstick and then scrubbing it off, before I finally headed over to his apartment on Twenty-Third and Second Avenue, my heart beating like a drum.

The place was a typical student bachelor bad—pizza boxes, beer cans, a couple of faux-leather sofas in front of a huge plasma-screen TV, back when flat-screen TVs were a new thing. Tom was by himself, sprawled on one of the sofas, eating a slice of pizza.

"Help yourself," he said, gesturing to a couple of slices of pepperoni still left in the grease-stained box. "Sorry, what's your name again? Melanie?"

"Mia," I whispered, and perched on the edge of the sofa. I didn't take a slice of pizza; my stomach was already writhing like a pit of snakes.

"So, Market Outcomes," Tom said as he chewed. His hair was rumpled and he hadn't shaved that day, and even slumped on a sofa, slurping a string of cheese from his pizza, I thought he looked gorgeous. "You know I'm a computer science major, right?" he asked with a laugh.

I shook my head. I didn't really know anything about Tom Sullivan besides what so many on campus knew—that he was the star pitcher of the varsity baseball team, the NYU Violets. That girls loved him and guys wanted to be him, that he was a hard-partying jock who still managed to seem pretty nice.

"Well, I am. I mean, I'm getting an A in the class, but..." He shrugged. "It's not like it's my specialty. But I like Farris, so I thought I'd do him a favor." He grinned, and I managed a small smile back. I'd never deluded myself that he was doing this for anyone but our professor. He certainly wasn't doing it for me.

It started out badly, with Tom becoming impatient with my hesitancy, my nervousness. We were sitting on the sofa, a textbook on our laps, my voice coming out in squeaks and whispers, when Tom leaned back, raking a hand through his hair.

"Are you nervous or something?" he asked. "Because you don't need to be."

"Sorry," I whispered.

"Why are you doing so badly in the class, anyway?"

Hesitantly, I told him about my dyslexia; his expression softened in a way that made my insides melt.

"That's really tough. Sorry."

It felt like an intimate moment, but, of course, it wasn't. A little while later, his roommates, loud and laughing, came back with a couple of six-packs of beer; Tom tossed one to me before cracking one open for himself. I'd barely drunk any alcohol in my year and a half at NYU; I spent all my time studying, and parties scared me. I drank the beer.

Just the one, though. I didn't get drunk, and he didn't take advantage in the way that Daisy assumed. I hoped I'd made that clear to Daisy, that even though I was stupid and naïve, I was willing. Very willing.

Tom had another beer, and then another. His roommates

left for a party, and once again we were alone. The apartment seemed very quiet.

"I'm sorry you're missing a party because of this," I told him, and he shrugged the apology aside.

"Nah, you're good. I'm kind of done with the whole party scene, actually. Had enough. I'm graduating a semester early, I'll be finished next week."

"You are?" I hadn't known that, and disappointment swooped through me. "What are you going to do?"

"I'm teaching English in Thailand for a year. Wanted to do something different. Make it count, y'know?" I nodded, as if I understood and agreed, when I felt as if I hadn't made anything count, ever. "After that... I don't know. Work in the city, maybe? Something in tech."

"What about baseball?"

He laughed, sort of a snort, and shook his head. "No, I'm not good enough, not to play pro or anything. Besides, I injured my arm this year." He stretched his arm out, almost as if he'd put it over my shoulders, and for a second something flared between us—heat, awareness, or maybe just an acknowledgment that we were a man and a woman alone in a room.

Tom got up, started prowling around. He might have drunk another beer; I'd lost count how many he'd had, but while I felt no more than pleasantly relaxed from my one, he was well on his way to drunk, although I'm not sure I fully realized it at the time.

"Hey," he said, as he stood by the window, his voice soft. "It's snowing."

I scrambled off the sofa to see, and we stood side by side at the window, watching the big, soft flakes drift down. Snow in the city is its own kind of magic—the streetlights casting haloes, the snowflakes sparkling, suspended in air. Everything goes really quiet, a frantic world suddenly muted, like a fairy tale, a magic spell of silence.

Tom turned to look at me, and our faces were very close. My heart bumped in my chest, and I held my breath. He leaned closer, and I could smell the beer and pepperoni on his breath, but I didn't mind. Then, with a flicker of confusion, he broke away, headed back to the sofa.

"So, we should finish this," he said, and I tried not to let my disappointment show in my face.

Another hour passed as we laboriously worked through the economics; by that time, it was eleven or so, and I was feeling both wired and exhausted, having been on high alert for hours. Tom had drunk a few more beers.

"I probably should go," I finally said as I glanced at my watch. "It's kind of late for me to be out, taking the subway alone." I was such a good little girl.

"Aw, shit." Tom ran his hand through his hair. "I didn't even realize. Sorry."

"It's okay," I said quickly. "I don't mind." I watched as his gaze turned heavy-lidded and he leaned closer, peering at me as if seeing me for the first time.

"You're kind of cute," he said, almost wonderingly, and once again I held my breath. That time he did kiss me, a gentle, questioning press of his lips against mine, and I kissed him back, fumbling, incredulous, as his arms came around me.

In a matter of minutes, we ended up on the sofa, a tangle of limbs, grasping hands and mouths, my whole body exquisitely alive for the very first time. Tom was poised above me, his warm hand under my shirt, and then unbuttoning my jeans.

"You... you're sure..." he said, pausing for me to respond, the words half-slurred, and I nodded almost frantically. I had never felt so alive in my life. So *wanted*. At that moment, I had absolutely no regrets.

I don't think he realized it was my first time; I didn't give any indication how uncomfortable it felt as I struggled to hold onto that initial glow, the lovely feeling of being so wanted.

Afterwards, he rolled off me, and I lay there for a few seconds, sticky and sore, but still strangely happy. Satisfied in a way that actually had, in retrospect, very little to do with sex. Tom's eyes fluttered closed; he looked as if he were already falling asleep.

From outside the apartment, I heard the judder and ding of the elevator, and then the drunken laughter of a couple of guys —his roommates, I realized with a jolt of horror. I jumped off the sofa, straightening my clothes, brushing the tangles from my hair. By the time they opened the door, I had my coat on, hugging my books to my chest. Tom had managed to get to an upright position, pulling his jeans back over his hips with a sheepish grin.

"Hey, hey," one of his roommates said, and then took in Tom on the sofa, me by the door, and burst out laughing.

It was enough to make me run, ducking under someone's arm, sprinting to the elevator, while the laughter and good-natured ribbing of Tom continued behind me. To this day, I'm not even sure why I ran like that. Embarrassment, I guess. I wasn't feeling sad or hurt or rejected—not then. I simply wasn't prepared for that kind of situation, and I figured Tom would call me or talk to me when I saw him again, if just to say—what? Thank you? Are you okay? I wasn't sure, but I thought he'd say *something*.

But what I hadn't expected was to meet his gaze across the examination hall three days later and have him look completely, utterly blank. Not faking it, for the sake of ease, but with no acknowledgment of what had happened between us.

Just to check, I worked up the courage to approach him after the exam. "Thanks for tutoring me the other night," I said. "I think it really helped."

"Oh, yeah, sure." His tone was easy, utterly uncomplicated. "The exam went okay?"

I nodded, searching his face, but he looked completely

guileless, no uneasy guilt lurking in his eyes, no shuffling his feet or looking away, eager to get away from me. Could he not actually remember sleeping with me? I could hardly believe it, and yet the evidence was right there in front of me. "Good luck in Thailand," I finally said, and he looked startled.

"Oh—I told you about that?"

He'd mentioned his trip to Thailand hours before he'd kissed me. If he didn't remember that, I knew he must not have remembered the sex.

"Yeah," I replied woodenly. "But don't worry about it." And I walked away without a backward glance, my heart thudding all the while, feeling sick and dizzy and used in a way I hadn't before, when it had been actually happening.

I never expected to see him again. He was off to Thailand; I had two and a half more years of college. We hadn't even exchanged phone numbers, and he no longer had the NYU email address he'd contacted me from before.

It took another two months for me to realize I was pregnant, more from denial than naivete. I'd put missing my periods down to stress, and I didn't suffer from morning sickness or gain much weight. It was only when I felt a weird flutter—Daisy kicking—that it occurred to me what might be going on. I took a pregnancy test, and then was referred for an ultrasound by the student health center.

I was, according to the technician, already seventeen weeks along. I spent a week more or less reeling, while time ticked on and I knew I had to make a decision. An abortion, I was informed, would be difficult at this stage, if not impossible. In any case, I realized I couldn't bear to have an abortion. I also couldn't bear to tell my parents, but I knew I had to. I couldn't do this alone.

I went home for Easter, hiding my pregnancy with a baggy sweatshirt, dreading the deep disappointment I knew I'd face. When Kerry was out, because I didn't need to see her sorrowful dismay on top of my parents', I sat them both down. My voice shook as I told them I was pregnant.

My mother stared, looking utterly disbelieving, and my father shifted in his armchair, not meeting my eyes.

"Oh, Mia." She shook her head, more exasperated than sorrowful. "How far along?"

"Twenty weeks."

She pressed her lips together. "You'll have to give it up for adoption. We'll find an agency, a good family."

I nodded mechanically, grateful that she had a plan, even if it wasn't one I was sure I wanted. Then she leaned forward and put her hand over mine, saying the words that, whether she realized it or not, sealed my future, and Daisy's too.

"You've worked so hard, Mia. You've achieved so much, even though it's been hard. Don't ruin it now, when you've come so far. Your whole future is in front of you." She squeezed my hand while I fought back tears. They were the kind of words I'd been waiting to hear my whole life, and in retrospect I realized they weren't even that much. Still, I knew then I'd do whatever she said, and I did.

Even so, I didn't take into consideration how I'd feel as I finally started showing, as those first flutters became kicks. As I laced my hands around my bump and thought *my baby*. Still, I forced myself through the motions, for my mother's sake, as well as for mine. This had to be the best way. I knew I couldn't take care of a baby on my own.

My mother picked out an adoption agency and we went through the potential parents together. She was the one who saw Suzanne and Mark first, who said she liked the look of them.

"Financially stable, good, honest people," she said, as if you could tell from a single photo and a short bio. "Oh, but they live in the city. That might be a bit close." She started to turn the page and I stopped her.

"No—no," I told her hesitantly. "I like the look of them." Already, without me even realizing, I was thinking about staying close to Daisy. And I *did* like the look of Suzanne, her direct stare, the no-nonsense way she'd filled out the form. She wasn't gushing like some of the other adoptive parents, trying to show how cool or loving or educated they were. She just *was*. She reminded me of my mom, but nicer.

And it all seemed to go according to plan, more or less. I gave birth to Daisy, Suzanne holding my hand, and then I gave her up. The day after she was born, when Suzanne came back to visit, I suggested the open adoption. I'd read about it, but I hadn't fully realized that was what I wanted. Suzanne looked stunned, but she agreed with alacrity; in my more cynical moments, I wonder if she would have agreed to anything, as long as I gave her Daisy, but looking back, I am grateful for how willing she was to have me visit. She didn't have to be; there was no legal obligation, and yet she never said no.

And so we worked out a plan of visits, and I went back to college, my body still aching, my mind reeling. At the start, I saw her about once a month, hesitant at first, and then gaining confidence. We had a different relationship then, maybe because I was younger, less threatening somehow. She'd listen to me talk about my classes as I cradled Daisy and it felt, a bit, like visiting an aunt or even my mom, the way I wished she would be. It's funny to think now that maybe it was, at least in part, Suzanne who helped me to gain confidence in myself.

And I did gain confidence, did it with determination, because I no longer wanted to be that shy, stammering girl who couldn't even remind a guy he'd had sex with her.

So I transformed myself, just as I told Daisy. I cut my hair differently and I started wearing makeup. I dressed not to impress, but like I didn't need to, like I was on top of the world already. And it worked. Even when I didn't feel it inside, when I still wondered who on earth I was, it worked.

And then, four years later, I ran into Tom. He didn't remember me at all. We were at an alumnae event, a wine and cheese thing in midtown, and I knew I looked good. I had a well-paying job in marketing, and I was wearing a slinky black cocktail dress and stiletto heels, sexy without being vampy. I had confidence and poise, or at least the pretense of them. I saw his admiring glance as he ambled toward me.

"Did we know each other in college?" he asked with a sleepy half-smile, and in that split second, I smiled sweetly back and replied,

"I don't think so."

Why? Why did I lie? I could have said anything in that moment—I could have prevaricated, said I wasn't sure—*um, maybe?*—or, with my forehead wrinkling as I recalled those foggy days, answered slowly, "I don't know... I think you may have tutored me or something?" Anything, basically, other than what I did say. But at the time he was just making chitchat; I had no idea I would *marry* him. That he would fall in love with me, that we would have a whole future together, three beautiful girls. Three *more* beautiful girls. I couldn't have possibly known any of that then. And in that moment, all I remembered was how hurt I'd felt, how disbelieving, when I'd realized he hadn't remembered what we'd done together... and I knew I never wanted to feel that way again.

Of course, there were times—many times—in the years since that moment when I could have, *should* have, said something. I agonized over it constantly—during our third date, when I told him I had a biological daughter who had been adopted, and he accepted it all with an affable smile and shrug of his shoulders. He was tolerant but not interested. The words didn't come then.

When Tom met Daisy, after we were engaged, I thought of it as something of a test; if he got along with her, if, perhaps, some subconscious part of him *suspected*... I'd tell him the truth.

I promised myself I would. But he wasn't particularly comfortable with Daisy, only five at the time, and although he said he'd had a nice time, he clearly wasn't in any rush to go back. It was obvious he didn't see himself as some sort of father figure, never mind her *actual* father, and he didn't think Daisy was going to be a significant part of our lives together going forward, besides, perhaps, the odd weekend.

And since then? When we got married, when he was offered a great job in Raleigh, when we came for Christmas—Tom deciding to join me at the last minute—and my heart felt as if it could burst with both love and despair? The longer I left it, the harder it became.

And, at the same time, the more unreal it felt—almost as if I could convince myself that Daisy wasn't Tom's daughter, that she wasn't even *mine*. She wasn't the wrinkled, reddened baby I gave birth to. She wasn't the damp-skinned newborn whose head I kissed. She was... I don't know who she was, but she was someone I kept separate, out of necessity, even as I loved her and ached for her... until now.

Now, when she is going to live us with for a *year,* when we've repainted Avery's bedroom and bought bunk beds for her and Ella, and I've filled out a registration form at Cary High School and Tom is smilingly calling us a family of six? Now I need to tell him. I know that, I absolutely do. I just have no idea how.

THEN

MIA

September 2008
13 years ago

"Daisy, my darling Daisy!"

Mia holds her arms out as Daisy comes hurtling down the hallway and leaps into them, both of them laughing as Mia spins around, her hair flying out, her arms holding her daughter tightly. She loves these moments. She lives for them. From the corner of her eye, she sees Suzanne come into the hallway, smiling, although the way she holds herself seems stiff.

"Mia. How have you been?"

"Good, thank you. Really well." Carefully, she sets Daisy down on the ground; the little girl wraps her arms around her knees and, laughing, Mia gently pries her off.

"Come in, come in," Suzanne says. "I've made tea."

"And cookies!" Daisy pipes up, and Mia murmurs her thanks and lets Daisy lead her by the hand into the living room.

At the beginning, when she felt so lost and aching, she appreciated Suzanne's efforts to make her more welcome and comfortable. She curled up in one corner of the sofa, a cup of tea cradled in her hands, and chatted with Suzanne about her own mixed-up life while Daisy sat and gurgled at their feet, content in her little seat. Four years on, however, she is starting to wonder if Suzanne's cookies-and-tea routine is more about control than comfort. If they all sit around and have tea and cookies, Mia has less time alone with Daisy. She can't take her out somewhere, which is what she'd really like to do, just the two of them together, mother and daughter.

Still, her feelings are in too much of a ferment to bother with Suzanne's tactics today. She sits on the sofa, murmurs her thanks when Suzanne hands her a cup of herbal tea. Daisy clambers up next to her, resting her head on her shoulder, and Mia's heart squeezes hard with painful, impossible love.

A month ago, she saw Tom at an NYU alumnae event. They've had three dates since, the most recent one last night, when she worked up the courage to tell him about Daisy. Except, of course, she didn't really tell him about Daisy at all.

"Actually, I have a daughter," she'd ventured as they finished their main course, when Tom had started talking about his family and how messed up it was. "I gave her up for adoption when she was born." She'd seen the look of shock flash across his face before he'd arranged his features into something more accepting. "But I'm in touch with her," Mia had continued, stumbling over the phrases she'd practiced, that she'd so wanted to get right. "It's what's called an open adoption. I see her about once a month."

Again with that flash, and then the quick rearrangement. "Wow," Tom said, nodding slowly. "Cool."

And then he asked her if she wanted dessert.

Now, as Mia looks down at Daisy, her heart contracting with love, she wonders how she can ever possibly tell him the truth about her. Yet how can she not?

The first time he asked her out for dinner, she wondered if she should refuse. Run away rather than get involved with this man, when he'd broken her heart, or close enough, once already, and couldn't even remember doing it. And who, she knows, would be utterly shocked—horrified?—to find out he has a daughter he never knew about.

But she didn't refuse, because, the truth was, the minute she laid eyes on Tom Sullivan after nearly five years, her heart skipped a beat and then started double time. When he began to flirt, gently, his face full of appreciation, her battered confidence came out swinging. Besides, she *liked* him. There would be time later to explain about Daisy. Except, time has marched on, they've seen each other three times, they've laughed and joked and kissed, and she still hasn't told him the truth. How can she? Would he even believe her?

"Mia?" Suzanne's voice, edged only slightly with impatience, interrupts her thoughts. "You're miles away there."

"Yes, sorry." She laughs lightly.

Suzanne cocks her head, her eyes narrowing. "How's everything going?"

Mia hesitates, then decides to tell Suzanne. Test out the idea of Tom. He didn't offer to meet Daisy when she told him about her last night, which had been disappointing, even though Mia hadn't really been expecting him to suggest it. But he might one day. She offers shyly, "I'm seeing someone. A guy I met at one of NYU's alumnae events, actually, although we didn't really know each other in college." She realizes she doesn't want Suzanne to suspect that Tom is Daisy's father, although Mia doubts she would. "Tom," she says, imbuing his name with import, unable to keep from glancing at Daisy. "He's really nice."

Suzanne looks surprised, but then she smiles quickly. "How lovely." She, too, glances at Daisy. Mia wonders if she is worried how this might affect Daisy—a man in Mia's life. What if Suzanne knew Tom was actually Daisy's father? What if she became concerned it might change things, and then restricted Mia's access to Daisy? They both know it would be entirely legal for Suzanne to do so; Mia is here on her and Mark's good will, and that is all. If Suzanne were afraid that

Mia might apply for custody, ask for the adoption to be reversed… Mia's heart gives a sudden little leap at the possibility. You heard about those stories, didn't you? It could happen… especially if Tom wanted Daisy in his life. He never had any say in the adoption, maybe he could contest it in court…

Her mind is racing, racing, leaping ahead to a golden-hued scenario she never dared to imagine before, where Daisy is hers, *really* hers, and she and Tom are living together, mother and father. *A happy family.* She catches her breath, and Suzanne gazes at her narrowly.

"Daisy started preschool this week," she says, and Mia forces the reverie back. There will be time to dwell on such happy details later, to embroider them with both hope and love.

"Did she?" She turns to Daisy. "How are you finding it, darling girl?"

Daisy shrugs, and Suzanne prompts her, "Why don't you show Mia some of your paintings, Daisy?"

Obediently, the little girl hops off the sofa and trots off to find her artwork. Mia doesn't like when Suzanne does this. It makes her feel like a maiden aunt Daisy has to impress, no more than a stranger to be polite to. What she really wants is to take Daisy away—to the park, or maybe the library, when it's just the two of them, walking hand in hand, needing no words, and she can think about all of this more.

Daisy comes back into the room, bearing a piece of construction paper weighed down with blobs of paint, thankfully dried. Mia oohs and aahs over it appropriately, even though it always gives her a little twist of sadness, to see the evidence right there in front of her that Daisy is living her life without her. It's ridiculous to feel this way, she knows, because of *course* Daisy is living her life without her. She visits maybe once a month, if that, although there was a period, a few years ago, when she tried to visit more. With work, she hasn't been able to continue that level of involvement, but she still comes alive on these Saturdays, still looks forward to them with every part of her being.

What if it didn't have to be just once a month? What if... *what if she got Daisy back?*

She glances down at Daisy's face, searching her beloved and familiar features for some trace of Tom. Is it there, in the shape of her eyes? Daisy looks so much like she does, and Mia loves that, but right now she wants the evidence of Tom, even if only she can see it.

But what if he does? She is jumping ahead again, past date number four or five, to the time when she brings him to meet her, his daughter. Should she tell him the truth before? After? What if he suspects—or what if he is not interested at all? What if he's angry? There are too many unknowns. It could all go so badly wrong. It's so much risk.

Daisy pulls on her sleeve.

"You seem distracted," Suzanne remarks dryly. "Are you sure everything is all right?"

Mia clasps Daisy's hand in hers. "Sorry, sorry. I'm fine. Actually... I was hoping to take Daisy out for a bit."

Suzanne hesitates as their gazes meet, clash. "She's had quite a busy day today," she says after a moment. "I don't want her to become overtired..."

Maybe she shouldn't have a busy day when you know I'm coming, Mia thinks, but of course doesn't say. "Maybe just a walk to the reservoir and back, then," she says, a steely-voiced compromise.

"Daisy?" Suzanne looks to Daisy, no doubt hoping, Mia thinks, that she will refuse or drag her feet, giving Suzanne the perfect excuse, but to Mia's satisfaction, Daisy claps her hands.

"Yes! I want to go with Mia!"

Suzanne's expression doesn't change, but Mia still feels her flinch. *You have her twenty-nine days out of thirty*, she thinks. *Can you not let me have a single afternoon?* But maybe that's part of the problem; when they first discussed open adoption, it wasn't about carving up Daisy's time like a pumpkin. It was about sharing experiences, resources, ideas, all for Daisy's sake. It sounded so wonderful, at the start: two women working together for the sake of the child they both loved. What could be better, or nobler, than that?

And yet Mia is honest enough to recognize that within a few months of Daisy's birth, that was not how she felt. Some elemental part of her has felt in competition with Suzanne, and as much as she tries to suppress or even deny that truth, it is there, like a thorny root. They are both trying to be mothers.

And maybe having Tom in her life will change things. Maybe she can be a proper mother, all of the time… is it wrong to dream? Is it dangerous?

Suzanne rises to fetch Daisy's coat and shoes while Mia walks to the door, hand in hand with Daisy.

"We won't be long," she promises, and Suzanne manages a smile and a stiff nod.

Outside, they walk along, swinging hands as they always do. The air is touched with autumn, a smell of sunshine and dead leaves that makes Mia think of school buses and new beginnings.

She thinks of Tom's latest text: *I had such a great time. When can I see you again? Let's make it soon!* Her heart thrills to know he's not just interested, he *likes* her! She can barely believe it; she is filled with wonder, with hope. When she tells him about Daisy…

And yet, just the thought of doing so makes her stomach clench. She recalls a throwaway comment he made during their date, how he didn't want kids for a while. How his own family's turbulence—a messy divorce when he was twelve, years of acrimony—made him cautious about having a family.

She'd done her best not to think about such remarks, or at least not to imbue them with any real meaning, because he didn't know the truth about Daisy. And when he did…

What *would* happen?

For a few seconds, she dares *not* to dream. She forces herself to imagine Tom's horror, his anger even, the demands about why she didn't try harder to tell him. Or what if he isn't angry, but horribly indifferent? What if he walks away, from Daisy, from her, because he doesn't want the responsibility of a child? What if he rejects her —again?

Daisy pulls on her hand. "Ice cream?" she asks hopefully, and Mia's lips tremble as she smiles. It's four o'clock, close to dinner, but surely one little ice cream won't hurt, and Suzanne might not find out about it anyway.

"All right," she says, and they head over to an ice-cream cart by the park entrance.

As Daisy takes her ice-cream cone, licking happily, Mia's mind continues to spin and whirl. What if Tom doesn't want to have anything to do with Daisy? What if he resents the time she spends with her? What if she loses not just Daisy, whom really she has already lost, but also Tom?

SUZANNE

When I meet Peter at the park, he is holding a wicker picnic basket and a bottle of champagne. He must see the surprised look on my face, for he says quickly, "Not meant to be over the top—just fun. You can't go to Shakespeare in the Park and not have a picnic."

"No, I guess not," I agree after a pause.

Despite my resolutions to mark this as the beginning of a new life, I feel out of sorts and depressed. As I left the apartment, I heard Daisy talking to Mia on the phone, her voice all high and girlish, in a way it's never been with me. I called good-bye, but she didn't even answer.

"So, how *are* you?" Peter asks, as if he really wants to know the answer, once we are seated on a blanket in the meadow and he is opening the picnic basket, taking out crusty French bread, a wheel of brie and a little tin of pâté.

I take a deep breath before blurting, "Mixed, I guess. Daisy has decided to live with her birth mother Mia for her senior year of high school."

Peter nods, looking sympathetic but neither shocked nor horrified, as I still am. And why should he be? He told me before that his sons had lived with his wife for their last years of high school. If Daisy had wanted to live with Mark, would I feel this devastated, this judged?

No, I realize, of course not. Because he is her father, he has watched her grow up, they have a normal, parental relationship... unlike Daisy does with Mia. And, I acknowledge, I feel this way because, at the heart, the very root of my relationship with Mia, there has been this sense of competition, of feeling threatened, that comes from us both wanting to be Daisy's mother. I haven't wanted it to be there, and I've done my best to suppress it, to act as if I don't feel it. I've smiled back when she's called Daisy "my darling Daisy"; I've enthused about how generous she is when the hundred-dollar gift cards come rolling in. I never minded that Daisy's favorite childhood toy, the stuffed panda she had to sleep with, was from Mia. I've told myself that more of Mia and more of me is good for Daisy.

But I don't think I've ever really believed it.

"I know it's hard," Peter says as he hands me a cracker spread with pâté, "but could it be possible to view this as a liberation? Someone else gets to be responsible for a little while. Someone else is going to be the one who is blamed or shouted at or ignored."

"You sound like my ex-husband, telling me I'll enjoy a bit of a break," I reply, trying for wry, but it comes out with an edge. This won't be the first time I'll have been away from Daisy, but it will certainly be the longest. The worst.

Peter smiles and shrugs. "Isn't there some truth to that?"

I glance up at the sky, the blue just starting to darken at the edges, the peach hues of the setting sun streaking over Belvedere Castle like fireworks. "You don't stop being a mother, just because your child isn't with you."

"No," Peter agrees equably, "but you stop having to bear the heavy lifting, day in and day out. That can feel like a relief sometimes, can't it? I'll admit it does to me. And the important thing is, your status doesn't change. You *are* Daisy's mother, regardless."

I nibble the cracker as I consider his words. Rather perversely, I've resented Mia for not having to do the heavy lifting, for getting to be the one to sweep in and save the day, be fun and exciting. For doing only the easy bit.

But now, I reflect, *I* get to be Mia. I can send the gift cards, take Daisy out for lunch, be chatty on a Zoom call—if Daisy even bothers to call me. Maybe it *will* be a relief, at least a little bit.

But then it occurs to me if I get to be Mia, then Mia gets to be me. And if my status doesn't change, then neither does hers. We are, I acknowledge, *both* Daisy's mothers. I have been fighting against that truth all of my daughter's life, even as I've pretended to espouse it. Maybe if I finally, truly, acknowledge it, accept it, I can make peace with it and then I can let it go.

"You never told me why your son isn't speaking to you," I tell Peter, and he looks slightly startled before he glances down, slathering some pâté on a cracker.

"He resents the fact that I gave his brother money," he tells me, his head still bent. "It's a bit like the story of the prodigal son." He glances up, eyes glinting, although there is a sorrowful twist to his mouth. "Do you know it?"

"Mainly from art."

Peter nods, casting his gaze heavenward. "Let me think... *Return of the Prodigal Son* by Rembrandt?"

I let out a little laugh, impressed. "Very good."

"It's a beautiful painting."

"It is." I've always loved the tenderness of the father's hands on his son's shoulders, the way he is bending over him so gently, bringing him back into the fold. *Come home, all is forgiven.* It feels especially poignant right now. "So what happened with your sons?" I feel as if I've told him so much of my story, and yet I know very little of his.

Peter sighs, a soft sound of sadness I haven't heard from him before. "My younger son got into a bad crowd when he was a teenager. Of course, you want to blame other people, don't you? Someone else's children, not ours. Not us. But he chose the bad crowd. We let him. I can't help but wonder if things might have turned out better if we'd forced him to take more responsibility, or maybe if we'd taken responsibility ourselves. I don't know, even now." Another sigh. "We managed to push him through high school, get the grades to go to college, hoping that would straighten him out, and in the middle of it all, we were splitting up. I'm sure that didn't help, and in any case, it was foolish, in retrospect, thinking he'd do better in college." He lifted his head, a new bleakness in his eyes. "Why would he do any better away from us?"

The question causes me a jolt of recognition, a pang of fear. I've just about convinced myself Daisy might do better away from me. What if she doesn't? I've been so worried that I might be the problem, but what if I'm not?

"So what happened, then?" I ask quietly.

Peter lifts his shoulders, drops them. "It got worse. *He* did. Spiraled out of control, dropped out, disappeared for a few months, which really scared his mother and me."

I feel as if a hand is clutching my heart, squeezing hard. I can't imagine losing Daisy in such a way, and yet the truth of it is, I *can*. I just don't want to imagine the pain I'd feel, how I would be able to bear it, if she did something similar. Having her merely flirting with rebellion has been hard enough.

"And now?"

"Now I've learned to let go. Melinda, too." Peter smiles, but there is no humor in the curving of his lips, no joy. "We've both had to. When he resurfaced, we told him we'd pay for rehab. An expensive program, one of the best, but we would have done anything... *anything*." For a second, his face crumples, the wrinkles looking deeply carved, reminding me of

Rembrandt's father's face. *Come back*. "He dropped out after two weeks."

"I'm sorry."

Peter nods. "That was a year ago. He disappeared for a while, resurfaces now and again. He lives in Philadelphia, picks up some work here or there, texts or calls on occasion to let me know he's alive."

"That must be hard." And yet I might be facing something similar, at least in terms of how much I see of my daughter.

"Yes, but like I said, you learn to let go. You have to. It's either that or go mad with guilt and grief." He meets my gaze, his own lacking his usual charm or lightness. I feel the weight of his grief along with my own. It's all so *hard*. Does it ever get any easier, for anyone? Or do you simply get used to bearing the weight?

"And what about your older son?" I ask slowly. "You said he wasn't speaking to you."

"He's angry because of all the time and money and attention we've showered on Rob. We've neglected him, even though we didn't mean to. He asked for help with his mortgage—he's just married, wanted to buy a house in Westchester—and I gave him what I could, but it wasn't enough. He feels he's been treated unfairly, and maybe he has. If I hadn't paid for Rob's rehab, I'd have had more money to give to him. But it's hard, when Rob is practically out of the picture, to be at odds with him too." He straightens, manages a smile. "Anyway. Enough about all this. I've got champagne and I think we should drink it." He reaches for the bottle and pulls the wire off the cork.

I watch as he pops the cork, discreetly, because drinking alcohol is technically illegal in the park, although plenty of people bring a bottle of wine with their picnic. As Peter pours us both plastic cups of fizz, I feel a sweep of melancholy, a stirring of hope.

I'm sad for Peter, for all he's endured, but it's also strangely encouraging, in an odd way, to know other parents struggle as I do—they feel the overwhelming love, the utter powerlessness. The deep, abiding hurt. But maybe that's just what parenting *is*. What life is, in all its mess and glory, and there is no escaping it. Rather than running from the pain or always trying to brace myself for the impact, maybe I should just let go, the way Peter has learned to do. Maybe I won't even have a choice. Daisy *is* going to Mia for her senior year. I've already booked her tickets; she leaves in three weeks. There's no changing that now.

The next afternoon, I travel to Montclair to see my mother. The evening with Peter was enjoyable in the end, watching the play as the sun set and the world turned dark. As we strolled out of the park afterward, we had a rousing discussion about *King Lear*—was he wrong, to ask his daughters to prove they loved him? Should Cordelia have spoken up sooner?

"Typical teenager, to be so stubborn," Peter said, shaking his head, and I laughed. The air was soft, reminding me that a summer evening in New York is a magical time. My muscles loosened, and I tilted my head back to the night sky. For a few seconds, I let my mind skim through possibilities, glimmers on the horizon I'd never considered before. Freedom, romance, maybe even love. If not with Peter, then maybe someone else. I wasn't that old, after all, was I? When I lowered my head, Peter caught my eye and smiled.

He didn't kiss me goodnight. By the time we'd cabbed it uptown, I was back to my usual uneasy self, and I think he could tell. He smiled and touched my hand briefly in farewell, and I was glad we left it at that. I still felt happy though, in a way I hadn't in a long time.

Now, as I head into the nursing home, the aide Tina stops me. "She's talking about Helen again," she tells me in a low voice. "And she seems pretty agitated."

I am already shaking my head. "I really have no idea who Helen is—"

"I know, but if you could just play along, it might help." She grimaces in sympathy. "I know it may sound weird and even wrong, but trying to explain reality to patients with dementia just frustrates or frightens them. This really is the best way."

I twitch a little, something between a nod and a shrug. I really don't want to do this. "I'll try," I tell her, even though everything in me resists.

My mother doesn't recognize me as I come into her room. She's in bed still, although it's the afternoon, a blanket around her shoulders, her bobbed gray hair tangled about her flushed face. Tina was right when she said she was agitated.

"Hey, M—" I stop myself in time. "Hello," I correct with a smile. "I haven't seen you in a long time."

My mother's eyes narrow with suspicion. "Who are you?"

I swallow hard. From the doorway, I see Tina give me a thumbs up. "Why, Elizabeth," I say, practically choking on the words, "you remember me, I'm sure, although I know it's been such a long time." I pause, glance again at Tina, who nods her encouragement. "I'm Helen."

"Huh!" My mother leans back against her pillow, eyeing me critically. "You have a lot to answer for, you know."

"Yes, you've seemed troubled about... about that," I say. I feel like I'm flailing in the dark. "Do you want to talk about it?" I inch into the room and perch on the edge of the chair by the window.

My mother folds her arms. "What is there to talk about now? It's all too late."

"Why is it too late?"

My mother gives me a look of scathing disbelief. "Because we already have her, don't we? And, you know, Philip isn't happy about this at all. He had no idea she would be so difficult.

He goes out most evenings, just to get away from her screaming."

My mind is scrambling, trying to make sense of the words. "Whose screaming?"

"Don't tell me you've forgotten already?" my mother scoffs. "Suzanne's."

For a stunned second, I feel as if the floor has dropped away, as I'm dangling in mid-air. I stare at her, open and close my mouth once, twice. "Suzanne," I repeat faintly. "Yes, of course."

My mother makes a harrumphing sound while I try to think of something more to say.

"So why do you think she is screaming?" I ask, my voice wavering even as I try for a mildly curious tone. I have no idea what my mother is remembering. When was I *screaming*?

My mother shrugs. "How should I know? That's where *you* come in, Helen. You said she was as good as gold. That she wouldn't be any trouble at all."

"I... I thought she wouldn't be."

Another harrumph. "Well, you were wrong."

I am trying to organize my thoughts, to shape my mother's words into a narrative I can understand. Who is Helen? Why would I be screaming? Or is this nothing but a jumble of scraps of memory, brought together to form a confusing whole?

"Tell me more about Suzanne," I invite, trying to keep my voice from shaking.

"I feel sorry for the poor thing, of course," my mother says, straightening in her bed. "She's clearly had a troubled start in life, and I've never been one to shirk my Christian duty. But Philip and I didn't think we'd have any children, you know, marrying so late. And we weren't prepared for all the havoc she'd cause. The screaming in the middle of the night! Neither of us can sleep, and I have no idea how to calm her. She just goes on and on."

I have no idea why my mother would be saying such things.

A troubled start in life? My mother is looking at me pointedly, waiting for me to respond. "It must be very difficult," I murmur.

She gives another harrumph. "The funny thing is, she's as quiet as a mouse during the day, wouldn't say boo to a ghost. But she hides food—it's appalling, really. I've found all sorts of moldy things under the bed, and one time she put cabbage down her pants, can you believe! She must have been starving before, poor thing." My mother's face droops with sadness. "Poor little thing. I want to do my best by her, I do, but it's so very hard."

"It... it must be." I feel the acid tang of bile in the back of my throat, and I have to grip the arm of the chair to keep upright. The room feels as if it is spinning. *If what my mother is saying is true...* "So, Elizabeth," I force out, "what do you mean by... by before?"

"Before we took her in," my mother says impatiently. "Of course that's what I mean." She suddenly lunges forward, scrabbling for my hand, my arm. "I feel so guilty, for being annoyed with her. I want to do my duty—"

I pat my mother's hand mechanically. "So what you're telling me is..." The words feel thick in my mouth. "Is that Suzanne is adopted?"

My mother pulls away as she glares at me. "You should know! You arranged it all. You placed her with us."

"Yes, of course." I stumble over the words. "What I meant was, can you remind me how... how old she was when you adopted her?"

"She had just turned four. Her birthday is in April and we got her in May."

"Right." *Four.* I was adopted when I was four. How could I not have known this? How could I not have remembered? Somehow I manage to focus on my mother, who is starting to look suspicious.

"Why are you asking me these questions?" she demands. "You are Helen, aren't you?"

"I just wanted to reacquaint myself with the facts." I force myself to meet her gaze, the corners of my mouth turning up in a smile that feels like an awful rictus. "I'm very sorry it's been so challenging for you, Elizabeth, but I'm sure things will settle down soon. Remind me how long has it been since the adoption took place?"

"Three months, but it feels like forever." My mother leans forward. "I want to love her, you know, I really do. And I think I can, but it's so hard right now. And Philip has just about had enough. I'm afraid... I'm afraid he might leave me." Her face crumples with sadness and worry, and my heart aches for her, despite my own gasping shock.

"Now, now, I don't think Philip will leave you," I tell her, reaching over to pat her arm. I know that he didn't. "Just... just keep on trying. She'll soon settle, I'm sure of it." I did settle, didn't I? I don't remember being unhappy when I was a small child. But clearly I don't remember much.

"She really is such a quiet little thing," my mother says sadly. "And she won't let me touch her. Not a kiss, not a hug. I know I'm not the most demonstrative person, but it's strange in a child, isn't it?"

But we've never been a hugging family, I think with something like panic. It wasn't that I didn't want to be hugged, it was that my mother never hugged *me*. Wasn't it?

"Just keep trying," I murmur. I don't think I can take much more. My head is buzzing and I feel as if I could be sick. Why has my mother never said any of this before? Why has she fixated on this time of life? Was it because it was so upsetting? Because she felt guilty? What does she need to hear now, to release her from the prison of her memories, her guilt and her fear? "She'll come round, Elizabeth, I promise," I tell her as I pat her hand. "And I might have a lot to answer for, it's true, but you've done the right thing, adopting her. She's going to grow up to be a lovely young lady, a real credit to you, and have a family of her own."

My mother's face clears, her eyes brightening with hope in a way that makes me want to sob. "Do you really think?"

"I know it," I assure her, my voice choked, and with one more clumsy pat of her arm, I walk out of the room, blinking back tears.

16

MIA

Somehow the weeks slide by and I never find the right moment to tell Tom about Daisy. I rehearse openings in my head —*remember when we were at college?*—but it is such an enormous leap from him believing we never knew each other during our NYU days to telling him he fathered my child. I do not know how to cross that chasm. And as the summer days pass in a lazy, hazy montage, I tell myself there is still time.

In the beginning of August, just a week before Daisy is due to come, we spend a weekend at the beach—long, lazy days in the sun and sand, splashing in waves and eating picnics gritty with sand. The last night, after the girls are asleep, Tom and I sit out on the balcony with glasses of wine, listening to the gentle shooshing of the waves. It feels like now or never.

I've registered Daisy at Cary High School, and Avery and Ella were excited to share a room—at least they were after I promised they could redecorate it, new bunk beds, the walls painted purple. Sophie is also thrilled, seeing Daisy as a built-in playmate, one who will, I suspect she thinks, obey her every command. And as for Daisy herself—she's been great. Surprisingly, sweetly wonderful. We've talked most weeks, and it's been amazingly easy. There have been no tough questions, no difficult conversations, just easy chat about what we're looking forward to about the year ahead, light and breezy.

Tom has got into the spirit of things too; he's arranged for Daisy to have driving lessons, and bought season tickets to the Raleigh Firebirds, even though we don't actually know if Daisy likes basketball.

It's all going so well, and yet I still haven't told Tom. I have not found a moment, although I recognize that one does not actually exist; I have to make it, carve it out of silence and awkwardness and ignorance. Yet I cannot even think how to bridge the gap between his lack of awareness and my own secret knowledge. I should have, I know that full well, but it has just felt so impossible—like taking a flying leap over the Grand Canyon, or all the way to the moon.

And so, as we sip our wine and gaze out at the moonlit beach, I tell myself that time is now. Yet how to begin?

"I was thinking about NYU the other day," I tell him, cringing at how forced it sounds. I can't see Tom's expression in the dark, but I feel his bemusement at the random remark.

"Oh, yeah?"

"It's your twentieth reunion coming up, isn't it?"

"Not for nearly two more years." He definitely sounds bemused.

"Well, perhaps we could make a trip of it, take the girls to the city, show them the sights."

"Okay..." He's waiting for more, because I am sounding so odd. I know I am.

I take a deep breath. "I was actually remembering that we knew each other, way back then."

He stills and I glance at him, glad it's too dark to see his face. "At college? We did?"

"Yeah, although not very well, admittedly. You tutored me in an economics exam, I think."

"What...?" The words come out in a breath and in the ensuing silence I know he's trying to think back. "When?"

"December, right before you graduated."

He lets out a huff of laughter. "I can't believe you haven't told me this before."

I shrug, not wanting to lie outright by pretending I've only just remembered. There's been enough deception, surely.

Tom blows out a breath and shakes his head. "Sorry, I don't remember. Are you sure?"

"Pretty sure." I try to inject a teasing note into my voice, but I can't quite manage it. "You were quite the big man on campus, you know. Baseball player. Frat boy."

"Zeta Psi is a good fraternity," Tom protests, laughing a little. "I know I partied quite a bit in college, but that was a long time ago. I've changed."

"I know. And I'm not surprised you don't remember me. I was pretty different, then."

"A little mouse, or so you've said." He reaches for my hand, his voice full of affection, but I pretend I don't see as I sip from my wineglass.

Inside, I am still shaking with fear, but I also feel a surprising streak of anger, like lightning, burning through me. Does he really not remember at all? Yet why should I be surprised? He didn't remember then. He's not going to remember now.

"Why are you bringing all this up now, Mia?" He sounds serious again, reaching for my hand once more. This time I let him take it. "What's made you think of NYU after all this time?"

Daisy has. I swallow, close my eyes.

Tom threads his fingers through mine. I am so close to telling him; I feel as if I'm on my tiptoes, legs flexed, poised to leap into the unknown, fall or fly. *I'm telling you because we actually slept together back then and Daisy is your daughter.*

The words are a pressure in my chest, which is getting tighter and tighter so I am struggling to breathe. Just say it. *Say it.*

I open my mouth. Tom squeezes my fingers encouragingly. "Well," I say, a tremble in my voice that I think he must hear. "It's because we actually—" And then I stop, because suddenly I am not thinking of how Tom will react, but how Daisy might. No matter how angry or shocked or hurt he is, he'll want to tell her, I know that much. He won't be able to keep it a secret, he shouldn't even have to, but then what?

How will Daisy feel, knowing that all these years we were building our family without her? That she has as much right to be one of the Sullivans, with her photo on every step of the stairs, as Ella, Avery, or Sophie do? How will she feel, knowing I've been lying —to her, to Tom—all along? Realizing I withdrew from her life, at least in part—in *big* part—because it hurt too much to keep this secret, seeing her so often, knowing I was living a lie? All these years she's missed out because I couldn't bear for anyone to know the truth, because I didn't know how to handle it. How will she feel—I know the answer already.

She'll hate me.

"Mia?" Tom asks gently, his fingers still threaded through mine.

I force a smile, although my lips feel funny. "Oh, just because I'm feeling nostalgic. Daisy will be applying to college this year, and she reminds me of me in a lot of ways." The words spill out, shamefully easily, and I feel Tom relax.

"I can understand that," he says gently, and I nod, hating myself, my cowardice, my lies. *I made my choices and I am doing my best to live with them.* It is what I've told myself all along, yet it has never felt as hard as it does now.

THEN

SUZANNE

October 2007
14 years ago

It is October, nearly Halloween, and Suzanne meant to have a costume for Daisy. She meant to have cookies too, and decorations, and most of all, *cheer*. But she's managed none of it, not that Daisy really knows or cares. The whole concept of Halloween isn't one she fully understands yet; she's only three years old, after all. But Suzanne understands, and even though she has never cared all that much about Halloween as a holiday, she feels she has failed.

Mark went into work this morning, grimacing in apology. He's taken too much time off this last week, he told her, full of remorse. He has to show his face. He made sure she was all right; he kissed her cheek and squeezed her shoulder while Suzanne sat silently, her face like marble.

Mia is coming this afternoon, though, taking time off work to see Daisy in her costume and accompany them trick or treating through the apartment building. It is the first time Daisy will have gone. When

Suzanne looks at the calendar, she sees that Mia has come at least twice or three times a month for the last year and a half. Suzanne had half-wondered if the visits might taper off once Mia had graduated from college and got a job, but it hasn't happened that way at all. She's been working for some marketing firm in midtown for a year now and, if anything, the visits have increased—several Saturdays a month are held hostage to Mia, and Suzanne tries her best not to resent it.

Back at the beginning, she'd convinced herself Mia's involvement could be a good thing, and it has been, in many ways, but there are times when Suzanne feels like asking her to come just a *little* less often. To just give them a little space to breathe, so Daisy won't miss her so much, but perhaps she would miss her more. Mia's absence, Suzanne fears, would not be the cure-all she sometimes thinks it would. In any case, she never says any of it because it feels so petty and ungrateful, so wrong. Mia gave them her own *child*, and she can't manage to give a few Saturdays back?

Except, Suzanne reflects, sometimes it feels as if Mia hasn't given her Daisy at all. Sometimes it feels like a tug of war, with Daisy as the rope, and that is something Suzanne does her best to avoid. She says nothing when Mia calls Daisy "mine," telling herself there is no need to be possessive about a person, a child they both love. She has never refused one of Mia's visits. She even invites her sometimes—to Thanksgiving or Easter, holidays Mia usually misses to be with her own family, which might be why Suzanne invites her. She reminds herself that Mia is only twenty-three, practically a child herself. All of this helps Suzanne to greet these visits, if not with outright enthusiasm, then with something approaching equanimity. She feels sorry for Mia, and she wants to help her. She wants to be the kind of person who would help her. Until today.

Today she can't summon the smiles, the cheerfulness. Today she is sitting on the sofa in her bathrobe even though it is nearly noon, and Daisy is watching her third consecutive hour of *Dora the Explorer*.

Today it has taken all her energy simply to sit there and try not to weep.

She's failing at that, anyway; the tears slide silently down her cheeks, but, fortunately, Daisy doesn't notice. She is glued to the television, hardly able to believe her good fortune at having such unfettered access to glorious cartoons. Before today, Suzanne has rationed screen time in fifteen-minute mind-numbing dollops; a single episode of *Dora* is an unimagined luxury. Now Daisy has had—what? Six, seven? And Mia is due in just ten minutes. Suzanne knows she should get dressed, but she can't make herself move from the sofa.

She never thought she'd feel this way—the dawning joy, the incredulous hope, and now the soul-sucking despair. She gazes at the back of Daisy's dark head and her heart aches and aches. She doesn't move. She can't.

The minutes pass, and then Suzanne hears the insistent buzz of the intercom. Daisy's head jerks up, and she is instantly alert, practically sniffing the air. She scrambles from the TV, Dora momentarily forgotten.

"Mia?" she asks, tugging on Suzanne's arm. "Mia?"

"Yes, Mia is here," Suzanne says wearily. She can't even summon a smile. She shuffles to the door, feeling like an old woman, and presses the button to unlock the front door downstairs without even saying hello first, as she usually does. Daisy stands by the door, alert and ready.

They both hear the creak of the elevator, the groan of its gears as it labors upward. Daisy stands on her tiptoes, hands clasped in front of her, her face radiant with expectation, while Suzanne sags behind her, struggling simply to stand.

Then the creak and bang of the elevator door, the light knock, and Daisy hurls herself towards the knob, twisting it eagerly.

"Just a minute, Daisy, just a minute." Suzanne unlocks the door, standing back to open it while Daisy springs forward.

"Mia!"

"My darling Daisy!" Mia swoops her up in an extravagant hug, shaking her shiny dark hair behind her back. She is wearing a white blouse and a gray pencil skirt, and she looks young and chic and pretty, so much more confident than the shy college girl she was just a short while ago. Suzanne is more conscious than ever of her bathrobe, her unwashed hair, the sadness that oozes from her pores. She usually tries to make such an effort for Mia—to make her feel welcome, but also to make herself feel better. She can handle Mia's visits better when she is neatly dressed, her hair done and the apartment tidy and welcoming. She has not let herself consider too closely why that is the case.

Finally, Mia turns from Daisy, and she can't keep a look of startled dismay flashing across her features as she takes in Suzanne's appearance. "Suzanne…"

"Sorry, it's been a hard day. A hard few days." Her throat thickens as she says the words and she turns away quickly. "Coffee? Tea?"

"Um, coffee, please, but I can get it—"

"No, no." Suzanne waves her away as she hurries into the kitchen. "It's fine." Her voice sounds clogged. She can feel Mia watching her for a few agonizing moments and then, from the corner of her eye, she sees her take Daisy by the hand and settle her in front of the television once more, where the map is singing its cheerful, irritating song. Then Mia returns to stand in the doorway of the kitchen. Suzanne's hand trembles as she measures scoops of coffee into the top of the machine.

"Suzanne… is everything okay?" Mia asks quietly. "Has something happened?"

Suzanne doesn't reply for a moment, focusing on making the coffee, because she is afraid if she starts speaking, she will sob. She never expected to feel this way. She had no idea this hope and grief had been waiting for her, and so the depth of her emotions has caught her completely by surprise.

"Suzanne?" Mia's voice is gentle.

Suzanne is reluctant to tell her, because she has never really shared confidences with Mia. She has always presented herself as completely capable and resilient, telling herself it was because that was what Mia needed, and yet now she wonders if it was what she needed, too. She does not want to be seen as weak. She never has.

And yet right now, she feels a deep, aching need to tell Mia what happened, to validate her grief. "I was pregnant," she says in a low voice, staring at the floor. "I lost the baby at fifteen weeks." She glances toward the living room, where Daisy is sitting cross-legged in front of the TV, completely absorbed. "We hadn't told Daisy or anyone yet, I suppose because it felt too good to be true." She swallows hard. "I didn't think I could get pregnant at all, you see. It was so unexpected…" Her voice breaks and she draws a shuddering breath. "It happened three days ago. I had to stay in the hospital overnight…" She can't say anything more. She is remembering the cramps that banded her middle that felt like contractions, because that was in fact what they were. She'd been scheduled for a D&C once they hadn't found a heartbeat, but her body had expelled the beloved, lifeless form from itself first. A tiny, translucent, perfect baby, one you could hold in the palm of your hand.

"*There was nothing wrong with her*," the doctor had said, as if that made it better, when in fact it made it worse. "*Sometimes these things just happen.*"

"Oh, Suzanne…" Mia looks aghast, but also discomfited. She has never had to comfort Suzanne before; their roles are strangely reversed.

"I'm sorry I'm such a mess." Suzanne wipes at her cheeks. "Mark tells me I need to get out and about, or at least dressed. There's nothing actually *wrong* with me, you know. It's not like I gave birth." Except it is. She glances up at Mia, and sees, for a second, how stricken she looks. *Is this how you felt?* she wonders with a sudden appalled understanding. *This loss, this grief, but so much worse? Because you held Daisy. You cradled her in your arms, and then you let her go.* Until this moment she realizes she has never truly and fully appreciated the sacrifice Mia has made, the grief she must have felt, the utter depth of it. "I'm sorry," she blurts, and she does not even know what she is apologizing for.

"You don't need to be sorry," Mia says, laying a hand on her arm. "I think you need to take it easy. Be kind to yourself. I'm so sorry this happened, Suzanne. Really, I am."

The sincerity in her voice makes tears spring to her eyes and Mia steps forward, enfolding her in her arms. The hug takes Suzanne by surprise; she'd never been much of a hugger, but as Mia's arms come around her, she realizes how much she needs this comfort. She bites her lip. "I would have loved for Daisy to have a little sister or brother."

"It will get better," Mia says softly, and Suzanne understands she knows exactly what she is talking about.

"Thank you," she whispers, and they stand that way for a few seconds more, Suzanne feeling as if Mia is propping her up, before Mia steps away with a small, self-conscious smile.

Suzanne reaches for a mug for Mia's coffee and Mia stays her, putting her hand over Suzanne's.

"You don't need to wait on me. Look, why don't you go rest? Or take a bath? Whatever you want. I can sit with Daisy. You take care of yourself." Mia smiles, and Suzanne knows she means what she says, but still she hesitates.

It feels wrong, somehow, to walk away from both Mia and Daisy. Of course, she's done it over the years, for Mia's sake. She's let her take Daisy to the Starbucks around the corner, the park, the Central Park Zoo. Occasionally, Mia has made vague, hesitant suggestions about bigger trips—taking Daisy to the beach or having her at her apartment for a weekend. Suzanne has replied with noncommittal noises, because Daisy is so young, and she's not ready for that level of trust. When Daisy is older, she thinks, things will get easier. She's not sure how—their roles will be more established, perhaps, or maybe Mia will back off. Somehow, she tells herself, it will all become easier.

"Please, Suzanne," Mia says. "Let me help you."

Too tired to resist anymore or analyze her own feelings, Suzanne relents. "All right," she says. "Thank you."

Mia beams as Suzanne shuffles off; by the time she reaches her bedroom door, she can hear Mia's singsong coo to Daisy. "Guess what I brought you, Daisy? Yes, your favorite…"

No doubt Mia has brought her some treat—a muffin or cookie. Every time she comes, there is something—candy or cookies, a coloring book or a small toy. Nothing too over the top, nothing Suzanne feels she can protest against or resent, and yet… And yet.

She goes into the bedroom and closes the door.

The room is quiet and dark; the window looks out over the alleyway and so it is never light, but right now Suzanne is grateful for the dimness. She had thought she might take a bath, but as she sits on the bed, she finds herself leaning back, curling up into a ball. She was barely showing, but she still feels empty, different. Two weeks before she started bleeding, they'd heard the heartbeat for the first time, that wondrous, galloping sound.

They'd just begun to feel cautiously hopeful, amazed that they'd arrived at this place at all. They'd talked about how to tell Daisy. Suzanne had ducked into a maternity store on Madison Avenue, thrilled to peruse the stretchy leggings and oversized shirts. She wanted nothing more than to have a big, round bump she could run her hands over, feel the flutter and kick of the little one cocooned inside.

Now none of it is ever to be.

"We still have Daisy," Mark had told her as they'd taken a taxi home from the hospital. They'd left Daisy with a neighbor, something they hardly ever did. He was being staunch when she was usually the one who rallied, but she couldn't. She simply couldn't.

Now her hands creep to her empty middle and she feels the slight sag of empty flesh. She closes her eyes. From the living room, she hears Mia's murmurs, Daisy's laughter. She knows she should be grateful that Mia is here, that she is helping—and she *is*, she tells herself, she is—but in this moment all she can feel is sad.

She drifts off to sleep without realizing, only to wake with a start. The room is no longer merely dim, but dark, and outside night has fallen. The air feels cold; she has not adjusted the thermostat, now that the nights are drawing in. Suzanne scrambles off the bed, feeling groggy and disorientated. It is, she sees, just after five o'clock in the evening. She's been asleep for four hours.

As she reties the sash of her bathrobe, she wrenches open the door and hurries out into the hall; the apartment feels not just quiet, but empty.

"Mia?" she calls, and there is no answer. Suzanne turns the heating up and then heads into the kitchen, where the warm, comforting smell of stew is wafting from on top of the stove. She lifts the lid to see chicken and dumplings bubbling away. There wasn't even chicken in the fridge, she thinks, her mind spinning in circles. She feels as if she has entered a fairy tale, stumbled into an enchantment.

As she walks through the rest of the apartment, she sees little evidences of Mia's touch. The rooms are tidy, tidier than they were before Suzanne fell asleep—pillows plumped, magazines organized into neat piles. Daisy's toys have all been put away. Where is Daisy? Suzanne wonders. She feels a lurch of panic; has Mia *taken* her daughter? But no, she's being absurd; she remembers the stew. She's coming back. Of course she is.

It is not until twenty minutes later, when Suzanne has turned off the stove so the dumplings don't burn, that Mia finally returns home, bringing in a gust of cold air from the hall. Daisy runs ahead, into the kitchen. She is wearing the kitten costume Suzanne had made, sewing on the ears and whiskers herself with painstaking care, as she is not naturally a crafty person. She has the plastic pumpkin basket for her candy that Suzanne had bought looped around one wrist, and her face is smeared with chocolate.

"You took her trick or treating?" Suzanne asks Mia dumbly, for of course it is obvious.

"We didn't want to disturb you… I saw a sign in the elevator that said trick or treating was from five to six, and I didn't want Daisy to miss it." Mia smiles uncertainly. "Was that okay?"

"Yes," Suzanne says after a pause where she struggles to keep a pleasant expression on her face. "Yes, of course." What she really feels like saying, shrieking, is *You didn't think to wake me up? To ask me? To consider that I might want to be involved in this moment?* She tells herself it is no big deal; she hadn't even been entirely sure about taking Daisy trick or treating in the first place. She herself never went as a child, and was it simply too much candy? Besides, so many children dress up as devils and ghouls; it's a little creepy, really. *This is not something to get upset about.*

"I took some pictures on my phone," Mia offers, brandishing the sleek silver cell phone she has. Suzanne's cell phone does nothing but text and call; Mia's has games and gadgets. Wordlessly, she watches as Mia brings up the photos—one of Daisy beaming proudly; another of the two of them, cheek to cheek. She smiles and nods. "I made dinner, too," Mia says, and Suzanne wonders, bitterly, if she wants a pat on the back.

"I didn't know there was any chicken in the fridge."

"There wasn't, but I took Daisy out to the grocery store. It was fun."

Suzanne nods, rather mechanically. She feels as if Mia has taken over, nudged her aside, and shown her up all at once. And she feels so petty and small for feeling that way.

Blindly, she turns to the sink, wets a rag. "Come here, Daisy," she says, a bit too sternly. "Your face is covered in chocolate."

Mia watches as Suzanne scrubs Daisy's face, before she runs off to the living room and her basket of candy.

"I'm sorry," Mia says after a moment. "Maybe I shouldn't have made dinner. Or taken her out. I didn't mean to... interfere."

Suzanne can tell it costs her something to say this, and she feels herself soften and yield. How can she be so small-minded? It's only because she's feeling so raw herself. "It's fine, Mia," she assures her. "It's wonderful, thank you. I don't think I was up for trick or treating, seeing all those children, and dinner was going to be takeout. You've been so kind. Really. And Daisy looks like she had so much fun." She glances at her daughter, who is digging through her candy.

"No more before dinner, Daisy," she calls, and Daisy looks up hopefully.

"One more, please?"

Suzanne lets out a small huff of laughter as she meets Mia's rueful gaze. "One more," she relents, and they both smile. "Would you like to stay for dinner?" she asks, even though Mark will be home soon, and she wants it to be just the three of them, cocooned in their family. She feels she owes it to Mia, and she wants to be kind.

Mia's gaze flits longingly to Daisy and then back again. "Sure, thanks," she says. "That would be great."

17

SUZANNE

For two whole weeks, I do nothing about my mother's revelations. I try not to even think about them; it's as if my brain is rejecting her words, the whole idea. Every time my mind skates close to that dark, shocking truth, it darts away again, so no thoughts can land, and then take flight. No realizations can occur as long as my thoughts are soaring, distant. I am simply not ready to face any of them.

Besides, I need to prepare for Daisy's year in North Carolina. She needs new clothes, since there will be no uniform at Cary High School, and I need to organize her paperwork, talk to Mia about money. Daisy might be living with Mia, but she's still my daughter, and I will provide for her.

Then there are the vacations to plan; Mark is taking Daisy to the Hamptons again, and I have suggested we have a week in Maine right before she leaves, which Daisy, somewhat surprisingly, agreed to. We haven't gone on vacation together in several years; she'd had her week with Mark, and with Stirling's tuition money has been tight. I plan the week meticulously, splurging on a shingled cottage in Northeast Harbor, outings to Freeport and Bar Harbor, hikes and kayaking trips in Acadia.

Then, towards the end of July, when Daisy is away with Mark, I finally force myself to face the truth. I am adopted. I was adopted when I was four years old, and I never, ever knew. I spend hours trawling through my early memories, hazy and distant as they are, looking for clues, because I cannot believe I didn't know, that I never even suspected.

There are no baby pictures of me, but I recall my mother saying people didn't have cameras the way they do now—as if it were the 1940s rather than the 1970s, and a simple Kodak was a luxury. "I was too busy to take photos, anyway," she'd say, and I believed her, because it was exactly the sort of thing she'd say —and do. I never questioned the absence of photos, although now I dig out the few albums from my mother's things in the cupboard and gaze endlessly at the scattering of photos there are—my fifth birthday, my first day of school, a Christmas when I was about seven, standing in front of a tastefully decorated tree.

I can't help but notice how serious I look in all of them, my dark eyes trained dolefully on the camera, my hair in a single, mousy brown braid. My mother used to say I was a quiet child, which makes it hard to believe that I once aggravated her and my father with my screaming. That's not me at all. That's not the me I've known, the me I believed myself to be—quiet, well-behaved, polite, reserved, capable. But maybe that's the me I became—why? Because I had to?

I've seen my birth certificate several times—when I got my driver's license, my passport, my marriage certificate. Like with the photos, I dig it out now, from a filing cabinet in the old maid's room behind the kitchen, but it reveals nothing beyond what I already knew—I was born at Fitkin Hospital in Neptune, New Jersey, in November, 1972. My parents are listed as Elizabeth and Philip Everett. There is no other information, no hidden clues to what happened to me, where I came from, who my birth parents were. They have been erased; *I* have been erased, or at least the me before I was adopted. Who was that baby, that child? What happened to her? I have no idea.

I look through a box of my mother's old papers, kept in a cupboard since she went into the nursing home. I sift through old bills, birthday cards, receipts—all detritus from a life forgotten, but nothing reveals the truth of my history.

And still the questions keep coming—firing through my brain, relentless and overwhelming. Why did my parents adopt me, if they seemed so reluctant as my mother indicated, thought themselves so old? They married in their forties, I know; my mother had been a teacher, my father a bank manager. I'd always assumed, if I thought about it at all, that I was a surprise blessing.

But, more importantly, why did they never tell me? The enormity of the secret is breathtaking, especially considering I ended up adopting a child—a daughter—myself. Why couldn't my mother have told me then, at least, when I was about to adopt Daisy? Shared her experience, her wisdom, even her heartache? I can almost hear the answer in her voice, sniffy and stern: *When you make your bed, you have to lie in it.* No, she wouldn't have changed course then, or ever. Once a secret, always a secret. Except it has obviously been bothering her all these years, since it's all coming out now, in half-remembered memories, anxiety and agitation, although I know she's most likely already forgotten about her conversation with "Helen."

My mind whirls emptily as I go through the days on autopilot—going to work, coming home, making dinner, staring into space. I struggle to make sense of any of it, to hold onto a thought and keep it there. On Wednesday, I take the afternoon off work to visit my mother, and amazingly, she is lucid, remembering me, knowing who I am, which, after what happened before, is both startling and a relief.

"Suzanne!" Her smile is genuine. "My dear, you really

should do something about your hair." I still haven't had it colored.

I raise one hand to my head self-consciously, and then drop it. Now that I'm here, I have no idea how to begin. *Mom, I figured out I'm adopted and I want to know why you never told me.* I have no idea how she'd react, if she'd be upset or confused or simply nonplussed. *Why on earth are you bringing all that up now?* she might demand, irascible. Or she might look blank. *Adopted? Who? I didn't adopt anyone. Who are you, again?*

"You're right, I do need to get it seen to," I tell her and I sit down next to her, trying to smile. She gives me a funny look.

"You're not unwell, are you?"

"No." My eyes are filling with tears even though I don't want them to be. I feel a rush of emotion so powerful it is like a tidal wave, dragging me under, consuming me utterly. It's a combination of anger and sadness, of regret and confusion and pure, raw grief. I stare at my mother and I realize she will never be able to tell me about who I was, where I came from. Those memories, lucid and factual and real, are lost forever in the tangled web of her disordered mind. I'll never know them, know her, know *me.* The realization, on top of the knowledge I am adopted, feels like a double betrayal, a double loss. My mother frowns.

"Well, if you're coming down with something, don't get too close," she warns, drawing her cardigan about her throat, and I let out a choked sound that I think may be a laugh.

"I won't, Mom," I manage in a husky whisper, and then I reach for her hand. She looks at me in surprise, even suspicion. We're not a touching family, and never have been. Is that because I was adopted? I think of what my mother said about how I didn't like to be touched. Why? What happened to me? I will probably never know.

"Suzanne, is everything all right?" she asks, her tone caught between concern and irritation.

No, nothing is all right, and I don't know if it ever will be again.

I smile and squeeze her hand. I know I can't bring this up with her, not when it is usually minutes, if not seconds, before she slips out of lucidity once more. "I'm fine, Mom," I say. "I... I missed you." I mean it in so many ways.

Her frown deepens, as if she doesn't quite believe me, and then she turns to look toward the door. "Tina said there was bingo today."

"Do you want me to take you to the day room?"

She shrugs her assent, and I rise to get her wheelchair. I feel a surprising, sudden rush of not just emotion, but love, deep and true—she might be tetchy and stern and not particularly affectionate, she might have kept a life-changing secret from me for her whole life, but she's my mother and I know she did love me, no matter that it might have been hard at the beginning. I think of the thousand-piece jigsaws we did together on rainy summer days; the beaming look of pride on her face when I graduated from Vassar. I remember how we held each other up at my father's funeral, together in our black coats in the sleeting rain. I might not remember the first four years of my life, but I still have memories that can't be taken away, even if I am the only one left who remembers them.

I am not, I realize, going to squander whatever time my mother has left drowning in recriminations for what she did or did not tell me, the struggles she faced. But I still want answers.

Answers, it turns out, might not be as hard to find as I feared. On Friday evening, the day before Daisy returns from the Hamptons, I fortify myself with a glass of wine and open my laptop. It only takes me a few minutes to discover that while many states require a court order to access sealed adoption records, New Jersey is thankfully not one of them. I click on a link to the instructions on how to access the records, only to have to trawl through a page of bureaucratic forms—from applications for asbestos management to ones for the sterilization of a pet.

A long, weary breath escapes me as I scroll down through the list, half-amazed that such a significant event for me—the ability to know where I came from—is sandwiched somewhere between an application for certification to handle oysters, clams, or mussels and one for a bulk milk hauler permit, whatever that is.

And then I find it, and my breath catches. *Application for an Uncertified Copy of an Adopted Person's Original Birth Certificate.* I scan through the instructions, my heart thudding as if I am running a race. My palms are damp and I take a slug of my wine. All I need to access my adoption records is three forms of ID and a check for twenty-five dollars. It will take four to six weeks. What I will receive, I read, is the original birth certificate "for informational purposes only," and any medical, social, or cultural records pertaining to my adoption. My breath leaves me in a rush. In about a month, I could know who I am.

I do all the paperwork that evening, and mail it in the next morning, before Daisy arrives home. I've already decided I'm not going to tell her I'm adopted, at least not until I have found out more information. I tell myself it's because I don't want to take the focus away from her right before she goes to Mia's, but I also know it's because I couldn't bear the dismissive response I fear she'll give. *Yeah, and so what?* Or *You're telling me this because...?* I can already picture her bored look, hear her teenaged drawl, as she dismisses my experience, my confusion, even as I am feeling a new, deep empathy for her own situation. *We're alike, you and I, we're both adopted,* I imagine myself saying, to Daisy's scorn.

No, I will keep it to myself, even though it feels as if this new knowledge is burning a hole right through me. I have an urge to blurt it out to almost everyone I see—colleagues at work, strangers in the street. *I'm adopted! And I never knew!* Of course, I never say anything, at least not until two weeks before Daisy leaves, when Peter asks me out for dinner.

We haven't seen each other since Shakespeare in the Park; he was busy at work and then he was on vacation and, in truth, I've come to realize while he's a friend, I'm not ready for romance. Still, I say yes, clumsily making it clear we're just friends, to which he laughs.

"I could always use a friend, Suzanne," he assures, and I let out an embarrassed laugh of relief that we're on the same page.

Now, as we sit at a cozy table for two in a little hole-in-the-wall Italian restaurant on Second Avenue, the words finally tumble out of me, and it is both a relief and a terror to say them out loud.

"I just found out I was adopted."

His eyes widen and I hasten to explain the story, my mother's confusion, the mysterious Helen.

"And you never knew?" Peter shakes his head slowly. "I know adoptions were closed back then, but that really is quite something."

"You could say that." I swallow hard, the realization hitting me all over again. Every time I think I've come to terms with it, I realize I haven't. At all. I haven't even begun to; I've thought about my mother, Elizabeth Everett, but I haven't let myself think about my birth mother yet. She had me until I was *four*. The same age, I have realized, that Mia started absenting herself more and more from Daisy's life. Are we alike in that, too, both of us reacting to a loss without remembering or realizing?

"Have you told Daisy?" Peter asks.

I shake my head. "I will one day, maybe one day soon, but right now, with her about to leave, it feels too complicated..." Part of me hopes I might find a time when we're in Maine together to share some confidences, but that feels like nothing more than a hazy dream right now.

"It could help to bring you two together. You've both had a similar experience—"

"But we haven't." The words practically burst out of me. "I was open with Daisy from the beginning. I *had* her from the beginning. And her birth mother has always been involved. Daisy has always known that she was adopted, she was chosen, she was loved." My throat thickens. "At least, I hope she knew that."

Peter's face softens with sympathy. "But the feeling of grief, of loss," he says quietly. "Of losing someone, of not knowing who you are..."

I shake my head, more to get him to stop talking than in denial of anything he's said. He's completely right, that *is* how I've felt, but I haven't fully understood until now that that's how *Daisy* might have felt. *At the heart of every adoption is loss.* I read it in a book, I agreed with it completely, but I didn't really understand. I didn't *feel* it. And no matter how many books I've read, however expert I thought I was, no matter that I did as best as I could, or thought I was... I realize I still didn't really understand anything. The thought leaves me feeling despondent—is there any way to get parenting right—yet also hopeful. *Now I know.*

"I will talk to her about it," I tell Peter. "Just not yet. I need to process it first... and I need more information."

"That's understandable," Peter says. "And whatever happens, Suzanne, whatever you find out... I'm here for you."

I know he is being sincere, I can see it in his face, and yet I find I can't reply. I don't know who I am anymore, and I realize I want to talk to someone who really knows me, who can remind me, and the only person who can do that now is Mark.

Yet can I really bring this to him? Will he want to hear?

. . .

That night, I lie in bed awake, staring at the ceiling, wondering who my birth mother was, and why she gave me up when I was four years old. Did she die? Am I an orphan twice over, my mother all but gone to me? Or did she run into difficult circumstances, feel she had no choice? Aged nearly fifty, I am falling prey to every adopted kid's fantasy—*I'm secretly a princess. My mother's looking for me. My father's coming back.*

The reality, I suspect, is not as romantic as being a lost princess or having my mother hand me over to an adoption agency, heartbroken and weeping. No, the reality, I fear, is that I was taken away and put into care. My mother's words hammer into me: *I feel sorry for the poor thing. She had a terrible start in life.*

I have a memory, hazy and vague, of starting school, my lunchbox banging against my knees, a feeling of trepidation that now feels far more significant and poignant. It can't have been that long after my parents adopted me.

I think of the story my mother used to tell me, about stuffing cabbage down my pants. I remember it as being funny, getting rid of the evidence because I didn't want to eat it, but now it takes on a whole new, sorrowful complexion. If what my mother said was true, I was squirreling food away because I was afraid of going hungry.

It's so *strange* to think of myself this way, almost as if I am thinking of an entirely different person, a different me. I find myself staring into space, lost in vague memories that I can't trust—am I making something up because I am so desperate to fill the gaps, or did it really happen?—or staring at my reflection in the mirror, as if my own face can tell me a truth I've never known.

When Daisy returns from the Hamptons, I try to talk to her, the knowledge of my own adoption like a pressure building in my chest, but she's focused on moving to Mia's and barely spares me a glance, never mind a whole conversation. I tell myself we'll reconnect in Maine, but I don't really believe it.

The first week of August, we drive up to Maine. As we head north, the weather turns crisp and clear, the sky a hard, bright blue that hurts to look at and yet I want to keep drinking it in. The sunlight is bouncing off every green leaf, every blade of glass. The world feels pure in a way it never does in the city, and I feel a fragile shoot of hope pushing through our stony silence.

I've rented a cute little cottage right on the shore in Northeast Harbor, an enclave of old-money privilege with the "cottages" having ten bedrooms or more. Ours only has two, as well as a kitchen/living area, with a screened-in porch overlooking the rocky shore. By the time we arrive, dusk is falling and there is an autumnal chill in the air even though it's only August. Daisy flops on the sofa on her phone while I scuttle around, gathering firewood for the wood stove and digging out the veggie curry I brought for our first dinner.

"This is nice, isn't it?" I say brightly, too brightly.

Daisy murmurs something that could vaguely be considered assent. I glance at her sprawled on the sofa, determinedly indifferent. Would it be so hard, I think with a spurt of bitterness I don't usually allow myself to feel, for her to *try*?

"Could you please set the table, Daisy?" I ask, and she looks up in wary surprise.

"We never eat at the table."

Which is my fault, but somehow I want to change things, even if it is almost too late. Two weeks from now Daisy will be gone. "We are tonight," I tell her firmly. "The silverware is in the drawer by the sink."

We eat dinner in virtual silence; I mention a hike tomorrow, and she shrugs. I try to make conversation about her new school, the weather, the book I'm reading, anything, but her answers are monosyllabic, accompanied by something bordering a glare.

I finally break, something I never do, and place both my hands on the table. "Daisy," I ask, trying to keep my voice calm rather than resentful or pleading, "do you even want to be here with me?"

She looks surprised, although she quickly masks it with the usual boredom. "It's not like you want to be here with me, Mom," she throws back at me, and I can't help but gape a little.

"Why do you think that?"

"Please, no more therapist questions, okay?" She rolls her eyes. "I think that because it's obvious."

How, I wonder, *is it obvious?* "Daisy, that's simply not true," I say. My voice wobbles and I take a deep breath to steady myself.

"Oh, please," she says, her lip curling. "You're not exactly shedding tears over me leaving for a whole year, are you?"

"What—" I am utterly astonished by this assessment. Did she want me to break down, beg her to stay?

"You can't wait for me to go. Fine, whatever, okay? Just don't make this my fault just because you feel guilty." She rises from the table and flounces off even though she's barely touched her dinner.

I stare at my plate, my appetite vanished, my stomach seething. Is she just trying to hurt me, I wonder, or does she really believe what she says? And could there possibly be any truth in such awful accusations—I realize I fear there is, if only a grain. I'm devastated that Daisy is going to North Carolina, but I have also begun to wonder if it could be better for her, and, yes, for me. And I *do* feel guilty. I feel like I've failed her some-how, for us to end up like this—and now I am wondering if it's because of who I am, where I came from. Memories I've forgotten yet have still been crucially, horribly formative, making me deficient somehow. Maybe it's futile, and there's nothing I can do now. No way to reach her.

And yet, even though I fear Daisy doesn't want me to, I have to try. I rise from the table and walk to her bedroom, knock on the door, open it.

"Daisy."

She is lying on her bed, staring at her phone, and she doesn't even look up as I come into the room.

"Daisy, when it comes to North Carolina... if you want to go, go. I won't stop you. But I'm not *glad* you're going, and I will miss you. Very much."

She lets a snort of disbelief and for a second I fight the temptation to yell, to scream, to ask her to stop scoffing for just one damned second.

"That is the truth," I say, but, of course, it's not all the truth. The truth is, I'm tired of fighting, of trying, of every moment being a battle. I want some relief and I want her back and I want space to sort out my own feelings. But I don't know how to say any of that, or maybe I'm just not ready.

In any case, Daisy doesn't even look up from her phone, and so, wearily, once again I turn away.

I feel despondent, because I don't know how to make either of us change. Maybe it is too late, after all. Maybe I should just give up. Maybe, I reflect with a pang of grief as I close her door softly, I already have.

18

MIA

A week after our weekend at the beach, I am at the airport, waiting for Daisy to arrive. I don't feel as anxious about her arrival as I did when she turned up at my front door a few months ago, far from it. But I still am nervous. There are a lot of unknowns.

She hasn't asked about her birth father since that day at the spa, but it has felt as if it is hovering between us, a pressure inside me that I am struggling to ignore, or at least live with. I'm half-expecting her to ask about it as soon as she gets off the plane, although I tell myself that's ridiculous. But she will ask at some point, and I have no idea what I'm going to say.

I have been kicking myself all week for not telling Tom when I had not quite a chance, but something close to it, even as I recognize I couldn't really do anything else. It's too late for the truth, I tell myself, and it will cause too much damage. This is the best way. It has to be.

And then Daisy is there, coming through the doors, and I start forward, my heart jumping in my chest. I call out to her and she waves and then we hug, and as my arms close around her, I tell myself it can all still be okay.

She hasn't got her suitcases yet, and so I help her lug them off the baggage carousel—two huge ones, which she laughingly tells me is just about all the clothes she owns.

"I meant to only bring one," she says with a laugh, "but then I'd see something else I just felt I had to pack."

"I think you did well to only bring two," I tell her. We haven't actually talked about when, or if, Daisy will go back to New York—for Christmas? Easter? I assume she will, but I don't actually know. Suzanne deposited a significant amount in my bank account to cover Daisy's expenses, and wrote me a formal thank you letter for having her, but we never actually hashed out the practical details. In any case, I realize as we walk out into the muggy sunshine that I haven't let myself think too much beyond this moment. I've been so busy getting ready for her arrival, worrying about Tom, that I have not considered just how this year—*a whole year!*—is going to unfold.

On the way back to Cary, I suggest a stop at Starbucks for grande lattes and some time to reconnect before we return home and Daisy is besieged by Sophie, Ella and Avery.

"How's your mom?" I ask once we're seated with our lattes, and she shrugs.

"She's been the same." She purses her lips and shakes her head. "No, worse, actually. We had this boring week in Maine where she basically blamed me for not trying hard enough." She rolls her eyes. "I think she's angry at me for coming here." She lifts her chin. "I don't care."

Yes, you do, Daisy, I think with an ache in my chest. *Of course you do, no matter how hard you try to pretend you don't.* "Did she tell you she was angry?" I ask.

"She doesn't have to."

"I don't want this year to come between you and your mom," I say gently, and Daisy gives me a look that is half irritable, half guilty.

"It can't. I mean, it's not as if we've ever had a real relationship."

"Daisy!" I am shocked into sounding scolding. "I know that isn't true. I remember visiting you when you were little—I visited a lot, you know, and I could always tell your mom loved you. The way she hugged you, looked at you..." I shake my head. "She was a really good mom to you."

"I can't remember the last time she hugged me." Daisy speaks flatly, but there is a hurt look in her eyes that has my own stinging. Is that really true?

"Have you wanted her to?" I ask.

"Yeah, sure, back when I was a kid. But then I stopped wanting her to because it would just be so incredibly awkward, and it's obvious she doesn't want to. She's always looking at me like... like I'm a problem she has to solve." She hunches a shoulder. "I know I don't always make it easy for her, but she doesn't make it easy for me either."

Which is the story of every parent and child ever, I reflect with an inward sigh. And I wonder, now that I am basically taking Suzanne's place for a year, if I'll be the one who can't do anything right. I certainly haven't started out well with this conversation.

"Maybe you need to talk to her—" I begin, only for her to cut me off with a quick shake of her head.

"I don't want to talk to her." Daisy sounds impatient, rotating her cup with abrupt, jerky movements, her head lowered. "I came here to get away from all that."

"I know." I swallow, wondering why I felt the need to press Suzanne's case when I never have before. Maybe it's because I don't want Daisy swinging her spotlight onto me. Or maybe I really do feel for Suzanne, for once. She hasn't had it easy. "Sorry."

"It's okay." She looks up, her gaze hooded, uncertain. "Look, I wanted to tell you, after we had that conversation at the spa...

it's okay about my... my birth father, whoever he is. I get that it might be complicated. You don't have to tell me if you don't want to. I mean, if you feel you can't." She takes a deep breath and lets it out slowly. "I'd understand."

This feels like such an unexpected gift that for a second I can't speak. Can it really be that easy? One word from Daisy and all my anxieties go away?

"That's really... understanding of you, Daisy," I manage. "It hasn't been easy for me, so I... I appreciate you saying that. Thank you."

She nods, but her expression has turned stiff and I see the flash in her eyes—a cross between anger and hurt. She was not expecting me to take her up on her offer, I realize with a lurch of guilt—as well as alarm. She wanted me to reassure her, that of course I would tell her, I've been meaning to, and I can't do that.

"Yeah, sure," she mutters, looking down at her cup, her dark hair swinging in front of her face. I gaze at her helplessly, my chest tight, my heart aching. *Oh Daisy...*

"I'm sorry," I tell her. "I'm not trying to keep secrets from you..." Except I am. "I just need to handle it all carefully..." Or not at all, which has basically been what I've decided to do. Guilt twists my insides into knots. How can I keep living like this? And yet how can I not? It's too late, it has to be. And yet what if it isn't?

"Yeah, I get it," Daisy says quickly, and then she lurches up from the table. "Shall we go?"

I nod, feeling miserable, and we ride in silence back to the house. The mood seems to improve a little when we get out of the car, and Sophie runs out of the house to tackle Daisy about the waist. She laughs, putting her arms around Sophie, and Ella and Avery come out too, both of them smiling shyly, with Tom following behind.

"Hey, Daisy!" His smile is wide and easy. "We're so glad you're here."

Her answering smile is as shy as Ella and Avery's. "Thanks."

Sophie is already tugging at Daisy's hand, telling her to come in and see her new room. Daisy will be in Avery's old room this time, which is a little bigger than Sophie's. I gave it a proper redecoration, with the promise to Avery that she could re-redecorate it once again after this year. The walls are a pale green—Daisy chose the color online—and the bedding is a soft, sumptuous cream. The room is still smaller than her room back in New York, but I hope she likes it and feels at home. Even though I'm writhing inside, I still want this to work.

And it does, or seems to—Daisy is pleased with her room, and after she's unpacked, the girls beg her to play Monopoly, which she does, while I make dinner. It's all so sweetly innocent, so perfectly pastoral—the four girls around the table, three blond heads and one dark, good-naturedly arguing about trading properties. At one point, Sophie scrambles onto Daisy's lap, and she puts one arm around her naturally, almost absently.

Tom comes into the room, his expression softening at the sight of them. He comes over to me and slides his arm around my waist. "Amazing, huh?" he whispers.

I nod, not trusting myself to speak. *My family*, I think, and I am filled with wonder, with love—and with fear.

My family... and I'm the only one who knows.

The next few weeks pass with thankful uneventfulness. I breathe a little easier. I tell myself the past with all its secrets doesn't actually matter, what matters is what is happening now: Daisy pushing Sophie on the swing, painting Ella's nails, going driving with Tom. Even though I still feel as if I'm tiptoeing over eggshells, no one else is. We are finding a rhythm. We are making it work. I let myself relax, if only a little.

And then the blips start, like little tremors rippling through our lives. Nothing too alarming, nothing worth even getting upset about, and yet. *And yet.* I find myself starting to feel off balance, struggling to stay steady, and after only a few weeks of seeming normality.

The first tremor happens the week Daisy starts school, she comes home at nine p.m. without telling me where she's been. She smells of cigarettes, and Ella, who came downstairs for a drink of water, is wide-eyed as Daisy saunters into the kitchen.

"Next time," I say as lightly as I can, "can you tell me where you are and when you'll be back?" I'd prefer for her not to be out so late on a school night, and yet I don't feel like I have the right to say that. She's almost eighteen, and even though I gave birth to her, she's not actually my daughter. Not that way. Can I really impose a curfew?

Daisy is wide-eyed, apologetic. "Sorry... I didn't even think."

"No problem." I tell myself it's all sorted, but there is something almost smug about Daisy's expression that makes me wonder. There's a challenge in her eyes I don't like to see.

Then, a few days later, Sophie comes downstairs with a full face of makeup—pancake foundation, glitter eyeshadow, carmine lips. "Daisy did it," she says happily, twirling around, and I feel a headache start at my temples.

"Very nice," I say diplomatically, although I think it looks awful, like one of those disturbing child beauty queens, and I dampen a cloth to wipe it off. "But your skin is too sensitive for this, sweetheart." Already I can see the red patches of her eczema coming out on her cheeks.

Once again, I tell Daisy lightly, so lightly, to check with me before putting makeup on the girls.

This time, her eyes flash before she gives her apology, and I grit my teeth because I know it's insincere and she's angry, but then I am, too. Maybe I shouldn't be, maybe neither of us should be, but there we are. We're sparking off each other already, butting heads, and part of me wonders if Daisy is forcing it. If some part of her actually wants a confrontation... but why? Is she angry with me about not telling her about her father? Or is it something else? Is this, I wonder, what Suzanne has been dealing with? What she feels?

I don't feel I can tell any of this to Tom, because he's so delighted with how well everything is going, and I'm pretty sure he'd think I was paranoid, or worse. So I keep silent, finding myself becoming watchful, wary, almost as if I am waiting for the next thing to happen.

That weekend, Daisy goes out to a party. While part of me is pleased she's made friends already, I am still apprehensive, especially when she comes home at two o'clock in the morning, stumbling in loudly enough to wake up Sophie, and clearly drunk.

I don't bother addressing the issue that night—I just settle Sophie, get Daisy a glass of water, and help her to bed. She mumbles something unintelligible as she pulls the duvet over her shoulders, and somehow I don't think it was a thank you.

"She's a teenager, remember," Tom tells me sleepily as I climb back into bed and he snuggles close. He didn't even get up, leaving me to handle it, as I knew he would. "They get up to some wild stuff."

You did, I think resentfully but don't say. I didn't go to a single party during my high-school years, and hardly any during college, either. I swallow the words down and close my eyes, trying to relax into Tom's warm embrace.

The next morning, I ask Daisy if we can talk, and she looks both annoyed and wary as she agrees. Tom is playing with the girls outside, so we have a little space to address matters, although I'm not even sure what I'm going to say.

"Mia, she's almost eighteen," Tom told me this morning, when I voiced my concerns about her staying out, getting drunk. "She's practically an adult. We can't boss her around."

"She's living in our house, with three very impressionable

young girls," I reminded him, my tone severe. "While in our house, she needs to obey our rules."

He looked amused. "You sound like your mom, you know."

And maybe for once that was no bad thing. "Aren't you concerned, Tom?" I asked. "Do you really want Ella seeing Daisy stumble in drunk, thinking it's okay?"

He shrugged. "Not particularly, but if Ella had an older sister living with us all the time, she would probably see that anyway. Sophie will, when Ella's older—"

"So getting drunk at parties is a given? Something for our daughters to aspire to?" Then I really did sound like my mother.

"Not a given, but teenagers are teenagers, Mia. They're experimenting. They're learning. It's all part of growing up."

"And they need guidance." I took a deep breath. "I can't have a year of Daisy doing her own thing, flouting rules, getting away with whatever she feels like. She wanted to live with us, not by herself. We should have put some guidelines down at the start."

Tom shruggingly agreed, as amenable as ever. I wanted him to take charge for once, to be a bit more authoritative, but that had never been his style. So it fell to me, on that bright Saturday morning, cradling a cup of coffee in my hands, to tackle it head-on.

"So I realize we probably should have discussed some house rules," I begin, keeping my tone friendly, as if I am talking to one of my clients. "Just to make things simple, right?"

I wait for a response, but Daisy merely folds her arms.

"Stuff about curfews, helping out, that kind of thing." I am trying to talk like it is no big deal, but Daisy is not fooled.

"Like what?" she asks flatly.

"Well, let's take curfews, for a start." I take a quick, steadying breath. "What time do you think would be reasonable for a weekend?"

"Two a.m.?" she drawls, and I struggle not to show surprise

on my face, because she has never used that tone with me before—like I'm stupid, like she can't be bothered to spell it out for me.

"I think two a.m. might be a little late," I reply lightly. "How about midnight?"

"*Midnight?*" The word is full of scorn. "You must have really been a loser in high school, Mia, if you think midnight is reasonable."

This time I can't keep the surprise, and even the hurt, from showing, because I can't believe she's throwing that at me.

"Whether I was or not, we're talking about you right now," I tell her, and I hear an edge to my voice that I've never used with her before. It's as if the gloves are coming off for both of us, or perhaps the masks are slipping.

She smirks at me, and I wonder if this is what she wanted—for me to lose my temper. *Why?* Why is she pushing me like this?

"Well, midnight is not reasonable," she tells me, her arms still folded, her expression not quite a glare. "Tom would tell you the same thing. He stayed out way past midnight when he was my age."

She speaks with authority, and I try not to grit my teeth. *Thanks, Tom, for that.* "Fine," I say as evenly as I can. "Why don't we compromise? One a.m.?"

She shrugs, and I decide to take that as a victory, even though I feel defeated.

"There's also the issue of drinking," I continue, and she rolls her eyes. "I know teenagers drink, I get that, but you're underage and it's still illegal."

"Seriously?" She shakes her head slowly, as if she can't believe how utterly ridiculous I'm being.

"Yes, seriously. Look, I'm not trying to make things difficult, but there are three young, impressionable girls in this house—"

"Oh, of *course*," Daisy says in that same, sneering drawl. "I should have realized this was about them."

I open my mouth, close it. "That's not fair, Daisy," I say quietly. "I'm having this conversation because I care about you." She gives a snort of disbelief and I continue steadily, "I won't say absolutely no alcohol, because I understand about parties, but I do not want you coming home drunk, stumbling and slurring and the rest of it. Okay? I think that *is* reasonable."

A resounding silence greets this little speech, while Daisy just glares at me. "Is that all?" she finally asks in a bored voice, and I am half about to bark that, no, that is *not* all, when I decide I need to pick my battles.

"If I think of anything else, I'll let you know," I say stiffly, and I watch in both frustration and despair as she flounces away.

A few minutes later, Tom comes bounding in, all endearing eagerness. "How did it go?" he asks, and for a second I feel like slapping him.

"Not great, actually," I tell him tightly. I wonder if this is how Suzanne feels, this mix of anger and grief, resentment and guilt. "She was really difficult about it all."

"She's a teenager—"

"Oh, *enough* with she's a teenager," I snap, throwing up my hands. "*I* was a teenager, and I didn't act the way she did. I'm not telling her anything unreasonable, and yet she's acting as if I'm some cruel jailer, or really, like I'm so... I don't know, *ridiculous*." I suddenly feel near tears, and I blink them away angrily.

"You've never had to enforce these kinds of rules before," Tom points out, which is nothing I haven't already thought myself. Telling an almost-eighteen-year-old not to get drunk is different from telling an eight-year-old to eat her dinner. "I guess you can expect a little pushback."

"And how about you?" I retort. "You seem happy enough to be her buddy, telling her what you got up to when you were her age, but what about exhibiting a little responsibility, Tom? A little authority?"

Tom blinks at me slowly. "I guess I haven't really felt I had that right," he tells me quietly. "Since I'm not actually her father."

That clams me up completely, and I turn away, not trusting the expression on my face. Not trusting anything. Right now, having Daisy here feels like a horrible, horrible mistake.

It doesn't get any better when, a week later, I open my purse to find the hundred dollars I took out from the bank a few days before is missing. Five crisp twenties, all in a white envelope, taken out to pay our cleaner. I stare at the empty envelope with a sinking sensation in my stomach, a tightening in my chest. I feel guilty that my mind has immediately leapt to Daisy, but who else could it be?

Even so, I investigate all options. I text Tom at work to ask him if he took it, which isn't utterly out of the realm of possibility, and he texts back almost immediately *No, are you sure you haven't spent it?*

Yes, of course I'm damn well sure. I don't bother replying to his text. I think back over the last few days, to make sure I haven't actually spent it, but I know I haven't. The house is quiet, the girls all at school, as I stand in the middle of the kitchen and try to think. Did Daisy really steal a hundred dollars from my purse? Am I wrong to jump to that conclusion?

After a few seconds where my mind is simply spinning, I go upstairs. I check Avery and Ella's room first, because I tell myself it's not impossible that Ella took it, although I've never caught her stealing before. Still, in her nine-year-old mind she might have justified it, or not realized how much money it was, or *something*. I know I am grasping at the flimsiest of straws, but I still have to try.

I don't find any money in the girls' room, besides a couple of wrinkled dollar bills and quarters in their respective piggy banks. I stand outside Daisy's room, debating whether I should go in and poke around. It feels like a terrible invasion of her privacy, and yet, *one hundred dollars.*

I open the door. The room is a mess, with a sickly-sweet smell of body spray that has me cracking open a window. I start to make the bed, and then leave it, because I don't want Daisy to know I've been in here. Do I? Or would making her bed be a courtesy, a kindness?

I shrug the question aside as I look around for where she might have hidden a hundred bucks. *If* she stole it, and yet the heaviness in my stomach tells me she has. As it happens, it doesn't take long to find it; I open the top drawer of her bedside table and there they are right on top, five crisp twenties, almost as if she *wanted* me to find them.

I sink onto the bed as I stare at the money and realize I have no idea what to do now.

THEN

MIA

September 2005
16 years ago

It's Daisy's first birthday, and the dining room is full of streamers and balloons, the table piled high with presents. Suzanne smiles self-consciously as Mia comes into the room to survey the scene.

"I told myself I wasn't going to make a big deal of her first birthday, because she won't even remember, but somehow it got away from me." She laughs, and Mark slips his arm around her waist as he gazes down at her tenderly.

Mia watches them, feeling a pang of envy, a rush of satisfaction. This was what she wanted for Daisy, after all. She turns to look at her little girl—yes, *hers,* she thinks, at least a little bit—and smiles. Daisy is in her high chair, a pink bow affixed in her fleecy dark curls. She is wearing a pink dress of sprigged muslin and white leather booties on her chubby little feet. She looks adorable, and Mia's arms ache to scoop her up, nestle her close, breathe in the warm, clean scent of her.

Suzanne must sense this, because she turns to Mia with a smile. "Why don't you give her a birthday hug?" she suggests, and Mia takes the opportunity, both glad for and resentful of Suzanne's under-standing. She doesn't want her permission, but she knows she needs it.

Navigating this first year has been hard, but they are still managing it. In the beginning, Mia felt tentative, shy; she was still reeling from the birth and dealing with her parents, who wore their disappointment with her decision to have an open adoption, as if she'd meant to hurt them personally with her choices. And on top of all that, she was trying to maintain her GPA as a junior in college and not think too much about Tom Sullivan, who as far as she knows is still in Thailand.

She wonders sometimes what she would say, if she saw him again. It's not impossible that she might, considering how he said he'd work in the city after he did his stint in the Far East. She knows she looks better now; she has been taking care of herself more, doing her hair and makeup, picking clothes that flatter her figure. It feels like a game of pretend, but judging from the sparks of admiration she sees in other people's eyes, it seems to be working.

Suzanne has noticed too, and has warmly complimented her on her looks, which makes Mia glow, almost as if her own mother had delivered such praise, which she never would. At the beginning of their relationship, she found herself trying to win Suzanne's approval, the way a child might, but a year later, she realizes that is starting to change. She sees Suzanne not quite so much as a mother figure, although there is still that, but a woman in her own right, a competitor, even, although she knows that's not the right way to think about her.

It's hard not to, though, even as she scoops Daisy up, cradling her close to her, her back to Mark and Suzanne. She's just pressed a kiss to Daisy's cheek when she starts to squirm away, her face crum-pling and going red as she lets out a long, awful wail. She's never done that before, and Mia stiffens in surprise, in horror. *Daisy…?*

"Oh dear," Suzanne says, biting her lip, looking genuinely regretful, although Mia wonders if she's secretly pleased. "She has gotten a bit clingy lately, but I'm sure it won't last. Come on, Daisy, it's Mia…"

Mia thinks she sounds half-hearted, but maybe she's just being paranoid. Daisy squirms, her chubby arms held out to Suzanne, who glances at her uncertainly.

"Should I…"

"Fine." Mia can't manage to sound gracious as she hands Daisy to Suzanne. She settles her on her hip with a grimace of apology. Daisy has quieted, arms looped around Suzanne's neck.

Mia stands there, struggling not to show the devastation she feels on her face. For the last year, Daisy has always been happy in her arms. Yes, she might have been a bit unsure at the start; Suzanne had to show her how to give her a bottle, but Daisy knew her. Daisy always knew her.

One of the birth moms at the support group she's attended sporadically told her that children always knew. "They smell you," she insisted. "It's like an instinct. They know you're their real mother. They always will."

She'd taken comfort from that, an almost savage satisfaction. *She'll always know*, she'd thought, except now it seems she doesn't.

"Shall we have the cake?" Suzanne suggests brightly. "Or presents first?"

"Presents," Mia decides, trying to move on from Daisy's rejection. She places her own present in its expensive gift bag—more than she could afford—in the center of the table.

"Daisy can open yours first," Suzanne says with a smile, and Mia nods her thanks, grateful for her kindness even though she's still struggling not to show how upset she is.

Daisy, of course, can't unwrap the presents on her own, although when Suzanne takes out the lumpily wrapped parcel she pats it experimentally, and when she tears a bit of the paper off, Daisy pulls at it, her interest caught. Mia watches, her breath held, her heart aching, as Daisy and Suzanne unwrap the present together, and then Suzanne coos at the sight of the toy inside—a panda bear, its fur silky soft, with a pink plush nose and dark, shiny eyes. Mia had seen it and fallen in love with it; she liked the idea of Daisy having a special toy that she gave her, one that she would always love and remember.

"I thought it could be her special teddy bear," she tells Suzanne, unable to keep a slightly pleading note from entering her voice. "You could keep it in her crib. She could sleep with it every night."

"Oh…" Suzanne glances at Mark, and Mia sees something wordless pass between them that makes her tense. "That's such a lovely idea, Mia. Thank you."

She gives the panda to Daisy, who hugs it tightly to her before chucking it onto the floor. Mark lets out a little laugh, and Suzanne gives that same apologetic grimace that Mia is starting to hate. Of course Daisy didn't mean anything by it; she's a baby, after all. But Suzanne's grimace makes it seem as if she did.

"Whoops, Daisy," Suzanne says cheerfully and bends down to scoop up the panda and put it on the table. "Now, onto the next present." She reaches for a brightly wrapped box.

Daisy has got the hang of it now, and tears at the paper eagerly, while Mark videos the whole happy scene. Mia watches as Daisy opens a baby doll, the kind that coos and opens and shuts her eyes, and then hugs the doll to her, even going so far as to press a sloppy kiss to her plastic cheek.

"Oh, look!" Suzanne exclaims, delighted. "She knows just what to do." She kisses Daisy's cheek, and Mark laughs again. Mia tries to smile.

It's not Suzanne's fault she feels this way, she knows. She and Mark have done their best to include her, right from the beginning. When Mia was still recovering in the hospital, Suzanne had brought her a care package of thoughtful essentials—body lotion and fleecy socks and herbal teas. The first time Mia worked up the courage to visit Suzanne at her apartment, to actually see her as Daisy's mother, Suzanne had done her best to make her comfortable—fetched her coffee, offered up Daisy easily, almost eagerly.

It wasn't her fault that Mia hadn't quite known how to hold her daughter, or that she looked so unfamiliar in her pink fleecy slipsuit, the cotton as soft as velvet. It wasn't her fault that Suzanne had seemed such an expert, draping Daisy over her back, patting her back gently to get her to burp. Mia hadn't returned for two long, awful weeks, because she simply hadn't expected it to be so hard.

No, none of it has been Suzanne's fault, she knows that, but it has not made it any easier. And yet still Mia persists in these visits, as much as they hurt her, because she can't not go. She cannot let go of her daughter, because if she does, it will feel as if she'll fall into an abyss, an emptiness—she'll just keep falling and falling and falling.

So she tells herself to stop feeling resentful or annoyed or lost. She tells herself that it's good to be here, good for Daisy, good for her, good for Suzanne and Mark. From the beginning, they'd all said they would make it work, and they will. They will make sure of it, together.

Daisy has finished opening their presents, and she is getting tired and irritable, rubbing her eyes, letting out squawks of discontent. Even though they haven't had their cake, Suzanne decides it's better to put her down for a nap.

"I'll do it," Mia suggests. "If I can? I can give her her bottle." She sounds pleading, she knows. Yearning.

Suzanne's tense expression softens.

"Of course, Mia," she says. "That's a good idea."

Mia waits, eager and apprehensive, as Suzanne warms Daisy's bottle. She takes the warm, heavy weight of Daisy into her arms, drawing her against her body, settling into her. Daisy lets out another squawk, but then Mia sticks the bottle in her mouth and she relaxes, sucking greedily, her dark lashes fanning her plump, rosy cheeks, her whole body already softening into sleep.

Mia rises to take her into her nursery, where she knows there is a rocking chair. She longs to sit there with Daisy, cocooned in a world of softness and quiet, just the two of them, together.

"Wait," Suzanne calls out as Mia heads to the door, and she stiffens. *What now?*

Suzanne's voice is gentle as she tucks the panda bear into the crook of Mia's arm. "Don't forget this."

Mia nods, gulping, feeling suddenly as if she could cry, and then she heads into the nursery, closing the door on Suzanne and Mark.

19

SUZANNE

The information comes in the middle of September, right before Daisy's birthday, in a plain brown envelope, return address the New Jersey Department of Vital Records. It's thick enough that the mailman had to wedge it into the letterbox, and as I wriggle it out, I feel my heart start to thud. It's only been five weeks; I wasn't expecting it yet, even as I checked my mail every day with both eagerness and trepidation, hoping, and yet now I'm not sure I want to open it. To know.

Daisy has been gone for nearly a month. In all that time, I have had no communication from Mia, and only two texts from Daisy, both in response to my own inquiries, both virtually monosyllabic. I've checked Mia's Instagram, but she hasn't mentioned Daisy at all, just the usual posts about motivation and lifestyle and how *you can do it, ladies*! At first, the not knowing bothered me, filled me with dread, but nearly a month on, I've relaxed into it. Maybe it's better not knowing, but simply letting it happen.

I've gone out with Peter a couple of times, just as friends, and met up for coffee or wine with Lynne. Lynne and I even went away for a weekend, antiquing in Connecticut, to see the fall color. I bought a lovely little jug, over a hundred years old and made by the New England Pottery Company, in an antique store housed in a red barn near Cornwall. It sits on the windowsill in my kitchen and looking at it makes me happy in a simple, easy way that I haven't experienced in a long time.

Life's little pleasures have taken on new resonance, a greater poignancy. The emptiness of the apartment is starting to feel peaceful rather than echoing. My evenings are quiet, but I don't mind that. I'm not sure how or why this has happened; it wasn't an active effort on my part, more simply a new way of being that happened around me as much as in me. I miss Daisy, sometimes unbearably, but I recognize that I have to truly let her go. I'll always love her, I'll always be her mother, but she is almost eighteen and I can't control her or the nature of our relationship. Finally and truly understanding and accepting that has been the greatest relief, but one tinged by sadness, even grief. Nothing happened the way I thought and hoped it would, but I wonder if there is a person alive who doesn't feel the same.

Yet now this envelope, with all its information, threatens my newfound equanimity. I'm afraid of what I'm going to find, and yet I know I need to discover it. I take it upstairs, leave it on the kitchen counter while I change into comfortable clothes, make myself a cup of coffee.

Then I take it to the dining-room table, drawing out a chair in a way that feels ceremonial. I sit down, stare at the envelope for a few moments, and then I open it.

I look at my birth certificate first—*Suzanne Davies, mother Cheryl Davies. Father Not Known.* The rest of the details are the same. I put down the certificate, take a few deep breaths. *Cheryl Davies.* The name means nothing to me. I pick up the next sheet; it is a typewritten case record of my adoption, the language clinical, emotionless.

First Reported Incident: Neighbor called police when baby, eight months old, was crying for several hours. The Child Welfare Department visited mother, who said baby was colicky.

Second Reported Incident: Baby, fourteen months old, taken to hospital with fractured arm. Child Welfare Department visited.

Third Reported Incident: Toddler, twenty months old, left alone in apartment...

The visits go on, about ten in total, a list of injuries and neglect that makes my heart ache for this poor, unloved child —*me*. I know Child Protective Services weren't nearly as good or well-resourced back in the seventies as they are today, but I am still shocked, even angry by how long it took for them to see the pattern. According to the report, I suffered multiple fractures; I was malnourished, neglected, developmentally delayed and often dirty. I was placed in foster care twice, before I was returned to my mother each time, only to suffer the same kind of treatment. By the time I was placed with Elizabeth and Phillip Everett, they had chronicled several years of persistent abuse. The last record is merely noting "a successful placement." It is signed Helen Woods.

I drop the paper, my temples throbbing, my body feeling as if I've taken a physical blow. Even in my hesitant, vague imaginings, I never thought it would be as bad as this. I take a few minutes to simply stare into space, letting this new, unwelcome knowledge seep into me. Was this why my mother never told me I was adopted? Because it had all been so traumatic? Maybe she saw it as a mercy. I find that I can't really blame her, and yet I continue to reel. If Daisy had suffered similar treatment, would I have told her about Mia? It's an impossible question. I can barely take in my own history, never mind the alternate realities that are buzzing through my brain.

I don't know how long I sit there, simply trying to absorb what I've learned, but at some point, I stumble up from the table and reach for my phone. I feel as if I am blind, or perhaps drunk; I am not fully aware of what I am doing even as I swipe for Mark's number.

"Suzanne?"

"I... I need to talk to you." My voice sounds strange to my own ears, like it's coming from outside my body.

"Suzanne? What...?" Mark's voice rises sharply in concern. "Is Daisy...? Is everything all right?"

"It's not about Daisy," I say, although part of me thinks it might be, in a roundabout way. "It's just... I need to... I need to talk to you." My voice wavers, breaks. "Please."

Mark is silent for a moment and I scrunch my eyes closed, my knuckles gripping the phone so tightly they ache.

"Okay," he says gently. "Why don't I come there?"

"No." I realize I want to move, escape the confines of this apartment, its memories. "I'll come to you. If that's okay."

"If you're sure—"

"Yes."

Five minutes later, I am out the door, in a cab, the brown envelope and its contents bundled in my bag. I don't remember the drive to midtown; I stare into space, unmoving, while the driver glances at me apprehensively in the rearview mirror every few minutes.

Mark's building is a soulless skyscraper, full of identical one-bedroom apartments, boring and boxy and small. It's all he could afford, what with me keeping our classic six and Daisy's tuition. I realize, perhaps for the first time, what a sacrifice he made, to get away from me. *Was I really that bad?* I am starting to wonder.

He greets me at the door, looking at me in alarm, although I don't know how I seem. Shell-shocked, maybe.

"Suzanne... for the love of... What's happened?"

"I'm sorry, I didn't mean to alarm you." My voice comes out lifelessly. I feel as if I am merely inhabiting my body, as if part of me is hovering somewhere else—back in some squalid apartment in New Jersey, crying in a crib. I shudder, and Mark reaches one hand out as if to touch me, and then lets it drop.

I step into his living room, a long, narrow room with plain white walls and black leather sofas, a coffee table of glass and chrome. He has lived here for over two years but he has not done anything to personalize it or make it homey, save for a couple of photos of Daisy. The whole place looks like it came directly from IKEA, already assembled. For the first time, I wonder why. Does he not want this to be his home? Is he waiting for something—someone—else? I collapse onto the sofa while Mark stares at me in concern.

"I discovered something," I tell him in that same, strange, lifeless voice. "Something my mother told me when she was in one of her less-than-lucid moments."

Mark lowers himself onto the chair opposite me. "What was it?"

I take a deep breath, let it gust out of me. "I'm adopted. And I never knew."

His mouth opens, closes.

I hand him the envelope. "It's all in there."

Leaning my head back against the sofa, I close my eyes as he begins to read. I hear a soft gasp, and then another, but I am too tired to respond, or even to open my eyes. It's as if all the knowledge has caught up with me, and I am exhausted—too exhausted to cry, or even to care. I just feel numb. So numb.

"My God," Mark says quietly when he's finally finished. "How truly... horrific. There aren't... I'm so sorry, Suzanne. I can't even imagine..." He lapses into silence.

"I don't know how to feel," I tell him. I force myself to open my eyes, lift my head from the sofa to look at him. "I don't know how to be. I don't even know who I am."

"This doesn't change who you are—"

"It *does.*" Suddenly I sound fierce. "Don't you see that, Mark? All right, maybe it doesn't change who I am, but why I am. *This* is why I am the way I am. It all makes sense now and I... I don't want it to." And abruptly, without me even realizing that it is happening, I am sobbing, gasping and choking for breath, the sounds loud and ragged in the still room. I fold over double, my arms wrapped around my waist, as the animal sounds tear out of me, shocking us both.

Then I feel Mark's arms come around me, his body pressed close to mine. We haven't hugged since we divorced, and I realize how much I miss the feel of him, even the smell of him, aftershave and laundry detergent. Familiarity. Comfort. I close my eyes as the sounds continue to rip out of me, one after the other. I want to stop, but I can't. Mark murmurs nonsense words like I'm a child, a baby, as he strokes my hair. I think I love him as much in this moment as I ever did.

Eventually, even more exhausted, I slump against him, my eyes closed, my face streaked with my tears. "I'm sorry," I mutter.

"Don't be sorry."

"I didn't mean to drag you into this. I just... I needed to talk to someone who knew me, and you're... you're the only one left." My voice hitches on a sob and I manage to draw it back in. I thought I'd accepted it all, I'd found a fragile peace with Daisy gone, I was letting go of my grief, but it's all collapsed like a house of flimsy cards, no more than a desperate illusion. I haven't made peace with anything. I have even more grief to bear now—the grief for the loss of my mother, my daughter, the life I once had and the life I thought I'd had all along. Everything. Absolutely everything.

"I don't know what to do," I tell Mark in something close to a whimper.

His arm tightens around me. "Suzanne, I can understand why you feel lost right now, but learning about your childhood doesn't change who you are or what you've done. You've been a good mother to Daisy. Your own childhood has no bearing on that."

"But it does." I sound sad, but right then I feel strangely calm. I straighten, moving slightly apart from him as I wipe my face. "Tell me something," I say. "Why did you divorce me?"

"What?" Mark looks both blank and guarded. "Why are you asking me that now?"

"Please, just tell me. The real reason, whatever it was, because I don't think I ever understood, but maybe now I can."

He shrugs, a twitch of his shoulders. "Suzanne... I..." He sighs heavily. "Are you sure you want to do this now?"

I nod, feeling an almost surreal sense of calm, as if someone has twirled a dial and the world has suddenly come into blazingly sharp focus. "Yes, I do."

"I was tired of feeling like I was getting nothing back," he says after a moment, his gaze on a distant, unfocused place. "When we first met, I loved how calm and in control you were. After the turbulence of my parents' lives, my mother's histrionics, my dad's alcoholism, their awful break-up... you felt comforting. Safe. Like I could trust you not to... not to go off the deep end, I guess, the way my mother so often did."

I nod, accepting, because he's told me this before, and I've always liked it. "But?" I prompt.

Mark winces a little, like he doesn't want to hurt me. "It's just you never give away *anything*, Suzanne. Your emotions, your feelings... even physically." His wince deepens, so he's practically cringing away from me. "It felt as if you never wanted me to hug or kiss you."

I open my mouth to protest—I *know* that's not true—but he holds up a hand to stop me.

"You tolerated it, I know, you accepted it, but... it felt as if you never welcomed or instigated it. Not even once, not really."

Can that really be the case? I try to think back. Did I never put my arms around Mark first, snuggle with him in bed? I *wanted* to. I'm sure of that. But, I realize, it felt foreign, like a language I'd never learned. I didn't know how to begin; I was afraid of being rebuffed, rejected. *Just like with Daisy.* I realize Mark is speaking the truth, but I never, ever saw it that way.

He sighs again, a sound of apology. "I'm sorry. I'm not trying to hurt you."

"I know." I nod, jerkily.

"You never told me you loved me, either," he continues. "Not even a 'you too' when I said it." He grimaces. "I know how it makes me sound—needy and pathetic, and maybe I was, but I hated that I felt that way. That you made me feel that way, even if you didn't mean to."

I nod again, accepting his words like hammer blows. Another way I haven't wanted to be rejected. "I'm sorry. I..." Even now it's hard to say it. "I did love you. I always did."

He nods, looking only sorrowful. "I know you did. It wasn't even as if you were cold, Suzanne. We had fun together. I remember the good times, you know, and there were a lot of them."

A thousand memories tumble through my mind—skating at Rockefeller Center on one of our first dates; spending an entire evening simply staring in wonder at six-week-old Daisy. *This is better than a movie*, Mark had said, and I'd laughed in agreement. Thanksgiving dinners where our eyes met over the turkey, full of love and gratitude; the time he held my hair out of the way when I was bent over the toilet, struggling with morning sickness. How we knew how to make each other's coffee perfectly—lots of milk and no sugar for him, a drip of milk and a quarter teaspoon of sugar for me.

It felt like he threw it all away in a moment, but now I understand how much more must have been going on. "So if I wasn't cold," I ask, "what was I?"

Mark is silent for a long moment. "You were just so self-sufficient," he says at last. "As if you'd never even think of needing me. I remember I went away for a business trip for a week, and when I came back, I said I missed you, and you... you laughed, sort of in disbelief."

"I didn't—" I protest. I can't even remember it.

"Not meanly. Just... like you couldn't understand why I would, or why anyone would miss anyone." He sighs and rakes a hand through his hair. "I'm sorry. I feel like I'm criticizing you, and I don't mean to. I didn't tell you all this before, because I didn't want to hurt you and I knew you couldn't change."

I blink slowly, absorbing the wound of his words. "Can't I?" I ask quietly.

Mark winces. "I'm sorry, I didn't mean—"

"No." I shake my head. "Maybe you're right."

He looks pained. "Suzanne..."

"And Daisy?" I ask, cutting him off.

"What about Daisy?"

"Do you think I was... the same... with her? In not showing affection?" It hurts so much to say the words, like tearing my heart out and offering it to him on a plate. I might not have shown affection, but I felt it. I loved Mark. I love Daisy. *So much.* How could they not have known? How could they have not seen it blazing out of me? Everything I ever did was out of love for both of them.

"Not exactly," Mark says slowly. "Certainly not at the beginning. When she was a baby, you adored her. We both did, but you had a special bond, like a mother should."

I let out a breath, relieved by this small nugget of information. I remember cuddling Daisy as a baby, burying my nose in the sweet curve of her neck and breathing her in. It was easier, I realize, when she was a baby, when I knew she loved me back.

"I'm not sure when it changed," Mark continues. "Maybe when she got older. She was impatient, wriggly, the usual toddler stuff." He pauses. "In retrospect, having Mia come so much at the start might have confused her."

"Because Mia was so affectionate." I remember the sweeping hugs, her darling Daisy. "And I wasn't, not in the same way." I know I could have never, ever been like Mia.

"You're two different people—"

"Trying to be the same mother." I shake my head slowly. I can't blame Mia, not entirely, anyway. "Do you think this is why Daisy acts like she hates me? Because I've been so... distant? Tell me the truth, please. What you really think. I need to know."

Mark rakes a hand through his hair, looking conflicted enough for me to realize that he must believe it is the reason, at least in part. "She's a teenager, Suzanne..."

"Don't fob me off with that. Not again." A new, unwelcome thought occurs to me. "Is that why you've always said that to me? Because you didn't want me to blame myself, for not being a good mother?" The words break me, but my voice is flat. *I tried so hard. I read every book. I've loved her so much.* Has none of it mattered, in the end?

"I don't think anyone should blame anyone," Mark insists. "And you are a good mother, Suzanne." His voice throbs with feeling. "I really do believe that."

"But Daisy doesn't."

Mark shakes his head. "I think she does. Maybe not right now, in the middle of all this stuff, but deep down... Look, we've all done the best we could, and we've all made mistakes. I know I have. I should have been more honest with you all along. I know I backed away, probably starting years ago. I felt guilty for being the one that had the fertility problem. I didn't always know how to deal with the Mia stuff. I was worried about any kind of confrontation, because of the way my parents were. I've had my own issues, just like you have, like anyone does. Everyone's hurting, Suzanne. Everyone's doing their best to heal." He pauses, and when he speaks again, his voice sounds the way I am feeling—broken, lost, reeling. "Maybe I should have told you all this before, but I don't think I'd ever verbalized it, even to myself." Another pause as he looks at me, his eyes dark with regret. "Maybe if I'd been more honest... we could have made it work."

His words fall into the stillness, creating ripples of memory, of feeling. On our wedding day, holding hands. I was affectionate then. Sharing a laughing look at a crowded party, knowing we were thinking the same thing: *Let's get out of here.* Quiet dinners when I thought we were happy simply to be. "Do you really mean that?" I ask quietly.

"I don't know," he admits. "I'm just sorry for the way it's all happened. I'm sorry for the pain you're feeling now. I'm sorry our daughter is in North Carolina, choosing to be away from us, and neither of us are sure how any of us got to this place." He shakes his head, raking one hand through his hair again, mussing it even more.

"So am I," I whisper. "Sorry for all of it. So much, Mark. *So much.*"

We gaze at each other, both of us grief-stricken, abject, lost in this new reality. Then slowly Mark reaches across the sofa and holds my hand, clasping my fingers in a way that feels both familiar and strange. We sit there in silence, needing no words, or perhaps simply not having any left. The silence speaks for both of us.

20

MIA

I don't tell Tom about the money. I don't tell Daisy, either. In fact, I put those twenties back in the drawer and act like I never saw them, like I never even noticed they were missing. As I'd stared down at them in my hand, knowing with an instinct I hadn't realized I'd possessed that she must have left them there on purpose for me to find, I knew that this was not just about me and the secret I was keeping. This was something deeper, darker and more painful, and I had to figure out how to deal with it. How to deal with Daisy.

So I scour message boards and websites, looking for information on the trauma of adoption. It feels like nearly two decades too late, and I know I definitely should have looked at this stuff before, but for so long I was trying to only see the positives of the choice I made so long ago. Now I need to understand the ongoing effects of adoption, the reality of what Daisy has been dealing with, simply because she is adopted. What I learn isn't all that comforting, but I know I need to hear it.

It seems that many adoptees, whether their adoptions were open or closed, from birth or later on, rebel in their teenaged years. Not everyone, of course, but enough. They struggle with questions of identity, of abandonment, of belonging. There is a theory—controversial, it is true—that there is such a thing as "Adopted Child Syndrome"—i.e. every adopted child, no matter how healthy the adoption or loved the child, experiences trauma of some kind, simply by being adopted. *At the heart of adoption is loss.* I never wanted to believe that, and yet I realize I might have to, now.

I find myself thinking back to the day after Daisy was born, when I asked Suzanne if we could have an open adoption. There had been a brochure on them at the agency, and it had sparked something in me. I knew I couldn't raise my little girl, but I still wanted her in my life. I know Suzanne was surprised, but she agreed readily enough. Did either of us have any idea what we were getting into—how difficult it would be for both of us, as well as for Daisy? And yet who's to say just because something is difficult, it is also wrong?

I'm not going to blame my insistence on an open adoption for what's happening with Daisy now. Life is too complicated for that, I know, even if it played a part.

But I had never anticipated how complicated it would all get, right from the beginning, even before Tom came into my life. Even before decisions were made—my marrying Tom, Suzanne and Mark divorcing. I hadn't realized that the very nature of our situation was fragile, papered with cracks as well as with good intentions. But maybe that's *every* situation—I think of Tom's family, or my own, or anyone's. The nature of life itself, I realize, is brokenness. Brokenness and then, God willing, healing.

And so I decide to do what I can to address the brokenness in Daisy's life. I plan a surprise dinner for her eighteenth birthday, and I compose a lengthy, emotional post for my Instagram feed. Neither is revolutionary or even very big, and they might not change anything, but these are the practical steps I can take now, to show Daisy she is loved. Because she is, very much, despite my conflicted feelings, despite how complicated and challenging I've felt everything to be.

It takes me hours to compose the post, as I labor over every word. I don't want to make too big a deal of it, but I know Daisy checks my Instagram. She's asked me about my lifestyle-coaching business, and I've told her a few anecdotes about the women I help. My heart beats harder when I think of her seeing this. I've already asked her if she is okay with me mentioning her online, and she said yes. Still, I doubt she's expecting a post like this.

> *Hey everyone, Time for an honest and heartfelt post, because this young woman means more to me than I could say, or have ever said before. I've shared my life with you in so many ways, but I haven't shared about this as much as I should have or wanted to, and there have been reasons for that—reasons that maybe aren't as complicated as I thought they were. The truth is, this lovely woman is my daughter. My biological daughter, whom I gave up for adoption when I was just twenty years old. I stayed involved in her life, with occasional visits, cards, phone calls, but I always wanted more even as I settled for less, because it felt easier, or less complicated. But like what I said before about things being complicated? Maybe that's my fault, because I didn't let them be simple. I didn't tell the truth to my daughter or my own heart as much as I should have. But I want to shout it loud and clear now—because Daisy is my daughter. My gorgeous, funny, wonderful daughter whom I love so much. And it's time I finally shouted out the truth!*

The accompanying photo is of Daisy—just Daisy, because this is about her, not me. I took it a few weeks ago when she wasn't looking, so she's staring off into the distance, a faint smile on her face, seeming young and vulnerable and so very beautiful. I'm going to post it right before her birthday dinner. It's not quite a present, but something close to it.

I get the girls in on the preparations—Sophie makes a birthday card dripping with glitter, and Ella helps me pick out a piece of jewelry, a single sapphire on a silver pendant, Daisy's birthstone. Avery writes her a poem and Tom makes a reservation at Maximillian's Grill and Wine Bar, one of the nicest restaurants in Cary. I'm excited for the event, for Daisy, for all of us. Suzanne and Mark have sent a present too; I asked Daisy if she wanted them to visit, and she snorted her disbelief at such a suggestion, which made me wince in sympathy for them, even as I was glad she wanted to be with us. With me.

At least there haven't been any eruptions in the last week, since I found the money. Daisy hasn't stayed out late, hasn't snarled at me, hasn't pushed the limits or tested the boundaries. She's been quiet, a bit watchful, perhaps; I'm not deluding myself that this is the end of all the trials, but I'm hopeful it can be a beginning. Because tonight, after our dinner, I'm finally going to tell her and Tom the truth. Together.

My heart flutters at the thought, and not in a good way. I'm terrified I might be risking everything—my marriage, my family —but I know I have to. It's impossible to be honest and keep a secret at the same time. And I know it will be such a relief, to have finally admitted it all, even if there is fallout. Which there will be, of course. I just hope they can both understand and forgive.

The birthday dinner starts off well. I put the message on Instagram, my stomach doing a little flip as I press post. Tom tells Daisy to dress up, but not where we're going. The girls are in their Sunday dresses, bouncing in the backseat with excitement, as we lead Daisy, blindfolded for silly effect, out to the car. She's laughing a little, wearing one of the dresses I picked out when we went shopping—a simple sheath in forest green that brings out the hazel in her eyes.

"Do I really need to be blindfolded?" she asks and the girls all screech, "Yes!" Tom and I share a smile.

We drive to Maximilian's, and we take the blindfold off in the parking lot, but tell Daisy to close her eyes as we guide her to the table prepared in a private room—complete with balloons, streamers, the works. Admittedly, it's not a huge party, there's just us, but that's how I want it to be. *Us.* Our family.

When Daisy finally opens her eyes, we all yell, "Happy Birthday!" and she blinks in surprise, looking for a moment like she might cry, but then she smiles instead.

"Wow," she says. "Thanks. Thanks so much." And then she hugs each of us in turn, and when my arms come around her, I hold her tight, wanting to imbue her with my love, with the truth of my feelings. *The truth.* It will finally come out tonight, and I am glad. At least, I am trying to be.

Looking back, I wish I could have stayed in that moment. I wish I could have pressed pause, or maybe rewind, maybe back to the day at the spa, or maybe all the way back to the beginning. Who knows? But I wish—oh how I wish—that things didn't turn out as they did.

But that moment passes like any other, like any split second where you have to make a choice, and you move on, not yet knowing what the repercussions will be.

We sit down and Tom orders champagne, sneaks Daisy a sip. We toast her, her year with our family, life itself. Everything feels like a promise.

I can just about make myself believe that somehow all the issues from before have been solved—or, at least, that they *will* be solved. All the issues we were dealing with—the money, the makeup, the drunkenness—were just symptoms of a problem we're solving now, we're going to solve. Together, with love and patience and understanding. In that moment, it almost seems simple.

But, just like before, just as I had always feared and known it would, it all falls apart in a single, split second. We've wolfed down our appetizers, made our way through the bread basket, with some laughter and jokes, the girls getting a little too excitable and so I'm busy managing them, and I don't hear Tom ask Daisy what she's thinking about in terms of college.

I do hear her response, though, that she's thinking of NYU, like me. Innocent, innocuous stuff, but some part of me must realizes the danger, because I stiffen as the world seems to go in slow motion, as if I am watching a car crash from afar, and there is nothing I can do, no way to stop the collision, the casualties.

"You know I went to NYU, too," Tom says with a smile, and Daisy stills.

"You did?"

"Yeah, Mia and I didn't really know each other back then, though, at least not that I can recall." He shoots me a fond look while I sit there frozen, appalled, watching it all unravel and yet too stunned to do anything to mitigate the damage. "But apparently I tutored her," he adds with a laugh. "In economics. I was a computer science major, though. I don't remember it at all." He glances at me. "Was it just the one time?"

I don't reply—I can't—as he reaches for the last slice of bread, and Daisy turns to look at me, her eyes like two dark holes in her face, burning into mine.

I know the truth is written all over my face in stark, agonized letters. I open my mouth, but I feel as if I can't speak, can't move, can't even think. "Daisy..." I finally manage, and then her chair scrapes back so hard and fast, it falls to the floor, and Ella, sitting next to her, jerks in surprise. Tom leans forward, one hand extended to help her; he thinks she's had an accident or something, I realize, and for one split second we're all frozen in this terrible tableau, and then Daisy hurtles out of the room, the door slamming behind her, leaving us in stunned silence.

Tom looks around the table, bewildered. "What the hell...? Why...?" He stands up. "I should go check if she's all right."

"No," I say quickly. My heart is hammering so loudly I can hear it in my ears, and my voice sounds tinny and strange, as if it's coming from faraway. "No, I'll go."

"What happened, Mommy?" Avery asks in a small voice, but I just shake my head.

"Don't worry. It's nothing to do with any of you."

Tom's eyes narrow. "You know what's going on?"

I take a deep breath. "Yes," I say simply. "I'll explain later." And then I go after my daughter.

Outside, it is already growing dark, and I see Daisy sprinting down the street as if away from a fire.

"Daisy!" I shout, and start running after her. "*Daisy!*"

I've almost reached her when she whirls around, so suddenly that I rear back, and then she plants both hands on my shoulders and pushes me, hard enough that I start to fall, throwing a hand out to stop myself, breaking the skin along my palm.

"All this time," she chokes. "*All this time.*" And then she whirls back around and keeps running.

By the time I've scrambled back up, she's around the corner, and by the time I reach the corner, she's gone.

I am still breathing hard, bruised and shaken, when I return to the restaurant. Tom rises from his seat, where the girls have gathered around him, an appalled look on his face. Belatedly, I realize how I must look—my hair has come out of my artfully messy bun, my hand is bleeding, and my dress is torn.

"Mia, what the hell is going on?" he demands, and I shake my head. "Where's Daisy?"

"She's..." *Gone.* I shake my head. "She ran down the street. She's... upset."

"What happened?" Tom demands. "What did I say? Why

is she upset?" The questions fire out of him, demanding answers.

Briefly, I close my eyes. *I was going to tell you both tonight.* It feels so unfair, so needlessly painful, to have this happen just hours before I would have told them the truth. But maybe it would have unfolded like this anyway.

"I'll tell you later," I say. "Let's..." Eat? My appetite has vanished. My girls are looking woebegone. And I have no idea where Daisy is. "Let's just go home," I say wearily.

Sophie tugs at my hand. "What happened, Mommy?" she asks tearfully. "Why is Daisy mad at us?"

"She's not mad, sweetheart. She's upset. And it has absolutely nothing to do with you." I swallow hard. *It has to do with me.* With my secrets and lies.

I glance instinctively at Tom, and find he is staring back at me with that narrowed, assessing look.

"What's going on, Mia?"

"I'll tell you later."

"Do you know where Daisy is?"

"She's... going home, I hope. Let's go, so we can be there when she is."

We are a sorry group, leaving the restaurant, the streamers and balloons, our entrées ordered but not arrived. Tom pays the bill, tight-lipped and silent. The maître d' gives me the cake I'd brought over earlier, a grimace of apology on his face. I take it with miserable, murmured thanks.

When we get home, Tom turns to me as soon as the girls have gone upstairs to get ready for bed.

"So tell me what's going on."

"I will later, when it's quiet." I shove the cake onto the counter. "Let's deal with the girls first."

"Mia—"

"Tom," I cut him off. "It's not a quick or easy conversation, so please, can we just put out the fires first?"

Wordlessly, he nods. I have a reprieve, but it's not much of one.

The next hour is spent putting the girls to bed—I read Sophie a story, brush Avery's hair. They are all docile and timid, on their best behavior as a matter of instinct, or maybe self-protection. Even Ella doesn't ask me any questions. I've just tucked her and Avery into bed, kissing them both, reassuring them that everything is going to be okay, when I hear the front door open and close. My heart stops and then starts beating again, double time.

Ella sits up in bed. "Daisy—"

"Go to sleep, sweetheart," I say gently, a waver in my voice. "It's going to be okay." I so desperately want to believe that.

Daisy is in the hall as I come down the stairs, her expression tight and closed. "Daisy..." I don't even know where to begin, how to reach her.

She shakes her head, a quick, angry movement. "I don't want to hear your excuses," she says, and moves past me, up the stairs to her room.

"Daisy," I protest, but it's only half-hearted because I'm not strong enough to force this conversation, not when she's still so angry. I tell myself I'll wait for her to cool down, when we can talk rationally. She slams her bedroom door, loud enough that Avery peeks out of their bedroom down the hall.

"Mom?" she calls, her voice wavering.

I hate this. *I hate this.* "It's okay, sweetie," I tell her as I head back upstairs. "Go to sleep."

I tuck all three girls back into bed, giving them extra hugs and kisses, and then I hesitate by Daisy's door, straining to listen, but there's nothing. Finally, I go to our room, where Tom is waiting, sitting on the edge of the bed, his arms folded. *Oh, Lord.* I can't face this now. It's nine o'clock at night, the girls are all still awake, Daisy is fuming, and Tom wants answers. I simply can't face it. We need to have a quiet, rational, private, *painful* conversation, and there is no time or space or energy for it, but I know Tom won't be fobbed off any longer.

He gives me a level look. "Tell me what's going on, Mia."

I take a deep breath. Close the door. "It's between Daisy and me, Tom." They are not the words I meant to say, but they're the ones that come out.

"Are you serious? She runs out of her own birthday party, you guys have a bust-up in the street, our own daughters are freaking out, and it's between the two of you?" He rises from the bed, his voice rising too. "Are you *serious*?"

"Quiet," I hiss. "They can hear you, and there has been enough drama already."

He shakes his head slowly. "Why can't you just tell me what's going on?"

"I will." I close my eyes. "I was going to tell you tonight, as it happens."

"Tell me *what*?"

I open my eyes to look at him. I look at him hard, trying to see if there is some spark of suspicion in his eyes, some subconscious knowledge of the truth, a distant memory he's buried for nearly twenty years, but he looks only bewildered. Bewildered and angry.

"That you're Daisy's father," I tell him, my tone weary, defeated. I've dreaded saying the words, I've imagined this moment a thousand times, but in the end, it falls flat. There's no thunderbolt, or melodramatic music, or anything. Tom simply stares.

"What..." he finally says, the word escaping like a hiss. "*What*? No."

"Yes."

"*No.*" His voice rises sharply, and I press a finger to my lips. "We... we didn't."

"We did. You just didn't remember it."

He gapes at me for a few seconds, then starts to shake his head, stops. Finally, the words coming in something of a gasp, "And you never *told* me?"

I open my mouth to reply, I'm not sure what, when we both still at the sound of a knock on the door.

Sophie peeks in, tangle-haired, hesitant. "Daddy? I'm thirsty."

"I'll get you a drink, sweet pea." Tom shoots me a fulminating glare before he shepherds Sophie out of our room.

I sink onto the bed, my head in my hands. My head and heart both ache, and my stomach seethes, yet at the same time I feel completely, utterly flat. The truth is finally out, and I have no idea what will happen now. I feel too tired to find out.

In the end, nothing happens, at least not then. Tom comes back after a few minutes, moving stiffly, rigid with affront. "I'm going to sleep downstairs," he announces, and I swallow something close to a laugh. That's the conclusion he came to?

"Fine," I answer, because I'm too tired for all the explanations. If he wants to be the offended party without even thinking about where I am coming from, then fine. I have enough guilt to be getting on with, anyway.

He pauses by the door. "I still want to talk. I want answers. But I just need to...' His voice wavers, breaks, and my eyes sting. "I just need to process this," he says, and then he's gone.

The room feels empty without him, the whole house quiet and still, watchful and waiting. I let out a sound that is half sob, half weary huff, and then I drop my head into my hands. I never meant this to happen. And yet it was what I'd been fearing all along. I hate that I kept it secret for so long, and yet even now I wonder if I could have done anything differently.

Feeling like an old woman, my whole body aching, I get ready for bed. I curl up under the duvet, my knees to my chest, my eyes scrunched shut as if I could block the whole world out. Eventually I must fall asleep, because I wake up early, a gray, predawn light filtering through the curtains I forgot to close, and hear my phone, lying on my bedside table, pinging with messages. *Ping. Ping. Ping.*

I open my eyes, one hand scrabbling for my phone, feeling exhausted even though I've just woken up. It takes me a few moments to focus on the messages coming up on my screen, longer to read them as I sound the words out slowly. *So sorry, Mia... I think maybe we should postpone our session?... Whatever you're going through, I hope you figure it out... I'm sorry, I'm going to look elsewhere for coaching... I didn't realize what a BITCH you are. I'm adopted, did you even know that?*

What?

I scramble to a seated position, my heart thudding as I swipe my phone to check my Instagram. Why am I receiving these messages? What has happened?

And then I see my profile, and I suck in a hard breath. Daisy has posted underneath my heartfelt message, one of her own:

> *So you want to know the TRUTH about Mia, my birth mother? She LIED to me my whole life, telling me she didn't know who my birth father was. She couldn't tell me... she would if she could... she was SO sorry... ALL LIES. The truth is she is MARRIED to him, and has been for ELEVEN YEARS!!! And she never told him the truth either. She has lied and lied and lied, and pretended to care about us, but the truth is she is COMPLETELY FAKE. So if you think she is going to tell you the truth and help you with her stupid lifestyle coaching shit?! Well, she WON'T. This is the real Mia.*

Underneath, she has posted a photo of me giving the camera a finger. It's Photoshopped, it must be, because I've never posed like that, but I look laughing and smug—*when* did she take that photo of me? And then I realize *I* took it—it's the selfie from the baseball game, but Daisy has edited herself out and added the obscene gesture.

Well, I knew she was good at Photoshopping. She told me so herself.

I toss the phone aside, my fingers trembling. There are already over two hundred comments underneath Daisy's post, probably because she added about a hundred hashtags, hoping it would go viral. Maybe it already has. Clearly from the messages I've received, people are reading and responding.

My screen lights up with another message, this one from someone I don't know. *You are pure evil.*

I flinch before drawing a shuddering breath and climbing out of bed. I should turn off the notifications, or at least make my profile private, but then I realize Daisy's post on my page might be only the tip of the iceberg. She's probably plastered her version of events all over social media—Snapchat, Reddit, who knows. I don't know what to do, so I take a shower and dress, giving myself time to think about how to respond. Do I take down my Instagram page? Do I find Daisy? I'm not even angry at her—well, not much—but more just sad and sorry that's it come to this. Although, I realize as I do my makeup, I *am* angry. She didn't need to do this. She didn't need to try to ruin my life.

But what if you ruined hers?

Impatient with myself and my thoughts, I toss the mascara tube onto the counter and turn away from my reflection. First things first—I need to talk to Daisy.

I find her downstairs, curled up at the kitchen table, cradling a mug of coffee. It's not much past seven in the morning and yet she's already dressed, her hair rumpled, her gaze downcast. The younger girls are all still asleep. I glance outside, the gray light of early morning giving way to pale blue sky. It's Saturday, and we'd normally have a lazy morning, with gymnastics and swimming in the afternoon. I can't imagine going about our usual activities now.

"I saw your post," I tell her as she lifts her chin up to give me a flat look I cannot decipher. "And all the comments." No reply, but her lip curls and there is a gleam in her eyes that looks like satisfaction. "Was that really necessary, Daisy?" I ask evenly. "Couldn't we have spoken first? Couldn't you have tried to understand?" And then I realize I'm not angry, after all; I'm *hurt*. Desperately hurt.

"Understand what?" she throws at me, her voice as flat as her glare. "That you're a liar?"

"Understand why I didn't tell you the truth."

"I already understand that. You didn't give a shit. You never have." Her mouth twists and she turns back to her coffee.

"That's not true. I admit, I've made mistakes, I've admitted that before. But I cared. I *care*." My voice throbs.

"As if. If you really cared, you wouldn't have kept it a secret for so long. We could have been a fa—" She breaks off, pressing her lips together. "All you've cared about is the cozy little life you've built for yourself here, with your stupid coaching thing and those *stupid* photos—don't you know no one takes those portraits anymore, everyone in jeans and white shirts? You're like, from 2005." I would have laughed at this insult, so ridiculous in light of everything else, and yet I can't, because Daisy is trembling, her eyes full of hurt, her voice full of fury. "You deserve to have it all blown open, so people can see what you're really like. What a total scheming *bitch* you are." She rises from her chair, moving toward me aggressively, one hand raised as if to strike.

I'm not scared, not exactly, but I'm alarmed. I realize I have no idea what she is capable of. "Daisy..." I lift one hand to ward her off—is she actually going to *hit* me?—and she sneers as she drops her hand.

"You're pathetic. I hope your business completely tanks. I

posted your stupid flowery message and my reply everywhere, by the way. So good luck trying to convince people you're so *authentic*."

"I don't care about my business," I tell her, although I do. I'm proud of what I've accomplished, and regardless of what I've kept from Daisy, it was real. I have always cared about the women I help—and I care about her. Even now, when I'm fighting a fury that rivals her own. "Daisy, please. Let's talk rationally about this, give me a chance to—"

"Mommy?"

I whirl around to see Sophie standing in the doorway, holding her teddy bear by one arm, blinking sleepily, her hair rumpled.

"Sophie..."

"Hey, you know what, Sophie?" Daisy's voice is pitched pseudo-friendly, and I tense. "Your mom is a liar. Did you know that? Did you know she lies?"

"*Daisy*." I turn back to stare at her, willing her to stop this senseless destruction. "Please—"

"My mommy isn't a liar," Sophie says in a small voice, her eyes filling with confusion as she glances between the two of us. "Why were you shouting? Why did you run out yesterday?"

"Because your Mommy *is* a liar," Daisy flashes back, and I realize she won't stop, that she can't. That in her anger and hurt right now, she wants to destroy my family. She wants to hurt as many people as she can, and I cannot let her.

"Daisy, stop this," I say, and she gives me a look full of fury. "Stop this right now."

"What? Telling the truth?"

"No. Lashing out. Trying to hurt us—"

"Well, the truth *does* hurt, doesn't it?" she retorts triumphantly.

Sophie whimpers, and I break.

"Get out," I tell her flatly. She recoils a little bit, shock flashing across her face, as if she didn't expect to be able to push me this far. "Did you think you could just push and push and push and I'd take it?" I demand, my voice vibrating with the raw force of my feeling. "Well, I won't. If you aren't going to listen, I'm not going to try to explain anything to you. So get out." I point to the kitchen door. "Get out right now."

She glares at me, and I almost take it all back, but then I see Sophie behind her, looking so small and scared. I wait, and after a few taut seconds, Daisy whirls around. She grabs something from the kitchen counter, and then she storms out of the kitchen. I sag against the table, the breath leaving my body in a trembling rush. *How did that unravel so fast?*

It is only distantly that I hear the front door close. Twice. A few seconds later, I lift my head at the sound of the car starting. Did she actually take my keys from the counter? She doesn't even have a driver's license yet. And then I register that Sophie is no longer standing in the doorway either.

I hurl myself towards the front door, running outside, the grass damp on my bare feet. Daisy is reversing bumpily out of our driveway, the back wheels going onto the grass, leaving muddy tracks.

"Sophie!" I scream as I glimpse her small face in the back-seat window as Daisy guns the engine and speeds down the street, away from me.

THEN

MIA

September 2004
17 years ago

The room is sunny and cheerful, with a view over the Hudson River, if Mia cranes her neck. The nurse who has settled her there is friendly and bustling, and she takes her blood pressure and listens to the baby's heartbeat, smiling at the galloping sound.

"Everything looks just as it should be," the nurse assures her as she pats her hand. "I'll leave you to settle. You're expecting someone…?"

"Yes," Mia says. "Suzanne Thompson. She's the… the baby's adoptive mother."

Mia doesn't miss the flash of sympathy in the nurse's eyes. "How lovely," she says. "I'll bring her in as soon as she arrives."

Alone, Mia paces the room, feeling nervous, though nothing has happened yet, not really. Her water broke this morning, a gush all over the bathroom floor, and when she called her OB, she told her to come in, that "they might as well get this baby out." Her due date is in three days.

Mia had already arranged with Suzanne to be there at the birth; she didn't want to ask her own mother, who didn't offer anyway, and neither did she want to be alone. Suzanne had looked as if she'd given her the best present in the world, and Mia had to pretend that she'd asked for Suzanne's sake, and not her own. In any case, she's glad she's there. At least she thinks she is.

The truth is, she's scared. She's not quite sure how she managed to get to this point, nine months pregnant, her parents acting as if she'd better clean up the mess she's made. She's waddled around the city for months, taken summer classes while avoiding the curious stares, and tried to forget about Tom Sullivan. She knows he's still in Thailand; a few months ago, before she was really showing, she worked up the courage to ask a guy she recognized as one of his roommates when he'd be coming back.

The guy had looked startled; he hadn't recognized her, either. "Man, I don't know. I think he was going to stay there for, like, a year."

"A whole year?" she'd asked, unable to keep from sounding dismayed and he'd shrugged.

"Yeah, he likes being useful, I guess." And then he'd walked off and forgot about her all over again.

The baby kicks, a hard, sharp jab. Mia rests one hand on her bump. Hard to believe she won't be pregnant soon, that she'll have a baby—except, of course, she won't. But she likes Suzanne and Mark; she believes they'll be good parents. They have plenty of money and they live in the city, a fifteen-minute subway ride from her apartment. Suzanne in particular has always been so kind.

It's going to be okay, she tells herself, and then the baby—a little girl, she decided to find out—kicks again.

"Mia?"

She turns to see Suzanne coming in the doorway, looking both tentative and eager.

"I can't believe it's actually time. How are you feeling?"

"I'm not even having any contractions yet," Mia says, an apology. "It might be a while."

"That's okay."

As Suzanne comes in the room, Mia sees she is holding a bag, one of those expensive hessian ones.

"I brought you some things," she says. "I hope that's okay?"

Mia shrugs. She doesn't know how she feels about anything.

Suzanne starts taking them out and putting them on the table by the bed. "Potpourri—it smells like cinnamon, which you said you liked? I would have brought a candle, but they're not allowed."

"Thank you," Mia murmurs, touched despite her ambivalent feelings about Suzanne.

"And fuzzy socks, because I've read that your feet can feel cold when you're in labor."

She continues to take out her gifts, detailing each one—several Hershey bars, Mia's favorite, to keep up her energy; a couple of novels by authors Suzanne knows she likes; a tube of body lotion that smells like lilies; a little brown jar of Vitamin E oil that's meant to help with stretch marks; an oversized T-shirt in soft, pink cotton "for after"; a couple of snack bags of trail mix.

When she has finished emptying the bag, she turns to Mia with a smile.

"Thank you," Mia says. "That's so kind."

Suzanne has been far kinder than her own mother; she's been genuinely thoughtful in a way that makes Mia want to cry, out of grief or gratitude, she's not sure. She's glad Suzanne is here; she knows she'll help. Mark, Suzanne has told her, will come after the baby is born; Mia hadn't wanted him in the delivery room. It felt too intimate. She thinks of how Suzanne will see her, grunting and groaning and *pushing a baby out of her body*, and she is filled with both wonder and terror. The next few hours feel like a mountain to climb. She cannot see to the other side.

.   .   .

The hours pass slowly. A nurse comes in again, to take Mia's vitals and assure her the baby is fine. Then her OB comes in, a brisk woman with curly hair, and informs Mia she's actually been having contractions for a while, without realizing; when she checks, with Suzanne looking away discreetly, she is already four centimeters dilated. Mia doesn't really know what that means.

"Baby will be here soon," the OB says, and Mia is seized by sudden panic. She's not ready. She's not ready to have this baby; she's not ready to give her up. She thought she was ready, or at least resigned, but right now she knows she isn't.

As the OB leaves, she turns to Suzanne; her terror must be on her face because Suzanne reaches over and holds her hand. "It's okay," she says. "I'm here."

Mia clings to her hand, needing her strength, looking to her for guidance, even as she recognizes that part of her doesn't want Suzanne there at all.

An hour later, the contractions start to hurt. Mia picked this hospital because it has a natural birthing center, and she liked the sound of that. Suzanne and Mark are paying the medical bills, so it didn't really matter anyway, but right now she wonders if she made a mistake, because she wants something, anything, to take away this blazing, blinding agony.

But then Suzanne is there, holding her hand, talking her through each wave of pain that crashes over her, threatening to drag her under, before leaving her gasping on the other shore. She focuses on Suzanne's steady voice, warm and sure and so wonderfully calm.

"You're doing great, Mia. So great. You're amazing. The doctor says you'll be able to push soon…"

She didn't even realize the OB had come back. Everything is a dazzling haze of pain, the world is dark at the edges, blurred at the center.

"How long?" she gasps out, clinging to Suzanne's hand.

"Not long now." The OB is calm and cheerful while Mia stares at her blearily, her body convulsing from the inside out. "Don't push yet, Mia…"

Don't push? She has to push. Her body is expelling this baby whether she wants to or not, and it hurts so much that she is sobbing and grabbing onto Suzanne's hand like a lifeline, an anchor. She wants her mother. She wants this to be over. She wants anything but this.

"Almost, Mia," Suzanne says, her face close to her, her expression comfortingly tender. "Almost, I promise. You're doing amazingly. Really, you are."

And then a cry splits the air—at first, Mia think it is her; she has been crying and grunting and sounding like an animal for a while now, but then she feels a sense of emptying, of release, and the OB places something on her chest—something warm and red and slimy. A tiny, wrinkled face peers up at her and then lets out another bleating cry.

Dear God, Mia thinks, *it's a baby*. Somehow, in the midst of being pregnant, of arranging the adoption and going to classes and just waiting for it all to be over, she had not quite computed that she was actually having a baby. That there is a baby right here, squinting up at her, and it is hers. *Hers.*

Except it isn't.

Then her body is taken over again, as she expels the placenta— something she'd never even *thought* about before—until she feels completely wrung out, her body no more than a sagging husk, utterly empty.

"Would you like to cut the cord?" the OB asks, and Mia doesn't know who she is asking. The cord is something else she has never thought about before.

"You can do it," she tells Suzanne, and Suzanne moves eagerly over to the OB, who hands her a pair of medical scissors. Mia tenses, expecting to feel something, but she doesn't. She reaches one hand down to touch her daughter's head. It is damp and soft and so very, very small. She cries again, a sound that tears at Mia's heart.

She glances at Suzanne, who, having cut the cord, is standing at her feet, watching respectfully, yet unable to hide the longing so evident in her face. Mia forces the words out that she doesn't want to say.

"Do you want to hold her?"

"Oh, but…" Suzanne bites her lip. "It's so soon. Don't you…" The words trail away.

Awkwardly, her whole body aching, she scoops her baby up in her arms. She's never held a baby before, at least not one this small. She feels scrawny rather than plump, and her legs remind Mia of a chicken, and yet she's the most beautiful thing she's ever seen. Mia kisses her head and her daughter snuffles against her chest. She feels as if she could hold her forever, and yet surely it's better if she doesn't. If she gets this moment over quickly, like tearing off a bandage, letting the wound begin to heal.

Wordlessly, she extends the bundle of baby to Suzanne, who springs into action. Mia has to turn her face away as Suzanne cradles her expertly, as if she's been practicing. She probably has. She hears Suzanne coo nonsense words as the baby lets out another bleating sound and then quiets.

The OB tidies Mia up, and then they are alone in the room, just her, Suzanne, and the baby. Daisy. She wants to call her Daisy. She's never told Suzanne that, but maybe she will. Maybe she'll ask her if she'll call her that, for her sake. That's not too much to ask, is it, considering?

"Do you want to hold her again?" Suzanne asks, and Mia fights a flicker of resentment that already it has changed, and Suzanne is now the one asking her.

She nods, and gently Suzanne places the baby—her daughter—in her arms. She has been wrapped up since Mia last held her, in a pink, fleecy blanket, a little knitted cap on her head and tiny mittens on her hands. She is nothing more than a pair of dark blue eyes peering at her unblinkingly, a stranger. She could be anyone's baby, Mia thinks, and then she lets out a sob.

She didn't mean to; it erupted out of her, from the depths of her being, impossible to contain. And then another, and another, and somehow she is weeping, her body racked with sobs, and Suzanne puts her arms around her, and Mia clings to her and holds her baby and grieves for everything she has already lost.

21

SUZANNE

The call comes at nine in the morning. It is a Saturday, and I am sitting in the kitchen, staring out at the sunny September morning, wondering what I am going to do with my day. It has been a week since I went to Mark's, since the past became a place I no longer recognize, so the present has become a foreign landscape, too. Where do I go from here? I keep asking myself the question, but I cannot yet come up with any answers.

And then, the call. An unrecognized number from Cary, North Carolina. I take it immediately.

"Yes?" My voice is sharp.

"Mrs. Thompson?"

"Yes?" Sharper still.

"Are you the mother of Daisy Thompson?"

My world free-falls, explodes. The room around me reels. *Oh God, please don't let this be one of those calls.* "Yes," I say for a third time. This time, I am whispering.

"I'm afraid she's gotten herself into some trouble." Now I register the syrupy Southern accent, the censorious tone.

"What kind of trouble?"

I can barely take in what the man says next—driving

without her license, an accident, an injury. "She's hurt?" I demand.

"No, your daughter's fine, Mrs. Thompson, but the girl she was travelling with was injured pretty badly. We've got Daisy here at the station. We need someone to pick her up." A pause. "There will be an investigation into the accident, of course. There is a witness to say she was driving recklessly. And, of course, she didn't have a license."

What? I can't take it in. Daisy driving? And who was the other girl in the car? And why isn't Mia involved in any of this? She hasn't texted me since last night, when I messaged about the birthday party she'd told me she'd been planning, trying not to feel both jealous and hurt that Daisy wanted to celebrate her birthday with Mia and her family, and not me and Mark.

"So you need me to pick her up?" I say dumbly. I'm in New York, I think. Does this police officer realize that?

"Yes, ma'am."

The answer, of course, is instant, obvious. "I'll be there as soon as I can."

I pack a bag, throwing random clothes in a holdall, calling Mark as I do so, but it goes directly to voicemail. I blurt out what's happened, or as much as I know, which feels very little. Then I try to call Mia, but her number goes to voicemail, as well. Where is everybody? *What has happened to Daisy?*

The first flight to Raleigh isn't for two hours, and I make it to the airport in forty minutes, wait in line, my leg jiggling. It isn't until they're calling out seat rows to board that I think to check Mia's Instagram. I blink as I take in the post, Daisy's response, the photo—is it Photoshopped?—and the six hundred comments, ranging from cautious sympathy to utter vitriol.

Tom is Daisy's father? *Tom?* I can hardly believe it, and yet at the same time I realize I can. I think of Mia shooting him such apprehensive looks, the first time he met Daisy. How she came less and less after she met Tom—perhaps not because she was building her own life, after all, as I'd assumed, but because she was trying to hide the truth? And now Daisy has found out. And something terrible has happened, I'm not even sure what and I am terrified to imagine.

My seat row is called, and I slide my phone into my bag.

My mind continues to whirl for the nearly two-hour flight to Raleigh. Why hasn't Mia called me? Why was Daisy driving? Who was hurt?

At Raleigh, I rent a car, and just twenty minutes later, I am pulling up to the Cary Police Station, hardly able to believe I am here. It has been five hours since the telephone call this morning, and it feels like an age.

The sergeant at the desk asks for ID, and I fumble in my purse for my driver's license before I am taken through to see Daisy, my daughter. She's been kept in a police cell, which infuriates me. Really? She's a *criminal?* But I don't say anything as he unlocks the door and Daisy lifts her head from her knees, her hair tangled, her face blotchy.

"Mom..." she whispers, and it sounds like the sweetest thing I have ever heard.

"Daisy."

The police officer leaves us alone and I step towards her.

"I didn't think you'd come," she says miserably.

"Of course I came." And then suddenly it is easy, obvious. I sit next to her on the bed and I pull her into my arms, the way I have wanted to do, for so long, but have been afraid she wouldn't let me. She rests her head on my shoulder as her body shakes with sobs.

"I've messed up so bad, Mom, so bad. I'm so sorry... I didn't even realize she was in the car..."

I smooth her hair away from her damp, flushed face. "It's going to be okay," I tell her. I mean it utterly. I will absolutely make sure it is okay for my daughter. "Tell me what happened, from the beginning."

And so the story comes out, amid gulps and sobs. How she discovered Tom was her father, how Mia kept the secret from him as well as Daisy. "All this time..." she chokes out. "All this time, my whole family has been living together."

I'm your family, I think, *Mark and I are*, but I don't say it. I understand her grief and confusion; they are not a slight against me. For the first time, I am not seeing Mia as some sort of a competitor for Daisy's affections; I am only seeing my daughter, desperately needing love. I keep my arms around her as she tells me more—how she posted on Mia's Instagram and all over social media to ruin her lifestyle-coaching business.

"I just wanted to hurt her the way she hurt me... I know I shouldn't have done it." She gulps and I stroke her hair.

"And the car?" I ask gently. "How did you come to be driving the car?"

"Mia told me to get out. I was so angry... so I grabbed her car keys. I was just going to drive around the block, freak her out a bit. I wasn't even thinking, not really..."

"Who was in the car with you, Daisy?" I keep my voice soft.

"I didn't even see her get in! She followed me out of the house... I didn't see her until I was driving... and then I went through a stop sign, I didn't *see* it..." She dissolves into sobs. "Is she going to be okay? The car hit her side... there was so much blood..."

I am chilled by her words, but I don't show it. "Whose side?" I ask, and Daisy clings to me.

"Sophie's," she whispers.

Sophie. Mia's youngest child, only four years old. I've never met her, but I can picture her blond ringlets, her big blue eyes.

Now I know why Mia isn't here, why she wasn't answering her phone. I keep my arms around my daughter.

"We'll get through this," I tell her. "I promise you, we'll get through this."

It only takes a few minutes to get Daisy released; the police officer tells me, rather ominously, that they need to be able to contact her for questioning. It doesn't end here.

"Of course," I say stiffly, and I give the address of the hotel I've booked into in Cary.

Half an hour later, we are in the hotel room, Daisy having a bath while I sit on the edge of one of the double beds and ease my shoes off. It's only three o'clock in the afternoon, but it feels like midnight, like the longest day of my life. Mark calls while Daisy is in the bath, and I take the call out to the little balcony that overlooks the parking lot. Even though it's the middle of September, the air is muggy, the heat sweltering.

"Suzanne? I'm so sorry, I'd switched off my phone. What's happened—"

Quickly, I explain. Mark is silent, the only sound his sharp intake of breath.

"And Sophie...?" he finally asks. "Will she...?"

"I don't know. Mia's not answering her phone, and I don't want to push."

"No." He lapses into silence for another long moment. "What will happen to Daisy?" he asks eventually.

"I don't know that, either."

We are both silent then, absorbing the enormity of what has happened.

"I'll come down," Mark says finally. "I'll book a ticket right now. I can be there by this evening."

I open my mouth to say it's not necessary, I know he has work, but then I close it again. Daisy needs her father here, and so do I. I've had enough of trying to be self-reliant, not needing or asking for anyone, just as Mark has.

"All right," I tell him. "I think that's a good idea."

When I come back into the room, Daisy has emerged from the bath, wrapped in the hotel bathrobe, pink-cheeked, her hair damp. I smile at her.

"That was Dad on the phone. He's coming tonight."

Her eyes fill with tears. "I'm so sorry," she whispers, and then lets out a hiccuppy sob. "This is all my fault."

"Blame doesn't help anyone," I tell her gently. "And, in any case, a lot of factors went into getting to this moment."

She frowns uncertainly. "What do you mean?"

I hesitate, then sit down on the bed and pat the space next to me. Cautiously, Daisy sits down. "I found out something recently," I begin. "About myself."

She frowns, not understanding, not yet. "What?"

"Granny told me something when she wasn't... wasn't quite herself. You know how she gets?"

Daisy nods. Although she hasn't visited my mother much lately, she has witnessed her descent into dementia.

"She told me I was adopted. I never knew, but I've been realizing that it has explained a lot of things about—well, about me. About the way that I am."

"You're adopted?" Daisy is incredulous. "How did you not know?"

"Granny kept it secret from me." I spread my hands helplessly. "I suppose she felt she was doing the right thing. My adoption was... difficult. I wasn't adopted until I was four years old, and I'd been taken away from my birth mother because of abuse and neglect." Daisy's eyes round, her lips parting silently. "Anyway," I continue hurriedly, not wanting to make this all about me, "the point is, I didn't know any of that, but it still affected how I acted. At least, I think it did. I'm realizing that I haven't... I haven't wanted to show I need anyone. I've been afraid of... of being rejected, I suppose, like I was when I was little, even though I've never remembered it." *At the heart of every adoption is loss*. "I didn't really understand that's how was I was acting, and I still don't understand it, not fully, but I'm trying. I'm sure it will take a while, and I'll need to process a lot of things. Anyway." Cautiously, deliberately, I place my hand over hers. She doesn't pull away as I might have once expected or feared her to. "Obviously, that has affected you, too. I think I may not have been as... as affectionate or open as I wanted to be, especially as you got older. I think I was trying to protect myself without even realizing I was doing it, and I'm sorry."

Daisy is staring at me in something like wonder. "I can't believe you're adopted."

I give a small smile. "No, me neither."

"I'm sorry," she blurts, and I know she's talking about more than me being adopted, or what happened today. Both of us have so much to be sorry for.

"So am I," I tell her, and squeeze her hand. "So am I."

We sit in silence for a few moments, our hands still clasped, a moment I couldn't have imagined even a few days ago. I'm grieved for what it took to get to this point, but at the same I'm so, so thankful we've got here. Not, I acknowledge, that it's all going to be easy from now on. This is just the beginning, and I know whatever is ahead of us, it will be very hard—for Daisy, for Sophie, for Mia, for Mark, and for me.

"Can you find out what happened to Sophie?" Daisy asks in a small voice.

"I'll try."

"And what about me?" Her voice is even smaller. "Will they... Am I going to go to prison?"

How can I answer that, when I don't actually *know*? I have no idea what Daisy might be tried for, convicted of. The thought of her in prison, at only just eighteen years old, is terri-fying. "What happened was an accident, Daisy," I tell her carefully. "The police know that, Mia knows that. Let's just take one day at a time."

Her face crumples. "I'm so stupid," she exclaims, pressing her fists to her temples. "I'm so *stupid*. Why did I do it, any of it? *Why?*"

Because you're just eighteen years old and you were hurting and confused and you needed to lash out.

I wrap my arms around her once more, drawing her hands away from her head. "Ssh, ssh," I murmur. "It's going to be okay. It *is*. I love you." And then, because they are the truest words I've said, the only promise I can genuinely give, I say them again. And again, only beginning to make up for all the times I wanted to say them, but didn't. "I love you," I tell my daughter. "I love you. I love you."

Eventually, Daisy falls asleep, and I take the opportunity to try to find out what's happened to Sophie. I call the hospital, but they can't give me any information due to privacy laws, and so I call Mia again, and then, when there's still no reply, searching through my contacts, I call Tom. He answers on the fourth ring.

"Suzanne?" He sounds both weary and incredulous.

"Hello, Tom. I'm so sorry about Sophie. Is there any news?"

A beat of silence. "How do you know about Sophie?"

"Daisy told me."

Another beat, and I have the sense that he had completely forgotten about Daisy. "Where is she?" he asks, sounding exhausted rather than angry.

"She's with me. I flew down to Cary. How is Sophie?" I hold my breath, because I have no idea what he is going to say, how bad it is.

"We don't know yet," Tom tells me. "The impact of the car —it hit her leg, crushed it, basically." His voice wavers. "She's in surgery now, but she might... she might lose her leg."

I suck in a hard breath. "I'm so sorry." The words sound glib, but I mean them. To lose a leg at four years old! And yet... her life isn't threatened. I am thankful for that, at least. For her sake, and also for Daisy's. "I'm sorry," I say again, because I have no other words.

"Mia said Daisy was arrested at the scene."

"She was, but she's been released." I pause, unsure how to continue because I can't tell anything from Tom's tone. Is he angry? Does he blame Daisy? "She's so sorry for everything. She didn't realize Sophie was in the car when she drove off..." I trail off, not wanting to make excuses.

"She shouldn't have been driving the car," Tom says wearily. "But then there are a lot of shouldn'ts in this situation, and not just Daisy's. I don't blame her, not really."

"Does Mia?"

He is silent.

"If there's anything I can do..."

"Thank you. I suppose... I suppose the best thing you can do right now is take care of Daisy." He lets out a sad, little laugh that he has to tell me that, that it has become that complicated, and yet that simple.

As I end the call, I realize how much is uncertain—for Sophie, for Daisy, for all of us. Will Daisy be prosecuted? Will she come home with me? What will her relationship to Mia—to her *biological family*—be like now? I have no answers. All I can do is simply be here for my daughter.

Daisy has slept most of the afternoon, and then we ordered a pizza in, eating slices out on the balcony. There is a sense of waiting, of expectation, but also—strangely—of peace. As anxious as I am for Daisy, for Sophie, for all of us, there is a rightness at the center of my being that comes from having been able to give my daughter what she needed. Finally.

When Mark arrives, a little after eight o'clock, tired and rumpled and dear, that sense of rightness expands, envelops us. He comes into the hotel room, looks at both of us, and then somehow we are all moving at once, as if choreographed, in time and synchronicity. Our arms come around each other as we stand together in a silent embrace, bound together by both grief and love.

22

MIA

Everything happens in slow motion and yet too quickly. It is all a blur, and yet certain moments are in painful, high-definition: Sophie's pale face, the mangled mess of her leg, the wail of the ambulance siren, cutting through a sleepy suburban morning. Another split second that changes everything.

Tom arranged for a neighbor to look after Ella and Avery so we could both go to the hospital with Sophie; I was too distraught, not wanting to leave Sophie for a second. Yet all we've done since getting here is wait, sitting on hard, plastic chairs, sipping tepid, tasteless coffee, our minds whirring blanks. We've barely spoken; we don't want to give voice to our terrible fears. As for the revelation of last night... it has become meaningless, and yet also the source of everything we are experiencing today. I can't bear it. I can't bear any of it, and yet I have to, a constant, crushing weight on my chest.

At some point, a doctor in scrubs tells us Sophie is in surgery. Her leg was basically shattered by the impact of a car plowing right into her side. Daisy had run a stop sign; the middle-aged woman driving the other car was shaken, but unhurt. It's only Sophie who is suffering. Only Sophie, four years old, utterly innocent, whose life might be forever changed.

As for Daisy... I can't bring myself to think about her. I am too numb to be angry, too afraid to care where she is or what happened to her. Tom said she was arrested, and part of me thought, *good*. Maybe that will be the kind of tough love she needs. But thinking that way makes me feel guilty, and I don't have the energy for that, so I end up not thinking about her at all.

"We're doing the best we can," the doctor tells us as we stare at him, blank-faced, silently reeling in horror. "But I've got to be honest with you. We may not be able to save her leg."

Her leg? The words don't penetrate; I can't let them. She is *four* years old.

Tom reaches for my hand and I cling to it tightly, in order to keep myself upright. I tell myself at least she's alive, she's survived, but it feels like only so much comfort.

"Why was she in the car?" Tom asks after we've been sitting in silence for over an hour after the doctor came out to speak to us.

"I don't know." I close my eyes, force myself to say more. "I told Daisy to... to get out. She took the keys... Sophie must have followed her."

Tom doesn't reply, but I fear I know what he is thinking. This is my fault. I shouldn't have lost my temper with Daisy. I shouldn't have told her to get out. I could have handled it better; I could have handled *everything* better. I cover my face with my hands as a sob chokes out of me. Tom puts his arm around me.

"This isn't your fault," he says quietly.

"Yes, it is." I mumble the words through my fingers, my shoulders shaking. "It's all my fault. If I hadn't lost my temper... if I'd told you from the beginning... if..." If. If. If. A thousand ifs, all of them pointless.

"Mia, stop." Tom tightens his arms around me. "If we're

going to blame anyone, then we have to blame everyone. Me for... for forgetting what happened between us. You for keeping it secret. Daisy for being so damned difficult and taking the keys. Sophie..." His voice breaks. "For getting in the car."

"Not Sophie," I protest, my voice little more than a whimper.

"All I'm saying is, it happened the way it happened. We're here now. Let's not waste time or energy deciding who's to blame, because that doesn't do anyone any good. Let's just... work together. For Sophie's sake."

And what about for ours? I don't have the courage to ask. I have no idea what the state of my marriage is now.

A couple of hours later, while Sophie is still in surgery, Tom tells me that Suzanne has called him. I haven't even looked at my phone; I simply don't have the strength. "Is Daisy okay?" I ask dully, and he tells me she is with Suzanne, in a hotel. She might be prosecuted.

"I don't know how I ought to feel about her anymore," he says, slumping back into the seat next to me.

"Because of what happened with Sophie, or because of me?"

"Both, I guess." He shakes his head slowly. "All this time..."

It's the same thing Daisy said to me, and it fills me with guilt. I turn to look out the window.

"Did you ever think about telling me?" he asks. "I mean, did you ever really try?"

"Yes. That weekend at the beach. I was working my way up to it."

"When you told me we knew each other, back then?"

I nod.

"That was only last month, Mia." He sounds weary, but I hear a sharpness under the words. "What about before?"

"I tried at the beginning, and then when you first met her, but..." My breath escapes me in a weary rush. "Can we not do this now, Tom? Can we at least wait until we know about Sophie?"

"Fine."

An hour later, the doctor comes out to tell us they've saved Sophie's leg. Mostly. It's been put back together with pins and screws, and she'll have to have a cast for over three months. There's the possibility of nerve damage, and she'll need skin grafts, and she'll almost certainly have a permanent limp, although one day she will be able to walk, maybe even run.

Tom and I collapse into each other, filled with relief, as well as a deep, pervading sadness. It's not as bad as we feared, but she is forever changed. We all are.

Tom goes back home to be with the girls, while I stay the night with Sophie. She's drugged up to the gills, deeply asleep, her leg encased in plaster from the hip to the ankle. My poor little girl.

For the first time, I let myself think of my other poor little girl. Daisy. I'm angry with her, I realize, but I'm also angry with myself, and it's an anger that feels more like despair. Why did everything have to happen this way? Why did Sophie have to be the one to suffer? I know Tom is right, that playing the blame game doesn't help anyone, and yet I can't keep my mind from going around in circles. Wondering. Wishing things had been different. That they could be different now.

I sleep badly on the pull-out bed next to Sophie's, in and out of sleep, waking up every time a nurse comes in to check her vital signs. At dawn, I do my best to tidy myself in the bathroom, and when I come back in the room, my little girl's eyes are open.

"Hey, sweetheart." I smile, although my heart is aching. Sophie looks impossibly tiny in the hospital bed, the cast on her leg so enormous and overwhelming, dwarfing her.

She glances at her leg, her eyes so big and blue, glassy with tears.

"What… happened?" she asks, her voice raspy.

"You had an accident, baby girl." I sit on the chair next to the bed, and hold her limp little hand in mind. "You had an accident and you hurt your leg, but you're going to be fine, just fine."

She stares at me, her eyes filled with confusion and fear, as a tear drips onto her cheek.

I squeeze her hand gently, do my utmost not to cry. I know I need to be strong, for her sake. "You're going to be okay, Sophie," I tell her, my tone turning determined, urgent. "I promise you, you are going to be okay, and I will be here with you, every step of the way."

Slowly, so slowly, she nods, and her little fingers squeeze mine before her eyes flutter closed and she drifts back into sleep. I stay there, holding her hand, as the tears silently slip down my face.

Later that day, Tom returns and I go home to have a shower, check on Ella and Avery. They're both anxious and tearful, clinging to me one minute and blowing up at me the next. I understand, I feel the same, but that doesn't make it any easier to deal with.

"What about Daisy?" Ella asks when I've had a shower and a cup of coffee and I feel slightly more human, although my brain is still fuzzy with exhaustion. "Is she coming back?"

"I don't know, sweetheart." I know I need to think about Daisy, find a way to close the distance between us, but right now my heart and head are full of Sophie.

"Why did she get so angry? Daddy wouldn't tell us."

"She was mad at me, for… for not telling her something."

"What?"

I need to talk to Tom before I tell Ella or Avery anything, I know that much. "I can't tell you right now," I say to Ella, and watch her fume. "But I will, as soon as I've talked to Daisy and Daddy."

She stomps away, angrier than she normally would be, every emotion rubbed raw. When will this end? I wonder. When will we ever feel as if we are back on an even keel, when things are normal? When all the secrets are dealt with, accepted and forgiven and put to rest?

That evening, while Sophie sleeps, Tom and I talk. I still haven't called Daisy or Suzanne yet, haven't found the energy for that conversation. I'm not sure I have the energy for this one, but I know Tom deserves answers.

"So tell me what happened," he says, his elbows braced on his knees, his head cradled in his hands. "I need to understand what... what I've forgotten."

I glance at Sophie, but she's sleeping deeply, peacefully. Our neighbor is watching the girls again; Trina, of all people, brought over a casserole this afternoon, has organized a schedule of preschool moms to provide us meals and babysitting for the foreseeable future. I don't even know how she knew Sophie had been hurt. News travels fast in small towns, I suppose.

There is nothing stopping Tom and me from having this conversation now, and yet, out of fear, or perhaps an old, half-forgotten humiliation, I resist going into all the details.

"Just what I told you. You tutored me. We slept together. You forgot."

"Mia." He lifts his head to give me a weary, hurt look. "Come on."

And so, haltingly, I make myself fill in the details. The roommates bringing the beers, the snow falling outside the window. That first, halting kiss.

He looks stricken, shaking his head slowly, not in denial, but in something like disbelief.

"I can't believe I forgot all that."

I shrug.

"Why didn't you remind me afterwards? Talk to me about it? I don't think I was that much of a jerk, was I? I wouldn't have blanked you or anything." He rubs his hands over his face. "I know I was a bit of a player, but I still had scruples, Mia. I tried to be a nice guy."

"I don't know why I didn't remind you." I stare into space, trying to remember the girl I was, that moment after class when he'd stared at me so blankly. "I was shocked and embarrassed, I guess. And... hurt, that you didn't even remember something that was so... important to me. I knew I was forgettable, but..." I trail off.

"You weren't forgettable."

"But I was—"

"I was just stupidly drunk. Jeez." He shakes his head, his face crumpling. "I feel like... like I attacked you, or something."

"No, it wasn't like that, Tom. I promise." I reach over to touch his hand, a brush of my fingers against his. "I was... I was thrilled, that you were paying attention to me. I had no regrets, not in the moment, and you were... you asked me if I was okay with that." I give a small smile. "You were a charming drunk, to tell you the truth."

He grimaces, unappeased. "What about after?"

"After?" I sigh. "I don't know. I suppose I wished you'd remembered. I thought we'd have an awkward conversation, not a complete blank. I was shocked, but I also thought I'd never see you again, and that it wouldn't matter. I didn't realize I was pregnant until I was nearly halfway through. You'd been in Thailand for months by then."

"And you didn't think to contact me?"

"I *thought* about it, but how? I didn't have your email

address or phone number. I didn't know anything about you. And I suppose... I suppose I was in shock. I'd never even had a boyfriend before we... This was totally new territory for me. It was all I could do to get through each day. I was focused on getting through it all, getting back to normal." Except, of course, that would prove to be impossible. There was no getting back to normal, not ever.

"All right, fine." He draws a deep breath, lets it out in a gust. "I can understand all that and I'm sorry for it. Truly, I really am. But when we met up again. When I asked you out. When you realized it was serious between us. *At some point...*" His voice breaks and he drops his head into his hands again.

"By the time I met you again," I tell him levelly, "Daisy was four years old. She was happy with Suzanne and Mark, they were her parents—her real parents in every way that mattered." The words throb through me, a truth I'd tried to avoid for so long. "And I had managed to, I don't know, separate myself from what happened, almost as if... as if Daisy wasn't really your daughter, or even mine. I can't explain it, it was just a coping mechanism I guess, but... it didn't feel like I was lying all the time. It was never like that."

"Only sometimes?" Tom retorts bitterly, and I sigh.

"Yes, sometimes, when it would hit me, and I'd... freak out." I think of the times I canceled visits, or sent a card instead. The relief I felt, along with the grief, at moving to North Carolina, easing off contact with Daisy. "It always felt so complicated, so hard."

"Yes, so you told me."

"Well, at least that's one thing I told you," I retort, my voice rising, "and I'm sorry, *very* sorry, I didn't tell you about Daisy, just like you're sorry you forgot you slept with me. Is there any way we can call it even?"

"I don't want to call anything *even*." His gaze is not quite a glare. "That's not how I'm looking at this, Mia. I'm just trying to understand how we got to this point."

"Okay, well can you understand how impossible it all felt for me? My parents were completely disappointed in me, that I'd gotten pregnant. They wanted me to clean up my mess, move on, and there was *no one* to support me. I felt alone, frightened, in the deep end in every way, because I'd barely been kissed before I was with you and now I was having a baby." My voice breaks and I force myself to go on. "And then later, when I saw you... I didn't realize we would date, fall in love, marry. That first moment when you flirted with me, I just wanted to save face. And then, the more time that passed, the harder it became. How could I possibly just drop this huge bombshell on you? At some point, I decided it was better for everyone if you didn't know."

His expression is both hurt and hard as he asks, "When was that?"

"When Daisy was five or six, I suppose," I tell him, my voice full of guilt and regret. Will he able to understand? To forgive? "When we were moving to North Carolina, and I knew we wouldn't see her as much. I think it was around then that I thought it would be better for everyone if we... drifted apart."

"But you kept seeing her," Tom points out. "You didn't end contact with her completely."

"No, I never could make myself do that," I agree heavily. "Maybe it would have been better if I had. Better for her, better for us, to have a clean break. I just wasn't strong enough to do it."

We both lapse into silence then; I stare down at my hands while Tom gazes off into space. Can he possibly forgive me?

Finally he speaks. "I just need to know... was any part of you not telling me because you were angry with me? For forgetting you? Was any of this... some kind of punishment?"

I open my mouth to say no, of *course* not, when I suddenly

stop. I've never thought I was angry with Tom, never looked at it that way, and yet... awful realization thuds through me. "Maybe, a little," I whisper. "On a subconscious level." Because I've carried the hurt of him forgetting for a long time. It's crystallized, ossified, become a part of me, and I didn't even realize it until this moment how hardened it was inside me. "I didn't mean for it to be that way. I never even thought it was, until you asked just now. But... it hurt, Tom. More than I've even admitted to myself." I bow my head. "I'm sorry."

He shakes his head, his shoulders slumped, his voice full of sadness. "I can understand why you'd feel that way. I'm sorry I was so... thoughtless, I guess. And stupid. I just..." He blows out a breath. "I don't even know. Regrets are pointless, at this stage, aren't they?"

"Yet we still have them."

He is silent for a long moment, and I feel as if I am balancing on a precipice, waiting for judgment. Then he looks up at me. "We're going to be okay," he says, his voice firm, and I let out a huff of surprised relief and gratitude as tears start in my eyes. I believe him, and I am so glad. "But," Tom continues, "you need to talk to Daisy."

I nod slowly. I know I need to talk to her, my firstborn daughter. I need to ask her forgiveness and offer her mine. It won't be easy, but it is necessary, and maybe, one day, it will even bring us closer together.

I don't actually talk to Daisy until three days later. By that time, Sophie is settled on the pediatric ward, where she'll be for another week, before she can be released home. She's awake and talking and getting around in a wheelchair, and it's so much more progress than I was expecting at this stage.

I call Suzanne, find out they are still staying at the hotel, although they are planning on returning to New York on the weekend. Daisy, Suzanne tells me, has been charged with reckless driving with serious injury, but because of her age, her record, and extenuating circumstances, they think the worst she'll get is a fine and community-service hours. She'll be coming back to Cary in a few months for the hearing. I am relieved for Daisy's sake; I never wanted to see her punished. I am also relieved, I realize, that she is going back to New York. As ever, my feelings are tangled and complicated.

"I'm so sorry," I tell Suzanne. "I suppose you know about what happened? Why Daisy was so angry?"

"Yes, I do." She sounds as calm as ever, but I can tell this time it costs her. Perhaps she's not quite as unflappable as I once thought. Perhaps we are more alike than I ever realized.

"Can I see Daisy? Talk to her?"

"I think that would be a good idea," Suzanne says.

We meet in Downtown Park, off Academy Street, a neutral location, away from prying eyes. Daisy and Suzanne are sitting together on a park bench, heads tilted up to the autumn sunshine, and somehow they look more *together* than I have ever seen them before. As I approach them, I am reminded of all the visits over the years—the tearoom, the park, the afternoons in Suzanne's living room, the three of us having to navigate every moment. It feels different now, but I am not yet sure how.

"Hey, Daisy." My lips are stiff as they turn up in a smile. "Suzanne."

Suzanne smiles back at me, and Daisy gives me a guarded look. Does she think I'm angry with her? I know I'm not, not anymore. But she might be angry with me.

"How is Sophie?" Suzanne asks, and I glance at Daisy as I answer.

"She's a lot better. She'll be coming home next week, I hope."

"And her leg?" Daisy's voice is low as she stares down at her feet. "Is she... Is there going to be any lasting damage?"

I hesitate, and then decide for the truth. Always the truth now. "They're not exactly sure yet. She might walk with a limp, and there might be some nerve damage, but you know Sophie. You can't keep her down for long."

Daisy nods jerkily, her gaze still on her feet.

"Hey." I speak gently as I sit next to her, the three of us on the bench. "Daisy, it's not your fault. I hope you realize that. At least," I amend, determined to be truthful, "it's not your fault more than it is anybody else's. There were a lot of choices that got us to that moment, and now this one. I don't want to blame anyone. I just want to move forward. But I do accept my own responsibility—I should have told you about Tom. I should have told Tom about you. It just felt so hard..." I trail off, unsure how to put into words how impossible my situation felt, for so long. "I told Tom it didn't feel like I was lying all the time. I sort of separated it in my mind—you and him. And," I continue, glancing at Suzanne, "by the time he was back in my life, you were four years old, and with your family, who love you very much."

"Yeah," Daisy whispers as she turns to give Suzanne a small, sad smile. "I know."

"I don't know where we go from here," I tell them both. "I want you to know we'd still very much like you to be a part of our lives. It might look different now, but hopefully in a good way. The girls love you. I love you. Tom loves you, and he did even before he knew he was your biological dad. And I know your parents love you, too. That's a lot of love," I finish with a small, hopeful laugh.

I meet Suzanne's gaze and she inclines her head with a small smile of acknowledgment—and gratitude. For the first time, perhaps, I feel we are working together, as we both imagined all those years ago. We are finally, truly on the same side. On Daisy's.

Did it need to take a tragedy to make us whole? Or is it just part of life, anyone's life—the cycle of brokenness and healing, people bound together by both love and grief, making mistakes, finding a way forward, however they can? I don't know, but as I sit on that bench with my daughter and her mother, I feel a loosening inside me, the tightly held parts of myself finally easing, freeing.

There are a lot of unknowns in our future—what will happen to Daisy, to Sophie, to Tom's and my marriage, to all of us. But for the first time, I am truly hopeful, deep down, right through. Something good can come out of the brokenness. Something that is both hard and healing.

I meet Daisy's gaze, and she smiles at me. And we sit on the bench, the three of us, needing no words as we bask in the sunshine and seagulls wheel high overhead, their calls borne away on the wind.

THEN

SUZANNE

May 2004
17 years ago

Mia asked her to meet in the park, a neutral location. She's coming to the apartment on the weekend, to officially meet Suzanne and Mark, the first time they'll all be together now that Mia has chosen them as the parents of her baby. But when Suzanne got the call this morning, asking her to meet just her, alone, she agreed immediately. She even understood—this was from one mother to another. Something sacred, a matter of trust.

She sits on a bench by the entrance to the Central Park Zoo; a man is selling balloons outside the gates, another is sketching carica-tures for ten bucks apiece. A few seagulls stalk the ground, pecking for crumbs as the warm May breeze blows over the city.

Suzanne is nervous. She is on her best behavior, but she also wants to be honest. Real. She feels she owes that to Mia, and also to herself. And she hopes Mia feels the same, that she will be honest, too. She wants this meeting to work; she longs for them to be friends.

They are going to have a long-term relationship, especially if Mia wants some form of ongoing contact, which the agency consultant hinted at, although nothing has been formalized. Still, Suzanne feels, they're on the same side. They both want what's best for this baby. Their baby. She's sure of that.

She looks up, and she sees a young woman coming down the walk. She has dark hair and is wearing a baggy T-shirt, loose jeans. The roundness of her bump is just visible when the wind tugs her shirt against her body. Suzanne hasn't seen a picture of Mia, but she knows this is her. She recognizes her somehow, and not just because she's pregnant.

She half-rises from the bench, waves. Mia smiles shyly, lifting her hand and then dropping it. Suzanne realizes she is smiling widely, and she tries to rearrange her expression into something slightly more sober, but she's so happy to have got to this moment.

"Suzanne?" Mia asks as she comes to stand in front of her, her voice husky and soft.

"Mia."

Then they are both smiling, and Mia lets out a little, uncertain laugh. "So," she says, and she laughs again. "Nice to meet you."

"Yes." Suzanne nods, and then she reaches out and clasps Mia's hand. Mia gazes at her with dark, serious eyes as they remain like that for a moment, recognizing the significance of this moment, the beginning of their life together, the life they will share.

Then Suzanne finally lets go.

"It's so nice to meet you, too," she says, and Mia smiles.

EPILOGUE

ONE YEAR LATER

"A couple more steps…"

My dad is puffing as he and Tom navigate their way up the narrow flight of stairs, the minifridge balanced between them, towards my bedroom on the third floor. I'm following behind, practically bouncing up the steps. It's early September, and I'm a freshman, about to start at NYU. I can't even believe it, that I got this far. That we all did. My whole family has come to help move me into my dorm off Washington Square, and I mean everyone—my three sisters, Ella, Avery, and Sophie, my two fathers, Tom and Mark, and my two mothers, Mia and Suzanne. I joke sometimes how I have two of everything, and in the last year I've come to realize how that really is more, not less.

Not that it's been easy. Sometimes it's been really, horribly hard. The hearing back in North Carolina. The community service hours—I was more than willing to do them, but I got looks. Whispers. All that stuff. And then there was having to face down Ella and Avery and Sophie, who were all so suspicious of me, and how could I blame them after what had happened?

But I wanted to have a relationship with them, along with

Mia and Tom. Not my real parents, but my birth ones. And thank goodness, despite how everything happened, they wanted to have a relationship with me. It's come in fits and starts; I flew down for a visit after Thanksgiving, and then we all met for a weekend in Baltimore at New Year's. Sometimes it's been awkward, sometimes it's been fun, but we're all trying.

"Pretty good room for a freshman," Dad says as he deposits the fridge by the window. "Nice view."

"Yes, you can almost see the arch." Mom moves to the window, and Dad joins her there, to see if he can get a glimpse of the impressive white marble.

I watch them, feeling hopeful. They're still divorced, but we've been spending a lot more time together—Sunday brunches, Wednesday dinners, the occasional Saturday afternoon, the three of us. And once I came home from school and Dad was in the kitchen, sipping coffee, my mom leaning against the stove and smiling. He jumped a little, looking embarrassed, like I'd caught them or something, and I just grinned.

Still, it hasn't been all sunshine and rainbows. Early on Sophie got some kind of infection in her leg and she had to go back into hospital, have more surgeries. I felt guilty all over again, and for a while Mia and I weren't in touch all that often. I understood why, but it still hurt. Even now Sophie walks with a limp, but her big, bossy grin is just the same.

This last year I ended up going to a high school on Eighty-Seventh Street that still had some spaces. It was a far cry from Stirling, but that was okay. I found a group of friends and I worked hard to bring my grades up so I could go to NYU.

"Can you see the arch?" Tom asks, and Dad gives a small laugh. "A tiny bit. Almost." He smiles at my mom, who smiles back. I feel kind of childish for hoping they get back together, but I do. I really do.

I know my mom has been having counselling about her own adoption, which still blows my mind. It's brought us together in a way I could never have expected, because she actually *gets* it. We're closer now than we ever were before, not that it's smooth sailing all the time. We still argue; my mom can go all quiet and I can lose my temper. But we've actually sat together and cried, our arms wrapped around each other, which considering the way my mom used to be, all reserved and controlled, is pretty amazing.

"Daisy, is this your room?"

I turn to see Sophie racing into the room, faster than her sister despite her limp, followed by Mia. I grin, and Sophie runs towards me, wrapping her arms around my middle. Right from the start she has welcome and accepted me, and amazingly, that hasn't changed.

"Yep," I say as I hug her. I hear the pride in my voice. "It sure is."

"It's kind of small," Ella comments dubiously, and I laugh, because that is so Ella.

"I like it," Avery fires back loyally. I smile at her, at all of them. My sisters.

I glance at Mia, and I see how tearful she looks, and I know what she's thinking: *her daughters*. All of us. Then I look at Tom, who is looking a little misty-eyed too. Mia told me they'd been having counselling; I guess her keeping me a secret was hard for him—for them—just as it was hard for me.

Mia stopped her lifestyle coaching a few months ago. She told me I'd done her a favor, writing that post, which didn't make me feel that much better, because I know what a stupid, mean thing it was to do. I saw that she wrote one last heartfelt post for Instagram and then closed the account, the business, everything. She's volunteering now, at a charity in North Carolina for learning disabilities; she says there might be a possibility of a part-time job eventually.

As we all crowd in my tiny dorm room, I can't help but feel proud. Thankful. I've got my family all around me, and it feels good. Frankly, it feels wonderful. Maybe I don't deserve it, them, the second chance I've been given, but I'm so grateful.

"I'm hungry," Sophie announces, and I see Mia and Tom exchange laughing looks.

"And I think it's just about time for our lunch," Mom says. She's made a reservation for lunch at a nearby restaurant, a table for eight. For everyone.

"Shall we plug this thing in first?" Tom asks, and Dad bends down to plug the fridge into the wall. It comes to life with a satisfying hum.

"I think I'm pretty much unpacked," I tell everyone as I look around my room. I'm so excited, but I'm also nervous. This is a whole new chapter, and I'm almost ready for them to go, so I can start it—but not quite yet.

"Then let's eat." Dad puts his arm around me and I lean into him briefly before we all start down the stairs.

As I turn back, I see my mom and Mia exchange weighted glances, like they're having some kind of significant moment, or maybe just a silent acknowledgement of how we all got to this place at last. Then together they head downstairs after me.

A LETTER FROM KATE

Dear reader,

I want to say a huge thank you for choosing to read *The Child I Never Had*. If you enjoyed it, and want to keep up to date with all my latest releases, just sign up at the following link. Your email address will never be shared and you can unsubscribe at any time.

www.bookouture.com/kate-hewitt

I have always been fascinated by the concept of adoption, and particularly open ones. It seems like such a good idea, and yet so often our human frailties and insecurities get in the way. But as I was writing this story, I came to realize that that might be true for every situation in life, and not just adoption. I hope, through Mia and Suzanne, I have brought some empathy and understanding to both sides of a challenging situation.

I hope you loved *The Child I Never Had* and if you did, I would be very grateful if you could write a review. I'd love to hear what you think, and it makes such a difference helping new readers to discover one of my books for the first time.

I love hearing from my readers—you can get in touch on my Facebook page, through Twitter, Goodreads or my website.

Thanks again for reading,
Kate

KEEP IN TOUCH WITH KATE

http://www.kate-hewitt.com

 facebook.com/KateHewittAuthor

twitter.com/author_kate

ACKNOWLEDGMENTS

So many people's hard work goes into every book I write, and so I would like to thank everyone on the Bookouture team who helps bring my books to life—Isobel, my fabulous editor, who always has such brilliant suggestions to focus my story and bring out the emotion; Jade, my copy editor; Tom, my proofreader; and all the team at Bookouture—Sarah and Kim in marketing; Richard and Peta in foreign rights; and Saidah, Rhianna, Alba, Sarah, and Laura in editorial and audio.

I'd also like to thank my readers, for being so loyal and enthusiastic and kind, and, of course, for reading my books! It's such an honor and a privilege to write for you.

Thanks also to my writing friends who have been so encouraging—Katy, with our woodland walks and frank discussions and Jenna, who is always at the other end of a text message. Thanks also to the writers I met recently at the Writing Outside the Box retreat, led by Katherine Blessan and Jane Walters. I so enjoyed meeting and chatting with all of you! It reminded me how important it is for writers to be in community.

Lastly, thanks as ever to my wonderful husband Cliff, who listens to me moan about plot problems and is always willing to research anything I ask of him, plus take care of the business side of things. Where would I be without you? And to my children, who always get a shout-out—Caroline, Ellen, Teddy, Anna, and Charlotte. And yes, Charlotte, I am finally done with this book!! Love you all.

Printed in Great Britain
by Amazon